The OTHER COUNTESS

The OTHER COUNTESS

EVE EDWARDS

DELACORTE PRESS

Visit us on the Web! www.randomhouse.com/teens

Educators and librarians, for a variety of teaching tools, visit us at
www.randomhouse.com/teachers

Library of Congress Cataloging-in-Publication Data
Edwards, Eve.
The other countess / Eve Edwards. — 1st U.S. ed.
p. cm.
Summary: In the court of Queen Elizabeth I in 1582, Eleanor Hutton, an alchemist's daughter, and William Lacey, the financially ruined Earl of Dorset, fall in love just as Will is supposed to be courting a rich and socially acceptable heiress.
ISBN 978-0-385-74089-0 (hc) — ISBN 978-0-375-98974-2 (glb) —
ISBN 978-0-375-98337-5 (ebook)
[1. Social classes—Fiction. 2. Love—Fiction. 3. Kings, queens, rulers, etc.—Fiction. 4. Great Britain—History—Elizabeth, 1558–1603—Fiction.] I. Title.
PZ7.E25252Ot 2012
[Fic]—dc22
2010052241

The text of this book is set in 11-point Adobe Caslon.

Book design by Stephanie Moss

Printed in the United States of America

10 9 8 7 6 5 4 3 2 1

First U.S. Edition

For Alex Reid

With thanks for all those evenings at the Phoenix

PREFACE

1578

THE FIRST TIME ELLIE MET WILLIAM LACEY, she thought him terrifying. Like a golden-haired angel fallen among mortals, the newly created earl blazed with impatience as he stood beside his widowed mother in the hall of his dilapidated manor house. At fourteen, he was one of the youngest and most important nobles in England and clearly did not feel he should have to listen to Ellie's alchemist father as he offered his condolences for their recent loss. Ellie knew then that the earl hated Sir Arthur Hutton and all those associated with him—which unfortunately included her.

The earl may have held his temper had her father restricted himself to sympathy; but to Ellie's dismay, Sir Arthur would go on to be obvious about his wish for continued patronage from the family. Ellie felt her horror rising; it was like watching helplessly as someone stepped off a cliff. She wished her dear, unworldly father would just be quiet. Anyone could tell he was merely sewing his own shroud with each word he tugged from his vast store of knowledge.

The new Earl of Dorset tapped his foot; his fingers curled in fists on his hips and two lines formed above his nose as his brow furrowed. If he'd had wings they would've been beating with fury, like the tapestry in the church showing the Archangel Michael on the Day of Judgment. Though only two years older than her, to Ellie's eyes, the earl had all the glowering authority of his position—an adult newly chipped from the block with none of his corners yet smoothed.

Oh, Madre de Dios, *Father, please stop!* Ellie prayed, twisting the shoddy woolen fabric of her gray skirt in her fingers.

". . . and as you know, my lord, we alchemists believe we are not far from finding the secret of transforming common lead into gold." Sir Arthur sketched a vague shape in the air, his sleeve falling back to reveal his fingers and forearm scarred by his labors over the crucible. "With only a few more years of study, I am convinced we can unlock nature's secrets. Your honored father understood this—and dedicated himself to the pursuit. He—"

The earl held up his hand, blocking Sir Arthur's plea midflow. The alchemist blinked at him in surprise like an owl woken prematurely from sleep. Ellie slid further behind her father's long black robes, fearing the earl was about to launch a thunderbolt—or run them out of the county at the very least.

"I understand, sir," said the earl crisply, "that my *honored* father held open house for men of your profession."

Arthur gave a fond smile. "Indeed, he was most generous—"

"So generous that he spent the entire family fortune in this fruitless pursuit!" The earl spat the words as he would an insult. "If you alchemists are so close to turning base metal into gold, where is mine, pray? What have you leeches done with the gold earned from my fields and by my people?"

Anger flashed through Ellie at the earl's accusation. Her father was no leech! He sincerely believed in his search for gold; he spent little on himself, but dedicated everything he had, all that was given him, to what he saw as a higher cause. And he would do it too—he'd promised her. All he needed were people who would have faith in him. She ground the toe of her shabby boot into the stone floor, afraid that her feelings would get the better of her and she would blurt out a defense of her father, making things worse.

"The Lacey family has no more money to throw away." The earl signaled a servant out of the shadows, the intent to eject them clear. "You may spread the word among your fellow *scholars* that there will no longer be any welcome for alchemists at Lacey Hall—unless they wish the welcome of being chased off by my hounds."

"Will, please." The widowed countess placed her hand on her son's forearm. He was trembling with rage, fists clenching and unclenching at his side in a silent struggle to keep hold of his temper. "Sir Arthur has his daughter with him," the countess said in a gentling tone.

The young earl took a deep breath, mastering himself. He forced a smile. "Apologies, madam," he said to his mother. "I did not mean that I would take such steps against the man, unless he was foolish enough to return." His gaze sought out Ellie, finding her in her father's shadow, a small girl of some twelve years with a mass of long black wavy hair escaping from her coif. Ellie knew she looked a disgrace to her rank; her father didn't consider such things as dress important, and it was long since she'd had so much as a new ribbon.

"Mistress Hutton need have no fear; my anger is not directed at her." The earl touched his mother's hand lightly, reassuring her that he was not going to let his formidable temper loose.

"Then perhaps we could offer Sir Arthur and his daughter some food from our kitchen, before Turville"—the countess nodded to the servant—"sees them on their way?"

"Yes, that would be best. I'm sorry, Mother, I must get some air. The stench of alchemy makes me sick. Good day to you." William Lacey flicked a gesture towards the waiting Turville, passing over the problem of the visitors to him, then strode out, whistling sharply to his dogs. The pack clattered out of a doorway behind Ellie, brushing her skirts in a mass of white and tan and wagging tails. She clutched at her father's arm, fearful that the earl would not keep his word, but the hounds passed her without a second glance.

When she looked round, the countess had retired, leaving only Turville, a brawny man with sparse ginger hair and a choleric complexion, glaring at them.

"Out!" he said, jerking his thumb to the door.

"But—" spluttered Sir Arthur, not quite comprehending that his hope of employment had been dashed.

"I'm not as softhearted as them." Turville indicated the portraits of the family lining the walls. "You false-mongers have a lot to answer for. There'll be no food from me. Get your worthless hide off Lacey land. And take your little beggar's brat with you."

The insult to his daughter did penetrate Arthur's confusion. "Enough, you, you varlet! You must not speak of her in that fashion. She is a countess, the Lady Eleanor Rodriguez of San Jaime. . . ."

Turville snorted. "And I'm the King of Spain. Be gone or I'll kick your backsides from here to Cádiz."

Ellie tugged at her father's sleeve. "Let's go, Father."

Arthur seemed inclined to stay to defend her honor. Thanks to her deceased mother, a younger daughter of a minor Spanish noble, it was true that Ellie was in possession of a mouthful of titles, but none of them meant anything when you stood in a patched gown in an English earl's hall. Her father, who had once been a diplomat of wealth and respect in Madrid, had come home to descend into poverty, blind to all else but his quest for the elusive gold. Responsibility for all practical matters weighed heavily upon Ellie's slight shoulders, and they still had to find food and lodging for the night.

"Please," she begged her father, tugging at his sleeve. *"Por favor, mi padre."*

Arthur finally noticed the desperation in her voice and absent-mindedly ruffled her hair.

"We don't need these people's charity, do we, Ellie?" he said tenderly, slinging his pack over his shoulder. "The road to knowledge is full of briars and thorns to prick us on to greater efforts."

Or to make us hurt and bleed, thought Ellie glumly, picking up her own bundle.

"I do not bid you farewell," Sir Arthur said gravely to Turville. "You do not warrant such a courtesy." With a fine sweep of his cloak, he marched out of the open door like a king leaving his court.

Ellie took a final glance around the once-elegant hall, regretting that there would be no roof over their heads that night, not even a leaky one like this. She doubted she'd ever be back.

"Get thee gone, little Spaniard," jeered Turville, watching her suspiciously. "Or I will set the dogs on you."

Ellie tossed her head, pride not letting her show fear. "*Malvado!* Your master said you wouldn't—and besides, sir, he took the hounds with him." She was tempted to stick out her tongue.

"Not my Bart, he didn't." Turville clicked his fingers and an Irish wolfhound rose wraithlike out of the shadows by the empty fireplace. Almost as tall as Ellie, it turned its gray whiskered snout to her and a spool of saliva unwound to the floor. The servant watched with satisfaction as the girl turned pale. "And the master isn't here to see what I do."

Ellie ran.

Chapter 1

1582

"THERE'S NO MONEY LEFT," the countess announced, leafing hopelessly through the family accounts. "The harvest returns were not good this year, so we have already run through our reserves."

Will stared out of the window, the tiny panes of glass distorting the forked trees. The snow lay thick on the ground. Deer wandered in the park, undisturbed today by any hunt. His quarry for the foreseeable future had to be coin, not meat.

"What are we to do, Mother? Do we have to bring James and Tobias home?"

The countess rubbed the bridge of her nose, a headache gathering. As Tobias was sharing a tutor at another noble family's house, the fees for her youngest son's schooling were due and James was sending in hefty bills from Cambridge.

"And there's Sarah's future to consider too." Will scratched at the frost on a pane with a fingernail, writing his initials. "Thank God, Catherine's well married, but I still owe Huntsford part of the dowry. He said he'd give us time to pay, but it is a stain on our family if I cannot come up with the rest. He's a good friend—and to be frank, it's embarrassing."

Will turned to glance up at the picture of his father hanging over the fireplace in his study. *This is your fault,* he thought. *If you had paid more attention to your estate and your family, we would not now be in the mire.*

Everyone expected him to step easily into the role of earl, but more often than not, Will felt like Atlas, carrying the weight of crushing responsibilities. In his case, the duties were summed up in the title Earl of Dorset; this splendid-sounding noble strutted around keeping up appearances while he, the real Will, staggered underneath the burden, trying to keep his footing. He knew he wasn't up to the task, but had to go on acting the part as so many depended on him. He'd begun to hate this Dorset fellow, whoever he was, and dreamt of casting him off like a snake sheds old skin.

Did you feel like that? he asked the portrait. *Was that why you hid in your laboratory and let everything slide?*

"Well, my dear," the countess said, pushing the ledger aside, "there is only one avenue still open to us. You must go to court and repair our fortunes. You must either win the Queen's favor or marry an extremely rich young lady."

Amused, Will quirked an eyebrow. "Simple as that?"

"Oh my, that does sound rather mercenary, doesn't it?" admitted the countess. "I meant that you should do your duty by our beloved sovereign and aspire to win the heart of some worthy—"

"I know what you meant, Mother." Will leant against the casement, crossing his arms and ankles, trying to ignore the fact that his hose were darned at the knee. "But I doubt I can afford to make an appearance that would not have our family dismissed in disgrace." He gestured to his outmoded velvet doublet, inherited from his father's wardrobe. "Not exactly the glass of fashion, am I?"

His mother smiled proudly. "My dear, what you lack in clothes you more than make up for in personal attraction, even if I do say so myself."

"And mothers are known for their impartiality?"

"Of course." She rose and went to the iron-bound coffer that stood against one wall. Taking a key from the chain at her waist, she opened the lid and took out a satin pouch.

Will, already guessing what she intended, held his hand out to stop her. "No, Mother, you can't."

"I can. My ruby set; part of my dowry. This should raise at least a thousand pounds—enough to equip England's most handsome lord with enough clothes and staff for his season at court."

A bleak sadness settled like a cloak on his shoulders. "If you sell that, then we really will have nothing left. I thought you wanted Sarah to have it when she gets married."

"I did, but the rubies will be scant comfort to us when we contemplate their beauty and starve this winter with the house falling about our ears."

Will approached her and took the jewels. Leaning down, he kissed her brow.

"I don't deserve you."

She poked his ribs playfully. "No, you don't, you scoundrel. Now go sell those and woo us a pleasant, wealthy girl, someone whom I won't want to strangle within a week of sharing the house with her."

"I'll do my best, Mother," Will vowed. "I'll get us out of this, I promise."

A particularly graphic curse shattered Ellie's concentration. Muttering a mild rejoinder as the word she'd been hunting for floated out of reach, Ellie looked out the window of her chamber, tucked away in an obscure corner of Windsor Castle. Below, the carpenters were preparing the lists for the Queen's jousting competition, the highlight of the St. George's holiday after the ceremony bestowing the Order of the Garter on the sovereign's most trusted men. Sawing, hammering and swearing filled the air, distracting Ellie from the manuscript she was translating for her father. She chewed on the end of her quill as she watched one broad-shouldered laborer strip off his shirt, revealing a torso to rival that of a Greek god.

"Don't wander, Ellie," she chided herself, while sneaking a second look.

The work had been going on like this for the past few days. The Queen and her retinue would be arriving within the week; hundreds of extra people to cram into the castle. The young bucks would be expected to display themselves to advantage on the field of chivalry; the girls to dazzle their suitors with their superior beauty and fine apparel. Youth was in fashion in the court of the aging monarch. Elizabeth's old favorite, the Earl of Leicester, had taken the unforgivable step of marrying; the situation vacant, all the young men were buzzing to court like bees to the honeypot.

Ellie yawned and rubbed her nose, not realizing she was leaving an inky streak across her cheek. It was all so tedious because she was on the outside of the excitement. To enter into the select group of gilded youth you had to have money, or the appearance of it, and influence. A scholar's daughter with a suspect Spanish inheritance was stuck somewhere between the kitchen and the great hall, belonging to neither.

Tearing off a crust from her manchet, Ellie tapped the crumbs so none fell on the page she was painstakingly inscribing. She took pride in her penmanship—very few women could read fluently, let alone write. The Queen could, of course, and Ellie admired her for it, mirroring herself on the monarch's accomplishment of translating one text into three languages while still in the schoolroom. Her own mother, the Lady Marta Rodriguez, Countess of San Jaime, had been a noted poet at the Spanish court—that was what had first brought her to Sir Arthur Hutton's attention and led to their marriage. Her father hoped that the fame of his erudite daughter would sweeten the Queen towards his own pursuits. He had urged to complete her translation of a work by his favorite alchemist, Paracelsus, before the court arrived so he could make a gift of it to Elizabeth. Ellie found the task of translating the old Swiss windbag monumentally boring, and she still had five pages to go. Worse still, she suspected that the Queen would be far less impressed than her father anticipated. Favor was given out for calculated political reasons, not from an overflow of heart.

"Plague upon Paracelsus," she grumbled, picking up her pen again. "May his quill shrivel." Pleased with the mildly obscene curse, she returned to her labors.

At noon, the maid came to straighten the room Ellie shared with three other girls attached to Lord Mountjoy's household. Ellie decided it was time to take a turn about the grounds and blow away the cobwebs from her overworked brain. Locking her work in her little trunk at the end of her bed, she ran down the stairs. It would do no harm to go past the lists, surely? The sun was climbing and there was a good chance that there would be other torsos to admire—in a purely abstract way, of course. The scholar's appreciation of a healthy example of God's creation, she promised herself.

Chuckling, Ellie jumped the last few steps and burst out into the sunshine, humming a snatch of song. Her mother's favorite tune came naturally to her lips when, after the cramped hours in her cold chamber, she was swamped with the wonder of being alive. Blessings had finally found her. She was young, had been well fed for the last few months; she even had a new gown, a castoff from a noble lady, all thanks to the patronage of Lord Mountjoy, who shared her father's obsession with alchemy.

It hadn't been like this for so long. The years after being run out of Lacey Hall had been miserable ones. They'd taken refuge with a fellow scholar in Northampton, living on his charity and a few tutoring jobs he had passed over to Sir Arthur. That was until Ellie had bloomed sufficiently to attract a much less welcome attention from their host. She'd lived in fear for a few months that her father would insist that she marry his friend in payment for the years they had lodged there. The suggestion had been in the air until Sir Arthur fell out with his colleague over the best catalyst to use in the conversion of base metals. Ellie and her father had been out on their ear in the middle of the night as a result, their few belongings thrown after them, while the scholar shouted:

"A preparation of sulfur, you fool!"

He banged the door closed on them—and on any prospect of marriage.

Saved by sulfur, thought Ellie gratefully, walking slowly down a path bordered by yew hedges, taking full advantage of the unobstructed view of the lists in each opening.

It had been no paradise that they had left in Northampton, but nothing had prepared her for the months of wandering that followed. They had descended to a level little better than beggars until Lord Mountjoy had taken them in. The experience had left its mark on Ellie. Her youthful belief in her father, already dying, had finally withered, leaving only the husk of dutiful companionship behind. He would never find gold: she had accepted this truth. She could only pray that he too would wake up from the delusion before it was too late.

She headed to the herb garden, thinking the scents would be a pleasant change from the stuffy confines of her room. In Lord Mountjoy's household she had been able to consult the limner's drawings of the plants; perhaps there would be some new ones for her to see in the Queen's well-stocked borders? One of her dreams was to have her own patch of earth one day where she could experiment with growing different herbs for medicine and cooking. English food never tasted quite as good as what she remembered of her mother's recipes. She crumbled a rosemary twig in her fingers, breathing in the heady scent.

The crunch of footsteps on the gravel alerted her that she was not alone in this part of the garden. Looking behind, she saw three young nobles approaching swiftly from the direction of the stables, deep in talk. Three brothers or close kin, she guessed, from the resemblance between them. She increased her pace. Court politics were treacherous and deadly. Better not to be suspected of overhearing anything. But her much shorter legs could not outpace the three giants coming towards her. She chose instead to turn aside from the yew walk and sit in an arbor until they had passed. The scrap of dutiful sewing she kept in her pocket for such occasions provided her with excuse enough for being there.

"As much as I love you, Will, I really would rather not be dancing attendance on you," said the tallest of the three, tugging uncomfortably at the tight ruff scratching his neck. He was an imposing-looking young man with a mane of shoulder-length brown hair, his gait soldierly as he strode along. "How long do you think this mummery will be necessary?"

With a sick dread, Ellie recognized the golden-haired one referred to as Will, whom she'd last seen ordering her out of his house four years ago. Knowing her luck, she must have summoned him like a bad fairy by thinking about what had happened at Lacey Hall. She stabbed the cloth with her needle, yanking the thread through, humiliation boiling in her veins.

"I'm sorry, Jamie, but I must have a retinue. I cannot present myself to our sovereign with fewer men than a minor baron." The Earl of Dorset's voice was deeper now, at eighteen having lost all trace of the boy.

The tall one snorted. "Bloody foolish enterprise, if you ask me."

"Maybe, but we've run out of choices."

Bored with the sober talk, the youngest of the three, dark like his taller sibling, jumped up and tugged James's cap from his head. Ellie guessed he must be thirteen or fourteen, sprouting like a beanstalk, but with none of his brothers' bulk as yet. "Stop grumbling, Jamie! You sound like a boring old fart. There's going to be a joust—surely that must be better than staying in Cambridge?" He skimmed the cap up the path. It flopped on top of the hedge. Hooting with laughter, he raced after it, leapt to snatch it back and repeated the game.

"Idiot," muttered James. "Tobias, give that back!"

"Catch me if you can!" The boy sprinted away, the cap crushed in his fist.

"You'll ruin it!" James ran after him. "I'm going to beat you within an inch of your life, you Devil-spawned nuisance!"

"Like to see you try!" jeered Tobias, disappearing round a corner.

"Thieving magpie!" James put on an extra spurt of speed, determined to save his cap.

Will shook his head and stooped to pick up the feather that had fallen from his brother's hat in the tussle. It was then he realized they had not been without a witness. He bowed.

"Good day, little mistress."

Ellie stood up and curtsied. "My lord." She smoothed her forest-green tabbinet skirt, thankful that she at least looked worthy of a lord's bow.

He gestured in the direction of the vanished Laceys. "My brothers." The earl left that hanging as sufficient explanation.

"So I saw." She kept her eyes on her embroidery, relieved he had not recognized her. But why was he not leaving?

He tucked the feather in an eyelet of his doublet. "I am interrupting your employment."

"Oh, it is nothing." She shoved the cloth behind her.

The defensive reaction provoked his interest rather than dampened it. "May I see?"

Reluctantly, she held her sewing out. It was a wretched piece, not improved by the scarlet cross-stitch she had just inflicted on it.

"A sampler?"

"Yes, my lord."

He twitched it from her fingers and flattened it. "I fear it is somewhat stained on this corner." He lifted his eyes to her face. "As is the maker." He touched her cheek.

Could there be anything more mortifying than to be caught out by the Earl of Dorset of all people? Ellie put her hand to her cheek, trying to hide the ink smudge.

"Here, let me." He drew a square of linen from his pocket and dipped it in the fountain playing beside the arbor. Holding her gaze with his, he bent down and rubbed the mark away. "All gone."

Ellie couldn't breathe. He was standing so close she could smell the hint of cloves in his breath and feel the heat of his touch on her face. Could he be flirting with her? The idea was preposterous. Yet his blue eyes were speculative, smiling, but still with a hint of hardness that she expected from him.

"May I ask your name, mistress?"

"Lady Eleanor Rodriguez, Countess of San Jaime." Her voice sounded strangely husky.

His smile dimmed. "A Spaniard?"

"My mother was from Madrid but has been dead these ten years. My father is English."

His lips curved upwards again. "And he is?"

"I think you might know him." Ellie prayed for rescue. A sudden storm. The arrival of the Queen of Sheba—anything. "He is a companion to Lord Mountjoy—"

"'Swounds, Will, what's keeping you?" bellowed James from the far end of the yew walk. "We'll be late."

Will took a step away, but not before his thumb ran lightly over her jaw, touching the little dip in her chin. He gave his brother a long-suffering look.

“Ah, my apologies, mistress.” James swept off his now-restored cap and bowed. “I now understand completely what’s kept him from his appointment.”

“The Lady Eleanor,” Will said by way of introduction.

“Sir.” Ellie took advantage of her good fortune. “I will not delay you any longer.”

“Then I’ll look forward to seeing you again when we both have time to linger.” He kissed her fingers, his eyes holding her gaze.

“Oh, um, well then, good day to you both.” Flustered by his gallantry, she dipped a curtsy and hurried back to the safe haven of her room. How on earth, she wondered, could she avoid the flirtatious earl for the duration of her stay at court? She had not forgotten his temper and did not want to be near when the fuse was lit by unpleasant memories of her father.

Chapter 2

Will watched her go with regret. His attraction to the dark-haired lady with her execrable embroidery had taken him by surprise. She'd been laughing at his brothers—that was what had done it. Her eyes had sparkled with humor, her smiling lips just begging for a kiss.

Will sighed. He was here on serious business and could not afford to be distracted.

James scratched his chest and yawned. "Who was she, Will?"

"I'm not entirely sure. A connection of Mountjoy's."

"Money?"

Will shrugged.

"Oh well, with our luck she'll be either already taken or penniless," James said philosophically.

"She's lovely, like a spring morning."

James gave a mock shudder. "Spare us—write her the sonnet, but don't try it out on me."

Will rubbed his close-trimmed beard. He was rather proud that he was now of an age where he could sport one. "I think she might like a poem. She had ink on her fingers."

"An educated female—the good Lord defend us from that unnatural tribe."

"Careful, James. Remember whose court this is."

James was not so reckless as to dig a deeper hole for himself. They might not think they were overheard but, as the lady had just proved, they could take nothing for granted. One whisper in the Queen's ear against them and they would be out in the cold. "So if she's not eligible, what are you going to do about the lovely little lady?"

"I've just this moment met her, Jamie. Your thoughts are running away with you as usual." Will handed over the feather and continued walking.

"You could set her up as your mistress. A prime piece like that won't stay unclaimed for long: if you don't, someone else will."

"I'm here to find a wife, not a paramour."

"Then you don't mind if I try for her?" James expertly ducked the blow he knew he had coming.

"You don't go near her."

"Like that, is it?"

"Oh, shog off, Jamie."

"Yes, my lord."

Tobias was waiting for them by the steps to Lord Burghley's private apartments. All three Laceys were intrigued to know why Elizabeth's most trusted adviser sought this meeting. Among his many responsibilities, Burghley was Master of the Court of Wards, which meant he administered the Lacey estate until Will reached his majority at twenty-one. He doubtless enriched himself by creaming off some of the profits from his ward's income as was the accepted practice for a placeholder at court. Burghley was a man to keep happy, as to be on the wrong side of him was tantamount to losing the Queen's favor.

A clerk ushered Will into the inner sanctum, bidding his brothers remain outside. Will entered the brightly lit room, finding Burghley standing in a commanding position by the window, dressed in rich black velvet robes trimmed with gold buttons. A small ruff fitted snugly under his mink-brown beard. A cluster of white hairs sprouted at each corner of his mouth, reminding Will of cat's whiskers, alert and twitching for the presence of vermin nibbling away at the fabric of the kingdom. Dark eyes surveyed the young earl, weighing, judging and, fortunately, not dismissing him.

"My Lord Burghley."

"Dorset. Good to see you at court." Burghley gestured to a chair, taking his position behind his desk. Behind him on the wall was Saxton's new map of England and Wales, the first ever to show accurately the Queen's domains. Will's eye was drawn briefly to the spot on the Thames occupied by his own lands, lying just south of the center of the chart and not that many miles from Windsor. "How did you leave your lovely mother?"

"The countess is well, sir."

"But she's not come with you?"

They hadn't been able to afford the clothing for more than himself and his brothers. As Burghley probably knew, his mother and sister would have to wait until the family fortunes improved. But still the polite dance had to be performed.

"Not this year, sir. She prefers the quiet of the country."

Amusement flickered in Burghley's eyes. "That's not the lady I knew in her youth."

"Age mellows us all."

Burghley smiled at that. "Not all, young man, not all. I do not believe the Lady Dorset would ever mellow." He picked up a decanter standing on the desk and poured two small glasses of red wine, pushing one towards Will. A good sign. If he had fallen foul of canny Lord Burghley, he surely would not be offered refreshment?

Unless it was poisoned.

Will dismissed that wild thought. He'd been watching too many plays.

"I expect you are wondering why I requested that you call on me."

"Yes, sir." Will sipped, relieved to find no suspicious aftertaste.

"I'm always on the hunt for good men, Dorset, and reports about you have been favorable." He waved negligently to the pile of papers on his left-hand side. "Steady, making sensible steps to restore your family's wealth, loyal. In short, a fine young man. Your father would've been proud of you."

Will swallowed the bitterness that he always felt when the last earl was mentioned.

"Thank you, sir."

"The Queen is, as you well know, the fount of all favor at her court, and doubtless you are here to win her regard, but I do have some discretion to employ people under my own aegis."

Will's ears pricked up. "Sir?"

"How is the land around Lacey Hall at this time? Quiet? No sign of Catholic agents?"

"No, sir."

"The families of the old persuasion not brewing trouble?"

This was trickier. Will did not like to be put in the position of telling tales on his neighbors.

"None that I am aware of, sir." Which was true. Old Dame Holton's adamant rejection of the new ways in the parish church was a matter of local interest only, and no threat to any but the vicar's peace of mind.

"Good, good, that chimes with the other reports I have received. What would you say if I asked you to be my eyes and ears in Berkshire?"

Will swallowed. "I . . . er . . . would count it an honor to serve the Queen in any capacity Her Majesty wishes."

"This is my wish, Dorset. And I'm not asking you to betray the foibles of your friends and neighbors; I have no time to police everyone's conscience. I am requesting that you keep any questionable characters under surveillance and report any treasonous behavior to me."

Put like that, Will could hardly refuse. "Well, of course, sir."

Burghley held his wine up to the window, where it shone the color of newly spilled blood. "We continue to walk the knife's edge, Dorset. Spain and the Pope look on us with ravenous appetites. It is no easy matter to be charged with the defense of the realm. The threat and the plots are all too real, as Campion proved."

Will was well aware that the Jesuit had been executed in December with two other Catholic missionaries; their crime had been to try to upset the delicate religious balance in the country that Elizabeth and her advisers were adamant had to be maintained. No sensible person wanted to return to the bloodletting of Queen Mary's reign. Peace was an aspiration Will could fully support.

"I will do as you ask, sir. I would have reported any worrying signs to you without this request."

Burghley smiled. "I know, Dorset, but there's more. I'd like to do something for you. Climbing out of the debt your father saw fit to leave you will take a great deal of luck and persistence. This position working for me comes with a small reward—three hundred pounds a year. For that, I expect you to think as my man and act as my man."

Will shifted in his seat, uncomfortable with the offer. He knew Burghley to be an honest politician, as far as that was possible, but it sounded like selling his soul to him.

"My first loyalty is to the Queen, sir."

"And so is mine, so there should be no conflict, should there?"

Will tasted his wine to give himself a moment to consider the offer. He couldn't refuse, as to do so would mean he was out of court even before he had a chance to make his entry.

"I'm honored, sir, that you have decided to place your trust in me."

"Humph!" Burghley grimaced. "Don't lie, young man, you are annoyed at the necessity—just as I would be in your shoes. But you need have no fear. You will find my favor a boon rather than a hindrance in your affairs. I'm minded to like you—I even think better of you for the reluctance to give away some of your independence. But do not mistake the matter: you would have to give it to one or other of the factions at court if you wished to get anywhere near Her Majesty. You may think later that it was better me than any other."

Will warmed to the man's plain dealing. "I believe I'm of that mind already, sir."

"Good. Ah, here's my son. Have you met Cecil, Dorset?"

"I have not had that pleasure." Will rose to his feet as a youth of around his age entered. Dressed in the same black robes as his father, Robert Cecil was something of a pale shadow, crook-backed and thin, but his hooded eyes were astute.

Not someone to be dismissed, Will thought.

They exchanged bows.

"Has my father been putting you on the rack for information?" Cecil asked, passing his father a letter.

"And turning the screws. But I think he has exhausted my knowledge now," replied Will in kind.

"Young Dorset will be working with us, Robert," Lord Burghley said, cracking the seal. "Take him to Benton and ensure he receives his stipend."

"At once, sir."

Cecil led the way out of the chamber. "He must value you, my lord, if you've got the old man to part with some money. You should be flattered."

"Or terrified."

Cecil gave a darkly cynical laugh. "That as well. First time at court since becoming earl, I hear."

"Yes." Will tried to quash the surge of self-doubt at his lack of knowledge. He had a fleeting impression of himself as a mariner wandering an ocean without a chart.

"Then I hope I can be of assistance. The place is full of vain Devonshire peacocks; it will be a refreshing change to have someone of my own age who is worth talking to."

Will could guess who the peacocks were who had made Cecil's life a misery. Walter Raleigh, a renowned son of Devon, fresh from the Irish campaign, had been cutting a dash recently. More fool him if he had spurned Cecil, for he had the ears of one of the most powerful men in the country. Will would not make the same mistake.

"I've never had many feathers to flaunt, Master Cecil, so I hope my conversation will not disappoint."

"You won't have to try too hard to beat the fools who fill the court with their galliards, capers and odes to their mistress's eyebrow."

"I can promise you I have never composed a line."

"Excellent. Leave that to Sidney and those who can rhyme." Cecil paused to bow to a sharp-faced nobleman dressed in severe black, a close-fitting cap covering his hair. "On your way to see my father, sir?"

"Indeed, Master Cecil. Is he within?" The gentleman's voice was soft but chilling.

"Yes, sir, and he is expecting you."

The man swept on with a swish of fur-trimmed robes around booted ankles.

"That was Sir Francis Walsingham," Cecil said aside to Will. "A useful gentleman for you to know. They're calling him England's Spy Master." He quirked a wry smile. "Not a man to cross."

"I hope you don't take this the wrong way, Cecil, but I pray I have no need to call on him. I intend to keep my lands free of plots and stratagems."

"Quite so, but the threat to the Queen's person is regrettably very real, else my father would not be paying you to keep Berkshire safe. Ah, here's Benton."

The clerk had Will's first pay ready in a pouch—three hundred gold coins. There had clearly never been any question in Benton's mind that the earl would be along to fetch it.

"Your brothers await you in the fountain courtyard, my lord," Benton said, marking receipt of the money in his ledger.

Robert Cecil bowed a farewell. "Until later, my lord."

Will tucked the heavy purse into his doublet and bounded down the stairs, wondering just what he had sold to Burghley.

"Well?" asked James, pouncing on him as he emerged.

"I'll tell you when we are alone," Will said swiftly, toppling Tobias from the fountain ledge to hurry him away. As they reached a quiet corner of the castle, he briefly recounted the interview.

"Three hundred! Gads, that's a fair purse!" Tobias exclaimed. "Can I have a new horse?"

"No!" Will and James replied in unison.

"I have to spend it on my appearance at the joust. As it was, I was going in our father's old armor on a broke-backed warhorse; at least now I can show myself to some advantage," continued Will.

"Give me the purse and I'll go see the armorer," offered James.

His brother's interest in all things military had already endeared him to the castle smith, so Will knew James stood the best chance of stretching their money a long way.

"I'm in your debt." He passed him the purse.

James took it and stowed it safely away. "We're in everyone's debt, Will; that's the trouble."

CHAPTER 3

LADY JANE PERCEVAL STOOD IN FRONT of the mottled glass in her chamber and surveyed her reflection critically. She adjusted the bodice on the tight stomacher of ivory damask to push her breasts up higher. Humming in disapproval as a small pox mark showed on the swelling mound, she dabbed her skin with ceruse, a paste of vinegar and white lead, ensuring all visible areas of skin were flawless white. Her honey-brown hair was looped over her ears and caught up in a pearl-edged headdress. Her lips were fashionably reddened by cochineal dye.

"Well?" She spun before her maid.

"You look very beautiful, mistress," Nell replied, knowing that failure to praise might result in a box on the ear. "You will be the loveliest lady at court. As fresh as a flower."

Jane bit her lip, trying to feel as confident as her maid. She had many people to face down that evening. Her father's lavish gift of a wardrobe for her appearance at court might have made her look as beautiful as a rosebud waiting to be gathered by some rich suitor, but she couldn't forget that she had already been plucked. Tweaking her bodice even lower, she comforted herself with the thought that though virginity was supposedly prized at court, few expected it these days in any but the Queen.

"The servants say that many more noble gentlemen have arrived this afternoon," Nell said, feeding her mistress's appetite for gossip, which was the main reason for her employment.

"Oh? Anyone we know?"

Nell turned her attention to the discarded clothes, folding them neatly. "Master Walter Raleigh is lodged near the Queen's apartments, they say."

"How fortunate for him," Jane said sourly.

Worse than no longer being untouched, in Jane's book, was the knowledge that she had been a fool, gulled by her brother's lustful best friend, Walter Raleigh. She scowled in the mirror, trying to dismiss her unwanted memories of the titillating courtship, culminating in a sweaty coupling in the home farm barn. With what she now knew was girlish naiveté, she'd thought he had been intending a declaration of love and a proposal of marriage; instead, she'd got a lost maidenhead and a moment of wild release before the horrid fact sunk in that she was just another warm body as far as Raleigh was concerned. He'd kissed her and patted her rump before riding away without a second glance.

I know better now, she told her reflection, confident that there was no outward sign of her lapse. Her monthly courses had come on time, so she did not need fear any further repercussions. Raleigh was a gentleman, or so he claimed, and comrade-in-arms of her brother, making his way as a soldier and adventurer; he surely would not reveal their secret? What would it gain him but her father's wrath and much shame for her?

Men are not to be trusted. They are to be used as they use us, she thought, drawing this teaching from her bitter experience. If she had not been so blinded by his dark good looks and sweet talk, she would have realized he was thinking with his codpiece, not his heart.

Her heart hadn't been involved either. It had been flattery that had wooed her; stupidity that had her allowing him to take it further. She'd learnt her lesson. Now it was time to make Raleigh and his ilk pay. She was going to be so dazzling, so desirable, he would be panting to have her again, and she would take great pleasure in refusing any further favors.

Jane fastened a string of matched pearls around her neck. Once she was wed, she might think again. Raleigh would make a good paramour for a woman with a rich old husband—for Jane was determined to marry someone who would conveniently die and leave her a wealthy widow while she was still young. Perhaps she would be like the Countess of Essex, who had managed to catch the handsome Earl of Leicester for her second marriage. Achieve wealth and power first time at the altar; choose the compatible bedfellow for later. If a woman didn't play the game to win, she would be trampled. Jane had no intention of being anyone's wifely rug.

"Tell my brother I'm ready to go down," Jane ordered Nell.

"Yes, my lady."

Nell picked up the linen towel, now soiled with smears of cosmetics, and went in search of Sir Henry. Lady Purity Perceval may think she deceived everyone with her behavior, but Nell knew the truth. Her mistress had taken a tumble in the hay with that Devon-born jackanapes last month and didn't want anyone to know it. Nell could've found some pity for her mistress being fooled by the man if Raleigh hadn't been so obviously a lusty buck after a quick swive. In truth, it was pleasing to see her mistress humbled.

The lady had always looked down her nose at others; now she's no better than the rest of us, thought Nell. The rigid ranks in their world were rarely breached, but a reminder that the Lady Jane was human would be good medicine for Her Arrogance.

Tugging her coif back to reveal the blond curls on her forehead, Nell knocked on Sir Henry's door.

"Come!"

She entered and dipped a curtsy. "My lady is ready, my lord."

Henry lounged on his bed and beckoned her nearer. Sandy-haired and stocky, he had the fighting spirit of a rough, wild bear. "Is that so, sweetheart?" He hooked his arm around her thighs and buried his face in her bodice. "Ah, you smell so good, Nell. Rose water?"

"Yes, sir." Nell glanced over her shoulder to check she'd closed the door.

"Because you know I like it?"

"It may have crossed my mind, sir." She ran her fingers through his hair coyly. Here was another exception that broke down the barriers between the likes of her and her betters. It made her feel powerful to have a man such as Henry lusting after her.

He nuzzled her midriff. "Do you know what's crossing my mind now, Nell?"

She giggled. "I can guess, my lord."

He tugged her down on top of him and ran his hand up under her skirt. "But we'll have to be quick. We shouldn't keep my sister waiting."

Nell squealed as he slapped her bared skin. "Oh no, sir, we couldn't have that. I've work to do."

"Then let us have no further delays."

•❁•

Jane paced the chamber, irritated that her brother did not immediately come on her summons. Henry was always like that, stubbornly keeping to his own time without regard to the wishes of others. Four years older and fresh from Ireland, where he and Raleigh had participated in the ruthless quashing of the Desmond Rebellion, he paid no heed to the views of his younger sister.

The door opened to reveal Henry lounging in the entrance. His hair looked mussed and his clothes askew.

"At last," huffed Jane. Pretending to be the innocent, she had to act as if she did not know the signs of copulation, but doubtless he'd been at it with that little hussy Nell.

"I got diverted, Janie. I apologize for keeping you." He mockingly offered her his arm. "You look splendid."

"You look a mess." Thinking of her family honor, she tugged his doublet straight and settled his gold chain across his chest. "Have many arrived yet?"

"Yes, there's been a rush today. Raleigh's here. Cecil. Sidney's around the place somewhere. The Mountjoys."

Jane smiled despite herself. "Good, I rather like Charles."

"Charles Blount's a good fellow but not enough coin for you, Janie. His father's wasting it all on some foolish alchemist. Or perhaps he has his eye on the man's luscious little daughter. I wouldn't mind learning alchemy from her."

Jane twitched the folds of her skirt straight. "Don't be crude, Henry."

Her brother smirked. "Oh, and the big news is the arrival of the Earl of Dorset. He's not had the funds to come to court before, but someone has provided him with the necessary. He's arrived with several gentlemen and twenty retainers in silk livery."

Jane rapidly calculated the cost of fitting out such a household. "How old is he?"

"Dorset? Eighteen. You should take a look at him, Janie. Perhaps his lack of coin will be made up by his handsome appearance. He'll be seeking a girl with a dowry like yours."

Jane dismissed the young earl as being far too likely to outlive her. She needed someone infirm and gullible. "And when does the Queen arrive?"

"Tomorrow. That's when the celebrations really begin." He rubbed his hands. "I can't wait."

Ellie sat at the end of the table occupied by Mountjoy's household. The banqueting hall was rapidly filling up, and the servers were having a difficult time keeping pace with the healthy appetites of the young lords and ladies gathered for the feast. Ellie did not think anyone was watching her so she enjoyed herself spying on the others as she cut her capon into tiny mouthfuls to prolong the savory taste, a marked improvement on her usual fare. The flavoring was thyme, with perhaps a hint of marjoram, roasted to perfection.

She looked along the table to see what other dishes were set out for them to try, wrinkling her nose at the soused herrings. She'd had enough fish during Lent to last her a lifetime. At the far end, in front of a dish of venison pasties, was her father, seated next to Lord Mountjoy deep in discussion about some obscure point of philosophy. He didn't notice that his sleeve was trailing in the gravy and that his meal was cold by now. His patron, a jovial gray-haired man with sagging jowls like a bloodhound, shared his fascination with the subject but did not let up from eating, allowing his companion to do most of the talking while he made his way through the meats on offer.

Up near the top table, the Earl of Dorset and brothers were sitting with Robert Cecil, sharing the mess of pottage between them, tearing off chunks of bread to soak up the thick soup. Lord Burghley usually chose to dine in his rooms, probably to avoid the frequent interruptions and petitions he would otherwise have to endure in the public chamber. Word was he was closeted with Sir Francis Walsingham, discussing high matters of state security. Burghley's son, however, had opted to join the other young people and for once looked happy in company. Ellie had exchanged only a few words with Master Cecil, enough to know that he was a man of wit and learning, even if his appearance was somewhat unfortunate. He had been quick to sound out her value, too, dubbing her Mistress Wisdom when he noticed her correcting an error in a Latin translation he had been reading. She had thought they might perhaps be friends if their paths crossed again, but now that he was close to the Laceys, she would have to avoid him.

At the other end of the table from Cecil sat Walter Raleigh and his companions. Raleigh slouched, legs spread, displaying his shapely calves in his rich navy hose for all to admire. His doublet was of the finest brocade, midnight-blue encrusted with pearls, his ruff tinged an azure hue to match. An earring dangled from one ear and he wore his black hair dashingly swept back. And the codpiece! Ellie almost snorted in her wine. He was such a popinjay, sporting the largest one that was deemed decent to wear. *Here I am, ladies,* he seemed to broadcast. *Come and get me.*

Dios, that man was transparently in love with himself! He would no doubt be on his best behavior when the Queen arrived on the morrow, focusing all his manly attention on her, but for tonight he was anyone's.

There was a lull in the conversation in the hall as two young nobles made a late entrance. The girl was dressed in ivory, the man in black: a clever contrast. Ellie knew them already—at least Sir Henry she had briefly met in Mountjoy's chambers, and she could guess the lady was his sister. Envying the material of the girl's apparel—it must have cost at least a hundred pounds, with all those pearls sewn onto the fabric—Ellie watched them sweep down the hall to sit with Raleigh. The girl hesitated slightly before accepting the seat at Raleigh's right hand. Was it Ellie's imagination or had Raleigh actually caressed her backside as she sat? Surely that was too forward of him? She decided she must have been seeing things. But then, she wouldn't put anything past that walking Priapus.

"Ellie, Ellie, my love!" Her father was calling for her attention. "What did Paracelsus say about the application of heat to base metals?"

Those at the table between her and her father fell silent, waiting with interest for her response. Wishing Sir Arthur to the bottom of the ocean, she gave him the answer as close to the text as she could remember.

"Yes, yes, that's it! Thank you, my dear: I always know I can rely on your memory." Sir Arthur turned back to his conversation, leaving Ellie the focus of much attention. Charles Blount, Lord Mountjoy's headstrong son, broke the silence.

"Well, Lady Eleanor, you are a veritable walking library! We stand in the shade of your towering learning."

The others chuckled at his lame joke.

"Thank you, sir, I will take your words as a compliment." Ellie toyed with the food on her plate, wondering when she could make her excuses. She knew that Charles disliked her, largely because of the influence her father had over Lord Mountjoy, but he had no liking for bookish girls on principle. It was like the Earl of Dorset all over again, though this time she was held to be part of the alchemical conspiracy to extract as much money from the family as possible. Then again, looking down at her dress, which she owed to the Mountjoys, she supposed he had good reason to think this.

Charles leant across the table, dropping his voice to a confidential level. "I was wondering if a woman's heart beat under that armor of scholarship you have donned. The doctors say that learning dries up the passions in a female, rendering her withered as an old apple and as sour to the taste. What say you to that?"

"Indeed, sir, I do not consider myself a very learned person." She opened her eyes wide with the appearance of innocent wonderment. "Perhaps you should direct your inquiry to one of greater wit than myself? Her Majesty, perhaps? I am sure you would be the first to admit that our sovereign lady is famed for her scholarship and understanding."

Blount sat back with a grunt of displeasure. "Clever, very clever," he muttered. "Lady Eleanor, I fear that your wit may prove your undoing. And I for one cannot wait."

"I beg you, sir, not to hold your breath for such an event. It may prove detrimental to your well-being." She piled a cheese tart on her plate, not because she was hungry but for something to distract from her shaking hands, and mashed it to pieces with her spoon.

Charles gripped her wrist, stilling her motion. "Lady Eleanor, my case is urgent. My father will hear no reason since yours seduced him with his promises of gold. He's like a sick man throwing off all covers, unable to see that the fever burns inside him and not in the room. You must take your father away before it's too late."

He was right—Ellie knew it. But if she had had any influence over her own parent, she would have long since exercised it. He'd had the fever first; Lord Mountjoy was merely unfortunate to have caught it from him.

"You're hurting me," she whispered, tears starting in her eyes.

Bully that he was, Blount didn't let go. "Will you do as I ask?"

"How, pray, may I achieve this thing? I am only his daughter, not his master. He'll not leave until your father tells him to go."

Blount released his grip with a snort of disgust. "You like your comfortable life here too much to try."

Ellie rubbed her wrist. "I pray you pardon me," she whispered.

"Pardon is not enough. There will be a reckoning. Pray God that he'll have more mercy on you than you have shown to my family."

"Excuse me, sir." She rose from her seat, leaving her plate full. She would not be able to force down a mouthful under his disapproving gaze.

"Go, go." He waved her off. "Unlike my father, I do not wish for your company."

Ellie bolted from the hall, cursing the day when Sir Arthur had first styled himself an alchemist.

Will watched the little black-haired lady depart in haste, wondering what had upset her. From the expression on the face of the gentleman she had been sitting opposite, they did not part as friends.

A lovers' tiff? He hoped not. He'd prefer her to be without attachments.

"So, my lord, are you intending to try your skill at the joust?" asked Robert Cecil.

"For my sins, sir, that is my intention."

"Then I hope you may win. There are some in this hall who royally deserve to be knocked off their perch." Cecil glared across the table at Raleigh, who, catching the look, raised his goblet mockingly in his direction.

"Why does he bait you?" Will wondered, not really meaning to speak the thought aloud.

"Because he's a foolish coxcomb drunk on the Queen's favor. His kind are two-a-penny at court."

"Then I hope I can pluck his plumage on the morrow."

"Amen to that."

"I wonder, would you be so kind as to enlighten me as to the name of that gentleman sitting at the lower table?" Will gestured discreetly to the Lady Eleanor's dining companion.

Cecil took a quick survey of the room. "That's Charles Blount. A fine fellow saddled with a foolish father. But you would know all about that."

Will's eyes wandered up the table to Lord Mountjoy—and then to his neighbor. "Good God, what is he doing here?"

Cecil perked up at the earl's scandalized tone. "Who?"

"That charlatan Sir Arthur Hutton."

"The scholar?"

"The bloodsucking flea who drained my estate of all its value. I hoped he'd be dead in a ditch by now."

"Far from it. He's with Mountjoy."

Will looked back at Blount. "Poor bugger."

Cecil hid his smile at the uncivil language. "I see you understand all too well."

"I must find out what I can do to help him. The scales never fell from my father's eyes. He died still believing he would get gold from nothing."

"Ex nihilo nihil fit—nothing comes from nothing."

"Indeed. I wish my father had paid attention to his Lucretius."

Cecil waved the serving man away, refusing to dull his wits further with more wine. "Speaking of Latin wisdom, there is one remarkable benefit in having Sir Arthur in your household."

"I can't imagine what that might be."

"He has a very scholarly daughter. An Amazon of learning. She corrected my Latin the other day." He lowered his voice. "I suspect she has knowledge of Greek."

Will had forgotten Hutton had a daughter. The scruffy urchin must by now have grown into a dry stick of a maid hunched over her parchment, boring everyone with her cleverness. He wondered if that was the reason why the dark-haired lady he'd met in the garden had ink on her fingers; he could well imagine the alchemist's daughter forcing the girls in Mountjoy's household to follow her pursuits in the same way her father trapped the master. Will decided he would be doing the lady a favor saving her from all that by getting rid of the alchemist. Girls no more needed learning than a fish a pair of boots. "I'm not sure I'd call that a benefit. The daughter must be terrifying."

Cecil smiled at the mismatch between this description and the reality. "Oh yes, she's terrifying."

Chapter 4

Too dispirited to sleep, Ellie begged a candle off a friendly serving man and finished her translation in the small hours. It was an act of desperation: she didn't really believe it would influence the Queen in her favor, but she had to do something to try to get out of this hole into which her father had dropped them both. He showed no sign he cared about the humiliating dependence he forced on them; he was happy playing with his scientific instruments on the floor of this deep well-shaft of lost opportunities. Ellie felt she stood at the bottom, staring up at the patch of sky. She could see the stars, so far above her, but no rope to climb.

"Ding dong bell, Ellie's in the well," she hummed. *"Who put her in?"* She paused.

The answers were many. Her father. Herself—perhaps she should have left him long ago; it might have shaken him out of his dreamworld. But to go where? Since her mother's death, all contact had been broken with her Spanish relatives, the distance and religious differences throwing up too many obstacles to continue the relationship. All she had left were a few Spanish phrases of her mother's; her jewels had long since been sold. Her father's English family had disowned him when they saw that his passion for alchemy had reached unmanageable proportions. If she had gone to them, would they have taken her in? She had felt too much love for her father and, to be honest, too much fear of rejection by her kin, to risk it.

"Alchemy put her in," she hummed. *"Who pulled her out?"* That would be no one. Her father was like a child, relying more on her than she dared trust in him. There was no knight in shining armor coming to her rescue.

The sleeper in the nearest bed shifted onto her back and began snoring, nose peeping out of the covers. Outside, two stable cats struck up a lively argument, screeching like out-of-tune viols played by the musically inept.

Wonderful: just when she was ready to turn in herself, the nighttime chorus began. Ellie wrapped her blanket more closely about her shoulders, blew out the candle and placed her head on her arms resting on her desk. She lay listening to the noises until she fell into an uncomfortable doze.

The movements of her friends woke her. Ellie sat up slowly, rubbing sleep from her eyes and gingerly revolving her neck on her shoulders, conscious of a painful ache across her back.

"Ellie, you lackbrain!" said Margaret Villiers, a cousin of Lord Mountjoy, laughing. She was a rosy-faced girl with tightly curled red hair, and also happened to be one of Ellie's favorite people. She was always cheerful, bearing her lack of good looks with good humor; as a result she was one of the most attractive ladies of Ellie's acquaintance, much sought out by the gentlemen for her lively company. "Why did you not come to bed?"

Ellie yawned.

"You've ink on your face."

Ellie rubbed her cheek. "Not again." Worried that she had smeared her manuscript overnight, she quickly checked her work. It was unharmed. She had merely lain on the blotter.

"I declare, it says something!" said Margaret in amusement. She tilted Ellie's chin to the light. "I think it says G-O-L-D—gold."

"Can you get it off me, please?" asked Ellie. If she were superstitious, she would see it as a sign. Her father's madness was now staining her skin as well as eating at her heart. She surreptitiously crossed herself, whispering a prayer to be free of it.

Margaret rinsed out a cloth and wiped the ink away. "Did you finish your work?"

All the girls knew about Ellie's great enterprise.

"Yes, I did. At about two in the morning."

"Oh, Ellie." Perceptive to the feelings of others, Margaret well understood what Sir Arthur was costing his daughter. "But that's good, isn't it?"

"For what use it will be, then yes."

Margaret gave her a brief hug. "At least you'll be free to enjoy the jousting."

"True."

"And watch the Queen arrive."

"Yes, I'm looking forward to that."

Margaret picked up her camlet skirt and slipped it over her farthingale, then tugged on her bodice, attaching the two together with ties. "Good. Now help me with my points at the back and I'll do yours."

Ellie deftly tied the metal-ended tags, closing the gap. The other two girls were doing the same over on the other side of the chamber, none of them rich enough to afford the attention of a personal maid.

"Good morning, Isabel, Katharine," said Margaret brightly, grinning her gap-toothed smile.

Isabel, Margaret's freckle-faced younger sister, groaned. "Maggie, how can you be so cheerful so early?"

"It's in my nature. You either laugh or cry at our absurd world, and I long ago chose what I would do."

Ellie decided she could learn a lot from her friend.

"And besides, there's the prospect of ogling scores of handsome men today. Why would any maiden at court be unhappy?" Margaret sighed. "Praise God for his wonderful creation."

"Amen to that," chorused Isabel, making the others giggle.

"Talking of the wonders of God's creation, did you see Master Walter Raleigh?" asked Katharine, a thin girl with long fair hair, which she was expertly braiding. "Isn't he perfect?"

Margaret snorted. "And knows it too. He's been strutting about like he owns the world since his soldiering in Munster. Eyes down, Katharine, he has his sights set on higher things than us." Margaret chose a set of sleeves from her trunk to match her petticoat. "My personal favorite was that new earl, Dorset."

"And his brothers," added Isabel, waggling her eyebrows suggestively as she fastened a garter round her silk hose. "I wouldn't mind a ride with one of them."

"Isabel Mary Villiers!" scolded Margaret without much rancor as the others hooted at her sister's bawdry.

"Don't worry, Maggie, I'll behave," Isabel promised. "But I fear we'll all be outshone by Lady Jane Perceval. Did you see her dress?"

"I could have fed the poor of London with what it cost to make that gown," said Margaret, who was always slightly disgusted by the flaunting of wealth that went on in court circles.

"Beware of the brother, girls," warned Katharine, settling her headdress on her blond coronet of braids. "He likes exercising his powers of persuasion on the ladies."

"In that case, I am insulted. I spent several minutes in his company yesterday morning," joked Margaret, "and he did not once try to seduce me. Remember, Ellie? You were there."

"He was too busy flattering Lord Mountjoy to bother with us." Ellie straightened her friend's tangled laces. "He's too shallow to have the good sense to notice you."

Margaret laughed. "I'll take that as a compliment, though I know what you're implying."

"He is a magpie, going for the flash and glitter rather than the things of value."

"My, my, aren't you the wise one. But I rather think him a wolf, and I should be happy he let this ill-favored lamb escape." Taking down her ruff, which she'd pinned to the curtain for safekeeping overnight, she passed Ellie the pincushion. "Fix this in place for me?"

Ellie spun her round to start the laborious process of attaching it from the back.

"You'll be careful won't you, Ellie?" said Margaret. "He's less likely to ignore you, and he did give you a rather ravenous look."

Grateful for her friend's concern, Ellie took a pin out of her mouth to reply. "Don't worry, Maggie. I know what to do with wolves."

"Oh yes? What's that?"

Ellie stabbed the starched cambric, anchoring it to the wire support attached to Margaret's collar. "Simple: shove Latin declensions down their throats till they snap their teeth shut and go off in search of less learned prey."

Laughter rang round the chamber again. After submitting to having her own more modest ruff pinned to her collar, Ellie hurried the last few steps of her dressing, tucking wayward strands of hair under her velvet cap, then gathered up her papers.

"I'll take this to my father and meet you later at the joust," she promised Margaret.

"Very well, Ellie. But if I find you dragging your heels in some dusty corner of the castle, poring over another book, I'll have serious words with you."

"Maggie, you have me all wrong." She tapped a finger on her chin. "Handsome young men or books? Hmm. The handsome men win every time."

"I'm pleased to hear it. And, Ellie"—Margaret lowered her voice so the other two would not hear—"do not treat it as a jest. We both know that marriage is the only answer for us. You should be taking a serious look at the young men at court."

Ellie knew her friend spoke the truth. She was in danger of slipping out of respectable company entirely if she did not find a husband to save her from her father before too long. Her foreign blood was nothing but a drawback in a court that hovered on the brink of war with Spain.

Ellie sighed. What had she to offer? With a dowry of abstruse learning and an empty title, she thought she would be very lucky indeed to attract the attention of even a minor figure at court. "I'll be there, Maggie."

Ellie knew exactly where to look for her father. Lord Mountjoy traveled with all that was necessary to set up a laboratory in every location in which he spent any time. As she guessed, Sir Arthur and he were cloistered in his private chambers, hovering over their latest experiment. Neither of them had bothered to change from their evening wear, which suggested they had been up all night.

"Father?" Ellie hovered at the door and dipped a curtsy to both men.

"Not now, Ellie," Arthur said in distraction. "We've almost found it—we're close!"

He always thought he was nearly at the secret. As usual, his face shone with enthusiasm, eyes feverishly bright. The sleeves of his robe were clipped back, revealing his thin arms with their red burns and pale scars.

"Just two drops of phoenix tears into the Venetian." Arthur uncorked a bottle of clear liquid and dribbled it into a glass vial. "Then apply heat to the mixture." He held it by long tongs over the little stove burning on the marble-topped table.

Bang! The vial exploded, showering the room with burning liquid and glass. Ellie and Lord Mountjoy ducked. Arthur was saved from serious injury by the tongs, but splinters speckled his arms. Oblivious to the pain, he wiped the blood casually away and picked out the bits.

"Hmm, interesting, very interesting." He rooted through the pieces on the desk. "Did it work? Can you see the nugget?"

Mountjoy actually went down on his hands and knees to find the elusive gold.

Ellie poured clean water into a basin for Arthur's scorched fingers. "Father?"

"What is it, Ellie? Can't you see I'm busy?"

"I know, sir, but I've finished the translation for the Queen."

"You have? Good, good. Put it over there and I'll have a look at it when I've time."

He'd been badgering her to complete the work for weeks and all he could say now was he'd glance at it when it suited him? Ellie swallowed her anger and disappointment—these feelings were nothing new when it came to her father.

"I'll put it in your room, then."

"Yes, yes, that would be best." Arthur had given up looking for a nugget and now was scratching his head, pondering this latest failure.

"Here's water for your burns."

"I'm burned?" Arthur looked down at his knuckles. "Good gracious, you're right." He plunged his hand into the cooling basin. "You're a good girl, Ellie. Now run along."

"Yes, sir."

Having left her manuscript in her father's tiny chamber, Ellie made her way out into the courtyard by St. George's chapel. The sun warmed the honey-colored stone, making even the row of grotesques above the first row of windows look funny rather than frightening: a monkey grinned down at her, a goblin pulled a face—cheeky expressions to have over the entry to a solemn house of prayer. The double row of windows glittered in the morning light. The walls were more like lace than sturdy supports for the vast roof, but there was hidden strength to them, thanks to the buttresses. It reminded her of the large ruffs that were now in fashion—a flimsy appearance held up by an undergirding frame and plentiful application of starch.

A ginger cat with a white stomach trotted over to Ellie and wound around her legs in a self-administered stroke. Ellie crouched down to rub its head. Inside, the choristers began practising their anthem to welcome the Queen. The music was so sweet Ellie could not bring herself to leave; she scooped up the cat and paused in the doorway and closed her eyes. Under her hands the cat's chest rumbled in a purr of contentment.

Men's voices alerted her to the fact that company approached. Turning towards the round tower in the center of Windsor, she saw the participants in the joust heading for the chapel, led by the chaplain. They must be coming to hear a blessing on their entertainments and prayers for their preservation as, even though it was but a game, noblemen were still injured in the lists. The cat scrambled free and strolled away to wash its paws in a patch of sunshine out of the thoroughfare. Thinking it had the right idea, she stepped quickly out of the way of what was a private moment for the men. As she did so, she came face to face with the Earl of Dorset, who had surprised her by arriving from the direction of the castle gates. Already partially dressed for the joust, he wore a beautiful gorget on his upper chest, engraved and inlaid with gilt, his compass cloak tossed negligently over one shoulder. He smiled broadly when he saw her. He at least was pleased to see her, even if the feeling was not mutual.

"Lady Eleanor of the embroidery bower." He swept her a bow. "May I take this as a sign that fortune favors me this day?"

"My lord, good morrow." Ellie dropped a neat curtsy and made to leave.

He caught her hand before she could escape. "Not abandoning me so soon, surely?"

"The service is about to begin. I would not wish to keep you."

"What need I of the priest when I have an angel to bless me?"

Ellie groaned inwardly at his flowery language. "I think perhaps you have more need of spectacles if you mistake me for one, my lord."

Her wit brought Will up short. He had expected an exchange of the usually courtly phrases, but she had pulled the rug from under his feet. He threw his head back and laughed.

"Sweet lady, you know not your own worth. I would count myself truly blessed if I could carry your favor in the joust this day. Your colors—a sleeve perhaps—to wear on my body as I hazard it for your honor?"

Dios! *You wouldn't ask if you knew who I really am,* thought Ellie grimly.

"I'm afraid, sir, I have none to spare," she excused herself, backing away.

Will's face clouded but he did not relinquish her hand. "You've not granted your favor to another man?"

She ignored the possible less innocent implication of the question, but it was clearly there in the earl's mind. "No, sir. I have not."

"Then there can be no objection." He pulled her a step closer. "If not a sleeve, mayhap you have, say, a piece of unique embroidery upon you? That will satisfy me." His lips curved in a smile.

"Embroidery?"

"I promise to cherish it and return it unsoiled. Well, no more soiled than it already is," he amended, daring her to share his good humor.

Ellie fingered the cloth in the pocket attached to her girdle. Would it do any harm to play the courtly game for as long as the earl's illusions about her lasted? She had never dreamt a noble lord would want to wear her colors at a royal joust. Did she not deserve the dream before it dissolved, leaving her with nothing again? "Well, I . . ."

He clapped his hand to his heart. "Please, dear lady, grant me this simple wish and I will die happy."

She laughed now. "There is no need for anything so dramatic, sir. Here, take my favor with my good wishes. May it serve you well."

He tucked the cloth into his doublet, then brushed his lips over her knuckles. "I will endeavor to honor your token."

He took his leave and followed the others into the chapel, where now the singing swelled in a psalm of praise. Ellie watched him go, wishing that she could rewrite their past dealings. If only she could work alchemists' magic on herself, turning her dross into gold worthy of a man such as the earl. Instead, he was her enemy but did not know it yet, while she was perilously near to being nothing.

Chapter 5

Only an hour after her expected time, the Queen arrived by barge—a vivid figure in dazzling robes sitting on a gilded chair, surrounded by her household and the musicians employed to enliven the river journey. Will stood with the other nobles on the landing stage below the castle to greet her, silently calculating the cost of maintaining such a large entourage. No wonder Elizabeth was always short of funds. First came the Yeomen of the Guard, then the sergeants at arms and gentleman pensioners, all charged with her protection, though Will thought the yeomen looked the most serious about the task: big, square-jawed men who seemed likely to know what to do in a fight.

They parted to allow Elizabeth to step ashore. The Queen's attendants, seven Ladies of the Bedchamber and four Maids of Honor, waited on the sovereign, dressed in clothing of black or white—foils to let their mistress shine out brighter. Elizabeth herself was splendidly attired, wearing a red velvet overskirt and a bodice trimmed with pearls, a white satin forepart and sleeves embroidered with gold, a lace-edged ruff framing her face. Will had not seen her at close quarters for some years and was privately shocked at how she had aged. She was, he reminded himself, a year shy of fifty. Her glittering garb could not hide the fact that her cheeks had hollowed, her shrewd eyes were surrounded by crow's-feet, her hair a false auburn. Blackened teeth did not improve her appearance, though she rarely smiled, keeping her thin lips closed as much as possible. Will thought of the contrast with the Lady Eleanor, whom he had met only a few hours before, and wondered what honest words of praise he could bring himself to lavish upon the Queen. He would have to find some, as it was expected of all single men to court her favor with the language of love.

Escorted by her most trusted privy councillors, Burghley and Walsingham, the Queen passed down the line of her nobles, starting with the senior lord present and moving to the junior figures. As an earl, Will was fortunate to be near the head of the queue. He bowed low as she drew level. Two jeweled toe caps stopped in front of him.

"My Lord Dorset, we are very pleased to see you at court at last."

"God save Your Majesty, I am deeply honored to be able to pay my respects to your gracious person. Every year I have been prevented from coming into your royal presence has felt like an age."

"Very good." A regal nod approved the sentiment. "I look forward to seeing more of you. Perhaps you intend to take part in the lists today?"

"Indeed, Your Majesty, if it pleases you I will test myself against the other noble lords."

"Excellent. I like nothing better than a holiday joust."

She moved on to the next lucky noble to catch her attention. Will heaved a discreet sigh of relief. That seemed to have gone well. She had lingered longer than he'd expected and given a sign of her approbation. He mulled over his words: no, he had not disgraced himself as he had feared.

The entourage slowly processed after the Queen, going up the hill at the pace she dictated. Will watched the gorgeous display with interest, particularly entertained to note the jester, dressed in motley, and two richly robed dwarf women, bringing up the rear. Elizabeth disappeared into the castle to her private apartments, giving the signal for everyone else to disperse.

He went in search of his brothers, who, in view of the lack of time before the joust, were helping Turville to polish the armor. The suit was on loan from the blacksmith, who had bought it from the estate of a disgraced lord. It had been lying in storage for some years.

"All well, Will?" asked James, breaking off his whistling to acknowledge his brother's return.

"Yes. Her Majesty spoke with me, welcoming me to court." He picked up a cloth to join them—no one in the Dorset household could afford to hold themselves above manual labor. It was tough enough keeping up the appearance of wealth as it was. The twenty silk-clad retainers he had hired the day before for his entrance had been dismissed, the livery packed away until the next occasion called for them.

Turville, who had grown fat over the past few years in Will's service, hung the breastplate on the wooden rack and picked up the helmet. He gave Will a disapproving look. He, for one, did not think an earl should polish his own armor. "My lord's horse is groomed and ready. I've a boy walking him in the field for you."

"You have my thanks, Turville. I see you are as efficient as ever."

"How long have we got?" asked Tobias, chucking a shoulder guard onto the sacking.

"Careful with that pauldron, young sir!" growled Turville.

"Peace, ye fat guts! I've not harmed it."

"Rather through luck than any judgment of yours," commented James, cuffing his brother for his rudeness to a trusted retainer.

"I should be on the field within the hour." Will began the laborious process of tying on the separate pieces, leaving only the heaviest parts to be carried to the lists so he could put them on just before the joust started.

Turville rushed to aid him. "Your father would be proud if he could see you, sir."

"Maybe." Will had never enjoyed what he would call a loving relationship with his father. The old earl had been too distracted by his mania for gold to pay much attention to his sons, and there had come a time when Will had simply stopped trying. Had he still been alive he probably would not even have noticed his son's appearance, but there was no point in saying as much to Turville, who idolized the family he served. Will pulled out the embroidery and transferred it to his sleeve before the breastplate covered his doublet.

"What's that?" Sharp-eyed Tobias tweaked it from his fingers. "Gads, this is a mangy piece of work!"

Will grinned and snagged it back. "I know."

"And you are carrying it about like a precious cargo because . . . ?"

"Because it is a jest between myself and a certain lady in the court. I wear her favor today."

Tobias hooted with laughter. "I hope her fortune is in a better state than her sewing."

"I fear not, but I do not court her for matrimony. I merely like the wench. She has a wit like Spanish steel, ready to cut down any puffed man who dare insult her intelligence with vain words."

James frowned. "You dragged me out of college to get you married off to advantage and you waste an opportunity like this to impress some rich young lady on a maid without prospects? Will, you need your head examined."

"It does no harm," Will said defensively, knowing his brother was right. He should stop flirting with the lady and settle down to a serious pursuit of a wealthy bride. "After today, I promise to stay on the scent."

"Lady Jane Perceval is your best choice." James checked his reflection in a vambrace. "Rich, comely and sent to court to hook a husband."

"I saw the lady last night. She is very fair." But there was nothing about her that sparked his interest.

"That's it, then. You should cultivate a friendship with her brother and seek an introduction to the lady. The sooner you get this business completed, the sooner Tobias and I can get back to our studies."

Tobias groaned. "Speak for yourself, Jamie. Take as long as you want, Will. This is far more fun than my tutor's lessons."

Will's suspicions were aroused. "I've never known you to be so studious, Jamie."

"That's because it is a certain goodwife of Cambridge that holds his affections," said Tobias.

Will rolled his eyes. "I pray I will not next hear of this in the bawdy court and find you doing penance in the marketplace."

James winked. "I pray that too—that you won't hear of it. But I cannot speak too highly of the charms of the older woman. My education is proceeding apace."

"You should try that line on the Queen," Tobias chuckled.

"Tobias!" James gave him a second cuff on the other ear to balance out the rattling of the brain. "Do not even jest about such things."

Laced into his armor with his brothers carrying his shield and helmet, Will made his way carefully down the inn stairs, movement restricted by his garb. They lodged outside the walls of the castle, the better to disguise their lack of retinue and to save money. Aware of the grand preparations going on in the upper room, the innkeeper and her maids stood at the bottom of the steps to watch them go.

"Godspeed, my lord!" called Mistress Gideon. Will and his brothers had become favorites of hers since their arrival—and of the starry-eyed maids, who gossiped about little else.

"Thank you for your good wishes." He thumped his mail-clad hand to his chest, unable to bow in his breastplate.

"Tell me why we're doing this?" he groaned to James once out of earshot of their hostess. "This armor is as comfortable as wearing a tinker's pots. I feel a fool."

"You don't look it." James was about to clap his brother on the back but thought better of it. "Very martial—a young Achilles. Still, you're right: it is a ridiculous sport with no relevance to modern warfare. Give me a company of harquebusiers and ample shot and I'd make short work of all you knights."

"But it is the romance of the lists, sir," chipped in Turville as they walked up the cobbled main street of Windsor to the castle gateway, their passage garnering the friendly cheers of the citizens. "I remember the stories about King Henry, how he used to dazzle the court when he took part in the joust as a young man. The Queen likes the old ways of chivalry."

Will knew this, of course: the sport was another display of the sovereign's power as her noblemen risked their necks in her honor, she the focus of their knightly love and duty. It was a rite of passage he had to pass through if he wanted to make an impression at court.

"I just hope I sustain the romantic illusion and don't end up flat on my back in front of the spectators."

"Think positively, Will. You're not a bad horseman," said James.

"But not as good as you, I take it?"

"Practice makes perfect, Will. You must admit you've not spent as much time as I have in the saddle."

"That's because I've been too busy scraping together the money to keep your horse in the stable."

Sensing that his brothers were about to descend into a round of their usual sniping about their respective employments, Tobias turned the subject.

"Will, did you hear about the explosion?"

"What?" Will clanked in his direction. "There's been an attempt on the Queen? When?"

"Not the Queen, Will. It was earlier. Some want-wit alchemist blew up Lord Mountjoy's bedchamber. It was reported to Lord Burghley and both gentlemen have been forbidden from doing any more experiments."

"Sir Arthur Hutton—it has to be him."

"Aye, that's the name. He's in disgrace."

"Sent away from court?" asked Will hopefully.

"No, just given a scolding and told to stick to making books rather than bombs. Lord Mountjoy was reminded that alchemical experiments were not permitted under the royal roof."

They arrived on the fields surrounding the tiltyard, already busy with noblemen and their attendants. Early competitors took runs at the rings or struck the target, avoiding the sack that whirled round to knock them from their saddles if they were not accurate or fast enough. Pennants rippled in the light breeze; armor shone; horses, resplendent in magnificent cloths of gold and azure, trotted past. Heralds bearing their masters' coats of arms preceded the most splendid of the contestants, crying out their lord's titles. The players in the masque that preceded the joust were gathering in one corner: white-decked maidens pretending to be vestal virgins, musicians carrying instruments decorated with ribbons, a horse dressed up like a dragon to carry the Queen's champion—it was a confusing but colorful mix of images and symbols.

Turville gave a shrill whistle. A lanky-limbed blackamoor boy approached, leading a huge white stallion draped in a caparison of Dorset's colors—emerald-green.

"I like the horse," marveled Will. "Whose is he?"

"Yours, for the moment. Belonged to the same disgraced lord as the armor," said James. "The blacksmith's been stabling him for a few months now. Ready to sell if you want him."

Will rubbed the velvet nose of the stallion. Oh yes, he wanted him.

"How disgraced was this lord, exactly?"

"He's in the Tower."

"Ah."

"Needs the money. Can't afford to keep paying for the upkeep of a horse he's unlikely to ride again."

"I'll give him a trial today, and if he proves as good a mount as he looks, I'll buy him."

Tobias gave a disgusted snort. "How come you get another horse when I don't even have my own?"

"Because he's the earl and you're not," muttered Turville.

"What's his name?" asked Will.

"Barbary. The boy comes with him if you wish." James indicated the groom efficiently controlling the creature among the noise and confusion of the crowd.

Will knew it was fashionable to have an African page but he had no money to waste on empty gestures, and besides, the boy was a bit too old to count as a fetching addition to his entourage. "I only want the horse." He took the reins from the lad and led the horse towards the mounting blocks, not noticing the crestfallen expression on the groom's face.

James tapped the boy on the shoulder. "Don't worry, Diego, he'll take you too. I know my brother better than he knows himself."

"Barbary and me, we are never apart," said the lad disconsolately.

"I'll explain it to him later. Do a good job today and I swear you won't have to worry about whether or not you'll have a roof over your head tonight."

Diego perked up and ran to assist the earl in the tricky business of mounting a horse in armor. Turville fitted the last pieces on his master, then stood back as Will climbed the specially constructed steps.

"I bet he's swearing like a fishwife in there." Tobias smirked, watching his brother's awkward progress.

Barbary was evidently well trained as he made no fuss when he received the weight of an armored knight on his back. James approached with the lance, the end padded to avoid serious injury to the opponent. Turville handed up the helmet.

"Put the lady's favor on my pauldron," said Will to his manservant. He struggled with the visor. "How on earth is anyone supposed to see in this thing?"

"I don't think you are," said James, climbing the steps to help his brother. "Just point and charge. Having fun in there?"

"Whose stupid idea was this?"

"Yours."

"Last sodding time, Jamie. You can uphold the family honor in future."

"Smile—pretend you're enjoying yourself. Raleigh and his company have just arrived."

Will fixed a debonair expression on his face. He had never been so uncomfortable in his life. The sooner this farce was over, the better.

"My Lord Dorset, that is a fine stallion you have there," called Raleigh from the back of his chestnut warhorse. His position as the Queen's favorite had allowed him entry into the exclusive sport of the nobility despite his lack of a title. He made the most of his humble origins, turning the handicap to his advantage. His armor was a serviceable plate-steel lacking adornment: a statement in itself. "You have much experience of the field of chivalry?"

Will knew Raleigh was making it plain to those listening to their exchange that he could not match the seasoned soldier in this arena. He did not make the mistake of pretending he could. "No, Master Raleigh. I am a novice in the art. I trust you will be gentle with me in my introduction to the sport."

Raleigh laughed. "You've come to the wrong place if you seek gentleness. Perhaps you should have stayed abed with your mistress this morning." The gentlemen of his company chuckled.

Will bared his teeth in a humorless smile. "You mistake me: I'm not afraid of taking a knock or two."

"Then I look forward to our encounter if we should chance to be set against each other."

With a superior smile, Raleigh rode on, garnering the lion's share of the attention from the spectators milling about the field. Will watched him go, at the same time noticing the change that had come over the tiltyard. The participants in the pageant were taking their places; the music swelling, drums throbbing in time to the clapping of the audience. Anticipation was high as people waited to see the cream of the court battle it out with blood and guts. A surge of excitement washed through Will: the game was afoot—time for him to prove himself in the hunt.

"What an ass! I hope you do meet him, Will," said Tobias angrily, glaring after Raleigh. "I hope you knock him into the next county so he can bray from his backside."

Laughing at his brother's rage, Will's spirits rose still further. "It's no matter. As long as I don't disgrace myself in the yard, I'll be happy."

Will urged Barbary into a walk to get used to the horse and his gait. The high pommel of his saddle helped Will keep his seat, but he wished he'd put in a few more hours of practice before attempting this in public. He'd jousted for fun with his brothers at home, but never with such a prime horse and before so many spectators. At the end of the first circuit of the exercise track, he spotted his little lady among a group of girls admiring the horsemen. He smiled to see her arm in arm with a carrot-topped maid, giggling at Sir Henry Perceval's high white plume, which kept dipping in his eyes and irritating him. Will drew up beside them, praying Barbary would continue to do him proud.

"Ladies," he said politely. "I hope you will be watching the competition."

The four girls quickly dipped deep curtsies, looking at each other in awe at being addressed by a lord. Three of them were clearly wondering who had been introduced to the new earl and therefore could speak to him. Reluctantly, Ellie stepped forward.

"Yes, my lord, we will be in the stands."

Will touched her favor on his shoulder. "I wear your token over my heart as protection."

"You'd be better off with a shield, sir." Again his lady turned his attempt at flattery to the practical, which amused Will greatly.

He winked. "I have one of those too. Wish me luck, ladies."

He spurred his horse forward and rode on.

"Ellie, you sly puss, you didn't say!" Isabel gasped. "How did that happen?"

Ellie tugged her friends towards the wooden seating lining the tiltyard. "It means nothing—just a joke between the lord and me."

"It's no joke to have your favor on display before the court," commented Margaret. "And what a lord—the armor, the horse, the man!" She pretended to wilt from heart palpitations.

"Put your eyes back in your head, Margaret Villiers," said Ellie. "We all know that for a lord like that to pay me any attention must mean he doesn't know who I really am. I think I just amuse him. His regard will not last." Not least because he had personal reasons to hate her.

The girls watched as Will next drew up alongside Sir Henry Perceval, seeking an introduction to his sister. The lady was dressed in buttercream silk, her ruff dyed gold so that she looked like a walking treasure trove.

"See what I mean? Rich girls never go out of fashion," sighed Ellie.

Margaret squeezed her arm. "But today it is your favor he wears, not hers."

But for how much longer? Ellie wondered.

Chapter 6

The first day of the joust ended reasonably well for Will. His appearance was much applauded in the procession past the Queen, and his initial meeting in the lists with three knights concluding with him having lost one and won two. He took the greatest pleasure in the fact that he had kept in his saddle.

Turville drew him a much-needed bath before the banquet. Will lay in the tub, knees bent double, relishing the warmth soothing his bruises, while his brothers dissected his performance. This postbattle analysis was the best part of the whole competition in Will's opinion, particularly when washed down with a mug of the hostess's best ale.

"You didn't keep your lance level," said James. "That's why Blount was able to get a hit."

"Hmm," said Will in noncommittal tone. It was easier to criticize than to play; his arm had been exhausted by the time he'd run up against Sir Charles Blount.

"Master Ass-Faced Raleigh was in the lead at the end of the day," mourned Tobias.

"Good luck to him," murmured Will, unperturbed.

"Bloody stewards must be blind. Perceval took him nice and sweet in that second run and still they gave it to Raleigh."

"Ah well, life isn't fair." Will squeezed out the sea-sponge and soaped his arms.

"I see you met the Lady Jane before the contest," remarked James, stretching out his legs and yawning.

"Indeed."

"You should ask to wear her colors tomorrow."

Will grimaced. It would be the politic thing to do if he wished to advance his cause with her. She'd seemed pleasant enough, beguilingly innocent and pleased with his flattering words, not like a certain sharp-tongued dark lady he could mention. Perceval seemed to favor the match and had been swift to make the introduction. Rumor had it that the father, Thaddeus Perceval, Earl of Wetherby, an old-fashioned nobleman with a fortune in wool and coal mines, had instructed Henry to catch the noblest lineage for his sister, so Will knew he stood a good chance.

"Perhaps I will. I'll see what happens at the banquet tonight."

This wasn't good enough for James. "Will, we're running short of time."

"I know that, but this is the rest of my life I am hazarding here, no small matter easily settled. I want at least to know something of the character of the lady I will eventually woo and wed."

Ever pragmatic, James sighed. "To be honest, Will, all that matters at the moment is the size of the dowry. We are skimming just an inch above ruin."

Infuriated at having his rest time spoiled by a reminder of their problems, Will threw the sponge at his brother. "I know that. But do I have to remind you that you were the one who persuaded me to take on that extra servant today?"

"Diego's a good investment—a wonder with horses."

"Only if we can afford to keep a stable. If you're so damned eager for a solution, go raid a Spanish galleon!"

James threw the sponge back so that it slapped into the water. "If you had the damned funds to fit out a ship, I would!"

Tobias rolled his eyes. His older brothers, so close in age, had always fought like cat and dog while remaining fiercely loyal to each other. Taking matters into his own hands, he jumped on a chair to gain their attention.

"I know what—I'll go found a plantation in the Americas and discover a gold mine!"

"Get down, you fool," growled James, though he began to smile at his younger brother's antics.

"No, I will not be silenced—I'm on to something here. You merely have not yet recognized my brilliance. Just you wait: I'll come home as rich as the King of Spain and buy you each an estate and myself three."

"Only three?" asked James drily.

"Yes. Never let it be said that I am greedy."

"Just deluded," added Will, hauling himself out of the tepid bath. "Come on, then: let's fit out our ships for the banquet and go plunder some rich lady galleons, if any cross our path."

"Cross? After your heroic efforts today, they'll be steering straight for you, Will," promised James, passing him the linen towel.

"Sounds a recipe for a shipwreck."

"That's a definition of marriage for you."

•❁•

Descending the stairs on her brother's arm, Jane felt sick—sick of the pretending, the shallow words of her many suitors, the lewd remarks of Raleigh. She already hated court, and she had only been at it for two days. She realized that it was a snare into which she had thrust her head willingly, thinking she would manipulate it to her purposes, but now she knew her struggles would only tighten the noose. Her family expected her to make a glittering match, had lavished money on her for the purpose, but she had lost her relish for conquest.

And why? Only yesterday she had contemplated her image in the glass and promised herself to win the marriage game; today she looked about her and found she wanted no one because no one wanted her for herself. Raleigh was part of the problem, with his knowing looks reminding her of her shortcomings every time she turned around. But it had really struck home when the charming but insincere young Earl of Dorset had showered her with pretty compliments. Not once had he actually looked at her properly, his eyes skimming her face only briefly, not meeting her eyes. He was not alone: every gentleman spoke to her in the same way, affecting an interest when their minds were on other things, usually the size of her dowry. She'd felt so depressed by the end of the day that she had even tried to explain it to her maid, but Nell had merely stared at her as if she were mad. She had been foolish to speak her mind so frankly, as she knew her maid had no liking for her. There was little sympathy to be had from someone so far beneath her rank. Any loyalty she got was paid for.

"Why the long face, Janie?" asked Henry. He held his right arm in a sling, having sprained it falling from his horse that afternoon.

"You'll curdle the milk. You should be pleased with yourself. So far you've been a great success."

"Thank you." Jane didn't bother to confide her thoughts to her brother, knowing he would dismiss her complaints as girlish nonsense.

"Father will be pleased to hear the Queen spoke to you."

It had been to approve the quiet color of her gown. The Percevals knew better than to risk the Queen's ire by setting their daughter up as a rival. The Countess of Leicester had had her ears boxed for that offense and been dismissed from court.

"Midnight-blue becomes you."

Jane hadn't wanted to wear this gown, but it had been specially commissioned for the banquet and too expensive to waste.

"I'm glad you think so."

"Raleigh wore that color last evening." Henry gave his sister a speculative glance. There was something between her and his friend and he wasn't sure he wanted to know what.

"Then I pray he won't wear it again tonight. We wouldn't want to be mistaken for a match."

"He has good prospects. You could do worse."

"I could do better."

They turned into the antechamber to the dining hall, pausing to rinse their hands in the silver basins prepared for the purpose. Servants carried food in from the outdoor kitchens to the servery: sizzling sides of beef, joints of pork, pies and roast chickens. Carvers lined up, ready to set to work once the signal was given that the Queen was on her way.

Jane wished the evening were already over. "We had better take our places; she'll be here anon."

But her brother had spotted someone he knew. He stopped before a black-robed man and a pretty dark-haired girl standing by the entrance as if uncertain of their welcome beyond.

"Sir Arthur, I hear you've been setting the castle on fire," Henry said jovially.

The alchemist shook his head. "An exaggeration, sir. Merely a little accident soon mended."

Jane stared in horrified fascination at the shiny burns on the back of the scholar's hands. A little accident?

"I hope you were nowhere near the conflagration, Lady Eleanor," her brother continued, turning his full charm on the girl.

"Not near enough to account it worth mentioning," the girl said, retreating a step, as if she was well aware of Henry's interest and wished to run.

Yes, thought Jane, she would be the sort to attract Henry: sultry brown eyes, complexion more golden than a fashionable white, but attractive nonetheless, a mass of raven curls inexpertly braided so that locks spilled free, teasing her neck and doubtless driving her brother wild. Had the girl done this on purpose? Jane frowned. If she had, then she deserved the petty annoyance of her brother's attention.

"I do not believe you've had the chance to meet my sister. Jane, may I present Sir Arthur Hutton and his daughter, Lady Eleanor?"

The girls exchanged curtsies, Jane's shallow, Ellie's deep.

"What did you do to your arm, sir?" asked Arthur, drawing Henry aside in conversation. "I hope it is not broken?"

Jane continued to look coldly at the girl, holding herself aloof.

The lady twisted her hands nervously. "I . . . er . . . admired your gown yester eve, my lady, but today you exceed even that. You look very well indeed."

Jane examined the girl's green skirt. It was clear that she had no others, as it showed dirt round the hem, probably picked up at the joust earlier in the day.

"A woman is more than her dress," Jane said, intending it as a put-down.

The girl, however, surprised her by smiling. "I'm glad you think that. All this fuss over what we wear is so tiresome, don't you think? If that was all that mattered, perhaps they should send the gown on the tailor's dummy to these feasts and give us a quiet night at home?"

The image was an extraordinary one and appealed to Jane's sour humor. She found herself smiling. "For that to work, you would have to send a herald to announce each arrival."

"Exactly. 'Make way, my lords and ladies, for the dress of her extreme importance, Countess of Everything, and his grace, Duke of All!'"

"Would save the Treasury a fortune in food."

"And raise the normal level of conversation to new heights."

Jane spluttered, then lifted a lace-edged handkerchief to hide her laughter. "Shh, don't! I'm supposed to be here on my best behavior."

The lady sighed. "Me too. But after Father exploded Lord Mountjoy's close stool this morning, I rather doubt anything I do will shock the company."

"He did what?"

"Blew up the privy. He'd managed a small explosion with a glass vial, but thought to repeat the experiment in a confined space to save himself further burns. He got rather carried away." The girl was regarding her father with the harried look of a desperate mother with a disobedient child. Jane's sympathy stirred.

"How serious are the repercussions likely to be?"

Lady Eleanor gave a tiny shrug. "We're not entirely sure we'll be welcome at Lord Mountjoy's table tonight. His son already hates us and his father is lying down, overcome by the fumes from the latest disaster."

"Sir Arthur seems in good health."

"Yes, my father is immune to injury, it would seem. Or at least, believes he is."

Jane glanced into the hall. Nearly all the seats were taken now, which meant the Queen was on the point of arriving. "I know Sir Charles Blount. I could speak to him on your behalf if you wish."

"No need, my lady. I'd prefer my father to feel at least some of the consequences of his adventure today. How else will he learn?"

It seemed an odd thing for a child to say in reference to a parent, but Jane guessed the relationship had long since been reversed.

"He's pinning his hopes on a gift I've prepared for the Queen," continued the girl, rubbing her arms as if cold. "A translation. But so far we've heard nothing from Her Majesty."

"So you linger here wondering if fortune will smile or frown on you?"

A sweet smile flickered over the girl's lips. "Exactly."

"I will pray for the former, then."

"Thank you."

Henry managed to extract himself from his conversation and offered his arm, leading Jane into the hall.

"We must stop making these late entrances," he said insincerely, nodding to acquaintances as they walked to their places.

"You love the attention, Henry," she replied, smiling through gritted teeth.

He handed her to her seat. "I'd be grateful if you cultivated the Hutton girl for me, Janie."

Struggling with the hoops of her farthingale, Jane forgot to smile. "I'm not your pander, Henry. I like the girl. Leave her alone."

Henry took a place beside her. "What do innocents such as you know of panders, Janie?" He lowered his voice. "Maybe not so innocent, eh?"

She shivered. "I don't know what you mean."

"If you wish to retain the claim to ignorance, then I suggest you do as I ask. I would hate to have to send back any unfavorable remarks to Father about your conduct at court."

"Judas," murmured Jane.

He took his knife from his belt and stabbed it in a loaf of bread. "At your service, but you're no Virgin Mary, are you, sister?"

A fanfare of trumpets announced the approach of Elizabeth. Everyone in the hall rose to their feet.

"God save Her Majesty!" declared the herald before sweeping into the hall at the head of the procession, the ushers walking backwards before the Queen.

Jane joined in the cheers. It was foolish to be jealous of the monarch—her position was unique—but Jane could not help but envy the Queen for that moment at the center of everyone's attention. Under no rule but that of God, Elizabeth kept the men dancing before her as she glided to her seat, her clothes an astonishing display of wealth and power—cloth of gold, ropes of pearls, a ruff of proportions beyond any other in the hall. The sovereign drew the eye like a jewel in a well-crafted setting, striking both fear and awe in her subjects. Jane mused that if she could but learn her Queen's secret for managing her unruly subjects, then maybe she would not have to fear her brother's threats or the prospect of marriage to one of the empty-hearted men who courted her. She also would be too clever for them.

But then, Elizabeth had never married—since ascending to the throne, she had never submitted to any man. The Queen understood that a woman's power lay in the courtship, not the wedding, and held off the threats to her person and realm by hinting but never committing. With a numb sense of hopelessness, Jane knew she could not use that behavior for her pattern, as she had no kingdom with which to bargain.

The Queen took her place and nodded to her chaplain, who droned a long, extravagant grace. When he finally finished, the Queen sat, and everyone else followed, a ripple starting with those nearest the center of power, spreading out to the lowliest knight at the far end of the tables.

"Raleigh's done well for himself," observed Henry, signaling a server to bring him a cup of wine.

Jane studied the placement at the top table and spotted him among the highest nobles near to the Queen, far above his station.

"His star rises. That should benefit us," Henry continued, piling a spoonful of lamb stew onto his plate, his movements clumsy, as he had to use his left hand.

On the other side of the hall from where they sat, Sir Arthur and Lady Eleanor approached the Mountjoy household, skulking along the wall in the knowledge that it was poor manners to arrive after the Queen. The girl looked as if she'd rather be anywhere but there, and Jane couldn't blame her. When Sir Arthur attempted to take his place at the end of the bench, Sir Charles Blount signaled his men to prevent him. The resulting whispered argument began to attract eyes to that obscure corner. Henry snorted his amusement as two of Blount's retainers forced Sir Arthur to retreat, escorting him out of the hall with the application of their firm grip to his elbows. That left his daughter stranded. She made to follow her father, but one of the girls at the table caught her hand and pulled her down beside her.

Henry tore the meat off a drumstick. "Plenty of room over here," he said through his mouthful. "Send her a message, Janie. Invite her to join us."

"She is well enough where she is, Henry. Leave her alone."

"Not for long, she isn't." Henry nodded his head to the two men who had returned from ejecting the alchemist. On a signal from Blount, they tapped the lady on the shoulder and jerked their heads to the door. Blushing, she got up and ran from the hall, her carrot-haired friend looking outraged on her behalf.

"Well, well." Henry threw his napkin down. "Think she needs a shoulder to cry on, Janie?"

"Henry, don't."

"Excuse me. I have an errand of mercy to run." He slipped away, disappearing through a side door behind the arras to avoid being noticed.

Jane stared at her empty plate, angry tears burning at the back of her throat.

Chapter 7

"My lord? My Lord Dorset, are you quite well?" Robert Cecil beckoned a servant. "Bring the earl a cup of wine."

Will looked down to find a goblet in his hands. He tossed it back and laughed without humor. "My thanks, sir."

"You are ill?" asked Cecil.

Will held the cup out to the servant signaling for it to be refilled. "There's nothing wrong with me. I was just taken by surprise."

Cecil returned to his plate. "Few surprises are pleasant ones."

"I couldn't agree more." Will snapped a wing off a roast duck. "Things seem fair but prove to be foul."

"I take it you do not refer to something you have eaten?" Cecil thought back to the moment when his companion's mood had changed. "The sight of Sir Arthur disturbs you this much? You need not worry: he's on his way out of court if my father has his wish. The man's a public menace."

"It wasn't the father I was surprised by." Will drained his second goblet, sending immediately for more. It was a lesson for him, he supposed: he should've been concentrating on his mission at court, not flirting with chance-met girls. Thank God he'd had his eyes opened before he had taken the relationship any further. He'd half feared before the feast that the Lady Eleanor had quite dulled his appetite for courting other girls. Now he realized what he should have suspected: his ink-stained maiden was the alchemist's brat.

"You refer to the Lady Eleanor?" Cecil frowned. "Ah, yes, she is unfortunate to have such a parent. Not the Amazon you expected, I'd hazard. A sweet maid. Blount did her wrong by sending her from the hall. I pity her for the shame she must feel."

"Shame?" Will nearly knocked over his cup as he reached for the salt. "I doubt she feels such a human emotion, else she would not venture among decent company."

"You do not like the lady? I have always found her pleasant and well-mannered."

"Then I take it that you do not know her well. She has the art of seeming other than she is."

"That's a grave charge, my lord." Cecil was evidently not pleased with Will's conversation. He looked to his neighbor on the other side, seeking more pleasant subjects.

Will refused to drop the matter. "Then how do you explain, Cecil, that I in my ignorance wore an alchemist's colors today at the joust?" He squirmed at the humiliation of having flaunted the hated Hutton's symbol for all to see.

Cecil turned back to him. "You did not know who she was?"

"I thought she was the Lady Eleanor Rodriguez, Countess of San Jaime."

"She is. Her mother's title, which she inherited—unfortunately without any lands to accompany it."

"Like a card cheat's sleight of hand, the wench uses an empty Spanish title to distract from her true name—Hutton."

"So she lied to you?"

"A sin of omission, but yes, I think she did."

"And she had reason to know that you would hate her on sight if you knew her true identity?"

"We last met when I kicked her and her father off my estate, so yes, she did."

Cecil smiled crookedly and raised his cup in a toast. "Then I say 'Well done, the lady.' She makes as fair a hand as she can of the poor cards Fortune has dealt her."

Will had to bite his tongue to stop himself arguing back with Cecil as he would one of his own brothers.

"In that case, I throw in my hand, Cecil. I'll have no dealings with a Hutton."

"I see you are a believer in the sins of the father being heaped on the heads of the children, Dorset." Cecil sat back to allow the servants to set the next remove of dishes. "Ah, apricot tarts—a favorite of mine."

Will settled for more wine, having lost his appetite for sweetmeats. "My own experience proves that to be true. You cannot escape the consequences of your parentage."

"You speak like an Old Testament prophet, Dorset. I'd dispute if our Savior would agree with you."

"I speak as I know."

"Hmm." Cecil glanced across at his own father, sitting at the Queen's right hand. "Then I praise God for blessing me with one of whom I can be proud."

No half-wit, Will saw that he was being offered an opportunity to restore the harmonious tone to their conversation.

"Indeed, your father is a remarkable man, a steady hand at the tiller of the state."

Cecil smiled. "Very good—my father as the Queen's helmsman—he'll like that. Now, my lord, tell me what you think of music."

Ellie ran as fast as she could away from the castle, taking refuge in the gardens she'd visited the previous day. The last person she wanted to see was her father; he no doubt would be wondering what he had done to deserve the ejection and would try to enlist her sympathy. He had not the faintest idea of how the world saw him—nor did he care. Let him take his complaints to Lord Mountjoy; she was sick of it all.

Ellie kicked the stone basin of the fountain where the earl had wetted his handkerchief only yesterday, feeling trapped and desperate. Hot tears traced scorching paths down her cheeks; she dashed them away with the heel of her hand, annoyed with the futility of crying. It never made anything better. No one heard, saw or cared when she was upset. She wanted to scream, to rant—but what would be the point?

"Lady Eleanor?"

Ellie froze.

A man walked out of the shadows. Not the earl, as she had half wished, half feared, but Sir Henry Perceval.

"Oh, sir." She dipped a curtsy, hoping he had not witnessed her unladylike kicking of the garden ornaments and praying it was too dark for him to see her tears.

"I noticed those knaves turn you away from the feast. As I told my sister, you'll always find a welcome in our party. She was adamant that I should seek you out to ensure that you come to no harm."

She had? Ellie felt touched that the Lady Jane had spared her a thought.

"Your sister is most kind, sir. I am . . . I am quite well, thank her for asking."

"I would not perjure myself with a false report." He took a step closer. The light was fading, his face was in shadow, but Ellie feared he would see hers too well if he came any nearer.

"Really, sir, I merely came out here to . . . get some air before retiring." She moved away, her skirts brushing the yew hedge at the back of the arbor.

Her retreat only encouraged the hunter to approach. "Fie on you, Lady Eleanor, you tell not the truth," he said softly, shaking a finger at her. "I see the tears those rogues have cost you." He reached out and traced the path they had left on her cheeks, letting his thumb brush past her ruff and come to rest on her collarbone. "See, the track runs to your heart." He trailed his index finger across her skin to the square neck of her gown, following it with his gaze.

Ellie was suddenly aware how far they were from other people.

"It is true, sir, that I was a little upset," she said, hoping formality would encourage him to step away. "So once again, I thank you for your good wishes."

He walked his fingers up her chest to rest in the hollow of her throat. She lifted her chin, trying to escape the touch of the back of the hand. "Sir?"

"Poor Lady Ellie," he sighed, the pad of his thumb feathering over the sensitive skin of her neck to where her ruff was pinned to her collar. "It doesn't have to be this hard."

"It doesn't?" Ellie wished her voice was less of a frightened squeak. Her eyes darted from side to side, looking for an escape route.

"There are those who would wish to make your path smooth, see those lips smile more than they frown." His thumb now brushed her mouth, tugging the bottom lip slightly. Not breaking eye contact with her, he lifted the thumb to his own mouth and pressed it to his lips.

Ellie shuddered. "I'm . . . I'm grateful to anyone who wishes me well." *I mustn't provoke him,* she told herself. *I must persuade him to leave this as a bit of harmless flirting.*

"I may not look like I can today," he said with what he probably thought was a charming smile, gesturing to his sling, "but I can protect you."

At what cost? thought Ellie. "I am under my father's protection, sir."

"He does a bad job of it, does he not? You are a jewel of great luster marred by a poor setting. If you were mine, I would dress you in silk, wrap you in lace, put satin shoes on your feet."

Does he ever listen to himself? Ellie marveled. It was evident he was far more intrigued by the unwrapping. He wanted to turn her into a high-class courtesan but made it sound as if it were a favor.

"You are the soul of generosity, sir, but I have no need of such things. If you do not mind, I wish to return to the castle now."

He smiled fondly at her, shaking his head. "Such an innocent. You have no idea of what I'm offering you, do you?"

He was a fool if he thought her that ignorant. "Please, sir."

He dropped his hand to rest on the curve of her hip. "I think, perhaps, I should show you a little of what I mean." He crowded her back to the hedge, arm clipping her waist to press her against him, lips seeking hers. Ellie tried to protest, but he took advantage and thrust his tongue roughly in her mouth. She shoved at his chest, but he just laughed and held her tighter.

"No, no, do not struggle, little bird." He rested his forehead against her, his breath heavy and hot. "Shh, now I'll not be unkind. Just a taste, something we can both enjoy."

"Please—"

He swooped again, convinced he could seduce her with a little coaxing. The hunter was not going to let the prey flee now he had her cornered.

Will had no desire to linger at the feast, and looked for an excuse to retire as soon as was deemed polite. The Queen departed for a private entertainment in her rooms with a select circle, so he was free to plead the next day's joust as an excuse when he left Cecil. As he stood, he recognized the signs of having had too much to drink, his legs unsteady, his mood dark. He waved off James and Tobias, telling them to stay as long as they liked. No need to spread his bad humor to them by denying them the pleasures of the evening.

"Don't forget the Lady Jane," murmured James, nodding to where the exquisite blonde sat on the other side of the hall.

Tobias snorted. "Her face looks like thunder."

"Peace," growled James, not wanting Will to put this off. "She just needs cheering up, since her escort was so unmannerly as to abandon her. Having a handsome knight ask for her favor should do the trick."

Will sighed heartily. "I've got a better idea. This lovesick knight, too abashed by his lady's blazing beauty, sends his herald"—he yanked Tobias up—"to win her over with honeyed words. Got that, Tobias?"

"Me?"

"Yes, you. Let's see if this expensive education I've been paying for has taught you the art of persuasion."

"Dammit, Will!" spluttered Tobias.

"Go to, be a very Cicero and plea my cause before her." Will shoved his brother in the shoulder blades, taking his vacant place beside James.

Walking stiffly, aware of his brothers' eyes, Tobias approached the lady.

"Not a bad bow," commented James.

Will waited for Lady Jane to look in his direction as he knew she would once Tobias began his pitch. He raised a cup to her in salute.

"He's doing well. She's already smiling," Will murmured, warming to this idea of distance courting. It seemed to be more successful than his attempts face to face.

"Aha! He's laid the bait and caught her." James thumped the table with his knife hilt as Tobias pocketed the sleeve she handed him. "Glad to see the lady came prepared with a spare one. She knows how to play the game."

Will suppressed a twinge of regret. Somehow the scrap of embroidery had seemed far more meaningful.

"There, he's done it: left her with a smile on her lips and the favor secured." James threw out his arm as Tobias approached. "Here comes the hero, back from the wars. How did you persuade her so quickly?"

Knowing they were still observed, Tobias reverently handed over the sleeve, which Will kissed and tucked in his doublet. With his back to the lady, Tobias grinned.

"'Twas a simple matter, Jamie. I said I had a brainless brother—a fusty nut with no kernel—who'd made but one sound judgment and that was to devote himself to be her knight, if she did but take pity on the poor fool."

"You did not!" groaned Will.

"Did too. She laughed and said I was a motley fellow who pleased her humor. She surrendered the sleeve without protest and wishes you well in tomorrow's joust."

Jamie chewed on a handful of raisins. "Unconventional, but it worked. Give the Cicero points for strategy."

"I suppose I brought that on myself. I'm to bed. Don't wake me up when you come in, and keep Tobias out of trouble, Jamie."

"Yes, my lord." James grinned.

"Shouldn't it be the other way round?" suggested Tobias.

"No, by appealing to his sense of responsibility I'm hoping you'll both turn up with all limbs and teeth intact." Will weaved his way out of the hall, wondering why the floor had suddenly become uneven.

"Walking like a seaman on land," commented Tobias.

"Yes, half-seas-over is our Will. Bed's the best place for him."

When Will stepped outside his dark mood returned, heightened by the fact that everyone else seemed to be enjoying themselves while he was miserable.

Scheming jade.

Deceitful witch.

He heaped insults on the absent lady's head, but it didn't make him feel better. A perverse desire to punish himself guided his feet to the spot where he had first seen her. He needed to learn the lesson that he should not make impulsive judgments, but should know a person's worth before offering friendship. He'd dishonored his family by sporting the colors of the very ones who had brought them low; it stuck in his craw to remember that. And he'd felt so smug, enjoying his little joke with the lady, while all the time she'd been laughing at him.

Arriving at the arbor, he stumbled in only to discover it was already occupied. Of course, it was the perfect place for a tryst.

"Apologies." He gave a staggering bow and tried to retreat before the couple could take offense. Unfortunately for his dignity, he fell over the bench and landed on his backside.

"Dorset? What the devil are you doing here?" cursed Sir Henry Perceval, annoyed, as well he might be, for the untimely intrusion. He clasped his lady's head to his chest, doubtless trying to protect her identity.

"Damned bad timing. Didn't mean to interrupt, but I'm a little in my cups. Give me a moment and I'll make myself scarce." Will rolled to his knees, then helped himself up by the bench.

The lady seemed to be trying to say something, but her words were muffled by Perceval's tight grip.

"Thousand pardons all," Will continued, finally finding his feet.

"Dorset, you're rambling. Westward ho, my good fellow."

"Absolutely. At once." Which direction was the inn? It was hard to remember when he had a problem remembering which way was up.

His departure was preempted unexpectedly by the lady kneeing Perceval in his crown jewels and pushing herself out of his embrace. She was shaking with outrage. Her companion by contrast was howling in agony.

"God's teeth, lady, that's harsh!" Will chuckled. His laughter dried up immediately when he found himself looking down into the Lady Eleanor's furious face.

She swiped the back of her hand across her mouth. "Not harsh enough. He . . . he assaulted me without invitation, my lord."

Strange how hatred can sober you up, reflected Will, finding his mind clearing like clouds shifting from the face of a full moon.

"Really? Is that what happened? Sir Henry, are you all right?"

Bent double, Perceval waved a hand, which either meant he was dying and needed saving, or that he was slowly recovering. Will decided on the latter.

Will's tone informed the lady without any more words that his attitude to her had undergone a complete transformation. He could sense her bracing herself for renewed attack.

"I see that you doubt me, but I swear it's the truth," she said, her dark eyes glistening with tears—a cunning trick to engage his sympathy.

"Oh yes, I understand now. You came innocently to this arbor, secreting yourselves away in the dark, and then were surprised when he explored your favors. Come, mistress, neither of us was born yesterday."

The girl's face crumpled and her trembling grew worse—a distressing sight if he had not known her to be a good actress.

"You play the injured maiden very well, mistress. My congratulations." Will treated her to a mocking bow. "But as your affections have so clearly passed to another knight, I will return that favor you so kindly bestowed upon me." He tugged the sampler from the pouch on his belt and held it out. When she did not take it, he let it drop on the grass. "I'll leave it there, then, for any man to take, like its maker."

The lady reeled back as if he had struck her a blow, but then gathered herself. Before he knew it, she had kicked him in the shin and taken to her heels. He hopped on one leg, then tumbled over, discovering his balance was still not at its best.

"All well, Dorset?" gasped Perceval.

"Bloody girl felled us both!" Will remarked to the stars, lying on his back.

"God, she's lovely. Not yours, then?"

"Not mine," Will said bitterly.

"Good. I'll go after her. Wish me luck."

"You'll need it," muttered Will.

CHAPTER 8

Too scared of the consequences of kneeing one lord in the groin and kicking another in the shin, Ellie dared not return to her room. She was left with no choice but to find her father, who, inadequate as he was as a protector, would at least stand by her if either man came seeking revenge. She found him sitting on a bench outside Lord Mountjoy's chamber, thumbing through his tables, which he noted in a pocketbook.

He looked up, pleased to see her. "Ellie! Enjoyed the feast, did you?"

Biting her lip, she shook her head. "They didn't let me stay." Unbidden, tears began to pour from her eyes.

"Ah now, my love, no need to cry so. Those men of Blount's are mere nothings, not worth your tears."

She began to sob, shoulders heaving. Arthur gathered her to his chest and awkwardly patted her back. "There now, sweeting, there now. I'll ask a servant to bring us something to eat. Would that make it better?"

He didn't know, couldn't conceive, that anything but an empty belly could trouble his little girl. How would he react if she tried to explain what had happened between her and the gentlemen in the garden? She could well imagine his angry response, storming off to confront them, but what good would that do? The earl, for one, would like nothing better than a chance to crush her father just as he had her with his insults; Perceval would probably laugh in his face. All that would result would be public knowledge of her humiliation, a fatal blow to her reputation.

"How about a piece of cheddar and an apple, eh? You always liked cheddar. Perhaps some quince jam to go with it?"

If only the application of jam and apples could fix things as it had done when she was little.

"There now, no more tears. You've quite drowned me."

Ellie pushed herself away from him and sat down, hugging her arms to herself.

"Better now?"

She nodded.

"I'll send for your supper."

She placed her hand on his arm to stop him leaving. "Please, sir, I'm not hungry."

"No?"

"But, Father, can we not leave here? Please? Go someplace where you can study in peace. A little house—a bit of garden."

"You . . . you want to leave court? But why?" He was genuinely puzzled. "The Queen has only just received your manuscript. This is our moment, Ellie; we can't run away now!"

"Can't we?" Her brief flicker of hope snuffed out.

"Lord Mountjoy needs me—we're getting somewhere with our investigations, Ellie, I am convinced of it. It would be a crime to leave." He leant closer. "Besides, you know we couldn't afford a place of our own just now. When we're rich again, I'll buy you the finest house in the land, and the loveliest gowns if that is your wish."

Ellie leant her head back against the wall behind her and closed her eyes. "You won't leave?"

"No, of course not."

"Could I go? Would Uncle Paul welcome me?"

Arthur frowned at the mention of his estranged brother. "You want to leave me for him?"

"No, Father, I want to leave court."

"Ellie, that is very selfish of you. I need you here for when the Queen asks to meet you."

"Selfish?"

He nodded, fingering the binding on his notebook, his mind already leaping ahead to the imagined interview with the sovereign. "You are alchemy's ambassador, my dear."

She got up and paced, her hands clenched. "You think me selfish?"

"You do not understand the great role you have been given. How could you? So young—so limited in your experience."

"I've stayed with you, Father, through everything. I've starved with you. Slept in barns—slept in hedges, even. I've lost nearly every claim to my birthright as a lady and have the hatred of half the court to battle each day, and you think I'm selfish?" Her voice rose at the end, close to complete breakdown.

Her father shook his head at her fondly, thinking her passion a mere childish mood. "Sit down, my sweet. I did not mean to offend you with my words. You're a good girl. I know I'm very fortunate to have you."

Screaming inside, Ellie stopped walking, staring at the blank wall in front of her. "Would Uncle Paul take me in, Father?" she asked with unnatural calm.

Arthur sighed. "I cannot tell you, my dear. When last we talked, he damned you as well as your mother to the outer darkness with me—that was when you were an infant before your good mother passed on to a better place. He's not a forgiving man."

"What does he have to forgive?"

"He never understood why I had to mortgage our family home. He has the farm—why should he fret about the property in Gloucester? He even had the effrontery to take me to court, can you believe it? He's not getting a penny from me even when we do unlock nature's secret of making gold."

"I see." No hope there then.

"So, my dear, how about a little broth if you've no desire for cheese?"

"As you wish, sir," Ellie said, knowing now a new depth to her despair. She'd thought she'd visited all the levels, but there was always one more to discover. "Some broth."

Will woke at dawn to find he was lying on his back in the damp grass of the arbor. It took him a while to remember what he was doing there. He'd drunk himself into a stupor and stumbled over the lady and her new lover. Cracking open an eyelid, he saw that Perceval had gone, doubtless to win her back with honeyed talk and promises he had no intention of keeping.

Men and women: liars all.

Realizing that he was, in fact, very uncomfortable where he was, he pulled himself up and splashed his face with water from the fountain. His doublet was never going to be the same again after its soaking in the dew—something he could ill afford, considering the limits of his wardrobe. Another sin to place at the Lady Eleanor's door.

Sitting on the bench, he rubbed his aching temples, cursing the birds for breaking into their exuberant chorus. Damned feathered tweeters. He caught sight of a scrap of cream-colored linen lying trampled in the mud. Knowing already what it was, he picked it up, remembering the circumstances that brought it there.

Had he really been so unkind to the girl? The cold light of day had a way of revealing his actions in a new and unflattering light. Whatever her many faults, she had not earned such an insult from him. He had implied she was no better than a common prostitute.

But the lady had hit back. He smiled when he recalled how she had felled them both, then frowned as he wondered at the cause. He knew what he had done, but why had she kneed Sir Henry? Had it been merely a ruse to hide her embarrassment at being caught in a compromising situation, or had it stemmed from real distress? He had the sudden awful feeling that he owed her an apology. She was still the thrice-damned alchemist's daughter, but her fame was rather for scholarship than seduction. She had given no hint in any of their encounters that she had the experience needed to handle a man of Sir Henry's type. Even if she had allowed herself to be led here—foolish enough though that was—she may have for once been telling the truth about him assaulting her.

"Hang me to Hell and back," muttered Will. Far worse than owing a friend an apology was to be in debt to an enemy. To live with himself, he would have to seek her out and ensure that no harm had come to her last night, and then he would eat humble pie and ask her forgiveness.

But first he had a joust to survive. With a groan, Will heaved himself up and headed back to his lodgings. If the lady wanted him punished, then she only had to think what he would be enduring in his armor with a hangover to wake even King Arthur from his sleep.

A pile of starched linen in her arms, Nell paused in the doorway of the staircase leading to her mistress's rooms. Something was afoot in the stable yard, and she could earn extra tips for gossip. Lady Jane had many faults, but she was always generous with her money.

An old man in a long black robe was standing with his belongings piled at his feet, a jumble of boxes and books, his sparse white hair sticking up on his head like a crown of thorns. He was protesting at the top of his voice the unfairness of his treatment. A girl stood at his side, a bag beside her, her face a blank, as if she couldn't hear or see what was going on around her. Nell's lips curved in a cruel smile. She'd heard rumors that Henry had been distracted by the alchemist's daughter; it looked like that particular diversion was on its way out of the castle in disgrace.

"Sir Charles, this is an outrage! Your father needs me!" the alchemist wailed as more bundles were added to his pile by insolent serving men.

Nell recognized the tall nobleman overseeing the eviction as Sir Charles Blount, a favorite of her lady's.

"On the contrary, sir, my father needs only your absence," Blount said in a triumphant tone.

"He would forbid you from doing this if he knew."

Sir Charles gave a wolfish smile. "He knows, but my authority is not from him but from the Queen herself. All practitioners of the dangerous art of alchemy are to be removed from her presence immediately. My Lord Burghley had signed the decree on her behalf. Do you care to read it?" He dangled a parchment between finger and thumb tauntingly.

Sir Arthur Hutton looked genuinely dismayed and puzzled. "I am not dangerous! I seek only to expand man's knowledge of God's mysteries."

"I beg to differ—the damage you did yesterday speaks for itself. You must get yourself at least five miles from Windsor by the end of the day and not come within that limit as long as the Queen resides here."

Another man arrived in the courtyard, that ill-shapen fellow Robert Cecil. The maids whispered about him, but not unkindly. His thin bow legs looked rather pitiful in his fine hose.

"Master Cecil!" cried the alchemist like a drowning man spying a raft. "Please, appeal to Her Majesty on my behalf. I count myself among her most loyal subjects. My craft poses no danger to her. Indeed, when I succeed, her realm will reap the benefits like none other in the history of mankind."

Master Cecil's eyes were all for the damsel, not the man. "I fear, sir, our gracious sovereign must think of her immediate peril rather than the promise of possible riches in the future. You suffer much for your art, I understand, but it is a burden you must carry alone at a safe distance from others."

His respectful tone stole the heat from the alchemist's protests.

"Aye, maybe you have a point, sir. The philosopher works best in retirement, away from the frivolous and light-minded." The alchemist gazed down thoughtfully at his equipment, at a loss as to how to carry his life's work with him.

"But Her Majesty is sensible of your loyalty to her and appreciates the gift you made her yester eve. The translation is much admired." Cecil was now addressing the lady, who barely registered his courtesy. "She sent this purse to the fair scholar as a token of her high opinion."

Nell snorted as the crook-backed gentleman pressed a small leather purse into the lady's hand. It was highly unlikely to have come from the monarch. She'd heard from one of the Queen's chambermaids that the sovereign was often pestered with such gifts from her subjects and rarely had time to more than glance at any of them unless the person was someone of note. The girl's work was probably destined to start fires, not grace a study.

Cecil dropped his voice, speaking to the lady now in urgent tones. "Lady Eleanor, there's twenty pounds in the purse, enough to hire a horse for yourself and for the baggage. You should get as far as Maidenhead tonight with no trouble. There's a decent inn there called the Black Boy. Mention my name and the landlord will look after you."

The lady nodded, her fingers curling around the purse.

Thank him, you want-wit, thought Nell in exasperation. The man clearly liked the lady but she was doing nothing to capitalize on his interest.

"You'll be all right?" he asked, studying her face.

The lady gave him a frail smile. "Thank you, sir, yes. Strange, only last night I begged my father to take me away from court; now my prayers are answered, but not in a way I expected. We will manage somehow—we always do."

Nell had seen enough to earn her sixpence. She hurried up the stairs to her mistress's chamber, knowing Lady Jane would still be in bed.

"My lady, you'll never guess what's going on in the courtyard," Nell began at a gallop, throwing back the drapes.

Lady Jane yawned and rubbed her eyes lazily. "It better be worth waking me to hear."

Nell turned her back to lay out the clean linen, rolling her eyes so her mistress could not see. "I think you will judge it so." She quickly recounted what passed below.

Lady Jane surprised her by throwing back the covers and leaping out of the bed. "Quick, my gown."

Nell ran forward with the garment and held it out for her mistress. "But, my lady, there's really not much to see; just some old fool getting his comeuppance."

Lady Jane held still as Nell deftly fastened the bodice. "I've no time for sleeves. Bring me my long cloak. That will have to do."

Not even bothering with stockings, her mistress stuffed her feet into her leather shoes and ran out, leaving Nell gaping at her uncharacteristic behavior. She went to the window to see what caused her mistress to be so disturbed. Lady Jane rushed into the yard, oblivious to the fact she was half dressed, hair tumbling down her back, with an audience of stable boys and the two noblemen. She put her arm around the girl and began talking earnestly to her. The girl nodded wearily, then, giving in to weakness, rested her head briefly on Lady Jane's shoulder. Odd. Nell had never considered that anyone would see her mistress as a tower of strength in their troubles.

"What ho, Nell!" declared Sir Henry, slapping her bottom in a friendly fashion. "What've you done with my sister?"

Nell bobbed a curtsy then grinned up at him. "You must see this, sir." She gestured to the scene below. "My lady has rushed to the side of the mad alchemist's daughter."

Rather than be amused at his sister's impetuosity, Henry frowned. "What's this? Why are they out there?"

"The Queen's dismissed the scholar, sir," Nell said soberly, understanding that she stood to gain more from feigning concern. "The poor girl has to leave with him, of course."

Three more ladies joined the little party in the yard: a plain ginger-headed one and two others of Mountjoy's household. They joined in with tears and lamentations like a chorus. It really was almost as good as going to the play.

"No, they can't do this!" Henry strode out of the room.

Nell settled down on the window seat to watch; she found Henry in one of his rages very appealing, not least because he often came to find her afterwards to work off his temper. Dabbing her neck with some of her mistress's rose water, she followed the progress of her big bear as he stormed out into the yard. He was arguing with Blount now, near to blows as Sir Charles flaunted the Queen's decree in his face. But what most intrigued Nell was the girl's reaction; she shrank away from Henry, even picked up her bundle, eager to hasten their departure.

Interesting, my lady. You are no willing conquest, then, thought Nell.

Three horses were led into the yard. On Blount's order, the

serving men loaded them with the baggage. Master Cecil had drawn Henry to one side, playing the peacemaker. Henry would have to be witless to stand against an order from the Queen—and he was no fool, even if he raged that his latest tidbit was to be taken from him. He instead made himself known to the alchemist, commiserating with the man.

There was barely room for a rider in the saddle once all was stowed, but the old man appeared content to relinquish his seat if it meant he did not have to leave any of his books behind. Nell watched the girl mount, wave farewell to her friends and follow her father as he led two of the horses in a string through the gate. Nell almost applauded the end of the scene—drama and passion, very finely acted.

Hearing footsteps on the stairs, she quickly made herself busy.

"Bound for Maidenhead, you say, Janie?" asked Henry, following his sister into the room. "That's strange—the father rambled on about Oxford, saying he'd go where his genius would be appreciated."

"I wouldn't pay heed to him, Henry. Lady Eleanor is of a more practical bent. She confided that they had been given some funds and she hoped to find a cheap lodging not too far away. It's nearly forty miles to Oxford; the hire of the horses alone would put a dent in their purse."

He kissed his sister's hand. "The Lord bless the sensible Ellie."

Jane tugged her fingers free. "For God's sake, Henry, leave the girl alone."

He grinned. "Not likely, lass; she'll need a friend now." He turned to Nell. "Are those my shirts, wench?"

"Aye, my lord."

"Bring them to my chamber. I have some others for you to mend."

Jane turned to the window. "Since when did my maid do your mending, Henry?"

"Since I asked her to, sister. Do you have a problem with that?"

With a sigh, Jane shook her head. Alert to any shift of power in her favor, Nell sensed her mistress had ceded ground to her brother.

"Come away, Nell," beckoned Henry, already unbuttoning his doublet.

Bobbing a pert curtsy to her mistress, Nell picked up the shirts and followed him.

Chapter 9

"So, Father, what are we going to do now?" Ellie had saved her question until they were clear of the winding streets of Windsor. They were following the road along the river, heading upstream. The way was quite beautiful if she had heart to appreciate it: elegant willows dipping fresh green branches in the stream, leaves not yet fully emerged; daffodils and primroses gilded the hedgerows; bluebells brought a touch of sky to shady woodlands. Swans glided undisturbed, beaks dipping into the water with elegant poise. It was a scene she'd like to remember on cold winter days, but today it failed to thaw the ice that had formed in her chest at the thought of yet another uprooting.

"Hmm, what's that?" her father replied.

"Where are we going to go? We can lodge tonight at Maidenhead, but I was wondering, sir, if you'd thought beyond that?"

She had. Her aim was to get her father to suggest they rent a small cottage for the next few weeks until she could think of a better plan. The Queen's purse should see to the basics as long as her father did not take it for his expenses. But she knew better than to propose the idea—she had to lead him to believe it was his own choice.

"I'm thinking Oxford, Ellie. I'm tired of these noblemen who do not understand the benefit I'm trying to bring mankind."

"I see, sir." She let that remain in the air while they passed a wagon on its way to the market in Windsor, the farmer's wife smiling in anticipation of a good price for her goods now that the court had arrived.

"You'll like Oxford, Ellie. The scholars are pleasant fellows; they'll appreciate your learning."

"I'm sure I would like it, sir." She took a breath. Time to make her pitch. "But I was thinking that maybe you would be better received if you wrote up your latest experiments and prepared a treatise for circulation. I've heard that one fault of scholars is to be jealous of their knowledge. What would stop them from claiming your advances as theirs unless you have proof in writing that you thought of them first?"

Sir Arthur frowned and hitched his robe up out of the dust, where it had been dragging for the last mile. "You may be right, Ellie. I hadn't considered that."

"I was thinking that we might pause a while in Maidenhead and find ourselves lodgings, the better to prepare for our arrival in Oxford when you are ready to show the scholars the fruits of your researches."

Ellie hated manipulating her father, but it was the only power she had left. They were on a downward path, and this was the only way she could think of to halt the slide for a time. A reprieve was better than nothing.

"I'm not sure, Ellie."

"I could find a cottage for us—you wouldn't have to interrupt your work to deal with the arrangements. Master Cecil did say that your profession was suited to a more retired situation."

Sir Arthur looked up at his daughter on the back of her hired nag. It struck him that she should be seated on a white palfrey, dressed in the finest clothes; instead she was wearing a stained gown, and her young face was pinched and tired.

"What am I doing to you, Ellie, eh?" he said, half to himself.

The moment of her father's self-doubt knocked Ellie back as nothing else could. She bit her lip and turned her eyes away.

"You'd like a cottage, would you?"

She nodded.

He placed a hand on her knee. "We can't stay there forever, you understand? Just until I've written my treatise."

"I know, sir."

He gave her his gentlest smile. "You'll be rewarded for your faithfulness, my dear, when all this is over. We struggle through the valley of shadow now, but then we will be seated in places of honor."

Ellie did not try to destroy the dream that sustained him. What would be the point? "Then I may look for lodgings for us?"

"Yes, my dear. How much money was in the purse?"

Ellie swallowed. He was going to take it from her—spend their one resource on more books or alchemical equipment. "Twenty pounds, sir."

"Perhaps you should buy yourself material for a new gown with it. We can't have the Oxford scholars looking down their noses at you, can we?"

Astonished, Ellie could only nod, a burst of love for her

infuriating father taking her voice. She had to remind herself of these times when he was so kind to her to counter the bitterness of his obsession when it was at its worst.

"And I suppose we must think about finding you a husband," he continued. "A nice young man who will let you continue with your education. Oxford will be a good place for you as well as me, I'm convinced of that."

"I thought none of the scholars were allowed to marry," she said carefully.

"I wasn't thinking of them, but of the rich young men whom they teach. A young noble with an interest in alchemy would be perfect."

For whom? Ellie realized that her father's thoughts, though they had started with her, had ended as usual with the cursed gold. Of one thing she was absolutely convinced: she would rather die an old maid than marry any man who went near the alchemist's laboratory.

"Yes, yes, Oxford will do us both well," Sir Arthur continued to mutter, his thoughts now revolving round how he could turn his one remaining asset to his profit.

Will spent the joust in a foul mood. His hangover grew worse with every jolt, but he was too stubborn to retire. Perhaps this gave him an edge, because he was doing uncommonly well for a novice, winning his bouts against much more experienced men, taking savage pleasure when one of Raleigh's companions finished unhorsed, lying on his back like an upturned beetle.

He made sure he acknowledged the Lady Jane as he cantered

past her seat in the stands, her sleeve attached prominently to his helmet as he tried to wipe away the memory of the alchemist's colors he had borne the day before. He told himself that the lady was far lovelier than his first choice—her skin a fashionable white, her hair like ripe wheat, her gown magnificent and tasteful. No grass-stained hem and wilting ruff for her. Everything was new and pressed to perfection. All he had to do now was like her enough to propose, but something about her subtly repelled him. He feared it was the fact that she did not think much of him. Though he didn't ask for love in his marriage, he did want to be able to bear the company of his wife and for her to welcome his.

Despite himself, his eyes sought out Lady Eleanor, but he soon saw that she was not sitting among her friends. Neither was she with Sir Henry, who had bowed out of the day's sport due to his injury. He was propped sullenly against the wooden wall at the far end of the stands. Now that Will had failed to find her easily, he decided her absence another thing against her, as it meant he could not get rid of his duty to apologize quickly and with the least embarrassment to himself. He'd imagined doing it from the back of his horse, presenting her with her embroidery, which he had wrapped in silk as a way of showing he regretted the dishonor with which he had treated it the night before. He then could have ridden quickly away knowing he had discharged his duty.

Guiding Barbary back to his brothers, Will dismounted. Tobias and his new man, Diego, took the reins to walk the stallion until he cooled.

"Well ridden, Will!" exclaimed James, helping him off with his helmet and removing some of the armor so he could rest. "I can't believe it, but you are in the final pair."

"Against whom?" Will splashed water over his head, welcoming the cold trickle down his neck.

"Raleigh or Blount. They're about to run against each other now."

Will found he couldn't bring himself to care about the outcome. He lay flat on his back, staring up at the sky.

"Not that the competition was that strong with Perceval out of the running," continued James.

How like his brother to diminish his achievements, thought Will. That was what families were for—keeping anyone from developing too high an opinion of themselves.

"If it's Raleigh, you'd best consider if you want to topple Devon's favorite son off his horse. Our sovereign lady may not like that."

"Or she might," interjected Will, knowing that the Queen's moods were hard to predict.

"True. In that case, I'd just play it fair and see what fortune brings."

A loud "Ohhh!" went up from the spectators.

"What was that?"

"Blount just tickled Raleigh in the ribs, but he stayed on."

"Sir Charles is on form today."

"Certainly is. He's been telling everyone how he saw off that alchemist fellow this morning. Had him dismissed from the castle, thanks to Lord Burghley."

Will sat up so quickly, his head spun. "He did?"

"Yes. As he tells it, Hutton walked out with a couple of broke-backed nags, his daughter riding among the baggage like some camp follower."

Will swore.

"What's the matter? I thought you would've been delighted to see the back of them."

He flopped back on the grass. "Remember the Lady Eleanor?"

James grinned. "With much pleasure."

"That's her—Hutton's daughter. I didn't know until last night."

"Shame." James flicked the colors on the helmet. "Well, Will, there are always other ladies to woo—and you've got the Lady Jane already halfway there."

"I know, I know, I had no intention of pursuing the lady, but I did owe her an apology."

"What for? That girl's father ruined our family; I would've thought the apology should be the other way round—and I hazard you were thinking of many ways in which she could earn it."

"Don't talk of her like that, Jamie. The girl is virtuous as far as I know. In fact, that's the problem. I caught her fighting off Perceval last night but, like a drunken idiot, I suggested she was a common jade when I should've at least offered my protection."

"What did Perceval do? Did she escape?" James looked daggers at Sir Henry. Play the libertine though James might, he had a strong chivalrous streak and hated to hear of mistreatment of the fairer sex.

Will gave him a grim smile. "Aye, she did. Kneed him in the groin and kicked me in the shin for good measure."

James barked with laughter. "'Swounds, I love the lady. She's too good to waste on that madman, her father."

"When I came to my senses this morning, I knew I had to find her to make sure that no disaster had overtaken her. Perceval was still intent on pursuing her when we parted. But it seems we are both too late: she's gone."

"Then perhaps it's for the best."

"Except she's left with the impression that I'm an ill-mannered beast. Besides, I do not like to think that she might be forced into the most desperate circumstances because of her father."

"No, she doesn't deserve that," agreed James. "But you can do no more than offer the apology should your paths cross again. She's not your responsibility."

"I suppose not." It didn't stop him feeling like a louse.

James took Will's forearm and hauled him to his feet. "You're up next, Will. Put the dark lady from your mind and try to do honor to the fair."

"Who am I against?"

James checked the board that listed the scores in chalk against the names of the competitors. "Raleigh, God help you. Seems as though the judges are awarding all his way unless there's a clear hit. See what benefits being in favor brings?"

"Then I'd better do my best to dislodge him from his saddle, if not from the Queen's opinion."

Tobias brought Barbary alongside the mounting block. "You have to win, Will; I've pledged my silver-handled dagger on you beating him."

"I should lose just to teach you a lesson about gambling," grumbled Will, swinging up into his seat.

"He won't take it that far," Tobias told James. "Will he?"

Facing Raleigh at the other end of the lists, Will had a moment when he wondered what on earth he was doing. He'd come to court with the urgent but necessary task of restoring his family's fortunes, and he was now about to hurtle down a course divided by a wooden barrier in an attempt to knock the current royal favorite off his perch. The problem was, as James had put it, he had no idea if he was also destroying his one chance at winning approval from the sovereign. That was if he won. If he lost, he would be more likely to retain the Queen's good opinion, but he stood the chance of doing himself an injury, and he did not like that prospect much either.

"Damned if I do, damned if I don't," he muttered to himself.

Problem was, Raleigh looked the conqueror already. Will knew he made the more romantic spectacle with his white stallion and gilded mail, but Raleigh's sober armor marked him out for the real soldier rather than the holiday player. It was annoying and very bad for his confidence. But no one ever won if one went into a joust with the expectation of defeat.

His new manservant touched his stirrup. "Mighty and magnificent lord."

Will raised his eyebrows at that, imagining what cutting remark the Lady Eleanor would have made in rejoinder.

Put her out of your mind, Will, he berated himself.

"Yes, Diego?"

"I watch Rah-Lee. He looks well, but he has no power behind his weapon. He shifts to the left at last moment."

Impressed, Will gave the boy a closer look. The Moor's dark-brown eyes were intelligent and shrewd—no fool, this one.

"Barbary, he does not like to lose," added Diego, patting the horse's neck affectionately.

"Neither do I."

"Then all will be well. Lord Tobias will not lose his dagger."

"We'll see. Good work, Diego."

"Thank you, my master." The servant released Barbary's head and gave Will a deep, elegant bow.

Muttering a prayer for protection, Will settled the lance into the ready position and waited for the steward's signal. As soon as the red cloth dropped to the ground, Barbary was off. The surge was amazing; Will had not felt such speed since he and his brothers had sledged down Bowman's Hill in the winter of '76. The despondent fog that had settled around him since the night before lifted; his mind sharpened, all focus now on the quivering end of his lance and the man hurtling towards him.

Impact was brutal. Will was thrown back in his saddle as Raleigh's lance hit his shield squarely in the center. His own weapon struck his opponent's shield a little to one side. So Diego was right: Raleigh did shift at the last moment—probably as he rose up in the saddle to put his weight behind the thrust. Neither man had been unseated, but Will guessed they would both have numbed arms and new bruises. He reached the end of his run and turned to look at the judge's verdict.

Devon peacock, one; Berkshire impoverished earl, nil.

He returned to Diego and found Tobias ready to act as his squire, checking that the padding on the lance was still secure.

"Stinking garlic-eater, he's got the judge in his pocket!" fumed Tobias. "Make him eat dirt, Will."

"I'll try my best," Will said soberly, his side feeling as if it had fallen between Vulcan's hammer and his anvil.

Diego quieted the excitable Barbary. "My old master, he said that you can prick a man out of a saddle with a lance as a blade does a walnut in its shell. Under and up."

Will thought it a bad time to take lessons, particularly secondhand from a man who had ended up in the Tower.

"And who was this paragon of chivalry, Diego?"

"My Lord Leicester's last chief sergeant at arms."

As the country's senior military commander, Will imagined Leicester employed the best. Perhaps he would do better to listen. "Do you have any more advice for me, Diego?"

The canny Moor smiled. "Aye, my lord."

"Be quick. We are about to run again."

"Rah-Lee is too confident. He will not expect even a beginner's trick from you. Always you have relied on brute strength to unseat your opponent, not skill."

Well, that put me in my place, thought Will, amused. No wonder James liked the boy.

"And this trick would be?"

"Rise in your saddle and aim a little below center of the shield boss, allow for his shift to the left, then sit heavily, levering your lance up." He lifted his skinny shoulders and let them drop in a shrug. "Blade under walnut."

"That easy, eh?"

The Moor just smiled.

"If I come back in one piece, Diego, remind me to give you a shilling."

"And if you don't, sir?"

"Run as if the hounds of Hell are after you, because I won't be pleased."

Drawing Barbary to a halt at the far end of the lists, Will waited for the signal. The crowd cheered their man—far more waving Raleigh's colors than his, he noted. Some troublemakers from the

Devon man's circle set up a chant—"Ra-leigh! Ra-leigh!"—clapping and whistling their encouragement. Will closed his eyes, blocking them out. He could see the maneuver Diego had described in his mind's eye, although he suspected the execution would be much more difficult. But one encounter down already, he really had little to lose. He opened his eyes and focused, staring down the narrow channel that marked his course through the lists. Up and out.

The handkerchief fluttered to the ground and Will spurred the stallion forward, relishing the surge of power between his legs as the horse's muscles bunched. He couldn't see Raleigh's face behind his helmet, but he concentrated on the memory of the man's smug expression, letting his irritation with the favorite's arrogance fuel his smoldering temper. He was determined to unhorse the peacock and hold on to his seat by sheer bloody-mindedness if necessary. As they closed, he rose slightly in his saddle. Up and out. Knife under walnut. Remember the shift to the left.

Then it all happened so quickly. He let out a grunt as his arm took the shock of the clash of lance on shield. The point of Raleigh's weapon had merely glanced off. Sitting down abruptly, he levered up, his lance slipping between shield and arm so that his opponent popped out of his saddle as cleanly as a pea from a pod. Once lifted over the height of the pommel, Raleigh was thrown backwards by the momentum and ended up sprawled on the ground, watching the tail of his horse as it continued its canter to the end of the list.

A great cheer went up from the crowd. Where Raleigh's colors had waved, now the green of Dorset fluttered. Even the most biased judge would have to award this one to the earl. Will reined Barbary in and passed Tobias his shield and James his lance, then removed his helmet. With the restricted view the visor allowed, he had not been able to savor the full sweetness of his victory, but now he could see that Raleigh was still on his back, his servants removing his visor.

"I haven't killed the man, I hope?" murmured Will, wondering where he could find a fast ship to the continent if he had to flee.

"No, Will, he's just winded." James grinned. "Brilliant riding, my lord."

"If even you say so, then I must have been good." He watched the marshal approach. "What's this?"

"My lord, Master Raleigh cedes the encounter to you. He does not wish to run again," the marshal declared.

Will dipped his head. "Then I lay my victory at Her Majesty's feet." He tucked his helmet under his arm, knowing what was expected of him now. "My lance, James."

Kicking Barbary into a high-stepping walk, he approached the stands, where the Queen sat under a canopy. Dipping his lance, he waited before her as the victor's wreath was fetched.

"My Lord Dorset, you have surprised us all," the Queen said in a carrying voice, placing the wreath on the end of the lance. "Your youth has defeated more seasoned knights. We congratulate you on your performance."

"I dedicate my victory to you, Your Majesty," Will said solemnly. "God has smiled on this unworthy beginner."

Elizabeth's lips curved, knowing he was referring to his good fortune at the expense of her current favorite. "Perhaps He did so to remind the more experienced of their fallibility. Yes, that may be the way of it. You have also gained the purse." With a flick of her wrist, she signaled the marshal to hand over the prize money.

"The greatest reward is to know that I have pleased Your

Majesty," Will said gallantly, hooking the string of the purse to his scabbard. It felt delightfully heavy.

"A noble sentiment. We will be seeing more of you at court, I trust."

"Can the lesser planets keep away from the sun, Your Majesty? Do we not ever dance back to you in our revolutions through the sky?"

She actually laughed at that. "I see you are quite the charmer, Dorset. The ladies at court should be warned. And now I must visit your poor opponent and offer my commiserations." She rose, the signal for everyone else to get to their feet. Will waited for her to depart before riding back to his brothers.

"All well, Will?" asked James.

"Yes. Her Majesty was amused rather than displeased that I'd beaten her favorite. I think she appreciates the reminder to him that he is but a man, even if he does win her smiles at the moment." With a sigh of relief, Will swung off Barbary's back on to the mounting block. "Help me off with this armor, will you? I'm broiling in here."

With swift efficiency, James and Tobias unlaced the plate steel, removing the extra weight that he'd been carrying for hours, then the padding.

"Ah, that feels good," sighed Will, stretching luxuriously, plucking at his shirt to unstick it from his body.

"You need clean linen," commented James.

"I'll go back to the inn and bathe."

"No, I mean now—for when you greet the Lady Jane. You can't leave your field of triumph without furthering your courtship."

Will grimaced as he tugged his shirt off over his head. "I'm not sure it's courtship yet, Jamie."

"Better be."

Will donned the fresh shirt Tobias had found for him. "Please, don't ruin the moment for me. I want to enjoy this, not start arguing with you. I'll go return her favor and speak to the lady; let that be enough." He remembered the purse and drew out a gold angel, tossing it to Diego. With excellent reflexes, the Moor caught it from the air. "For your advice."

Diego laughed with delight. "You are most generous, O High and Mighty Lord of Dorset."

"Enough of that," said Will as Tobias sniggered. "'My lord' is quite sufficient, Diego. And Tobias, about that bet."

Tobias began to edge away. "What about it, Will?"

"What were the odds?"

"Ten to one."

Will grinned. "Glad you had the brotherly loyalty to back the underdog. Go claim your winnings, but next time, remember that I could easily have lost."

"You didn't though, did you?"

"Not this time." Will's eyes shifted to where the Lady Jane was sitting quietly, waiting for her champion to approach. "Not this time."

CHAPTER 10

OVER THE COURSE OF THE NEXT FEW DAYS, Sir Arthur decided he rather fancied the idea of a period of study in seclusion.

"Like Our Lord's time in the desert before taking up His ministry," he suggested to Ellie.

She made a noncommittal sound, though to her the sentiment sounded blasphemous.

Sir Arthur had repacked the horses so he could ride a few miles and was now enjoying the sights from the saddle.

"This is a lovely valley, isn't it, Ellie? We lived here once, do you remember?"

Ellie remembered all too well. Lacey Hall was only a short ride away, and all this land probably belonged to Dorset's estate.

"I have very fond memories of this place. I did some of my best work while I was living with the old earl. Shame the new one is so blinkered in his views. I think we should look for our cottage around here; the atmosphere is conducive to scholarship."

"I think we'd best ride on, sir. The earl does not want us anywhere near him."

Sir Arthur waved his hand in a dismissive gesture. "Pish! Does he own the air we breathe now? What would it matter to a great man like him if we lodge here? He's not likely even to notice. Besides, he's at court, his mind on other things than two poor travelers seeking temporary shelter."

The harder Ellie argued against it, the more her father stuck to the idea of finding a cottage in this stretch of Berkshire along the Thames.

"The villagers of Stoke-by-Lacey were always very kind to you," he continued. "They paid proper respect to a man of my rank. I would have thought you would see the sense of returning to a place that we know will treat us well."

"But we don't know that, sir. The earl threatened to run us off his lands if ever we returned."

"He meant his estate, Ellie. We are free to pass along the Queen's highway through the village, I am sure of that."

"But, sir—"

"Enough, Eleanor. I am your father; you will obey me in this." Sir Arthur frowned at her.

Ellie put her knuckles in her mouth and bit down on her riding glove to stop herself from giving vent to a scream of frustration.

"There was a lady there—a widow. Dame Holton, her name was. She always showed great interest in you, Ellie, and she has a fine house, plenty of room for lodgers. Let us start there and find out if she is still in the village."

Stoke-by-Lacey had changed since she last saw it; the cottages looked in better repair and the villagers wealthier than under the neglect of the old earl. The gray tower of the church had a new weathercock and some fine glass in the west window; the inn bustled with people; wagons stood fully loaded in the yard on their way to London. A bakery was doing a good trade in buns and pies, the enticing smells reaching Ellie as she rode by. Turning off the road, Sir Arthur led her down a winding lane bordered by garden plots. He stopped outside a timber-framed house, the walls a chalky white, the roof a thick thatch topped by a straw bird, giving the dwelling its name of Partridge Cottage. Blossom festooned the apple trees in the orchard; the kitchen garden flourished with herbs and neat rows of vegetables. A brood of chickens scratched about the yard.

"Wait here," Sir Arthur told her, dismounting. "Let me first ascertain if Dame Holton still lives here."

Ellie slid to the ground, her muscles protesting after two days of riding. She felt even worse, for it was her monthly terms and her stomach was aching, yet she was too shy to explain the problem to her father. He could relate to her brain but not to the demands of her female body, leaving the handling of such matters to her, embarrassed beyond belief when she mentioned such things.

Ellie sat on a log seat under the shade of a tree, remembering back to the first time she had been visited by the terms shortly before she turned fourteen. For all his learning, her father had failed to teach her that this was natural, and for a terrifying few days she had concluded she had contracted some horrible disease. When she had whispered her fear to Sir Arthur, he had blushed scarlet and paid a female servant to explain it to her and show her how to cope with the monthly inconvenience. They had never mentioned it again.

Luckily, the servant had also concluded that Ellie might be ignorant of other matters to do with childbearing and filled in the blanks in her knowledge with detailed and unembarrassed descriptions of what transpired between men and women. She had told the wide-eyed girl of the pleasures and pains of being a wife, concluding with some lusty advice on how to please her husband. Ellie smiled now to recall how her ears had burned at some of what the woman told her. It had been so hard to imagine that she would want to do any of those things with a man; but recently she had found herself daydreaming, speculating as to what it would be like.

Mind drifting, she pictured how it would be to be kissed by a lover, the feel of his hands around her waist, drawing her close, the brush of lips on hers. It would be so splendid to be cherished—protected by someone who had the strength and means to solve all the problems she faced daily. He would be handsome, of course, kind, caring, considerate of her needs; he would know how to heat her blood with his touch; he would be just like the Earl of Dorset. . . .

Ellie sat up with a snap.

"You idiot." She thumped her knees with her fist. "The earl is none of those things—and certainly not for you." Annoyed that her imagination could have betrayed her into thinking of him in such a way, she got up and paced. Better than indulging in fantasies would be to remember how he had treated her two days ago, leaving her to fight off unwanted advances.

"Ellie!"

She spun round, seeing her father coming down the path with a matronly woman on his arm. Dame Holton was a large, square-jawed lady with fading brown hair tucked under her coif. Her efficient, firm movements declared her one of those people who wrestled with life and usually made it succumb to her will.

Ellie dipped a curtsy.

"Hasn't she grown into a lovely young lady!" exclaimed Dame Holton, giving Ellie a firm pat on the cheek. "Of course you can stay. I'd welcome the company, truth be told. My girls have married and moved away. The plague took my dear boy with my husband, as you might remember, Sir Arthur."

"Ah yes, madam. Holton was a good man."

She smiled, tears glinting in her eyes. "And Gregory was a beautiful son. God's ways are mysterious; we all have our crosses to bear." She sketched a sign of the cross over her breast. "Come in and take your rest. Your daughter can help me arrange your rooms while you set up your study, sir."

Ellie found the house intriguing, unlike any other she had visited. It was crammed with little statues of saints, religious pictures, or fragments of paintings, and ornate crucifixes. There was not a ledge or wall that was free of the decoration. She studied a stone carving of the Virgin Mary, running her finger down the smooth cheek, while the dame took fresh linen from her press.

"Lovely, isn't she?" said Dame Holton, emerging from the chest with an armful of bedding. "I rescued her from the parish church. Lying in the gutter, she was."

"And the others?"

"All orphans, thrown out by the ignorant. I started collecting them and now the tinker knows to bring me bits and pieces he comes across in his travels." She pointed to an ebony cross hanging over the window. "That came from Blackfriars monastery, he said."

"They're beautiful. You have so many."

Dame Holton nodded. "That I do. I keep them for the day when error is corrected and people ask for them again. The vicar won't look down on me then—he'll be knocking on the door begging for her to come back." She patted the Virgin on the shoulder, one woman consoling another.

"Error?"

Dame Holton clucked her tongue. "Best we don't speak about that, my child. Come, let's set your room to rights. I'm giving you Gregory's. It has a lovely view over the orchard and good light for sewing and reading." The lady chattered on about the small matters of the household, the chores Ellie could help with, the neighbors. Ellie let the tide of information sweep her away. She had enough trouble with her father without worrying about the religious inclinations of her hostess. The word was not said aloud, but it looked like they had fetched up in the house of that most suspect of characters: a Catholic.

Will rode home to Lacey Hall buoyed up by his success at his first appearance at court. He'd won the joust, made allies in Burghley and son and begun tentative negotiations for Lady Jane's hand in marriage with her brother. The next step had been agreed—a visit by the Percevals to his home; all he had to do now was check that his estate looked in a fit state to receive his prospective bride.

"Pretty pleased with yourself, aren't you, Will?" James smiled, urging his horse alongside.

Will's lips curved in response. "Even you can't say I did badly."

"No, I have to allow that you weren't a complete disgrace to the family name."

Tobias jogged alongside, his hired hack no match for his brothers' mounts. "When you marry Lady Jane, then can I have a new horse?"

James lightly clipped him round the ear. "Can't you find something else to moan about?"

"You'd be the same if you were in my shoes," Tobias grumbled.

"You mustn't assume the match is going ahead," warned Will. His brother's reminder where this was leading lodged in his stomach like a badly digested meal. "The Percevals are rich enough to have their pick of any family. The brother may be convinced, but the lady is not."

Lady Jane had been friendly but cool towards Will, initially refusing the suggestion that she visit his home; she had accepted this invitation only after Sir Henry had persuaded her she should go. Will wondered what threat or promise her brother had used, because her agreement was very clearly a reluctant one.

"Won't she do what her family says?" asked Tobias.

"I'd prefer her to agree to the match because she wants it, not because others tell her to marry me."

"That's very enlightened of you, Will," chuckled James. "Remember that when it comes to arranging Sarah's future."

Will grimaced. "Don't—it was hard enough handing Catherine over to my most trusted friend; I don't want even to think about our little sister."

"Any husband has to know that if he doesn't treat them right, then he'll answer to us." James's voice dropped to a threatening growl.

"Anyone who marries Sarah will need our protection from her." Tobias laughed, with all the loyalty of the brother closest to her in age. "She's got a nasty punch."

"Only when provoked—and you're the only one who provokes her."

"She's sweet to you because she knows you and Will are silly when it comes to girls."

"We don't throw apples at her friends when they visit—or dress her cat up in her nightcap and call it Mistress Bagley."

"You have to admit it did look like the vicar's wife."

"That's not my point."

"So you think it did!" crowed Tobias.

"Maybe. Possibly." James frowned. "But what I mean to say is that you roundly deserved any punch Sarah directed at you."

"You always take her side," grumbled Tobias.

"That's because you are always in the wrong."

Will held up his hand. "Enough, please. My head is beginning to ache." They turned in to the long drive leading to the house. Will paused to take stock: this was the first view of his lands the lady would see. Would she be impressed? Elm trees lined the way, the roof of the house just visible over the rise. The deer park was well fenced, the herd healthy. They couldn't yet see the formal gardens by the house, but they too were much improved, thanks to his mother's hard work with the gardeners. She had saved them much money by propagating most of the plants herself in the glasshouse he'd had built for her.

"It'll do," said James, following his brother's thoughts. "She knows we need money. What she'll see is someone managing as best he can."

"I hope so. I could do so much more with even a few thousand pounds to invest in the land."

"A new horse?" interjected Tobias hopefully, then ducked as two hands reached out to box his ear.

The countess was delighted to have her boys home with so many good things to report. She grilled Will for every detail, then moved on to gossip and fashion, subjects on which he did far less well, having no head for such things. It made him realize how much she missed the interest of a life at court; a good marriage would benefit her enormously, allowing her to mingle with ladies of her own rank again.

Taking a late dinner well after noon, Lady Dorset made sure she milked them for every drop of news they could remember. Sarah had been allowed out of the schoolroom to listen, and she was trying to behave, sitting between James and Will, her eyes sparkling.

She was growing up too fast, thought Will. Her hair, the color of old gold with hints of bronze, was still worn down under her coif, but it wouldn't be long before she was putting it up and demanding to be shown at court herself.

"How did the Queen wear her ruff?" the countess asked Will.

"Um, it was big," he ventured.

Sarah rolled her eyes as her mother smiled into her napkin. "What kind of lace, Will? Colored or white? With beads or plain? Larger than last year or smaller?"

Will threw a frantic look at his brother but James was suddenly absorbed in carving his meat.

"Her Majesty looked very splendid," he managed.

"As if that tells us anything." Sarah tweaked her own ruff, a very small affair by court standards.

"Her gowns were exceedingly fine."

"Even worse," muttered Sarah.

Tobias took pity on the females. "When I saw her, she wore a ruff of Flanders lace, projecting about a foot on a delicate frame. She prefers white and doesn't wear any of the colored ruffs that some of the younger ladies favor. Pink is definitely out of fashion, as she believes it clashes with her hair."

Sarah gave her youngest brother a delighted smile. "And beads?"

"Glass ones, sprinkled like dew across a web."

"There!" Sarah rounded on Will. "At least someone in the family uses their eyes."

"What news in the village?" Will asked his mother, quickly changing the subject.

The countess sighed. "Well, the miller lost his eldest to a fever. I sent our condolences. The baker has asked if he can extend his ovens."

"I'll ask Turville to look into it, but I can't see why not." Will felt happier now he was on the firm ground of matters he understood.

"Mistress Newburton and Farmer Jacobs were ordered by the bawdy court to stand at the crossroads last market day for"—she glanced at Sarah—"the sin of . . . um . . . intimate congress."

"Mother, there's no need to be so coy." Sarah smirked at Tobias. "Who would have thought Mistress Newburton could attract an admirer? She's so old."

"She's only thirty-five," the countess pointed out.

"That's what I mean."

Will cleared his throat. "I hardly think this is a decent conversation for the table, ladies."

"Probably not, but you must admit it is more interesting than ruffs," quipped James.

Will decided he was fighting a losing battle for decency with his family and gave up.

His mother laughed. "We are a sad trial to you, aren't we, Will?"

"I believe there is no safe answer to make to a comment such as that, madam."

"At least I'm not as much of a trial as Dame Holton. She scolded the vicar for his treatment of the church fittings in full view of the congregation. I saw her carting home the old arras of David and Goliath last week, which he had seen fit to throw out. By the time he has finished, we'll all be staring at blank walls."

"That was my favorite tapestry!" wailed Sarah. "Now what am I going to do during the sermon?"

"Listen?" suggested James.

The countess grasped her daughter's wrist before she could throw a morsel of bread at her brother. "And she's taken in a most peculiar lodger. I'm afraid you're not going to be pleased, Will."

"As long as it isn't the Pope in Rome or one of his priests, I can't see that it is of any concern of mine," Will replied. He steered clear of Dame Holton as much as possible.

"Not a priest, thank the Lord. Not as bad as that. Do you remember that terrible old fellow who lived with us when your father was alive? Hutton, the alchemist?"

Will dropped his knife; James stopped midchew.

"I certainly do," Will said coldly.

"He's taken a room with her. Writing up his life's work, according to the dame." The countess leant forward and added confidentially, "I think she's smitten with him—an autumnal romance is in the air."

Her attempt at humor fell flat.

"Does Hutton have his daughter with him?"

The countess looked worried at whatever she was reading from his face. "You remember her? Yes, she's with him too. Quiet little thing. Very pretty, with nice manners. They speak well of her in the village."

Will shoved his chair from the table. "Excuse me, madam, but I seem to have come home to a problem with vermin. I must expel it from my lands before any more damage is done."

Ellie felt as if she had tumbled into her own little plot in paradise staying with Dame Holton. She had a motherly woman to gossip with as they went about the household chores; a warm bed in a lovely room she did not have to share with others; a large garden that she was free to roam. She was spending this sunny afternoon in the orchard, sitting on a blanket under the apple trees, reading from the dame's prized collection of saints' lives. For once she did not have to worry, knowing that her father was cloistered in the small back room of the cottage that the Dame had let him use as his study, all his equipment still packed away, his thoughts turned to summarizing his knowledge rather than furthering it with any more dangerous experiments. If only she could stop time and live like this forever, she would be truly happy.

She flipped past the grisly details of a martyrdom to find another tale to amuse her. Maybe she could encourage her father to notice the languishing looks the good dame sent him at the dinner table? Ellie fancied that the widow would rather like the honor of marrying a baronet, even one with her father's weaknesses. In fact, if anyone could curb his excesses, it would be a woman like Dame Holton. Ellie couldn't imagine her allowing Sir Arthur to spend the housekeeping money on alchemical supplies. If he dared dip into the pot, he was likely to have his ears boxed—and the shock of that might do him some good. And if that dream came true, Ellie could venture to think of a better future for herself, even marriage to some local gentleman farmer or man of law. She would have her own house and a good, loving man with whom to pass her days; children, maybe . . .

A shadow fell across the page she was reading. Ellie looked up, then scrambled to her feet, leaving her dreams tumbled with the book in the dust. She bobbed a curtsy.

"My lord." What stroke of ill fortune had brought him home so soon?

"Mistress Hutton."

The earl stood there silently. Ellie wondered what he was waiting for: an apology for kicking him on their last encounter? Our Savior would return before she gave him that, she vowed. Perhaps he wanted her to beg his pardon for her very existence?

He cleared his throat. "You are well?"

Surprised, Ellie's eyes flew to his face. He was looking at her with a mixture of emotions, none of which seemed to give him any pleasure.

"Yes, I am well," she replied quietly.

"I owe you an apology," he continued in a stilted manner, like a cat walking across a hot pavement, paws barely touching the stones. "I was inexcusably rude to you on our last meeting. You deserved my protection, but I offered only contempt. That was very wrong of me." He dug inside his doublet and pulled out a silk-wrapped package. "I wished to find you immediately after I came to my senses, but you had already left. I return your favor to you with my thanks and sincere regrets for the churlish manner in which I treated both you and it."

Ellie took the offered parcel, guessing already what was inside. "Thank you, my lord."

He took a step back, relief evident that this distasteful duty had been done. "May I inquire when you will be leaving?"

Ellie squeezed the material tightly in her fist. For one moment she had felt herself softening to the earl, but now his intent was clear. He was running them off again—this time with polite words rather than dogs, though those doubtless would come later if they didn't go.

"When my father has finished his treatise."

"How long will that take?"

"I don't know. Why don't you ask him?"

Will waved the idea away as if it were absurd. "I refuse to speak to the man. I will not be answerable for the consequences if I am forced into a position where I have to share the same room as him."

"Or the same village?" Ellie remembered her father's words about the earl not owning the air they breathed, her anger mounting.

"I see you understand. I trust you will convince him of the wisdom of moving on. You would not want your hostess to suffer for her kindness in offering you lodging."

Silken words, but they were wrapped around a threat. Ellie dropped his parcel on top of her book and started walking away, not trusting herself to reply.

"Mistress Hutton?" called the earl, surprised by her dismissal.

Ellie crossed her arms over her breasts. "Sir, I am the Lady Eleanor Rodriguez, Countess of San Jaime to you." She threw the words over her shoulder without even bothering to look back.

"Where are you going?"

"Someplace where you are not."

Hearing him approaching, she increased her pace, but then he caught her arm, his grip unyielding.

"Lady Eleanor, I must have your word that you will leave."

"I was trying to leave, sir." She looked significantly at his hand detaining her.

"I don't mean now—I mean from the village."

She swung round and batted his hand away. She couldn't help herself: something broke inside, causing her words to spill out. "You will not be content until my father and I are quite destitute, will you, my lord? *Drive them off with dogs, Turville! Dame Holton, fear for your life for hosting an old man and his daughter! Sir Henry, she's only an alchemist's daughter, and therefore, anybody's for the taking!*" She was shaking but she couldn't stop herself. "By all the saints, what did I ever do to you? Why will you not let me rest until you've ground me under your boot heel as low as I can go?"

"Mistress Hutton—Lady Eleanor . . ."

Tears were stinging her eyes but she refused to cry in front of him. "Do you think for one moment that I want to live like this? I hate alchemy—I *hate* my father's obsession with it—but I am not his master! It is not my choice, you hear me? If you want to drive us out, sir, you'll have to get your dogs—I'm not doing it for you." She pushed him away, gathered up her skirts and ran, leaving the earl alone in the orchard.

Chapter 11

Will stared after the lady as she ran for the house. With a sigh, he scooped up the book, parcel and blanket that she had abandoned in her hasty flight.

Well done, Will, you prize ass, he berated himself.

She had been magnificent in her anger, he had to give her that. And her words? Her words had cut him to the bone. It was easy to hate the alchemist, but, as she had so ably pointed out, any attack on him was a punishment of her—a splendid, spirited lady who deserved someone much better than her father. If Will drove her out, what would be her future? Poverty would make her prey to men such as Perceval and worse. Her father was unfit to look after such a treasure. She needed someone she could rely on.

The temptation to offer his less than honorable protection sneaked into his mind before he could dismiss it. It was what was expected of men of his class who took a fancy to girls like her. But there was something so admirable about her innocence that he would not insult her by tarnishing it. She deserved a chance at a good life, a decent marriage. While she might fulfill all his fantasies of the perfect material for a mistress, her character spoke against such an offer.

And he needed a rich wife, not a pauper.

Alarmed to find his thoughts had strayed so far, Will made himself return to the matter at hand: Sir Arthur. He glanced at the cottage. No explosions or strange smells emanated from the building. Will could not imagine Dame Holton allowing such goings-on in her respectable dwelling. For the sake of the lady, could he not stomach the man's presence for a while, give her the respite she craved?

Gathering her belongings under one arm, he approached the house.

"Good day!" he called.

Dame Holton bustled out of the front door, her pleasure evident that the earl condescended to call on her humble home.

"My lord, this is an unexpected honor! Is there a problem? Has your horse cast a shoe?"

"No, mistress. My groom has my horse and is walking him in the lane. I exchanged a few words with Lady Eleanor, but she forgot to bring these back with her." He held out the book and the blanket.

Dame Holton frowned to see her favorite tome so mistreated. "Ellie!" she shouted.

There was the sound of a door banging inside and Ellie ran down the passage from the kitchen, her face gleaming from the water she had just splashed on it.

"Yes?" She caught sight of Will. "Oh, it's you. Have you come to tell us to be gone?"

Dame Holton clucked her tongue. "That's no way to greet the earl, Ellie. He very kindly called by to return my book. What were you thinking, leaving it outside? It could've rained!"

Ellie flicked her eyes ironically at the cloudless sky. "I apologize, mistress."

"And why would he want you gone?"

"Why indeed. Shall I go pack?"

Dame Holton sighed. "Don't be silly, child."

Swallowing his prejudice and pride, Will took a step forward. "Lady Eleanor, I called by to welcome you to the village. I hope you have a long and peaceful stay." He would've smiled at her stunned expression if he hadn't been standing in front of one of the sharpest observers in the village. "Dame Holton, I hope you realize you are hosting a man of exploratory science. I pray that you will be careful as to what activities you allow him to pursue while under your roof. I would not like to have to dispatch the fire cart to put out the thatch."

The dame glowed under his attention. "My lord, I assure you I will have none of that dangerous stuff in my house. Sir Arthur seeks only a place to write."

"Excellent. Then I bid you good day." He gave them both a bow and set off for the lane. Unpalatable though this concession had been, he felt more than recompensed by the deep relief he'd seen on Ellie's face as his announcement sank in.

Confused by the sudden change in the earl's attitude, Ellie did not quite trust him to keep his word. She spent an anxious day or two looking for his servants to turn up and force them back on the road, but nothing of that nature occurred. The lane outside the cottage remained quiet with only the shepherd guiding his flock along it twice a day and the farmhands going about their ordinary business.

Tidying her bedroom, Ellie paused over the small chest of clothes that she hadn't unpacked, fearing that to do so would tempt fate to kick her out of her comfortable home. Could she relax and enjoy their quiet lodgings with Dame Holton? Used to being unwanted, she found it hard to get over the cautious habits she had learnt. No, it was too soon. The earl had a mercurial temper. He was all sunshine with the dame, but the next time he met Ellie he might revert to thunder.

Her chores done for the morning, Ellie decided to walk into the village to call on the friends she had made there. She hadn't gone far down the footpath when she came across a party of men repairing a wall. She stood to one side as a wagon rumbled by, a pile of stones on the back. As she watched, it lurched into a puddle, the weight sinking the axles deep into the mud. The huge toffee-colored shire horse was having trouble heaving the wheels out of the rut, provoking much cursing from the carter. The man cracked his long whip over the creature's head, seeming not to care that the horse's flanks were already streaked with sweat.

"Get on wi' it, you great brute!" the carter shouted. "We've not got all day!"

Ellie couldn't stand to see any animal mistreated and was just gearing herself up to intervene on behalf of the struggling horse when her words were taken right out of her mouth.

"No need to whip the poor creature, Taylor, he's doing all he can." The earl himself had stepped forward. Ellie hadn't noticed him because he was stripped to the shirtsleeves like his field workers as he gave them a hand with the wall. That must be a first: a lord of the realm doing an honest day's work! He dragged a wrist across his brow, leaving a muddy smudge behind. "We'll have to lighten the load before your horse can pull free." Putting two fingers in his mouth, he whistled to his men. "Lads, come over here. Pile up the stones by the trough. Taylor, come hold the horse's head while we do this."

Six burly laborers downed tools and came to carry out the earl's wishes. Ellie had mixed feelings about meeting the earl again so soon. Mostly she was afraid, unsure of his reaction, but a traitorous part of her was always on the watch for him. Caution won the day and she tried to slide behind the wagon to hurry out of sight, but she had not counted on the carter jumping down from his seat just as she tried to go past. The resulting collision ended with her in the hedge, fortunately just missing a patch of stinging nettles.

"Oh, lass, I didn't see you there." The carter recovered quickly and lifted her to her feet. "Did I hurt you?"

"It's nothing. Worry about your horse, not about me," replied Ellie, rubbing her toes, which he had managed to trample.

"What's going on, Taylor?" Of course, the earl would have to come see what the delay was about.

"Ah, your lordship. I knocked the lass over like a skittle but she says she's all right." The carter moved aside so the earl could see her.

"Lady Eleanor!" the earl exclaimed.

"Hang it all, a lady. Just my luck," muttered the carter, realizing how familiar he had just been with her.

The earl smiled warmly at her. "This is a pleasant surprise."

Ellie brushed leaves off her skirt. "Sadly, not so pleasant for me—"

His smile dimmed.

"I ended up in the hedge." She inspected a bramble scratch on the back of her wrist.

Relieved that no personal slight was intended, the earl frowned at her injury. "I see what you mean. Let me take a look."

Ellie cast an embarrassed glance at their audience of carter and six laborers, all of whom found this meeting much more interesting than moving a pile of stones. "There's no need, sir. I'll just get about my business."

"Come now, you're still half attached to the hedge." He gestured to the bramble caught up in her petticoats.

"Oh."

"Men, give the lady some room. Get back to work."

On their master's order, the laborers returned to their task and the carter went to calm the horse, which was still floundering in his harness.

"Please, let me free you." The earl knelt at her feet, trying to be discreet as he tugged the thorns free. Ellie looked down at the top of his golden head, wondering at the urge that came over her to run her fingers through his hair. She folded her hands together to make sure she didn't give in to impulse.

"There, all done. But I fear you may have some scratches down there too." The earl gestured to her ankles. "Not that I looked, of course."

Ellie couldn't think of a suitable reply to that, aware that her cheeks were broadcasting her feelings for her.

"Are you able to walk home? If you give me a moment, I can reclaim my doublet and offer you my arm."

Say something, you silly goose, Ellie chided herself. "No, no, thank you, I'm really not hurt. I'm on my way into the village—I'd better leave you to your task."

The earl's expression turned to one of disappointment. "Truly?

It's no trouble for me. The men know what to do—I was only directing the work because I hate sitting idle at home. Barker here is my foreman—he can do the rest." He waved towards a bald-headed man who was now ordering the unloading.

"But I'd spare you the humiliation of being seen with the alchemist's daughter, my lord," Ellie said quietly, lacing her fingers together nervously.

The earl cleared his throat. "Ah, I deserved that, I suppose. It would be no humiliation, but an honor. You know that I'm no admirer of your father, my lady, but I find that I rather admire you."

Ellie was flattered that the flirtatious earl she had first known at Windsor had returned. She smiled. "Admire a girl covered in leaves and bramble scratches? You have strange tastes, my lord."

"Guilty as charged." He gave her a playful bow.

Ellie bit her lip. "But why are you being so kind to me now?"

The earl reached out and plucked a dandelion seed from her hair. "You could say I'm mending fences today in more senses than one."

"Then you don't regret allowing me to stay?"

He shook his head. "Oh no. I offer you protection on my lands, Lady Eleanor, as long as you need it. And if your father comes as part of that package, then I will learn to live with it."

She suppressed a smile. "I'm afraid he does."

"Oh well." He smiled with a hint of self-mockery. "I'll try not to think too much about it."

Ellie dipped a curtsy. "Thank you, my lord. For everything."

"Good day, my lady, and welcome."

She walked on, aware of his gaze on her back until she turned out of sight. That had been an odd meeting, but reassuring. She knew now she need no longer fear the earl—at least not for his hostility to her father. What danger he might be to her heart was another matter entirely.

The next few weeks passed peacefully for Will. Preparations for the arrival of the Percevals went smoothly under his mother's guidance: two guest rooms were newly whitewashed and the hangings aired and patched as discreetly as the sewing women could manage. Tobias was dispatched back to his tutor, much reducing the noise levels in the house, and James returned to college, promising to come home as soon as term finished to help entertain the guests.

To all onlookers, the earl, as Will thought of his official persona, appeared to be going about his normal duties, reviewing correspondence, walking his fields, listening to his tenants' complaints. But inside Will knew it was definitely not business as usual. Against his better judgment, he could not keep away from Lady Eleanor and too often made an excuse to ensure their paths crossed. He felt as though his whole being was now revolving around that one little insignificant moon of a person, rather than the great weight of his earthly duties as the owner of a large estate and position of responsibility in the country.

Today was typical: he was supposed to be inspecting repairs to the windmill on Bowman's Hill; instead, he had decided it was imperative he speak to the dame about her failure to attend church the past two Sundays. Normally, he would have left such matters to Vicar Bagley, but the temptation to catch a glimpse of a certain pair of dark eyes was too much.

"Diego, walk Barbary a while," he ordered his groom, slipping nimbly from his saddle.

"Yes, O Great One."

Will shook his head. Try as he might, he could not persuade the Moor to drop his overblown terms of address. He even suspected the boy did it as a kind of jest, but he could hardly complain that his servant was *too* respectful, could he?

"I do not know how long this will take."

"No, master. The lady may not give you a kind welcome." Diego scratched Barbary's nose, causing the stallion to snort with delight.

"Dame Holton is always polite to me." Will tugged his ruff straight and ran his fingers through his hair, hoping it hadn't got too dusty on the ride over. He'd put on his claret-red velvet doublet with gold sarcenet peeping through the eyelets, one of his favorites, hoping it would make him look his best.

"I meant the little lady, O All-Powerful One. The one with hair like the berry of the elderflower and eyes like polished mahogany."

Will stared at his servant in surprise. Had he been that transparent? Were all his people talking about his attraction to Lady Eleanor—and if so, what damage was he doing her reputation?

"Where did you hear that, Diego?"

"I hear nothing, Great Lord. I watch." The boy's eyes rimmed with curling black lashes were dropped to his toe caps in a sign of humility, but Will could not fail to note the intelligence in his expression.

"Do others watch?"

"Everyone watches the magnificent lord of these lands, sir."

That was true enough.

"Do they gossip about the lady?"

Diego raised his eyes briefly, a glint of humor in his expression. "All talk all the time, my lord. They talk of the cow that gives birth, the flock of geese that escapes, the strangers lodging at the cottage."

"You know what I mean, Diego. I wouldn't want any harm brought to the lady because I occasionally call upon her hostess." Will slapped his gloves into his palm, irritated that he might have to give up this visit to protect her.

Diego shook his head. "I think not, O Kind Master. The lady is well-liked by her friends in the village and is considered a sweet-hearted maiden. No one speaks ill of her. You also are spoken of with much respect; they do not think you would pursue one of her nature with dishonorable intent."

"And they speak rightly. She is in no danger from me. I would thank you if you counter any words to the contrary and report the matter to me as soon as any malicious talk reaches you."

"Yes, O Great One."

Satisfied that he had done all he could, Will strode down the path to the cottage, feeling his heart lift in anticipation of seeing Lady Eleanor. He knocked on the door and was delighted when she answered it. He was pleased to note that her face no longer fell when she saw him, as she had come to expect friendly treatment.

"My lord." She dipped a curtsy. Will thought she looked quite delectable in her plain sage-green gown and apron, her hair braided beneath a neat coif with the same orange ribbon he had wrapped around the embroidery he had returned to her.

"Lady Eleanor Rodriguez, Countess of San Jaime." He bowed.

She laughed, her cheeks dimpling at the use of her full title. "Fences all mended, sir?"

"For the moment, I hope. Is Dame Holton within?"

"I'm afraid the dame is from home. She went to market."

Will rejoiced at this stroke of luck. He was spared the airing of an unpleasant subject with the stubborn lady.

"I merely came to ask if she had an excuse for missing church the past few weeks, but the subject can wait."

Lady Eleanor looked pensive, biting her bottom lip in a way that made Will want to kiss it.

"Perhaps she had a chill," Lady Eleanor said loyally, though they both knew that the indestructible dame would not be felled by such a common complaint.

"Then perhaps it is a matter best left for her to discuss with the vicar."

"Who is it, Ellie?" a voice called from within.

Will stiffened. The alchemist. So far he had avoided meeting the man.

The lady squeezed her hands together awkwardly, trying to think of a way of circumventing this confrontation. None came to mind.

"The earl, sir."

A tall figure in dark robes trimmed with ragged black satin emerged from a room at the end of the passage, quill pen in hand. "Where are your manners, Ellie? Invite him in. My lord." Sir Arthur bowed low, quite forgetting their last bitter exchange.

Will took a step back. "I cannot stay, sir."

"That is a shame, my lord. I miss the conversation of learned men here in my seclusion. The ladies are well enough, but no match for a man in debate."

Will marveled at the man's blindness. How could he possibly

have forgotten the distaste Will had for him and his so-called learning?

The poor Lady Eleanor—Ellie as he now thought of her—was blushing as red as a robin's breast. "I will see the earl out, Father."

"Aye, do that, Ellie. Show him that I have taught you some manners. Good day, my lord." Sir Arthur retreated back to his study, mumbling something about mercury solutions.

Will breathed freely once the man had disappeared.

"Thank you," the Lady Ellie said softly.

He moved aside to allow her to show him out. "For what?"

"For not speaking your mind. Father is"—she searched for a word—"childlike in his view of the world. He does not see himself as others do. He truly has no perception of the harm he did your family."

"Or that he does you?"

She reached to unlatch the gate, but Will leant against the slats, preventing her from opening it. The hawthorn that arched over the entrance made a pretty white-blossom frame for her dark beauty, and he wished to savor it. Looking more closely at her eyes, he saw the irises were flecked with tiny hints of gold.

"I don't know," she replied honestly, worrying her bottom lip again. "Sometimes he does realize, but it is like a drunkard with moments of lucidity; he soon tumbles back into his former state. I've given up hope of him ever sobering." She looked down the lane to where Diego was walking his stallion. "Oh, is that your horse? I saw him at the joust, I think."

"Yes, he's mine." Will was more than willing to let drop the painful subject of Sir Arthur. "Would you like to be introduced?"

"May I? He's magnificent."

"It would be his honor." Will whistled for Diego to approach.

"And your servant—where is he from?"

"North Africa."

"I've never seen anyone with skin as dark as his."

"Everyone in his country is like him, and people to the south are even darker. If you were there, you'd be the oddity."

She laughed again. "Yes, I suppose that's true. They would think me a very sorry specimen."

He doubted that. He could see her as quite a prize in some sultan's harem.

"Diego, this is the Countess of San Jaime," Will said as the boy came within earshot. "She wishes to greet Barbary."

Diego flashed her his broad smile. "Barbary likes the ladies, my lady," he confided. "He likes them to stroke his nose."

Will took her arm. "Approach from the side so he can see you." She advanced cautiously, her slight stature dwarfed by the huge stallion. Tentatively she reached out and gently fondled the soft skin around Barbary's nostrils. "That's it, Ellie. You have him charmed now."

She sent him a shocked look at the familiar use of her name, but he didn't regret it. That was how he was thinking of her. He hoped at least to be a friend if he could be nothing more.

"Would the lady like a ride, O Great Master?" Diego asked, his tone innocent, but Will caught the sly humor in the boy's eyes.

Ellie clasped her hands to her breast, bobbing on the spot with happiness. "Could I? He's such a wonderful creature!"

More than pleased to oblige, Will swiftly mounted, making a note to give the boy a shilling for the thought. "I'll take you down the lane. Come, sit in front of me."

Cheeks pink with a mixture of embarrassment and excitement, she took his hand and used his boot to climb up. She ended up sitting sideways across the front of the saddle.

"Oh," she exclaimed when she realized how close she was to him. "Perhaps I had better get down."

"Not if I have any say in the matter, my lady." He clicked Barbary into motion, removing that option from her power. "There's no one about to see."

As they jogged down the lane, Will had plenty of time to realize how perfectly they fitted together, her head resting just under his chin.

"Comfortable, my lady?"

"Yes, my lord. Barbary moves like a dream. I envy you such a fine horse." She turned to look up at him, her hair brushing his throat. "You've spoiled me now for the nags I usually ride."

"I know what you mean. I have ridden my fair share of swaybacked beasts that a farmer would be ashamed to own."

She laughed at that. "I cannot imagine you on such a creature."

"Believe it, lady." He reached out and snapped a flower from the high bank of the hedgerow to tuck behind her ear. "So, Ellie, what do you do when you are not torturing poor pieces of cloth with your needle? I've heard you have an excellent grasp of Latin."

"I like reading the ancient writers, particularly poetry."

"You have a favorite?"

She gave the question serious thought. "Ovid. His imagery is quite exceptional."

"Rumor says you read Greek too."

"A little. Nothing to speak of."

"I doubt that most sincerely. I'm beginning to understand you.

You are the Amazon of learning I first imagined, but you hide it well."

Her face fell at this description, reminded of her problems back at home. "It does me little good, my lord. My father hoped my skills would win the Queen's favor, but his activities put an end to that."

They had reached an open field. "A canter?" Will asked.

"Yes, please!"

With a whoop, he kicked the horse into a faster pace, using it as an excuse to increase his hold around the lady's waist. She was loving every moment of the ride, laughing as the wind whipped through her hair, the ends of her ribbon becoming completely entangled in the fancy buttons on Will's doublet. As they reached the hedge at the far end, he turned Barbary's head before the horse took it into his brain to leap. He was not going to risk the lady on such an exploit, tempting though it was to show off before her.

"You enjoyed that, Ellie?"

"You could tell?" she asked, eyes sparkling.

"Those squeals of pleasure betrayed you."

"I do not squeal!"

"Yes, you do. You are like my little sister, Sarah. I would wager you giggle too."

"Sir, you quite destroy my claim to gravitas with your false accusations." She gave him a frown of mock-censure.

"I'll have to call Barbary as a witness to back up my claim, then, as I'll not be accused of perjury."

She giggled at that image, quite proving his case for him.

Will nudged the horse back towards the lane. "I would ask you a boon in return for the ride."

"What would that be, sir?"

"That you think of me as your friend, Ellie."

"I do, sir. Now, at least."

"So will you call me Will when we are alone?"

She looked doubtful. "I suppose it was very wrong of me to agree to be alone with you, wasn't it?"

"I mean you no harm. You can trust me."

She nodded slightly, as if in response to an internal debate that had fortunately declared in his favor. "I think that I do, sir."

"Will."

"Will." She smiled up at him, and he could not resist brushing his lips across hers in the lightest of kisses.

"A gesture of friendship only," he said quickly, excusing himself.

She touched her mouth reflectively, then surprised him by reaching up to press her lips briefly against his for another kiss.

"To friendship, then," she said.

CHAPTER 12

LADY JANE DREW HER HORSE TO A HALT as the end of their journey came in sight.

"What do you think, Jane?" her brother asked, scratching a fleck of dried mud off the hem of his short velvet cloak.

"It is very fine. The family obviously had money at one time." She counted the chimneys with ornate pediments bristling from the roof—there had to be at least sixteen major rooms in Lacey Hall, almost as many as her own home of Stafford Grange. The walls were a pleasing golden sandstone, warm-looking even in the dull conditions of this cloudy day. A moat surrounded the dwelling, doubtless stocked with fish for the table.

"It's good land. Dorset will come around eventually, even without your dowry," Henry noted.

"But he could do with the money now." Jane sighed. She was no expert in land management, but she knew that it took investment to improve crop yields, establish markets and transport goods to the city.

"It's the way of the world. The earl would be a fine connection for our family. They say at court he has Burghley's favor."

"So you want me to grant him mine?"

Henry raised a brow. She had been making such comments with him since he had blackmailed her into coming to Lacey Hall. She no longer seemed to care to maintain the aura of innocence around him. "Not yet. We don't want to shoot our bolt too soon now."

Too late, thought Jane grimly. *Your friend saw to that.*

"And remember not to shock the countess with your ribald tongue, sister dear."

"You will have no reason to fault my manners. I am an accomplished actress, after all, as you have often pointed out."

Henry clicked his fingers and their retinue fell into position for their grand approach. "Ready?"

"As I will ever be, brother dear."

He smiled sourly at her acerbic tone and kicked his horse into a trot, knowing she would keep up so as not to be left eating his dust.

The earl must have had people on the watch for them, as the family emerged from the house to greet their guests in the courtyard even as they clattered under the gatehouse. A blackamoor groom ran forward to hold the head of Jane's horse, and the earl himself took her hand as she used the block to dismount.

"My lady, we are delighted to welcome you to our house. I trust your journey went well?"

"It was tolerable, sir." Jane felt nothing seeing him again, not even the slightest lifting of spirits, despite the fact he looked very fine in his severe black doublet and white hose.

The earl led her to the front entrance, where the family were gathered. "May I introduce my mother, the Countess of Dorset?"

An elegant woman in outmoded finery came forward, hands extended in friendly welcome.

"The Dowager Countess," she corrected her son genially. She had her son's golden hair, but her eyes were hazel.

"Madam." Jane dipped a deep curtsy.

"Lady Jane."

"Lady Dorset."

"Oh, you are a pretty thing!" the lady said in delight. "I can quite see how my son came to choose you."

"Mother!" growled the earl, embarrassed at his mother's forthrightness, but Jane rather liked her for it. They all knew what she was here for. It would have been dishonest to pretend this was anything but a marriage negotiation.

Undeterred, the dowager turned to greet her brother, beaming at him with similar genuine warmth, which even Sir Henry could not fail to return. He usually despised women unless they were of use to him, either in his bed or as a step to his advancement, but the dowager had him charmed within a few seconds of being introduced.

"My sister Sarah," continued Will. A fresh-faced girl of about twelve bobbed a curtsy, her eyes devouring the detail of Jane's riding habit—it was far from her finest, but the child seemed enraptured by the embroidery on the bodice. "And this, I regret to say, is my younger brother James," the earl said, taking Jane's hand and leading her to a tall gentleman she had seen at his side at court.

"My lady. I have admired you from afar and am honored now to make your acquaintance," James said smoothly, sweeping a charming bow, his dark hair falling forward and brushing her hand as he kissed it. She felt a shiver of awareness of him as a man, a reaction that disconcerted her.

"And where is your youngest brother?" Jane asked quickly,

remembering the humorous youngster who had wooed a sleeve from her.

James beat a fist to his breast. "You wound me, lady, preferring the company of that scamp over mine."

Jane smiled. "His manner was most refreshing."

"I believe he told you my esteemed older brother was an idiot."

She tried not to laugh. "He may have intimated something to that effect. Is he wrong?"

James grinned at his brother. "No, but you won't hear it from me. I fear him too much."

The earl groaned. "Don't believe him, lady. James fears nothing."

"Not true—our mother can box ears like none other. I live in mortal terror when I am at home."

It was impossible to imagine the lady reaching up to chastise her two grown sons, so Jane raised a skeptical brow.

"You believe me not?" asked James. "I will have to do something outrageous in your presence to provoke her to anger. The ladies of our family have terrible tempers."

"And the gentlemen are models of good humor?" she asked in a tone resonant of her disbelief.

"Of course. At least I am. I can't answer for my brother; he's an idiot, after all—not that you'll hear me say that."

Jane laughed openly at the brotherly banter, so unlike the casual cruelty that passed for a relationship with Henry. She was warming to this family, particularly James, who, it had to be admitted, sparked her interest more than his sober elder.

"My lady," said the earl, presenting her with his arm again, "rooms have been prepared for you. Perhaps you would like to refresh yourself after your journey?"

"Thank you."

"We dine at noon."

Jane gave a regal nod and allowed herself to be led into the house.

Nell stayed outside as her mistress disappeared within. The family's steward approached to ask about the luggage, and she was kept busy for the next hour ensuring all ended up in the right chambers. While she planned which outfit she would lay out for Lady Jane, Nell contemplated the household, potentially her new home if her mistress made the expected match with the earl. It was comfortable enough. The steward could be a possible catch for her, though she would have to find out if he was already married. He was a big man, far from comely, but that was not as important as power. It would be a shame to lose Sir Henry's attentions, but she had always known that they would be fleeting. Yes, all things considered, it may well be a decent place for her.

"Mistress, is there anything further you require for the lady?" the steward asked, dismissing the man who had carried up the trunk.

"No, I have everything I need, Master . . . ?" She stood close to him, letting him feel his superior height over her middling stature. Men liked that sort of thing.

The steward flushed slightly. "Turville. Affabel Turville."

"And I am Nell Rivers." She dipped her eyes demurely, hoping he would imagine her cheeks were modestly flushed.

Turville bowed. "Mistress Rivers. May I welcome you to Lacey Hall? If there is anything, anything at all, you require, you only have to ask me and it will be yours."

"Thank you, Affabel—I mean, Master Turville."

Flustered, the steward backed out of the room, then barked some unnecessary orders to a passing servant to impress her with his commanding presence. Nell chuckled. Landing him would be like tickling trout—almost too easy.

A hollow round of applause sounded behind her. Nell spun round quickly to see Sir Henry at the connecting door to his apartment.

"Excellent work, my little vixen. That's what I like most about you: your unashamed self-interest."

Nell shrugged and opened up the trunk. "I must think of the future. If my lady marries into this family, I'll have to make a place for myself."

Henry came up behind her and rubbed himself against the back of her thighs. "I have a place for you, Nell."

She smirked. "And don't I know it."

He hitched her skirts a little higher. "Do we have time?"

"No, sir." She shivered as his fingers touched the back of her knees.

"Good, I like a challenge."

"But I'm afraid it will have to wait, brother." Lady Jane sailed into the room, not even pretending shock at his antics with her maid. "I have more need of Nell than you do."

Henry gave Nell a wicked grin. "I doubt that."

"I will wear my rose damask silk," Lady Jane continued, ignoring the remark.

"Very good, my lady."

"And Henry, if you insist on debauching my maid, I request that you be more discreet about it."

"Oh, come on, Janie, the earl won't care."

"But I do. I find it . . . tasteless."

Henry guffawed. "Very well." He winked at Nell. "I'll see you later."

His departure left the two girls in an awkward silence.

"What will you do when he gets you with child?" Jane asked bluntly, before moving to the mirror to remove her cap. She cast it on the bed behind her.

Nell shrugged. "It's not happened yet, mistress."

"You can't trust Henry to look after you."

Nell carefully unpacked a new ruff, pleased to see the starch was still keeping its shape. "Then I'll apply to your father, mistress. He has enough by-blows to his name to not remark another one." Nell's tone was more carefree than she felt; she knew she took a big gamble. A child would tie her down, limit her choices, remove her power, and more than anything she wanted to be in control of her destiny.

"I should dismiss you, but I won't." Lady Jane sounded despondent, too tired for another battle.

Nell paused in shaking out the pink skirt. It was not like her mistress to sound so . . . well, so defeated. She preferred her when she was all spit and vinegar, even if she did have a rotten temper.

"Thank you, my lady."

Jane began yanking the pins out of her hair, letting the fair locks tumble about her shoulders. "I know you don't like me, but maybe another servant would hate me. Then where would I be?"

Nell had never considered that the lady thought her feelings of any importance and had no idea what to say.

"But what does it matter?" her mistress continued. "This whole business is a farce. So let's go play blushing bride and you demure maid. Perhaps God will strike us down where we sit and put an end to it."

Nell tackled the points fixing her mistress's stomacher to her skirt. "You are not pleased with the match, my lady?"

She gave a desperate sounding laugh. "Have you never wanted to be loved for yourself—not your looks or, in my case, my dowry?"

Nell grimaced. "I'm no romantic, mistress. I do what I do to survive as best I can." She tugged the skirt free and Jane stepped out of it.

"Then you are wiser than I. I still want something more."

"The earl is a fine fellow," Nell said, beginning to feel a little annoyed that her mistress did not value all the advantages of birth and fortune that she had.

"Indeed he is. I'm very blessed." She made it sound like the worst of all fates.

"You will get to know each other—friendship will grow—maybe love eventually." It was more than Nell could hope for herself. She'd jump at the chance to have someone like the earl woo her.

"Perhaps." Jane fingered a darn on the outmoded bed curtains. "Perhaps it will prove enough."

Ellie stood at the scrubbed kitchen table in the shaft of sunlight that spilled into the room from the open door. A mound of early strawberries sat waiting to be hulled, but Ellie was too distracted by her daydreams to get down to work. She held a berry to her lips, relishing the sweet scent, letting the taste tantalize her mouth. It savored of spring and Will's kisses. How wonderful it was, she thought, to snatch such simple pleasures and enjoy them, especially when her foothold in happiness was so fragile. She had no idea how long her friendship with the earl would last, but she intended to value every moment.

A shadow fell across the doorway waking her from her pleasant thoughts.

"Is the mistress within?" A thin gentleman with a head of sparse brown hair stood without, hat held in his hands.

Embarrassed to be caught for all intents and purposes kissing a strawberry, Ellie put it down quickly.

"I'll fetch her for you, sir. Who shall I say is calling?"

"John March. Please tell her I am a friend of a friend of hers."

Ellie found the dame dozing in the front room, a string of rosary beads caught in her fingers.

"Mistress Holton, there's a man at the back door—a gentleman, I think."

The dame sat up with a start and dropped the beads. "I was just praying," she excused herself hurriedly. "What's that?"

Ellie repeated the message.

"Let's go see who he is, then." The dame tucked her rosary back into her girdle and headed for the kitchen door. "May I help you, sir?"

The man cast Ellie a worried look. "I need to speak to you privately, mistress."

The dame pursed her lips, worry now furrowing her brow. "Ellie dear, run along and see if there are any more strawberries in the south-facing patch."

"I picked all I could find," said Ellie.

"Please go and check you didn't miss one."

Her presence was clearly not desired by either party, so Ellie took a basket and went out into the garden. She spent half an hour lingering in the strawberry patch before returning inside. Knocking hesitantly, she waited until Dame Holton invited her in.

"Find any more?" asked the lady as she served the gentleman a light meal of bread and cheese. He consumed everything she put before him with gusto, evidently ravenous.

"No, mistress. Well, one little one but I ate it, I'm afraid." Ellie rinsed her fingers in the basin on the table and turned to the pile of strawberries still awaiting preparation.

"Master March is going to be staying with us for a while," the dame continued, not meeting her eye. "He's a friend . . ."

". . . of a friend of yours. Yes, he mentioned that. Pleased to meet you, sir."

March smiled at her. "I'm delighted to find such a pretty houseguest. Mistress Holton explained why your father is staying here. She says he will enjoy the company of an educated man. I vow we will be a very merry party."

Ellie offered him a strawberry from the basket. "He'll like that. He's quite tired of my conversation."

March took the berry. "Then maybe I can take that burden from you. It is long since I spoke with a scholar of such learning."

"Our Ellie is a very clever girl too, Fa—Master March." The dame quickly corrected herself. "Speaks and reads Latin and all sorts of strange languages."

March regarded her with new interest. "Indeed?"

"My father's idea, sir."

"You can read the scriptures in Greek and Latin?"

"Latin easily. My Greek is a little weak."

"Maybe we can study together if you have the time? My Greek is rusty too, and I would enjoy a chance to polish it in such fair company."

"It would be my pleasure, sir."

"Run along now, Ellie. Master March and I have much to discuss." The dame flapped her with her apron to the door. "Go buy yourself a ribbon or two in the market. The tinker is in the village." She pressed a tester, worth sixpence, into her hand. "My treat."

Ribbons and sunshine or ancient Greek in a dusty study—no contest.

"Thank you." Ellie ran out, barely remembering to bob a parting curtsy in her eagerness. Her high spirits made the visitor laugh.

"Oh, to be that young again!" she heard him say. "Where happiness can be purchased for the price of a ribbon."

The village was bustling with people doing their weekly market shopping. There seemed to be more carts than ever. Ellie stopped by the baker's to greet Mistress Anne Smedley, his young wife, who she had known when she lived at Lacey Hall before. Ellie's return meant that they had had a chance to pick up their friendship where they'd left off.

"Good day! Anyone home?" she called.

"Ellie!" Anne, a short, chubby girl with a rosy face, emerged from the back kitchen, carrying her swaddled baby of three months. "Just let me put Dorothy somewhere safe. She's been fretting since dawn, making me feel eighty rather than eighteen." She hung the baby snugly on a peg on the wall, out of the way of danger, then came forward to hug her friend. Dorothy began to wail.

"I don't think she likes it," Ellie commented as the infant went bright red with anger.

"She'd have me hold her all day and all night if she had her way," Anne acknowledged. She adjusted the lacing on her bodice, her breasts plump with milk.

Ellie laughed and took the baby down to cradle her in her arms. The crying instantly ceased. "Quite right too, young lady. If you don't let the world know what you want, no one will give it to you."

Anne smiled. "Would you like a job as her nurse? You have a magic touch."

"Hardly. She just knows she'll get her way with me. Why all the bustle, do you know?"

Anne stacked a pile of fresh buns on a flat basket. "The earl is entertaining guests—a fine lady and gentleman, they say. The cook has ordered dozens of my goodman's fine pastries—I'm run off my feet keeping up."

Happy for her friend's good fortune, Ellie smiled as she skimmed a finger over the floury surface of the board, drawing a heart. "Who would've thought two people could eat so much?"

"Ah, but it's the retainers, the entertaining of local gentry to meet the guests—the list goes on. And I can't get any decent help—the girls are all preparing for the May celebrations and can't keep a sensible thought in their head for two minutes together."

"They're going Maying?"

"Aye, they've waited for the fine weather. We brought in the

May on the first, but it was too wet to dance. Didn't Bess tell you?" Anne asked, mentioning her younger sister.

"I've not come to the village for a few days—I've not seen anyone." Except Will, that was.

"They'd love you to join in, I'm sure. It's tonight—they're meeting at twilight on the green."

"Will you be there?"

Anne wrinkled her nose. "Sadly, no, not now I'm a respectable married woman. My last time was a year ago—but I don't regret it. I met Sam in the woods after the dance, and well, there's Dorothy as evidence." She blushed at the admission.

Ellie grinned and tickled the baby under the chin. "Why, Anne, you wild thing!"

"We were betrothed—as good as married, Sam said."

"I bet he did." Ellie giggled.

Anne broke into a laugh. "He marched me to church the next day to arrange for the banns to be read, bless him."

"I'd love to go. I've not been Maying for so long."

"Just keep out of the woods." Anne gave her a wink.

"Of course! What do you take me for, a wicked woman who meets her lover there, like some I could mention?" She raised an eyebrow at her friend in mock censure.

"No, you're too good, not like me. Too much a lady."

Ellie wasn't so sure about that, but there was only one man she'd like to meet, and he was unlikely to be found in the woods. "Shall I watch Dorothy for you? I've only come to buy some ribbons, and I know you have much to do."

Anne perched against the table and sighed. "Too true."

"Where's Sam?"

"At the mill fetching some flour."

"Then you take a rest—go watch the loaves rise—and I'll take Dorothy for a little wander."

Anne touched her friend's arm lightly. "You are a sweetheart."

"No trouble at all."

Taking the baby off the swaddling board and wrapping her in a shawl, Ellie went back out into the sunshine. The tinker was easy to spot, standing under the old oak in the center of the green, a crowd of young girls gathered around him as he displayed his rainbow ribbons. Anne's sister, Bess, a tall, thin girl with sleek brown hair like otter skin, greeted Ellie enthusiastically, repeating the invitation to join in the May dance that night. Ellie stood with her, debating the vexing question of whether she should purchase a raspberry-pink or a forest-green ribbon for the celebration. Or maybe both. She turned the tester in her hand, wondering if she would not be better saving it in case of need. She could live without ribbons.

But the dame had given it to her to spend on a gift, not to hoard.

"Go on, Ellie, buy one," urged Bess.

She reached out to take the two ribbons for closer inspection, letting them flutter in her hand. The tinker straightened up from his fawning over her choice and swept an elaborate bow, eyes fixed on something behind her. Bess bobbed a deep curtsy. Turning round, Ellie saw Will had arrived on horseback, accompanied by one of his brothers, Lady Jane and, worst of all, Sir Henry. It was too late to hide, not with her hands full and a sleeping baby strapped to her, preventing her from slipping away. She dipped a curtsy, catching Will's eye as he smiled to see her standing among the village girls.

"Lady Eleanor!" Jane exclaimed in shock, guiding her horse forward. "I had not realized you were here."

"Nor I you, my lady." She summoned a smile from somewhere.

Sir Henry cast a look at the baby, then the earl, his mind drawing unflattering conclusions. His lips thinned.

"My father and I are lodging here for a few weeks," Ellie continued. She took a step away from Henry, moving closer to Will and Jane.

"The child—not yours, surely?" Jane gave a scandalized laugh.

Ellie shook her head, blushing at the thought. "No, my lady. A friend's. I was minding Dorothy while her mother bakes her bread."

"A baker's child." Jane shook her head with amusement at the idea of a lady stooping so low as to mind a commoner's babe. "My friend, you are always a surprise."

Encouraged by the correction to his false assumptions, Henry swung out of his saddle and approached. "Lady Eleanor, it is a joy to see you again after the unpleasant scene at Windsor."

Ellie wondered if he was referring to their banishment or his attempt to force himself on her in the garden.

"Sir," she replied neutrally.

"You were about to choose a ribbon for yourself?" He tugged the raspberry one from her fingers. Bess smothered an excited giggle.

"As you see."

Will dismounted quickly and came to her other side. Henry held the ribbon up to her hair.

"Oh, this one suits you best. Raspberries—put me in mind of a sweet taste." He let his gaze drop to her lips. Ellie's foot itched to kick him again.

Will gestured to the green. "But that one goes well with your gown, does it not, Lady Eleanor?"

"You must let me buy both for you," Henry announced, feeling in his purse for a coin.

"No, no, I must insist I have that pleasure," Will countered. "These are my lands, after all."

"I do not believe that gives you the right to all the ribbons on it, my lord," Henry said, making it sound a jest, but his eyes were hard.

"Enough, my lord, Sir Henry!" Ellie held up a hand. "I fear you are both too late. My kind hostess has already given me the coin for the ribbons. This is her gift to me." She pressed the tester in the bemused tinker's palm. "Now I must return Dorothy to her mother. She will think I have run off with her."

She curtsied, but before she could leave Jane called out:

"Lady Eleanor, please do come and see me while I am in the district. I would value the chance to speak to a friend."

Ellie paused, wondering if there was any way she could visit Jane without having to bear the company of her brother. "Of course, my lady."

"I will send a horse for you tomorrow morning, and you can dine with us," the earl offered quickly, "if that is convenient?"

It was far from being so with Henry in residence, but to refuse would be rude. She would never hear the end of it from the villagers. "Yes, my lord. Thank you."

Jane urged her horse nearer so she could speak confidentially. "But I would also like to see you alone—there's so much I want to tell you."

Ellie met her eyes, reading the sadness so few saw under the perfect beauty of Jane's face. She wondered what had caused it. "I'd like that."

"Then when?"

A zany thought tumble-turned across Ellie's mind like an acrobat at the fair. There was something that might cheer Jane up if she dared. "Come tonight," Ellie whispered, keeping an eye out for Will and Sir Henry. They were too busy glaring at each other to listen in on the girls' conversation.

"Come where?"

"I'm going a-Maying—with the girls from the village. We meet here at dusk."

"Maying?" Jane licked her lips. "With common people?"

"Don't be such a killjoy." Ellie grinned. "You'll enjoy it. So much more fun than stuffy banquets at court."

Jane's gaze flitted lightly over the gathered villagers, then the green where they stood. "All right."

Ellie was amazed she had agreed so readily. "Really?"

"Yes."

"Wondrous. I'll see you later." Dorothy let out a wail, so Ellie turned to go. "Oh, and wear something"—she frowned at Jane's lush rose-pink damask petticoat with fine wool overskirt—"less . . . eye-catching."

"But I don't have anything of poorer quality than this."

Ellie rolled her eyes. "You can't go Maying dressed like a duchess."

"I'll think of something," Jane promised.

"Until dusk then, my lady." Ellie bobbed a curtsy and walked briskly away, aware that all eyes were on her back. The gossip would be lively now the honor of buying her ribbons had been fought over by two gentlemen in full view of everyone. She just hoped they wouldn't also get wind of the fact that she had persuaded one of the noble guests to join the girls that night; if they knew, there would be an outcry. But still, it would be rather fun.

Chapter 13

"Nell, I want to borrow one of your gowns this evening," Jane announced as she sat at her dressing table. "And tell the countess that I have retired early so will not join her in the parlor."

"A gown?" Nell stood in the doorway, waiting for her mistress to announce that it was a jest.

"An old one," continued Jane, taking down her complicated hairstyle and redoing it in two plaits. She fixed mismatched ribbons to the ends.

A suspicion crossed Nell's mind—her ladyship was planning something she shouldn't. Another secret rendezvous, perhaps? But with whom?

"Of course, my lady. I will fetch one from my trunk."

Jane stripped off her fine clothes and pulled on the simple brown woolen gown Nell had found her. The material was a little scratchy even through the fine linen of her shift, but it served the purpose. No one would ever guess that the fair-haired maiden was a rich noblewoman.

"My lady is going out?" Nell inquired, folding up the discarded garments.

Jane adjusted the bodice up so that the edge of her shift covered her cleavage and arranged a plain coif over her hair. "I am going Maying, Nell, but I would prefer you did not share that fact with my brother." She sounded almost proud of herself.

"Maying?"

"Yes. With Lady Eleanor. And the girls from the village."

For once, her mistress had managed to surprise her. Lady Jane had never shown any eagerness to participate in such low pursuits before.

"I wish you a good evening, then, my lady. Shall I wait up?"

"No, no. I'll see to myself when I return. But if you could arrange for the back door to the kitchen to be left unlatched, I would be grateful." Jane took a coin from her purse and handed it to Nell.

"Of course, my lady," murmured Nell.

Jane had already bribed the blackamoor groom to have her horse waiting for her. A pleasant fellow with a smile that lit up the stable when he heard what she was about, Diego had insisted that he accompany her to the village and look after her mount while "the ladies were playing," as he put it. Jane rather suspected he fancied the idea of spying on the girls' secret rites. Leaving him with her palfrey some distance from the green, she made the last part of the journey on foot. Only now did doubts begin to ambush her resolve. What if someone recognized her? This had to be the stupidest thing she had ever done. No, that was not true. Meeting Raleigh was far worse—this was merely a little bit naughty.

"Lady Jane!" Ellie had been on the lookout for her.

"Ssh!" she hissed, hoping no one had overheard.

Ellie grabbed her arm and towed her along. "I thought you would lack the courage to come."

"I don't lack courage, just common sense."

"Hush now, you'll love it. I last went when I was twelve—there'll be dances, and I'm sure there'll be lots to eat and someone will have smuggled in something to drink. It'll be great fun."

Jane glanced around at the cottages, all of which had windows overlooking the green. "We can't dance here, surely?"

"No, in the meadows by the wood, of course. You can't go Maying without spring flowers." With that, Ellie plonked a garland of daisies that she had strung together on Jane's head. "And now my lady's necklace." She looped a second wreath around her neck.

"Thank you, they're priceless." Jane laughed, admiring the humble flowers, thinking them quite the prettiest thing she'd ever worn. "What about you?"

Ellie pulled a few bluebells from the hedgerow and stuck them in her hair so they sprang out like the horns on a snail. She turned to let Jane assess the effect. "What do you think?"

"You look like a mad beetle."

"Excellent."

Jane found the other girls had decked themselves with similar inventiveness. As it was an all-girl occasion, they had strived to outdo each other in absurdity rather than worrying about what their male admirers would think. Everyone had flowers somewhere on her person. One girl had made a wig of lilac blooms; another, an apron of leaves. As Ellie had predicted, someone had brought a cask of the brewer's best ale, and a few were already giggling from its effects.

Ellie marched up to a tall girl, who appeared to be the unofficial leader of the festivities. "Bess, I've brought a friend along. She's visiting her aunt in Up-Hadley," she said, naming a village a few miles away.

Bess nodded to Jane. "Welcome. What's your name?"

"She's Pru—short for Prudence," Ellie said swiftly, giving Jane a sly wink.

Jane decided she would get her back for that before the night was over.

"I think we're all here now." Bess gave a shrill whistle, putting two fingers in her mouth. "All right, ladies, the fun begins here. Time to move to the meadow."

Jane noted that quite a few people appeared in the doorways to see the girls off, the older women smiling fondly as they remembered their own youth. The young men were gathered outside the inn, their looks rather more speculative.

"Don't wear yourselves out, girls!" called the blacksmith's apprentice. "We'll be in the woods later."

"You'll be so lucky," crowed Bess, giving him a jaunty swish of her skirts.

Having heard about Bess's sister, Anne, from Ellie as they passed her door, Jane wondered if there might be quite a few more weddings in the village by the summer.

A maypole stood waiting in the meadow, crowned with a wreath of flowers, ribbons tied to the stem in a bow.

"Gift from the boys," Ellie whispered. "They put it up each year. I think they hope it makes the girls feel charitable towards them."

Or aroused by the dancing, Jane thought, intrigued by a glimpse of a way of life she had never realized existed among the lower classes.

A blind fiddler sat on the ground, jumping to his feet when he heard the girls approaching.

"He's the only man allowed." Ellie bent down to tighten her shoelaces.

"Paid for by the boys?" Jane guessed.

"You're catching on," Ellie laughed.

"Now we get to choose our May Queen!" announced Bess. "The prize goes to the most deserving maid among us."

"Me!" called a stout, red-faced maid with a jolly smile.

"Never, Maud, you were caught with Hamnet, so you no longer qualify."

The girls hooted with laughter as Maud stuck out her tongue at Bess.

"This year, by a completely fair and open process known only to me," continued Bess archly, "the title goes to Ellie, for putting up with Dame Holton and generally charming the hose off everyone in the village. Agreed?"

"Agreed!" shouted the girls as Ellie blushed and flapped the compliment away.

"The lucky winner gets to wear the crown." With no ceremony at all, Bess chased a resisting Ellie round the maypole and dumped a sagging coronet of mayflowers and weeds on her head as the onlookers cheered.

"Speech!" called Maud.

Ellie cleared her throat with great self-importance. "Ladies, I am touched by your terrible sense of judgment and will ever treasure the fragrant honor you have bestowed on me this day." She gestured to her crown. "Thank you all."

"Long live the May Queen!" called Bess, echoed by all, even the blind fiddler.

The first tune plunged Ellie back four years to her last May dance. It was an old favorite—a single plait that took little skill but allowed the girls a chance to get reacquainted with the maypole. Bess marshaled them into position so they could weave the ribbons in pairs.

"There's a forfeit for getting it wrong: a kiss for Blind Martyn!" announced Bess.

The fiddler cheered. "Right, my dears, watch yourselves. I'm going to go so fast, you're bound to stumble."

They didn't, of course, not on this dance. But the challenge was as old as the tradition of dancing in the spring, and the fiddler knew his part.

The single plait was succeeded by the double, then the fiendishly tricky spider's web. Jane made them go awry when she tugged Ellie the wrong way, and they both had to kiss the fiddler's cheek, much to the amusement of the others. When they'd danced themselves out, they collapsed on the sweet meadow grass, sharing a batch of buns donated by Anne, and passed the time catching up on the latest gossip.

"So Pru, where are you from?" asked Bess, rolling over onto her stomach and kicking her feet in the air.

"London," Jane replied.

"You talk fine—almost as fine as Ellie."

Ellie snorted at this. Jane pelted her with twigs.

"I . . . er . . . serve a lady there," Jane explained.

"At court?"

"We go sometimes."

"You lucky thing." Bess turned on her back, watching the glow-worms flickering on the bank. "Life here is so boring. I'd love to see all the court ladies—the Queen herself. I mean the real one and not our May Queen."

Ellie smiled and pulled the crown off her head, letting it flop into her lap.

Jane yawned. "Court can be boring, too, if you spend too much time there. Very formal and stuffy."

Ellie thought Jane was giving too much away, sounding too much the spoilt noble. "But the gentlemen are always worth seeing, aren't they, *Prudence*? Did I tell you, Bess, that I went to a joust? The earl looked very well in his armor."

"Oh, I wager he did. He is just . . . just so handsome—and an earl—it's not fair. I wish I was the lady he's courting."

"He's courting?" Ellie met Jane's eyes as the reason for her visit suddenly became clear. She should've guessed.

"Yes, the lady you met this morning. I thought you must know, as you seemed to be friendly with her." Bess's tone was too innocent to be completely believable. She was watching the by-play between Ellie and Jane closely.

Ellie studied the shredded flowers in her lap. "No, I hadn't realized, but you're right, I should've known."

Bess's revelation had spoiled Ellie's mood as quickly as a frost in spring. Her relationship with Will had existed in a perfect bubble, floating unattached to duties or reality, but now that had burst.

Letting the conversation move on, she got up and brushed off her skirts. "I'd better get back."

"Not coming to the woods?" asked Bess with a gleam in her eye as she nodded to the shimmer of torches weaving between the trees.

"Not this year."

"I didn't think so."

Ellie said her farewells and started walking off across the meadow towards the village, not even waiting for Jane.

Bess turned to Jane. "What about you, Pru? Are you as strait-laced as your friend, or can we tempt you into the woods?"

No, she wasn't, Jane thought ruefully. But she wasn't going to share that fact—and she had a few things to explain to Ellie. "I'd better not. Thank you for letting me join you."

Bess smirked. "Any time. You're not really a servant, are you?"

Jane wasn't sure what to say.

Bess gestured to the girls lounging on the meadow around them. "We all got an eyeful of you earlier. Ellie may think you can fool us, but you're not easily forgotten, my lady, even with the change of gown."

Jane laughed. "I'm sorry for the deception, then. But I did enjoy myself."

"We're all glad you came. If you become the next countess, we'll know who to come to if the vicar tries to stop us going Maying."

"You can count on me." Jane waved a general farewell, then hurried after Ellie. It had been shocking to be on equal terms with girls she'd always considered beneath her. For the first time, she'd begun to think that maybe their life held attractions hers did not. Friendship, for one. Fun, for another.

"Ellie, Ellie, wait!" Jane caught up with her in the lane to the village. From the shrieks behind her, she guessed the girls had just gone into the trees. At least no one would be interested in what the two of them were doing with so much happening in the woods.

Ellie stopped but did not turn, her head hung low.

"That's what I wanted to talk to you about. I know that there's some . . . some affection between you and the earl. It was obvious this afternoon, and I'd suspected it before."

"No, there's nothing like that," Ellie said in a dull tone of voice. "We're just friends."

"I don't want this, but my family has commanded me to see if we will suit." Jane felt her annoyance rising—she'd found her first true friend and this was coming between them. The earl wasn't worth it, in her estimation.

"I understand—really, I do. I'm sorry to stride off like that. It's not my place to make you even think that you are doing something I don't approve of."

Jane threw her daisy chain at her. "Oh, hush up, Ellie. You and I both know that's not so. Out of character for me it may be, but I care what you think—what you feel."

Ellie managed a smile, resigning herself to something she could not change. The world had set her on one course, Jane on another. "Thank you . . . Prudence."

Jane half laughed, half growled. "*Prudence!* Couldn't you come up with something better than that? I vowed I'd get you for that, Lady Eleanor. Prepare for death by flowers!"

She chucked a handful of hedgerow weeds at Ellie, who responded in kind. The Mayflower crown hit Jane in the face as grass caught in Ellie's hair.

"You look like a dog with mange," mocked Jane; then she shrieked as her opponent managed to stuff a handful of leaves down her neck. Their hilarity grew as they pelted each other with weeds. They stopped only when Diego approached them cautiously, leading Jane's horse.

"Is all well, O Most Gracious and Most Gentle Ladies?" he asked, then looked bewildered when both collapsed into each other's arms, breathless with laughter.

"Oh yes, Diego, we're well." Ellie gasped.

"Just perfect," agreed Jane.

Chapter 14

Ellie checked her reflection in the little polished mirror for what felt like the hundredth time. She had cleaned her green gown, borrowed Dame Holton's ancient wedding stomacher of cream and gold thread and made herself a pair of new sleeves from another castoff of the dame's. The string of seed pearls around her neck also belonged to her hostess, but they had the unfortunate effect of making her old ruff look very dim by contrast. There was nothing she could do about that at this late stage. She knew she was going to be outshone by the ladies at Lacey Hall, but at least she wasn't an absolute disgrace.

A knock at the door downstairs announced the arrival of Diego with a horse for her. Taking a deep breath, she dipped into her father's study.

"I'm off now, Father."

"Hmm? Where to?" He looked up distractedly from his pile of books.

"Lacey Hall. I'm dining with the family."

"Oh yes, you did tell me. Enjoy yourself." His eyes were already directed back to the last line he had written.

Ellie knew better than to seek his opinion about her appearance, so she instead called on Dame Holton. She caught her hostess and Master March at prayer in the parlor.

"Oh, excuse me," she said, seeing them both on their knees. She had suspected March was of the same creed as Dame Holton, but had preferred not coming face to face with the proof.

"Why, Ellie, you look lovely," the dame commented, not at all abashed to be found in such a humble position. She crossed herself and rose, cupping Ellie's face gently in her fingers. "Hold your head high, young lady. You need not be ashamed of how you look today."

It took Ellie a while to coax Diego into talking to her as they rode to Lacey Hall. She knew from his banter with his master that he had a lively mind, but he was wary of showing it to an outsider. Yet he was one of the most interesting characters Ellie had ever met—so different from everyone else, not just in appearance but experience—and she had been impressed that he had willingly colluded with Jane the night before.

"Have you been in England long, Diego?" she asked.

"Not that long, mistress."

"Do you remember your homeland?"

"Yes."

Ellie would've laughed at his skill at giving minimal and uninformative answers if she had not feared to offend him.

"I've read of the deserts of North Africa in works of the ancient travelers. Is it true you can journey for days without sight of water?"

"Yes."

"And that the land is made entirely of sand?"

"Yes."

"Do you miss it?"

"Yes."

She would have to try another tack. "What do you miss most?"

Diego cast a searching look at her. "Why are you so interested in a poor servant, O Beauteous Queen of May?"

That did make her laugh. The wretch had been spying on them! "Do you address the earl like that, Diego, with flourishing titles?"

He couldn't hide a smile. "Yes, O Kindly One."

"I wager he loves it." She chuckled at the thought of Will being heaped with such flowery epithets.

"He is uncomfortable with the praise, mistress, even though it is most deserved. He is a very generous master."

"Which are your favorites?"

By teasing questions, she managed to draw out of him how he went about making Will squirm with embarrassment, though neither stated that that was what he was doing.

"And his brother James, does he groan under the weight of redundant titles?"

Diego shook his head. "Oh no, most bounteous and benevolent mistress, Master James would not allow it."

"Meaning the earl and I are both too softhearted to put a stop to it? You've obviously not seen my lord in a temper."

"Not yet." Diego grinned.

A servant waited for her at the door of Lacey Hall carrying a hand basin and comb so she could put herself to rights after the brisk ride from the village. Ellie frowned at her reflection in the large looking glass flanked by statues of nymphs—she looked every inch the poor relation, from mismatched clothing to dowdy ruff.

"Are the ladies' dresses very magnificent?" she asked the servant.

"Yes, my lady," the girl stated baldly, her expression just a shade mocking.

Ellie shrugged. "Oh well, I was never going to prevail in this competition, was I? They asked me to dine, so they get me, warts and all."

"I can't see any warts, my lady," quipped the girl pertly.

Ellie was startled into a bubble of laughter. "Thank you, I think." She tapped her empty pocket. "I'm afraid I have nothing to tip you for your compliment, um . . . ?"

"Nell, my lady. I serve the Lady Jane."

"Nell." She tweaked her cap straight. "Oh well, I'll have to do."

The steward came out of a nearby doorway, giving Ellie an unpleasant surprise. It was the same man who had threatened her with his wolfhound four years ago, and he looked far from pleased to see her today.

"Lady Eleanor," he said gruffly, giving her an abbreviated bow.

Ellie knew she should be feeling triumphant, being invited back as a guest of honor after her ignominious departure, but she couldn't quell the fear she felt around this big man with rough ginger hair and hard eyes. "Master Steward."

"I have been ordered to conduct you to the countess's glasshouse. The ladies are inspecting her flowers." His tone made plain it was only orders that forced him to let her set foot again on his territory.

"Thank you," Ellie said faintly. She cast a helpless look at the maid, only to find the girl had undergone a complete transformation. No longer the witty servant with a sharp tongue, she had her eyes trained meekly on the floor.

"Mistress Rivers, Sir Henry asks if you can attend him. There is some matter to do with a lost glove he wishes to discuss." The steward's manner to the girl was cringingly respectful.

"At once, Master Turville." Bestowing on him a sweet smile, the maid darted away.

"Lady Eleanor, if you would follow me." The steward swept his hand in the direction of the garden at the rear of the house. He kept a step ahead of her, opening doors and ushering her through, but she felt more like a bad smell he wished to expel from the house than a person of worth. His attitude raised her hackles.

"And how have your fared since last we met, Master Steward?" she asked brightly, forcibly reminding him of their last unpleasant encounter. "You look as though you've been very comfortable in your position." Overfed was closer to the mark.

"The earl is a very good master," he said stiffly.

"And is your dog still alive—that charming brute you introduced me to?"

"No, lady, Bart died some years back."

"Can't say I'm sorry to hear that."

"But his son, Tiber, is more than a match for his sire. Quite able to chase a man down should I give the word."

"How delightful."

He stopped in the door leading to the garden, barring her exit. "I know I shouldn't say this to you, you being here as a guest and all, but if you harm my master, you'll be facing more than Tiber."

Ellie gave a strangled laugh, her fingers touching her throat. "Me? What possible harm can I do him?"

Turville glared at her. "He's got this pretty young lady here to woo and wed. We don't want no interference from alchemists' brats."

She took a step back. "You are rude, sir."

He waved a dismissive hand at her. "You and I both know your family is poison to mine. I protect those I serve. There's more than one obsession that can make a man act a fool. Behave yourself and you and I will have no quarrel."

He thought the earl in danger of contracting an obsession for her? They'd reached a truce, that was true, and Will had admitted he admired her, but she doubted he meant more than to flirt with her. She wasn't sure she could say the same about herself.

"I'm here because I was invited, Master Steward, not because I forced myself upon the family. Who are you to question the will of the earl?"

"His good friend and protector. I don't need his permission to watch his back for him. Now get along with you and behave yourself with the ladies. Don't forget: I'm watching you."

Outraged by the man's unmannerly treatment of her, she flounced past him, wishing she had some cutting remark to prick his pompous hide, but just at the moment, nothing came to mind.

"Vile wretch," she muttered under her breath. "Lump of lard on legs." Pleased with that image, her lips curled in a smile. She tried an improvement. "Rancid rotund lump of lard on legs." Perfect.

"Lady Eleanor!" The countess emerged from the shrubbery where she had been showing Jane the newly planted border by the glasshouse.

Wonderful: she'd been caught mumbling insults to herself like an inmate of the madhouse.

"My lady." She swept a deep curtsy.

"To whom were you talking, dear?" The countess's eyes twinkled, and Ellie just knew that she had been overheard.

"Um, no one?" she ventured.

"Did someone vex you?"

Yes. "No, my lady. I was just . . . just repeating a rhyme I heard the other day."

"You like poetry, do you? We must read some together, then. I confess to a passion for it that none of my boys admit to sharing, though I do so want to suspect them of being closet admirers of a finely turned sonnet." She sighed. "At least, I hope they are, or I have raised three barbarians."

Jane came forward and kissed Ellie on the cheek. "Lady Eleanor."

Ellie smiled at the deliberate formality after the flower-battle the night before. "Please, Lady Jane, my title is little used at home, and means nothing outside Spain. I much prefer to be called Ellie by my friends."

"I hope your eagerness at meeting your friend, Lady Jane, does not mean you've tired of us already?" The countess beckoned her daughter to her side and tugged her coif straight. "This is Lady Sarah, my youngest."

Sarah took a quick inventory of Ellie's clothes, as sharp as any dressmaker. "I like your stomacher," she said. Meant as a pleasant remark, it came across more as a criticism of the rest of Ellie's clothes.

Ellie leant forward confidentially. "Not mine, Lady Sarah. Borrowed from the wedding finery of my kind hostess."

"Dame Holton? Must be ancient, then. Why aren't you wearing your own?"

"Sarah!" the countess warned.

"It's all right, my lady, I'm not embarrassed. I have no fine clothes, Lady Sarah, because I'm poor."

"So are we," said Sarah, nodding in understanding. "But Will always manages to find a few pounds here and there for our clothes, doesn't he, Mother?"

Rendered speechless, the countess looked quite mortified by her daughter's indiscreet tongue.

"Jane's the only one here with any money, and she has a splendid wardrobe—you should see it! I spent yesterday just admiring her shoes. She's got a pair of suede riding boots I would die to own."

Jane shifted uneasily. "Lady Sarah, Ellie and I long ago agreed that clothes were empty extravagances."

Sarah jumped on a stone bench, pretending to parade in a fine dress like a lady at court. "That's all right for you to say, you've a king's ransom in clothes in your trunks."

The countess had now found her tongue again. "Ladies, I apologize for my daughter. I obviously have been too sparing with the rod."

Sarah snorted. "Pish! I'm just speaking the truth."

"But not all truths should be spoken," the countess said severely.

Ellie laughed at this by-play. She thought the little lady quite splendid and likely to turn Will's hair prematurely gray.

"Lady Sarah, will you do this poor guest the honor of showing me your favorite parts of the garden?"

"Oh yes, please! Race you?" Sarah had obviously sensed a fellow partner for her mischief.

"Sarah!" her mother scolded. "Lady Eleanor is too old for such horseplay!"

Was she? Ellie didn't feel so when the sun was shining, and she had the prospect of a good meal ahead. She was only sixteen, not sixty. . . .

"Where to?" she asked.

"Sundial." Sarah pointed to the end of a hedge-lined aisle. "Marks, set, go!" She shot off the bench, hair flying out from beneath her coif like a golden flag. With a smile at the countess and Jane, Ellie set out in pursuit, lifting her skirts above her ankles to stand a chance of catching her. "Come on, Jane!" she called. "I dare you!"

"Madam?" Jane asked the countess, holding out her hand, her face brightened by a carefree smile.

Lady Dorset laughed. "Oh, very well, you hoydens!" She took Jane's hand and ran as fast as her heavy gown would allow. "Curse upon farthingales! I really need to shed a few layers if I'm going to do this!"

Ellie let Sarah reach the sundial first, then grabbed her hands to dance her round it, humming one of the tunes the fiddler had played for the maypole. Sarah squealed as Ellie spun her and then both let go and tumbled to the ground, giggling.

"Oh!" Ellie said, suddenly remembering. "I mustn't get grass stains on Dame Holton's clothes!"

The countess and Jane arrived at a run, their faces flushed.

"My!" said Lady Dorset, hand to her racing heart. "I haven't run like that for years!"

"What's this, Mother, dashing about the garden?" Will stepped into the grassy clearing round the sundial to find the four women collapsed in degrees of rumpledness on the ground. Sun making his hair shine, he had a tennis racket slung over one shoulder and was dressed only in a shirt and hose, no peascod velvet doublet to disguise the breadth of his shoulders and flat stomach. Ellie felt her mouth go dry, told herself it was the exercise and looked away.

"Yes, dear," said the countess. "I may be old at thirty-eight, but even I am not past exerting myself from time to time."

"Old, madam, never let that be said!" declared Sir Henry, following Will, his racket tucked under his arm.

James arrived on their heels. "What's all this?" he asked as he sketched a bow to the ladies.

"Mother. Running," Will said deadpan. His eyes moved to Ellie. "With our guests."

James held out a hand to help the countess to her feet. He continued the motion to scoop her up and swing her in a circle. "Splendid! I don't think I've seen such a smile on your face, Mother, since Father died."

The countess stroked his cheek affectionately.

"Me! Me!" demanded Sarah, wanting her turn to be spun.

"All right, pest."

Sarah got a violent whirl, which left her in a breathless heap.

"Any more takers?" James asked the ladies, his eyes on Jane.

Jane looked away, embarrassed. Eager to ease an awkward moment for her friend, Ellie quickly stepped forward.

Before James could oblige, Sir Henry advanced.

"Unfair, Master Lacey, why must you get all the lovely ladies? I pray you take my sister, and I'll handle this fair burden."

Before Ellie had time to think up an excuse, he took her firmly by the waist and twirled her round. It wasn't fun like the dance at the maypole—it was horribly like being trapped on a whirligig at the fair. She stumbled into him, the garden a blur of color.

"Hmm, lovely," Henry said in a low voice, letting his hands rove.

Ellie pushed herself away, in time to catch Will's gaze on the pair of them. He looked worried and angry, a fair summary of her own feelings being back in close proximity to Sir Henry. Fortunately, the countess was quick to restore sanity to their May-madness.

"My dears, enough of this before we scandalize the gardeners! Shall we proceed inside? We dine at noon, and some of us need to dress." She smiled pointedly at her sons. "Sir Henry, will you escort me?"

Reminded of his duty to his hostess, Henry turned from Ellie and offered his arm. Ellie breathed a sigh of relief.

"Lady Jane, Lady Eleanor?" Will held out a hand to them both. "May I?"

"Not fair, Will," grumbled James. "Leave one for me, won't you?"

"You can bring Sarah." Will winked at his younger sister still flopped in her heap of skirts. "Remind her to assume the role of lady before we reach the table, please."

Sarah grimaced at her brother and struggled to her feet. "Stupid skirts. Wish I could wear hose."

"No!" said Will and James in unison.

"Wasn't my idea to race—that was Ellie."

Ellie raised an eyebrow.

"All right, it was my idea—but she agreed."

James brushed the grass off her skirt, patting her rather harder than necessary on the behind. "Minx."

"Oaf," she retorted, dancing out of reach.

Will groaned. "Ladies, I hope you are not getting the wrong impression of my family. We can be very well behaved when we try. *Can't we, Sarah?*"

Ellie laughed. "I think Jane and I, the very pattern of decorum at all times, have exactly the right impression, my lord."

"Yes," agreed Jane, catching Ellie's eye across Will's chest. "They are hopeless, the whole pack of them."

"Tennis-playing terrors."

"Mad, mincing mooncalves!"

"Mincing? I take exception to that. I do not mince!" Will protested good-humoredly as they entered the house. He had led them into the family parlor, a fine paneled room with a view across the gardens. The sun bathed the chamber with rich warm light, making the oak glow. "Jamie might, though."

"Do not," growled James.

"But pardon me, ladies: we must dress ourselves for dinner." Will relinquished their arms and bowed. "If you would care to rest here awhile, the musicians will entertain you." He nodded to a lutenist and viol player hired for the occasion.

James towed Sarah with him, telling her that her skirt was beyond saving and she too would have to change. Jane watched the exchange wistfully.

"You like James Lacey, don't you?" Ellie said softly. She sat down on the cushions lining the window seat.

"Yes," Jane admitted candidly. "He's a wonderful brother."

Ellie glanced at Sir Henry, who was just taking his leave of the countess at the other end of the room. "They're a wonderful family. I envy them having each other."

Jane's face darkened. "Not all brothers are a blessing."

"I suppose not. But I've never had one, so I have never had the opportunity to be disillusioned." She reminded herself that Jane was destined to join the family and she owed it to her friend to ease the way. "The earl is very kind too."

"He's very polite. Very proper."

Not to her, he wasn't, thought Ellie, remembering the stolen kiss. "He'll make a considerate husband."

"Perhaps." Jane rearranged her skirts, picking a piece of grass out of a seam. "I suspect his affections lie elsewhere. If I marry him, I'll get only half the man."

In her situation, Ellie knew she'd happily settle for half. "I doubt he would do anything to disgrace you."

"No, but he'll never truly love me, will he?"

"I . . . I don't know." Ellie twisted her hands in her lap.

"If he looked at me with a scant part of the desire with which he looks at you, then I would have some hope for us." Jane's tone was matter-of-fact, no blame attached to Ellie.

"But I'm . . . we're not . . ."

"No, of course not, Ellie." Jane covered Ellie's hands with her own. "You can't help the fact he's attracted to you, but you must know he won't marry you. He's after a rich bride and I seem to fit the order. Shame for us both, don't you think?"

Ellie swallowed. "Yes."

"I'd prefer to marry an old man who'd croak before a month was out, leaving me free. If I do have to marry the earl, please tell me I won't lose your friendship? I have so few of them."

Ellie smiled bravely. Visiting Jane when she was the Countess of Dorset would be like voluntarily sticking needles in her flesh. "Of course, I'll remain your friend—that's if you still want to see me."

"I will." Jane pulled her hand away, resuming her pose of demure lady.

"You are very kind—very understanding."

Jane shook her head. "No, you've got me all wrong, Ellie. I can be a bit of an old witch." The words were shocking coming from the lips of such a perfect-looking lady. "Just ask my maid—or my brother, for that matter."

"Then they are wrong." Ellie frowned. "Or only partly right."

Jane choked in surprise.

"I just meant that I think we all have the capacity to be . . . um . . . witches when pressed."

Jane smiled at the embarrassed tone Ellie used to repeat her insult. "No, Ellie, there's a reason you were chosen as May Queen. You're nothing like me."

Ellie leant forward. "I kneed your brother in the . . . well, you know."

Startled, it took Jane a moment before she let loose her laughter. "And I wager he deserved it."

Ellie bit her lip and nodded. "I kicked the earl in the shin too."

"Good for you! But that still doesn't make you nasty like me. I'm quite coldhearted, you know. Vengeful too."

Ellie gave her a skeptical look. "If you want vengeance, I wager *they* deserve it," she said, repeating Jane's words.

Jane nodded. "Oh yes, definitely."

Chapter 15

Dinner was a revelation to Will. His future wife was more animated than he'd ever seen her before, quite on fire with wit in the company of Ellie and James. Their end of the table was by far the liveliest; he felt quite jealous. Why did Jane not smile and laugh like that for him? And why did Ellie have to be so . . . so irresistible in her borrowed finery and tumbled hair? She looked like she had just been rumpled by a lover, her stomacher coming unpinned and petticoats hooked up at the back. He didn't think she'd noticed but Sir Henry had. He was regarding her with the hankering look of a dog eying a bone, just waiting for the cook to turn his back so he could sneak it away. Foolishly, in the garden at Windsor, Will had made it sound as if he approved of Henry's designs on her. Now he would have to make sure his attention didn't lapse; he had to keep her safe.

"My lord?" Ellie was addressing him and by the tone of her voice, not for the first time. So much for keeping his attention fixed—he'd clearly been daydreaming for some time.

"Lady Eleanor?"

"The villagers say you expect more visitors. Is that true?"

He nodded. "Yes indeed. I believe you'll know at least one of the party. Master Cecil is touring the area with Sir Francis Walsingham."

Her face brightened. "Cecil? Coming here? Oh, that is good news. Now I have someone else with whom I can discuss Virgil."

This remark was followed by silence due to amusement on the gentlemen's parts and shock on behalf of the ladies.

"You read Virgil, my dear?" asked the countess, rather in the tone one used for confirming a terminal diagnosis.

"Um, yes?" Ellie replied uncertainly. "I've borrowed a copy from my hostess's new guest. The *Eclogues* are very . . ." She trailed off, realizing that she was only making it worse trying to explain.

"A veritable Sappho!" James declared, breaking the awkward silence and toasting her with his wine goblet.

"I hope without the preference for her own sex," muttered Henry.

"And who is this scholar, Lady Eleanor?" Will said quickly, changing the subject.

"A Master March, a friend of Dame Holton's. A gentleman who has been traveling on the continent until recently."

"He must make good company for your father," the countess said kindly.

Ellie nodded. "Yes, they debate long into the night. I think he knows many of the same men of learning that my father once knew when we lived in Spain."

"Not another alchemist?" asked Will, wary that Stoke-by-Lacey was becoming a haven for that detestable breed.

"No, no, I think he's quite skeptical of the art. He says that trying to make gold transgresses God's laws of creation."

"Sensible man. Perhaps we should invite him to dine when Walsingham and Cecil are here?"

"I doubt he would come. His circumstances are much reduced, and he says he wishes to remain in obscurity. It is a shame, for his Greek is much better than mine. Master Cecil would enjoy meeting him."

Will began to feel faintly jealous of this man who had Ellie's admiration.

"What manner of man is he?" he asked, rather more abruptly than he intended. "Young, well looking?"

James shot him a look, dipping his head towards Jane, who was absorbing every word that was said—and unsaid—in this exchange.

"Fairly old, I would guess. A little stooped, and his health is not good. About my father's height. Why, do you know him?"

Will shook his head. Nothing to fear from her cool description. "No, Lady Ellie, but tell him that he is welcome to dine with us if he wishes to break his vow of anonymity."

"Thank you. I will."

The family party lost much of its sparkle once Ellie returned home. Will played chess with Henry and then read aloud to the ladies, but time crawled by. Lady Jane retreated back into her shell of perfect lady, making polite conversation and venturing only the most conventional opinions on the subjects under discussion. James had abandoned them, saying he needed a vigorous ride to clear his head. Will couldn't blame him; he only wished his duties as host had not prevented him from accompanying his brother.

During the tedious afternoon, as moment by moment limped by like a beggar pacing St. Paul's Walk, he could feel his mother giving him concerned looks. He feared his partiality for their dinner guest had been too apparent. Had he also hurt Jane's feelings? He studied her calm profile over the top of his book: her blue eyes were dipped to the piece of needlepoint she was working in a frame, her milky skin untroubled by a blush or freckles, anything to suggest that she was a fallible human like the rest of them. She really was too perfect for his ramshackle family.

He turned to his mother's favorite poem.

"*My true love hath my heart, and I have his,*

By just exchange, one for the other given," he read aloud.

But he didn't have Jane's. The poetic words were a lie. For all Jane's glowing beauty, she left his heart cold. Could he survive a marriage built on such an icy foundation? Could the lady? He wanted warmth, love and laughter. He wanted Ellie.

He faltered in his reading. Saints in heaven—he'd gone and fallen in love with a penniless girl with a father he abhorred. Anyone more unsuitable he could not imagine. But his true love was someone quite different from the woman he was supposed to marry.

"Will?" the countess queried. "Something wrong with the sonnet?"

"No, no, Sidney's words are very fine." He cleared his throat and continued.

"*I hold his dear, and mine he cannot miss;*

There never was a better bargain driven."

Marriage was nothing but a bargain that both parties entered into with open eyes. Jane did not expect his heart, only his title and his respect. The problem was what to do about Ellie?

"My true love hath my heart, and I have his." He forced himself to read the last line as if his own heart were not crumbling in his chest at the thought of giving her up forever. He snapped the book shut. "If you will excuse me, ladies, I must exercise Barbary. I have quite neglected him all day."

He strode away before his mother could point out that he employed grooms for that purpose.

Outside in the twilight, he took a cleansing breath, rippling his shoulders to shrug off the cares of the earl. Weary of the situation in which he was caught, he wanted, just for a few hours, to be Will only. He gave a whistle. Diego bobbed out of the stable with admirable alertness.

"My lord?"

"Saddle Barbary for me. We both need the exercise."

Diego returned swiftly, leading the stallion at a trot. "If my gracious lord would wait, I will fetch a horse to accompany him."

Will waved him away. "No need. Go to bed. I'll see to Barbary when I return."

"I'll wait up," Diego said stubbornly, clearly of a mind that no one but he knew how to tend properly to the stallion.

"Suit yourself." He swung up into the saddle. "O Most Obedient and Humble of Servants."

He smiled as he heard Diego's laughter follow him into the night.

Will made no conscious choice to retrace his path to Ellie's cottage, but he found himself in the lane before he could think better of it. It was inky dark now; only the faint light from a nail paring of a moon preventing him riding completely off course. A number of times he had felt the hedge brush against his leg before he had steered Barbary back into the middle of the track. The air smelt of damp earth and lank weeds bursting into spring growth. Wild garlic grew somewhere close by—a scent that cut through the dust and faded perfumes of the family parlor, giving him a jolt out of his low spirits like a dose of smelling salts. Deciding the sound of hooves might give his presence away, he tied Barbary to a gatepost some distance from the cottage and completed the journey on foot.

What was he thinking? Will ran his hand over his face, breathing in the familiar scent of leather and horsehair on his glove. Lord of these lands, yet he was skulking around in the lane outside his love's house like a thief. What did he hope to achieve? Sing a serenade under her window? That would expose his unfortunate passion to the mockery of the dame and, by extension, everyone in the village. No, all he could hope for was to share the same night air with Ellie, be comforted by the knowledge she was hearing the same sounds, seeing the same sights from her window as he was in the garden below.

That was if she wasn't already asleep, which was more than likely. He felt vaguely irritated that love was making him such a foolish figure even to his own mind, but he couldn't help himself.

He approached the house through the garden, trying to remember if the dame kept a watchdog. He thought not. He would have to have words with the dame about ensuring her security. Maybe he could prevail upon Turville to lend her Tiber. Did Ellie like dogs? He'd never had a chance to ask her. He'd seen her with a cat once at Windsor, but there was so much to learn about her.

He stumbled over something, releasing the scent of crushed strawberries into the air. Idiot: he'd walked on the plants. Taking a step back, he stopped on the path. The upper story of the house was in darkness. He did not know which was the window to her chamber, but from the stillness within, it looked as if everyone was asleep.

Sounds carried in the night: the rustle of the leaves in the orchard, the bark of a distant dog, the trickle of the stream that bordered the lane. A door banged in the house. He was wrong about the inhabitants being asleep: at least someone was up. Was it too much to hope it was Ellie? He brushed his fingers lightly over his lips, imagining the goodnight kiss he wished he could give her.

James would laugh to see his older brother now, languishing over a girl. Or thump him. Will walked quietly back to the lane and approached the front of the house, pausing at the gate to take a final look at his lady's home. He couldn't indulge himself like this again; he had a duty to his family and his estate. His feelings were irrelevant.

Someone entered the front parlor, carrying a candlestick. His heart leapt, then sank when he saw that it was only the dame, doing the night round to check all was secure before she retired.

But no, a man followed her. Master March, Will guessed, going by Ellie's description. He was about to depart when his steps were arrested. March got out a crucifix and arranged it on a table by the window, then took a small flask of wine and a morsel of bread from a leather satchel.

"No." Will breathed. "Oh no." He watched in horror as the man read from a prayer book, going through the blessing for the Holy Communion. Dame Holton sank to her knees, listening intently, only raising her head when he offered her the bread.

Only a priest could offer communion.

Only a Catholic would conduct such a service secretly at night like this.

He was harboring an agent of the Pope in his village—the same pope who had excommunicated the Queen and said it was a Catholic's holy duty to assassinate her. He could put up with the dame's old-fashioned ways as long as they did not stray into treason; hiding a priest pushed her behavior far over the line into being a traitor. It was now his duty to arrest her and her household.

He ran back to Barbary, knowing better than to try this single-handedly. Was Ellie a party to the secret? She'd spoken freely of March—praising his learning. If she'd suspected, surely she wouldn't have mentioned it over supper? No, he could not believe she knew a thing about the guest beyond what she had stated. She would be all right.

A dark thought wormed itself into that comforting apple of a thought: he'd never asked after her views on religion, had he? What if he was so far wrong that she was a Catholic too? Her mother had been Spanish—it would follow she had been brought up in that faith.

He took a moment, leaning his head against the horse's shoulder, feeling duty and love ripping him apart. She had not hidden March's presence from him, he reminded himself; she had shown no sign of interest in matters of religion; he knew for a fact she attended the parish church and was well liked by the vicar. No, he was not wrong. Living under the roof of a Catholic did not make her one.

Her father? He would have to be questioned, but his interests were scientific rather than theological. Will doubted he was involved.

But that did not disguise the terrible truth that he had to put one of the oldest, most respected people in the village under arrest. God help the dame if she was guilty of more than softheartedness to a priest begging for shelter. God help them all.

Will did not pause even for his usual banter with Diego but entered directly into the house, casting his riding crop and gloves angrily on the table. Burghley had made him responsible for the security of Berkshire, and he had given his solemn promise to do so; any ill-placed leniency because he had known Dame Holton all his life would make him a traitor too. But he needed help. He couldn't carry out an arrest on his own. He needed James.

He bounded up the stairs and beat on his brother's door, praying he had returned from his excursion.

"This better be good," James called grumpily from within. "I'm in bed."

Will pushed the door open, then closed it behind him. "It's good—or should I say, very bad." James was lying in his nightshirt, fingers laced across his chest, looking far too relaxed for Will's humor. "Jamie, we've a serious problem."

James rolled onto his side and propped his head on his hand. "What? Lady Jane refused you?"

"No!" Will swiped the air. "Why must your brain always revert to that?"

"Because it's our best hope?" he replied patiently. "But come on, Will, spill the news. Something's eating you."

"I was in the lane outside Dame Holton's an hour ago."

Jamie sighed. "Will, you can't chase after Lady Ellie—"

Will held up his hand to stop the lecture. "It's nothing to do with her. I saw Dame Holton taking communion from a priest—that man March whom Ellie mentioned. The dame's giving shelter to a Catholic priest."

Jamie threw back the covers and sat up on his knees, running his fingers through his hair. "You're sure?"

Will gave a bitter laugh. "I saw him hand her the bread. What more proof do you need?"

James quickly ran through the repercussions, much as Will had done. "The Huttons?"

"Innocent, as far as I can tell."

James nodded. "That's a relief. So, how are we going to apprehend the man, and then what will we do with him?"

"We have to arrest the dame too, I fear."

James grimaced. He had no more stomach for the idea than Will. "Then what?"

"It is our duty to find out if this goes beyond one priest ministering to those remaining loyal to the old faith. I'd prefer to have the answers before Cecil and Walsingham arrive."

"When are they due?"

"Tomorrow evening."

James started pulling on his clothes. "So we make our move tonight?"

"I think it best. We can hold them in the dower house and question them in the morning."

"We must gather more men."

"I'll wake Sir Henry. You fetch Turville."

Will found Henry in bed with one of the maids. Her face was hidden under the blankets, so he just had to hope it wasn't one of his household.

"Sorry to interrupt," he said, his business too urgent to allow for any embarrassment. "I need you to come with me."

"You sound very grim, Dorset. What's afoot?" Henry pulled on his hose and dragged a shirt over his head.

"I'll explain on the way."

Free of any local loyalties, Henry heard the news with great pleasure.

"Trapped one of the Pope's boys, have you, Dorset? Excellent." He urged his mount into a trot, eager to get the job done. "What's the plan, then? Break the door down and arrest all inside?"

"I thought we would try knocking first," said Will drily. "James and Turville can cut off any attempt to escape from the back of the house. And we're only interested in the dame and her priest. The Huttons lodge there."

"The luscious Eleanor mixed up with Catholics?" Henry laughed. "The lady does have a talent for trouble, doesn't she?"

"It isn't a joking matter. And in any case, I believe she knows nothing about it."

Ellie had always been a fairly light sleeper, so she was the first to hear the firm knock at the door in the small hours of the morning. Such summonses rarely brought good news—illness or accident being the usual causes. Groping for her shawl, she wrapped it round her shoulders and ventured out into the hallway. Dame Holton's snores could be heard from her room—her hostess was deeply asleep.

The knock came again. Deciding to find out who it was before waking the household, Ellie padded downstairs in her bare feet to the front door.

"Who's there?"

"Ellie? It's me, Will. Open up."

"Will?" Ellie fumbled with the bolts. "What's wrong? Is it your mother?"

"No, no, nothing like that." He sounded urgent—annoyed, even.

Ellie put two hands to the big key in the lock. She then opened the door and took a step back, blinking in the light of the lantern he carried. To her surprise, Will wasn't alone. He had Sir Henry Perceval with him.

"Oh, um, my lord, what brings you here?" she asked, regretting how informally she had addressed him moments before.

"Step aside, Ellie. Go into the parlor and stay there." Will advanced into the house.

"What? Why?" Ellie didn't move, blocking the way to the upper floor. "Is it my father? You're not going to harm him, are you?"

"No, not your father and not you. I have business with your hostess and her guest."

"Business? At this time of night?" Ellie's voice rose in alarm.

"Ellie, who are you talking to?" Her father appeared at the top of the stairs.

"Sir Arthur, go back to your room, please. This doesn't concern you." Will brushed past Ellie to climb the stairs. Sir Henry did more: he picked her up bodily and deposited her inside the parlor with a pat on her head like she was some dog performing a trick for him. She didn't stay put but followed him back out into the hall. She could hear Will knocking on the dame's bedroom door.

"Mistress Holton! Mistress Holton!"

The door banged open and footsteps made the ceiling creak above Ellie's head. She could hear what was said quite distinctly.

"Mistress, I have come for your guest. I believe you are harboring a Catholic priest."

A priest? Ellie closed her eyes and sagged against the wall. Of course. She hadn't wanted to know, but she feared Will's suspicions were true. Had she given Master March away by carelessly mentioning him at dinner? Was this all her fault? She swallowed against the bile that rose in her throat.

"My lord, wh-what is the meaning of this?" The dame's voice was trembling, her indignation a cover for her fear.

"Please get dressed. I am taking you and Master March away for questioning."

"But we've done nothing!"

"If that is true, then you have nothing to worry about. I will step into the hall to allow you to dress."

Sir Henry appeared at the head of the stairs, dragging March with him. He'd not let the man don his clothes, so the poor scholar was clad only in a nightshirt. Ellie pushed past the pair without a word and rushed into March's room. The bedclothes were on the floor and the table overturned, the small vase of spring flowers broken, water seeping through the boards. Ellie grabbed March's hose, cloak and hat and ran quickly back downstairs.

"Your things, sir," she said breathlessly, ignoring the amused look Henry gave her.

"Thank you, dear girl," March replied with great dignity. "You must not worry. All this will be sorted out in the light of the morning."

Ellie attempted a smile but she felt horribly guilty. "The earl is a fair man; he'll hear you out." At least, she hoped he would. She'd never tested his views on religion; if they were anything like his prejudices against alchemists, then March was in deep trouble. But then, Will had never actually carried out any of his threats against them, had he?

"Better him than Walsingham," Henry interjected, clapping March on the shoulder and shoving him towards the front door. March had to hop on one leg, as he was only halfway through pulling on his hose. "Just your luck, priest, the Queen's chief minister is arriving tomorrow night. I was wondering why he was straying in our direction—maybe there's something brewing that we need to know about? So if I were you, I'd tell Dorset all you know, and quickly. He's likely to be far more merciful." He gave a whistle, signaling to the men outside that all was secure. "Just a thought, March. Walsingham employs his own specialist in extracting information. From the look of that stoop of yours, I imagine you're well acquainted with the rack. Think about that, won't you?"

March tried to stand up straighter but his body betrayed him, his hands trembling at his sides. "I have done nothing wrong," he stated again.

Ellie picked up his cloak, which had fallen to the ground, and buttoned it at his neck for him. She could feel him shivering and she didn't think it was from cold.

The earl appeared, preceding the dame, who was leaning on Sir Arthur's arm as he helped her down the stairs.

"What have we come to?" the dame wailed. "Arrests in the night—honest citizens torn from their beds!"

"I know, madam, it is quite, quite shocking," Ellie heard her father say. "But it will be sorted out, and you'll be back here without a shadow on your name. Catholic plots! Complete nonsense. Everyone can see you are honest and loyal to Her Majesty. Just tell the earl that and all will be well."

Ellie was by no means convinced that all would end as well as her father predicted. It was undeniable that the dame flouted the law by not attending church, and March was more than likely a priest, as Will had said. She was a little hazy about the legality of that—was it enough to condemn a man just for being ordained by Rome?

"My lord, what's going to happen to them?" she asked Will softly as Henry boosted March onto a spare horse with his hands tied before him.

Will pulled her into the parlor and took her hand to give it an apologetic squeeze. "I don't know. I saw evidence with my own eyes that March is a priest. I can't ignore that."

"If he is, will that get him killed?"

Will rubbed his face, his exhaustion evident in the slump of his shoulders. "That depends. I can't let him run around my county preaching sedition."

"He wasn't, was he?" To her annoyance, Ellie heard the childish squeak in her voice.

"That's why I need to question him." Will cupped her cheek with his hand and kissed the tip of her nose. "I'm sorry, Ellie."

"The dame?"

"I hope she's just guilty of stubborn adherence to the old ways. If she promises to reform, then things will go better for her."

"Reform? Dame Holton?" Ellie was incredulous.

"To save herself from prison or worse, who knows what she will agree to?"

Ellie wasn't so hopeful; the dame would stand her ground: it was her nature, ingrained in her like rings in an oak. "Please, Will, she's my friend. She's kind. Whatever she has done, she will have done for a good reason, not through evil or malice."

"Ah, but Ellie, do you not know yet that people do many terrible things for what they think are sound principles?"

"Like arresting old ladies in the night?" She crossed her arms.

Offended, he took a step back, assuming the earl once more. "Even that. I hoped you would understand."

She was being unfair: she did not have the responsibility to make a choice as he had done. She'd allowed herself the luxury of closing her eyes to what was going on under the roof where she lived.

"Forgive me, Will. I do understand. Please look after them both. They're good people at heart."

His spiky manner softening under her concession, Will stole a quick kiss, then rubbed his nose against hers. "I will take care of them, don't worry."

Ellie watched as a subdued dame and stoic March were taken away on horseback. Of course she would worry. She lit a candle from an ember in the banked fire and waited for her father to come back in from the lane.

"What a disaster!" Sir Arthur declared, sinking into the chair by the fire, the candle flickering on the mantelpiece between them. "I thought better of the earl than to do such a thing."

Ellie felt the urge to defend Will. "He has a duty, Father. He couldn't ignore Master March once his profession came to his notice."

"March is a decent person and a wise man. Did he do any harm while under this roof?"

"No, sir."

"So don't you excuse the earl to me, Ellie. And poor Dame Holton—arrested for extending a welcome to a traveler!"

"His lordship said she'd be safe as long as she promises to behave."

"Behave? She's a grown woman—not a child or a dog to be curbed!"

Her father's sentiments were too close to her own for her to argue. "What can we do to help them?"

Sir Arthur frowned, steepling his fingers in thought. "I don't know. I no longer have any influence with men of power. I'm nothing compared to an earl. But I'll see what a written appeal—an avowal of their good conduct—will do."

"I will send their clothes and other things they might need," Ellie said, her mind turning to rather more practical matters. "And make sure the poultry are fed."

"Quite right. Mistress Holton was a friend to us when we needed one; it is only fair that we should prove one to her now."

Chapter 16

As evening approached the following day and shadows lengthened in the lane, Will rode the short distance back from the dower house, where he had left his two prisoners under close guard in separate chambers. His spirits were rapidly tumbling into a profound depression like a rickety bridge giving way to a flood. He hated what he had to do, but the evidence was irrefutable. After long questioning, he was convinced that John March was a Catholic missionary with extensive experience of taking his message throughout the kingdom. But he was also a clever and amiable man; under any other circumstances, Will was sure they would have liked each other. Yet he did not have the freedom to allow his personal feelings to sway him. March was guilty of hiding his profession and ministering to Catholics; if his activities went further, to the encouragement of treasonous plots—well, that was much harder to determine. One thing was clear: Dame Holton knew nothing of such matters, and Will was convinced she would have trumpeted them if she felt them justified, as she lived without apology and without regard for the security of herself and others. Perhaps she just could not imagine being punished for keeping to what she had been told was right as a child. Whatever the case, his ears felt quite battered by her protestations of innocence and outrage.

He swiped at a nettle overhanging the track. Their staunch adherence to their faith made Will reflect on his own grasp of the great mysteries of life. He did not have it in him to be a fanatic, being too aware of other points of view, other possibilities. Will thought of himself as a staunch member of the Church of England largely, he had to admit, because it represented the best chance for peace in the country—a peace in which people could work out the distinctive flavor of their own beliefs. Extremists of both sides left him cold.

Lacey Hall came into sight, windows burning with the glow of a reflected sunset giving the illusion that the house was on fire. He muttered a prayer, asking for wisdom in dealing with this thorny situation. Will feared he had little of his own to offer.

With terrible timing, the second party of guests, Sir Francis Walsingham and Robert Cecil, arrived as twilight fell over Stoke-by-Lacey. Even if Will had wanted to keep his apprehension of the priest a secret, Sir Henry would have prevented him. In the confusion of horses milling about the courtyard, Perceval reached Walsingham before Will.

"Sir Francis! Good journey?" Sir Henry asked, gesturing a groom forward to hold the horse's head.

"Perceval, isn't it? Yes, yes, we endured." Walsingham drew his mouth into a disapproving line. A gaunt-faced, swarthy man, his long nose had a knot halfway down, evidence that it had previously been broken. His strand of strict Protestantism did not approve of the dissolute behaviour of Perceval and other young bucks at court.

He landed heavily on the ground and groaned, rubbing the small of his back.

Perceval was not daunted, seeing an opportunity to raise his stock with an influential member of the government. "You've come just in time, sir. The earl here has smoked out a Catholic priest right here in his village. We've got him locked up."

"A priest, you say?" Fire of interest flickered in the depths of Walsingham's eyes, his aches quite forgotten. "What's his name?"

Will hurried over, too late to smother the blaze. "Sir Francis, please do come in and take your rest in my house."

Walsingham bowed. "Thank you, my lord. But Perceval here tells me you have a priest in your custody."

Will cursed Henry silently. "Indeed, that is so. I have the fellow secured, and he'll keep. The ladies are waiting within to greet you."

At that hint, Walsingham nodded and deigned to follow Will indoors. Cecil and Perceval fell in behind, keeping a distance from each other like two wary dogs. Will heaved a sigh: this particular house party had the makings of a disaster.

Thank goodness for his mother. She swept upon Cecil and gave him a maternal kiss. "Robert! It is years since I saw you last. You probably do not remember me, but I was a great friend of your mother, Lady Burghley."

Cecil's pale face twisted into an unguarded smile. "Countess, of course I remember you. She often speaks of you."

The countess laughed and bent forward to whisper confidentially, "We were terrors in our youth, Robert. We had most of the men at court at sixes and sevens, trying to impress us."

"I can well imagine."

The countess turned to Walsingham. "And Sir Francis, it is long since we last met as well."

The chief minister's smile was genuine but looked ill-suited to his face, like a bow in a boy's hair. "Lady Dorset." He kissed her hand. "I see you've had a fine brood of children since that time."

On this hint, the countess introduced James and Sarah. "My eldest girl is married, sir, and my youngest boy is at school," she explained.

"Five healthy children!" marveled Sir Francis. "God has blessed this house." He accepted a glass of wine from a servant and drank to the countess, then the earl. "Forgive my eagerness, madam, but I really must hear more about this renegade priest your son has discovered. I'm not on a journey of pleasure, more's the pity; I must have a mind to the nation's security at all times."

"Indeed, sir. Then Lady Jane, Lady Sarah and I will leave you gentlemen together." The countess shot Will a warning look. She had been quite opposed to his holding Dame Holton.

"I am much obliged, madam," replied Walsingham.

The ladies retired, Sarah snapping the door closed behind her. Will suspected she would be listening at the keyhole if their mother did not tow her away.

Walsingham cracked his knuckles, then rubbed his hands. "Well, Dorset?"

Will gestured for them to take seats. Cecil looked vaguely interested, but he lacked the fervor plain to read in Walsingham's face.

"I saw the man—one John March—minister Holy Communion to his hostess, an elderly woman from my village. I immediately set in process their apprehension and have both of them in custody." Will got up to pace the room, disliking the feeling that he was reporting to a commanding officer. He reminded himself that he outranked Walsingham by virtue of blood, if not age and experience. He did not have to justify his actions to him. "I've questioned both today. I judge that the dame is guilty only of adhering to the faith of her youth."

"Only?" Walsingham's eyebrows shot up his forehead. "She's harbored a priest."

"In order to receive the sacraments and spiritual comfort. Are we to imprison every man for his faith?"

Walsingham studied the young earl with disapproval. "It is not the wrongheaded beliefs that most concern us. You can't have forgotten the Pope has ordered his followers to strike at the Queen and thus at the very stability of our country."

Will gave a jerky nod. Of course he knew this: the very reason he had proceeded with the arrests in the first place.

"You may tolerate their beliefs, but should they succeed in toppling order, you and I will be the first on the bonfires they'll light to purge the country of all but followers of their own Devil-spawned creed. They make no secret of their plans."

Cecil coughed discreetly. "But, sir, you must allow that only the most rabid of the followers of Rome advocate such a path."

"Must I?" asked Walsingham in an icy tone. "The Queen of the Scots sits in our prison stirring up plots with her very presence and most likely with her active participation. Our security is a frail thing that can be undermined by the action of even one man with the determination to strike at the heart of our realm. Queen Elizabeth's safety is paramount. We can take no gambles with so important a matter."

"That goes without saying," Will conceded. "But Dame Holton

has no desire to attack the Queen. Her attention is only on local matters. She is more concerned with the church furnishings than issues of state."

"Hmm," grunted Walsingham, not agreeing but dropping this minnow of an argument for the bigger fish. "I'd like to interrogate March myself. Hand him over to me and I'll see to his questioning."

This would mean a long spell in the Tower and close acquaintance with the rack for March. Will remembered his promise to Ellie. "I'd be delighted if you would assist me with my investigation, but I still have not had enough time to determine how far the matter penetrates into my lands. I am loath to send him away prematurely; he might be of great assistance in uncovering other threats to our peace and security."

His argument appeared to be correctly phrased to appeal to the chief minister. "You think you can persuade him to inform on others?"

Will didn't think that for one moment, but he wasn't going to admit to it. "I've only had the prisoner under arrest for a day; many things are possible."

Walsingham scratched his beard, smoothing it into a dagger-sharp point. "True. I find much use in informants and double agents. Often it pays well to let such people go in order to capture much larger prey."

Will hadn't thought as far as releasing March, but this was a promising avenue. "I will be guided by you in this. I have no experience in grooming an informant for my use."

"You'll have to learn, Dorset. Burghley says you're his man in Berkshire, so you'll need your own network. It's an expensive business, mind, and you'll get little from the Queen's coffers for the purpose." His face soured. "She likes the fruits of spying but is less keen on paying for the planting."

Will hid his grimace: the last thing he needed was more expenses. Burghley's purse was looking less generous now.

"Were there no others in the household arrested—servants and so on? Often they know more than their masters and mistresses suspect."

Will opened his mouth to deny the presence of maids when Henry was there before him. "There's an old alchemist—the man who blew up Lord Mountjoy's close stool, my lord."

"Him? So this is where he ran to! A dangerous fellow, as I told your father, Cecil."

"He's got a daughter too. By her own admission, she seemed to know March quite well." Henry gave Will a smirk. Cecil sat up in his chair as he sensed danger in the air for Ellie.

What was Perceval up to, Will wondered. Did he have some greater stratagem against Ellie?

"The girl is quite innocent of any involvement. I'm quite convinced of that," Will said quickly.

"You have the pair under arrest, then? Questioned them? Searched the house?" asked Walsingham.

Will paused by the window, watching Walsingham in reflection, the fire flickering behind him giving the illusion he was already on the bonfire he feared. "No, sir."

Walsingham got up and took a step to the door. "Then that was not well done of you. We must proceed immediately. Who knows what evidence they have had a chance to destroy?"

"But, sir . . . !"

"It must be your inexperience speaking, Dorset. You will never catch the Catholics if you are not as clever and ruthless as they. They pass our surveillance by seeming innocent and ordinary—never forget that." He turned to Perceval. "Where's this house?"

Henry stood. "I'll show you."

The situation was spinning out of his control. The last thing Will wanted was Walsingham to march into Ellie's house and turn the place upside down. What would she think of his promises then?

"Sir, this is still my estate—my land. I will show you the house if you insist, but I am convinced your suspicions are wrong. Sir Henry here, Master Cecil too, will vouch that the Huttons are harmless, the girl especially."

Walsingham slapped his riding gloves in his palm. "I sense a partiality here, my lord, one that is clouding your judgment."

"No, sir."

Walsingham gave a bitter smile. "You are how old? Eighteen? Your knowledge of the world must needs be limited. You should let me guide you in this."

"I will show you the house. You may make a search, but that is where it ends. The priest is the man of interest in this affair, not the innocent bystanders."

"We shall see."

For Ellie, it felt like a repeat of the previous night, though this time she was still up, reading quietly by the fireside as her father scratched away at his manuscript. First came the sound of hooves, then the firm knock at the door.

"I will answer," her father said, indicating that she should stay in her seat.

She nodded wordlessly, marking her place in the book with her finger as she strained to hear all that was said outside. A bloodred ribbon trickled from the book's spine, spilling onto her lap.

Her father returned, accompanied by Will and a stranger. More people crowded into the corridor beyond. Ellie stood and dipped a curtsy, looking to the earl askance.

"Apologies for the interruption to your evening, my lady," Will said stiffly. "This is Sir Francis Walsingham—you have heard of the gentleman before?"

"Indeed, yes." Ellie put the book aside. The Queen's chief minister—not a welcome visitor in any household under suspicion.

"How may we help you?" her father asked.

"The Lady Eleanor, Sir Arthur." Will completed the introduction without the use of her Spanish titles.

Sir Henry shouldered his way past the earl. "Come now, Dorset, give the lady her due: the Lady Eleanor Rodriguez, Countess of San Jaime. She had a Spanish mother, Walsingham, who bequeathed her the courtesy title. Sir Arthur lived in Madrid for many years."

Alarmed by this obvious attempt to discredit them, Ellie felt her heart begin to race. What was going on? Henry was stirring up trouble, but to what purpose Ellie couldn't fathom. She had not hidden her parentage, but it was now treated as a mark against her.

"A countess, eh?" The Queen's minister turned on Will. "Why did you not mention this fact? That changes everything."

"How so, sir?" Will asked curtly. "The lady's mother is long dead; there is no doubt in my mind that Sir Arthur and his daughter are loyal to the Crown."

Ellie's father finally caught up on the message underlying this exchange. "Indeed, sir, I wish to assure you of my honest and heartfelt admiration for our sovereign lady, gracious patron of the arts and renowned scholar, as well as wise ruler."

Walsingham sniffed at this pretty speech. "Fine words butter no parsnips, sir. I look to a man's deeds, not his protestations."

Sir Arthur went to Ellie's side and tucked her hand in the crook of his elbow. "We will withstand any scrutiny, sir. I'm ashamed of nothing I have done. I am a man of learning, an alchemist, seeking to unlock the mysteries of God's universe and bring honor and riches to this realm."

Ellie felt pride in her father's words: for all his wrongheaded notions, his motives had ever been pure—purer than any gold he would be lucky to extract from the ingredients of his craft.

"Then you have no objection to the examination of your papers?"

Her father stiffened. "None, sir. I merely ask that nothing be destroyed. I have labored hard over the account of my methods and practices."

Walsingham carefully pinched off his gloves, finger by finger. "I too have my methods and practices. The enemy can use even the most innocent-seeming vessel in which to pour the poison of Catholic rebellion." He moved to the desk. "These are all your papers?"

"Yes, sir." Sir Arthur let go of Ellie's hand and moved to hover at Walsingham's shoulder like an anxious parent over a child's cradle as a wolf prowled.

"And books?"

Sir Arthur gestured to the teetering pile. "I have a few others in my saddlebags."

"There is too much for inspection now. I'll take these with me."

Sir Arthur clenched his fists in frustration. "But how will I work?"

"Take a holiday, sir. They will swiftly be returned if they prove to be of no interest to this matter." Walsingham flicked at a paper. "Do you record here how to make explosions such as you carried out in Windsor?"

Sensing he was treading boggy ground, Sir Arthur rubbed at his throat before answering. "No, sir, I have not yet reached the section I projected on the application of phoenix tears."

"Good. I advise you never to commit that to paper. Far too dangerous in the wrong hands, would you not agree?"

Uncertain, Sir Arthur nodded.

"But I'd be interested to hear how it was done. It may have its uses in our fight against Spain and Rome."

"I am at your service, sir," Sir Arthur vowed, giving him a shallow bow.

Ellie shrank back to the wall. She didn't like this Walsingham. He would have her father either on suspicion of treachery or caught by his loyalty to the realm: either way Sir Arthur would end up his creature. Did her father not realize the danger he was in? He rarely saw beyond the matters pertaining to his craft, so she doubted he had the political astuteness to see how he was being pressed into service.

Henry sidled up to her, placing a hand against the wall behind her head. "Looks like things are not going too well for you, doesn't it, sweeting? Feel in need of some protection? My offer still stands," he said softly.

She glanced towards Will, but he was busy overseeing the

collection of papers, handing them to a servant under the fluttering presence of her father. Walsingham had turned his attention to the other books in the room—the dame's meager collection on a single shelf and the one Ellie had been reading when they entered, the *Eclogues* March had lent her.

"No use looking there for any help," Henry continued. "The earl is Burghley's man in this county, charged with ensuring that the peace is kept, so he can't oppose Walsingham on this." He caught one of her loose curls on his fingertip and pulled it straight to let it spring back against her neck. "But I can look after you. I've been trying to do so for some weeks now, and I'm getting tired of coming away with nothing."

Ellie tried to shift out of his reach, but he kept crowding her as he had done in the garden. She could feel the almost feverish heat of his skin only inches from hers. "Am I accused of anything, sir, that I would need a defender?"

"Well, you tell me, sweeting." He smiled, tapping each point out with a fingertip. "Living under the same roof as a priest, having a father who blows things up, bearing a Spanish title when this nation is fighting an undeclared war with that country: it doesn't look good, does it?"

Walsingham glanced up from the *Eclogues,* seeking her out. "Lady Eleanor, is this yours?"

Henry moved away, pretending he had only been reaching for another candle to light.

"I . . . I was reading it, sir," Ellie admitted. "Master March gave it to me."

"Gave it to you?"

"It is a loan."

"Are the annotations on pages four, eight, twelve, sixteen and so on in your hand?"

"Annotations? No, no, I would not presume to write in his books."

Walsingham took a step closer and thrust the volume under her nose. "So what did you understand by them?"

All other activity in the room ceased as attention fastened on her. Stomach clenching with foreboding, Ellie turned her eyes down to the page he had on display. She'd seen the faint markings when she was reading, but they had meant little to her, just a list of names.

"To tell the truth, sir, I paid them no heed."

"Did you not find it strange that these names only appear on certain pages and not on others?"

"Now you mention it, I suppose it is."

"Looks to me like someone is trying to hide a message. What do you think the names mean?"

Ellie bit her lip and raised her gaze to his implacable face. "I . . . I don't know, sir. Previous readers of the book, perhaps?"

He snapped it shut, making her jump. "Or a list of traitors? If so, why would he entrust it to you? Is your name among them? Is your father's?"

"Why would it be?" She looked to Will and found he had moved much nearer. "My lord, of what is it that I am accused?"

Will took her hand and pressed it comfortingly. "Nothing. Walsingham means only to test you."

"Is Master March truly a priest?"

"I fear so."

Walsingham tucked the book inside his doublet. "Very productive. An excellent night's work. I'm sure you will agree, my lord, that these two must also be taken into custody. We would not want either fleeing the county before I have had a chance to sound this matter to the bottom."

Will stood between Ellie and Walsingham, his back rigid. "What do you mean by that, exactly?"

"There is enough here to warrant more rigorous questioning, my lord. The moment I heard about the priest, I sent for Thomas Norton."

"The rack master? I'll not have innocents put to torture, sir—not on my lands."

"Ah, but they're not innocent, are they?" Walsingham picked up a pile of Sir Arthur's letters and let them drift back to the desk like autumn leaves. "Even at a glance I see here correspondence in foreign tongues—Latin and Spanish, to name but two."

"Hutton is a man of learning—surely it is no crime to exchange letters with fellow scholars?"

Ellie could feel her knees shaking, a damnable weakness, but she couldn't help it. The man meant to torture them for information of plots that they did not have. She'd heard tales of the rack—the cruel instrument that stretched a body beyond the point of all bearing: snapping sinews, dislocating bones. Many confessed to anything and everything just to be free of it. It was too much. Her heart pounded and her vision seemed to narrow down a dark tunnel. "Will, please!" she said faintly.

Hearing her distress, Will turned quickly towards her and caught her just before she crumpled.

"Ellie!" her father cried, rushing to her side, but she felt too distant to reply.

Will lifted her to his chest, catching her legs behind her knees.

"All will be well," he said calmly. "I won't let them touch you. Walsingham, I cannot allow you to distress a lady with your threats. I'll take the Lady Eleanor to my mother. If you wish to question her further, it will be done in the countess's presence and without force."

Ellie burrowed her head into the soft velvet of his doublet, not daring to open her eyes again. She was a coward to take refuge in such frailty, but right now it did seem her best and only strategy.

Walsingham snorted with derision. "Eve's wiles, Dorset. Young as you are, you do not see them for what they are. Woman first brought man to sin."

"By my thinking, sir, man's weakness brought him to sin. He had a duty to protect and care for his wife, not blame her for his own fallibility." With that, Will strode from the room and took Ellie into the fresh air.

The evening cool revived her a little. Her pride reasserting itself, she struggled to get down, but Will held her more closely.

"Wait a moment, darling. I want you safe and out of that man's sight before I release you. I had no idea what he had in mind. He really is a snake—I'll not trust him within six feet of you."

She snuggled closer to him, fingers stroking the soft nap of the maroon velvet, seeking comfort in his confidence as her own had been sapped. "What's going to become of us, Will?" The horrifying threats had left her feeling completely exposed, at the end of all her resources for survival. She knew she should be embarrassed for collapsing—letting him haul her out like a bolt of cloth—but she wasn't.

He sat on a wooden bench in Dame Holton's hawthorn arbor tucked into the thick hedge that bordered the road. Ellie could hear the others seeing to the loading of the horses beyond the thicket, stacking papers and books into panniers to be taken away for examination. She tried to slide down beside Will, but he tightened his grip, keeping her on his lap.

"Please, let me hold you," he murmured.

With a sigh of surrender, Ellie let her head drop back against his chest. She could hear his heart beating steadily and feel the rise and fall of his chest. Slowly, she let it soothe her.

"You mustn't fear, Ellie. I won't let Walsingham hurt you. I can't stop him asking you questions, though." He let silence fall for a moment. "So . . . so if there is anything, anything at all, that you need to tell me, say it now. I can protect you as long as I know the truth."

Ellie realized that he feared that she was involved in some small way with a plot, but still he promised to look after her. She wasn't sure if she should be offended by his doubts or grateful for his loyalty to a friend.

"There's nothing, Will, I promise. I guessed that March might be Catholic like the dame, but no more than that. And I don't believe he was here for any evil purpose. If there's a list in that book, it's likely to be of those who will offer him shelter, like Dame Holton."

He brushed his hand over her upper arm. "Good. Then you have nothing to fear. I agree with you, by the way; from my talk with him this morning, I don't think March plots against the state. I'll speak to Walsingham. It's just foul timing that brought him here at this very moment." He ran his hand down her arm to link his fingers with hers. "But you've another friend who'll support me in this."

"Oh?" Ellie looked up. His face was in shadow, only the faintest gleam giving away his eyes.

"Robert Cecil's with Walsingham."

"Good. I like Master Cecil." That was excellent news, unlacing another knot of anxiety in her breast. Ellie snuggled back against Will's chest, savoring for this brief time the feeling that someone was looking after her, standing between her and disaster. She loved Will's kindness, his strength, even his ridiculous temper—despite the fact that she had suffered from it on two occasions. His temper, she'd realized, was the reverse of the coin that made him capable of deep emotion. You only had to look at the way he behaved with his family to see his capacity for affection. To be loved by him would be a gift beyond anything she expected from this life, so she was grateful that somehow she had come within the circuit of those for whom he cared.

"Cecil has great admiration for you too. Thinks you quite the paragon of learning." Will ran his hand back up her arm to caress the sensitive skin at the nape of her neck. "Your ruff is a mess, Ellie."

"I know."

"Damn stupid fashion." He tugged at his own much more impressive collar. "Gets in the way when I want to kiss you."

Ellie went still. "Kiss me?"

She felt rather than saw his nod. "You are driving me to distraction, Lady Eleanor. I can't eat, sleep or think without worrying about you. I leave you alone for half a day and I find you in trouble. I'd feel happier if I had you somewhere I know you are safe."

"Why, Will? Why do you care?"

He gave a self-mocking laugh. "Because I am a fool. I've gone and fallen in love with you. My heart beats here." He gently placed his hand on her breast. "Can you feel it?"

Her heart leapt under his palm. "Yes, I can feel it."

"Good."

She too had a confession to make. "And . . . and I think that you might have mine." She placed her hand over his heart.

"My true love hath my heart, and I have his," murmured Will. He shifted his hold on her to raise her face to his. "May I?"

Ellie nodded, not entirely sure what she was giving him permission to do. His lips brushed once over hers, then settled back with firmer pressure, his tongue running lightly along her mouth, outlining her lips and the seam between them. She relaxed, letting him deepen the kiss as he gently explored, delicately flirting with her teeth and tongue, tickling sensitive places she didn't know she had. Compared to the crude assault of Henry's invasion, her only other experience of a man's kiss, Will's felt like a loving wooing, cherishing her and her taste. She was beginning to feel quite light-headed again.

"Ellie! Ellie!" From the lane beyond, her father sounded panicked. "No, Sir Henry, I refuse to leave without my daughter. Take your hands off me!"

She froze, the reality of her situation crashing back on her. Will broke the kiss, resting his forehead against hers for a moment. She took a ragged breath, realizing she'd been holding hers for some time now.

"Darling, you must remember to breathe," Will whispered, his mouth quirking into a smile against her cheek. "Come, it's time to go. I'll insist that you and your father be lodged at Lacey Hall." He helped her to stand. Her legs were oddly unsteady.

"Ellie! Where are you?"

"I have her here, Sir Arthur," Will replied. "She's recovering from her faint in the fresh air."

Recovering? Ellie felt ready to swoon all over again.

"My lord, please, is she all right? She must not worry—I won't let this man harm her. I'll . . . I'll . . ."

"Calm yourself, Hutton. I'll bring her to you." Will bent close to Ellie. "We have to go, but we must talk about this." He ran his thumb over her lips, cupping her face tenderly in his two hands.

Ellie nodded mutely, misery washing away the wonderful sensations the kiss had sent through her. What was there to talk about? Will had to marry wealth. He could offer nothing honorable to an alchemist's daughter now under a cloud of suspicion.

"Take my arm, darling." Will held out his elbow. "Be brave now."

She followed him out to the lane, feeling her courage spilling from her like flour from a hole in the miller's sack. She could almost see it, shining in the faint moonlight, marking the path back to the one moment when she had known what it felt like to be loved.

Chapter 17

Nell was helping Dorcas, the countess's maid, prepare guest rooms for the new arrivals. She shook out the worn sheets, noting the pleasant smell of lavender as well as the age of the linen. The house could do with an influx of Perceval gold before there were more darns than cloth. Tucking the sheet in tightly under the mattress, she wished her mistress would hurry up and settle the match so she could make further progress with her own plans to establish herself in Lacey Hall. She'd had enough of heavy household tasks.

Getting up quickly, Nell felt her head swim. She grabbed the bedpost to prevent herself falling.

"Are you quite well, love?" asked the matronly chambermaid. She ran a rough hand over Nell's forehead. "Not running a fever, are you? The tertian fever can be awful bad round these parts come summer."

Nell brushed her away, remembering to smile sweetly. "No, Dorcas. I just got up too quickly is all."

Dorcas tutted. "You should take more care of yourself, Nell. You hardly touched your dinner."

True—she'd been feeling out of sorts for a few days now. Nell rubbed her chest, her breasts feeling uncomfortable in her bodice.

"Maybe I am sickening for something."

Dorcas misunderstood the gesture and thought Nell was gesturing to her heart. She let out a gale of laughter. "Sickening for a young man, I've no doubt. That's what I was like at your age—never happy unless I had my admirer on a short string." She snapped a linen towel in the air and arranged it by the ewer and basin. "Who's caught your fancy, then?"

Nell could not think of a clever answer, because her thoughts had taken an unpleasant direction. There was more than one form of sickness a man could bring to a girl. Had her mistress been right in her warnings a few days ago? Was she with child?

No! It wasn't fair! Not when she was so close to getting what she wanted from this household.

But her body didn't lie. She knew the early signs and she now realized she had all of them. It had to be true. She kicked aside a whisper of fear, and her mind adjusted with its usual ruthless practicality to this new piece of information. A baby was a nuisance but didn't have to be a disaster. Most girls she knew were far gone by the time they wed—the only difference being they usually married the father.

"Nell, dear, are you listening?"

"Hmm? Um, yes, sorry, I was just dreaming—of my perfect man." Nell covered her long pause as handily as she could.

"Dream man? Yes, that's the only place you meet such paragons." Dorcas gave the room a final inspection, pleased with their handiwork. "Mind you, can't say I don't have no uses for the real thing, if you follow me." She made a crude gesture, which in her present mood. Nell struggled to smile at. "Aw, don't mind old Dorcas—I didn't mean to make you blush."

Nell hadn't been blushing, and she thought she could probably teach Dorcas a thing or two, but it suited her to sustain the illusion of innocence, particularly for what she knew she had to do next.

"I'm sorry, Dorcas, I'm just not used to such talk," she said humbly.

Dorcas patted her cheek. "Sweet chick. Let's go down to the kitchen and see if there are any leavings from the master's table."

"Thank you. I'd like that."

Nell followed the maid, walking demurely in her wake, all the while plotting the seduction that would have to come very soon. Her child would need a father, and Sir Henry was not that man. Master Turville didn't know it yet, but he had just been selected for the honor.

To Will's relief, Sir Francis Walsingham did not come down to breakfast the day after the late-night apprehension of the Huttons. News from his manservant was that he was laid low with a bout of illness exacerbated by the excitement of the previous evening. Responsible for dealing with the minor ailments of her household, the countess immediately left the table to go to his side and see how serious the problem was.

"Poor man." Lady Dorset caught her son just as he was about to ride for the dower house and drew him into her parlor to make her report on their guest's progress. "He's in great discomfort. Sir Francis suffers from a serious congestion of the bowels –"

Will held up a hand, knowing his mother was more than

capable of giving him a vivid account of what exactly this congestion entailed. "I can imagine, Mother."

She pursed her lips at her son's lack of interest in the finer points that fascinated her. She frequently told him that the human body was a marvel, its balance of humors so complex. "It's a wonder he can go about his business, riding the length and breadth of the country as he does."

"Indeed." Will tried not to imagine that in too much detail. "I swear, Mother, in another life you would have been a doctor."

She rolled her eyes at that unlikely prospect. "He quotes St. Paul, talking of his infirmity as a thorn in his flesh, but I fear he's not a well man, Will."

Well or otherwise, Will was selfishly grateful for the much-welcome opportunity to make plans. He now had time to counter the man's desire to use extreme measures against the suspects he had in custody.

"Then I trust you'll do all in your power to make him comfortable," Will said, kissing her hand. "I hope you can persuade him to stay abed."

The countess gave him a knowing look. "I gave him a sleeping draught. He won't rise till long after noon."

"Excellent."

His mother swatted his arm. "You should not sound so happy about another's misfortunes. It'll be you one day."

He kissed her cheek. "I know. But there are many kinds of misfortunes, and I now have a chance to unravel one particular set of them, which are more tangled than the thread in your workbox."

"Impertinent boy." His mother laughed, acknowledging the truth of it. She was not one for keeping her belongings tidy.

"Boy? I'm the earl, remember?"

"Not to me, Will." She tweaked his nose. "Now go and sort this out. I'll see to our guests."

Before they could separate, Robert Cecil came in from the garden, shaking the dew from his damp leather shoes. He had refused to be party to the raid last night and had treated Ellie and her father with pointed politeness when they arrived to spend the night at Lacey Hall, his actions reassuring Will that he would find support there were it required.

"Countess." Cecil kissed her knuckles.

The lady's cheeks dimpled into a smile at his courtly gesture. "Robert. I trust you have slept well?"

"Thank you, I did."

"Forgive me, you must excuse me. I have to go to my stillroom to prepare another draught."

Cecil glanced at Will. "Is someone ill?"

"Sir Francis," she supplied.

"Ah yes. Then I mustn't keep you." Cecil waited until the countess was out of earshot before gesturing to Will's outdoor clothes. "So, Dorset, off to see your other charges?" he asked astutely.

Will bowed. "As you see. With Walsingham confined to his bed with illness, I think it best to proceed with the interrogation."

"Before Norton arrives?"

"Indeed."

"May I come? I'd like a glimpse of this rabid priest Walsingham has been fulminating against."

"Rabid? As to that, I would value your opinion."

March was sitting in the window of his room when Will and Cecil entered, his eyes closed in prayer. He rose instantly when he heard them come in.

"My lord."

Will went straight to the point. "March, this gentleman is Robert Cecil. He has agreed to assist in this interrogation."

The priest's brows rose in surprise. "Sir." He bowed. "What has a lowly man such as me done to warrant the attention of the great Lord Burghley's son?"

"What indeed," replied Cecil, casting a look around the room. The only furnishings were a chair and a table with a quill and paper lying upon it, but March had not written anything on the blank page.

"Master Cecil travels with Walsingham, March." Will lobbed this fact into the conversation deliberately to see what effect it had on the man. Aside from a slight clenching of his jaw, March showed no sign of being unduly alarmed. "We confiscated all books from the dame's house last night and took the Huttons into custody."

March clasped his thin hands together, his consternation evident. "The Huttons? Why ever did you do that?"

"Lady Eleanor was caught reading a suspect book of yours."

March turned away to the window; the light washed across his pale face, leeching it of life so he appeared almost corpselike. "I see."

Will's anger rose like yeast set to prove. Walsingham had been right: there was something hidden in that volume, and March had thoughtlessly endangered Ellie by lending it to her. "You make no denial?"

"I admit to giving the young lady the *Eclogues* to read. They're a favorite of mine. I thought no harm in it."

"And the notes on the pages—the ones with numbers divisible by four?"

"The lady has nothing to do with them."

"But you do?"

"A list of names only. There's no ill intent to them, my lord, I vow that before God."

Will believed March did not swear oaths lightly. "So what intent do the names have?"

March closed his eyes for a brief moment before confessing. "Names of those wanting a priest's ministry, nothing more, my lord, put as marginalia to escape detection. That failed, I see."

Will paced the room, gathering his thoughts. "You must know that I cannot leave you free to continue your work, March."

The priest's face took on a resigned look. "I understand."

"Cecil?" Will looked to his guest, leaning in thought by the door.

Cecil pushed himself off the wall. "There is an alternative to execution, Dorset. I advise you send him to join the other priests interned at Banbury castle."

"Internment?" March shook his head.

"Better than death, I'd hazard," Cecil replied grimly.

"For some. You'd be cutting me off from what is God's work."

"To me, you work only for the Devil, spreading dissension in our country," Cecil said harshly, revealing the iron under his pleasant manner. "I strive to understand you, sympathize with your dilemma as a man of good conscience, but I foresee the results as you do not. There's no greater crime against God and a peaceful nation than promoting civil war, for that's what it will come to if we fall again to arguing about our faith."

March quivered with indignant rage. "So it is acceptable to spill Catholic blood on the scaffold, hanging, then quartering the living bodies of my fellow priests, all in the name of keeping this false peace? Far better short punishment now than an eternity of misery in Hell for following the broad road that leads to destruction rather than God's narrow way as defined by the Mother Church!"

Will's head began to ache. He hated this kind of argument, where two immovable opponents clashed like rams butting horns in a field. They needed to keep focused: this was about saving Ellie from being questioned on the rack.

"Enough, please. We will not agree on the principles, but perhaps we can find common ground on our aims. I wish to avoid the torture of innocents. Lady Eleanor and her father must not get caught up in your mission, priest. Even Dame Holton, annoyance that she is, does not deserve extreme penalties for offering shelter to you. Can you agree with that, March?"

The priest sighed and nodded. "Yes, lord. And I apologize for my angry words."

"Cecil?"

His guest scowled at the priest. "Yes, I agree that March should bear any consequences, not those he put in danger."

"So, I will propose to Sir Francis Walsingham that we send March to Banbury. But there must be some conditions, else I have no hope of persuading the Queen's minister not to question all my prisoners more severely. Master March, you must write and sign a confession as to the purpose of your stay in Stoke-by-Lacey, explaining the names in that book. And you must promise not to try to escape."

March swallowed, his face turning even paler. "You want my word?"

"Yes."

Silence fell in the room. Will prayed that March's concern for the other three caught up in this mess would outweigh his qualms about voluntarily submitting to this arrangement.

"Very well, my lord," March conceded, "I give you my word that I will not try to escape before I reach Banbury." He sat down at the desk. "But I won't incriminate others to save myself and those you have arrested. You cannot ask that of me." He dipped the quill in the ink and scrawled a confession across the paper. Will stood at his shoulder to read what he had decided to put down—that he was ministering the sacrament and hearing confessions; that he had no part in any plots to attack the English state; that his only wish was to pass peacefully about the kingdom.

"The book?" Will prompted.

March added a postscript, saying the names were those of old families of the Catholic persuasion. They had no knowledge of him, nor could he say whether they would have welcomed him. Will hoped it would be enough to clear Ellie of suspicion.

Will picked up the confession and waved it in the air to dry the ink before rolling it up tight. "I'll make the arrangements for your journey to your new lodgings."

March stood up and bowed. "Please tell Lady Eleanor that I'm very sorry for any distress I may unwittingly have caused her by lending her that book."

"I will."

"And thank you for caring enough to spare this poor servant another taste of the rack."

"Then hope I succeed. There's still a way to go before I can say that threat is truly passed."

Her father had been closeted with Walsingham for hours now. Ellie paced the hallway outside the sick man's room, listening to the soft burble of voices within and watching the shafts of sunlight mark off the hours on the wall. No shouting. No screams of pain. She had followed her father here when he had been summoned midmorning and she had stood guard over the door ever since, promising herself that she would burst in if she'd heard the least sign that her father was being abused. What could they be talking about? The man was supposed to be ill. The countess had gone in and out several times during the morning, tutting that Walsingham had not drunk her sleeping draught, her reports on his condition not favorable.

"My guest is too stoic for his own good," she huffed, giving Ellie a wan smile.

Arms hugging her waist, Ellie plucked at her elbows anxiously. "Is my father all right?"

"Yes, dear. They are talking about his craft." The countess wrinkled her nose. "I must admit, it takes me back to less happy days when my husband was ill. Your father was the only man he would admit to his chamber."

"I apologize."

The countess brushed Ellie's hair tenderly, a maternal gesture that made her ache with longing. "I never blamed you—or your father, for that matter."

"Will . . . I mean, your son does."

The older lady shook her head. "Will is Will. He saw it all through the eyes of a neglected boy, forced to take on responsibilities without the means to fulfill them, and he has yet to see those bitter days clearly. No, the blame was my William's—a lovely man, but weak." She bit her lip, eyes tearing though she smiled bravely. "I could not be strong enough for the two of us and he ended up dragging us all down."

Ellie knew how that felt. "I beg your pardon for the distress we've caused you," she repeated.

The countess caressed her cheek with a butterfly touch. "Dear heart."

After almost wearing a hole in the floorboards with her pacing, Ellie returned to her room. She discovered a posy of flowers on her pillow; a note attached read, "For the other countess in Lacey Hall, sweet dreams, Henry." She was glad that she had not been there to receive it. The man was like a beehive, thinking he promised honey when all he gave were stings. She toyed with the idea of calling on Jane but feared to run across Henry in his sister's apartments. His attentions were becoming harder to ignore, and she knew how rapidly he could turn ugly.

Ellie tossed the flowers out of the window, then leant on the sill for a moment. She felt trapped and confused, sick with love, paralyzed with fear, hunted by disgrace.

"Dios!" Ellie hid her face in her hands, the prayer tumbling from her lips in a desperate plea. "Show me a way out of this, I beg you."

There was no answer. Waiting in the silence, Ellie could not shake the impression that the house was suffocating her, the distant sounds of life mocking her own isolation. She couldn't bear it any longer. Out—she had to get out. Running from her room, she passed several startled maids as she escaped to the garden. Ignoring the gardeners, she kept going until the sweat streamed down her back and she felt her lungs would burst with the effort of sprinting in her heavy skirts. The wild thought of stripping off all layers and flying free seared her mind. Reaching the trees in the deer park, she ripped the ruff from her neck and cap from her head and tossed them to the ground.

Better, but not enough. Not nearly enough.

Next to go were her overskirt and her bodice, leaving her in her light shift and petticoat. She took her first proper breath. The madness was fading, and she had regained her senses sufficiently to feel embarrassed by her impetuosity. Had she really just stripped her gown off like some hussy going swimming in her shift? The heavy clothes lay on the grass, upbraiding her. Remembering her conversation with Jane about sending their gowns to the feasts without them, Ellie laughed and kicked her skirt.

"Go to, you killjoy!" she mocked. "I want to . . ." She looked around her. "I want to climb a tree!"

Finding a likely candidate in an old beech tree with lots of low, lateral branches, Ellie swung herself up into the canopy and began her ascent. For one glorious hour, she was going to cut free from everything that weighed her down.

Chapter 18

"Are you sure she went this way?" Will asked the gardener.

The old man scratched his head, then nodded. "Aye, master. The little Spanish lass ran off to the park like the hounds of Hell were on her tail."

"How long ago?"

"An hour. Maybe longer. I've hoed that row since I saw her."

Will noted the neatly turned soil—the man either worked fast or Ellie had been gone for a long while. "Very good. Carry on, Jeremiah."

"Aye, sir." The old man picked up his hoe and returned to whistling.

Will contemplated going back to the stables to fetch a horse, but it would take too long. He'd rushed back from the dower house to see Ellie, hoping to put her mind at rest and explain the deal he had struck with March, only to find that she had fled. He didn't know quite what to make of his mother's news that Hutton was closeted with Walsingham, but she had also reported Ellie's vigil outside the room. Perhaps she had taken fright? Being near Walsingham was enough to give anyone the horrors. Why else would she have run away in such a panic?

Reaching the edge of the park, Will was alarmed to find Ellie's ruff and cap cast carelessly on the ground. Alarm grew to real fear when he saw her skirt and bodice a few yards farther.

"Ellie?" he bellowed. Ugly visions of Perceval tracking her down filled his imagination. "Ellie?"

"Up here!"

It was her voice, but it appeared to come from overhead. He could swear he heard her muttering a series of Spanish oaths under her breath.

"Are you all right?"

"Um." He thought he heard a giggle. "Um, I'm fine, but you'd better not get any closer."

He moved to see her better. All he could glimpse was a flash of white near the top of the tree.

"How on earth did you get up there? Did someone—or something—chase you?"

"Not exactly."

Will felt ridiculous conducting this conversation from the ground. He was an earl: he shouldn't be reduced to this. He jumped to reach the first low branch and began to ascend.

"Don't!" warned Ellie. "I'm not decent."

"You should've thought of that before you went climbing, love," he growled back, not slowing. He wasn't going to take her word that she was unharmed until he saw for himself.

"Please, Will, I'm embarrassed enough as is."

He began to have an inkling of what might have transpired.

He grinned. "Not embarrassed enough, Ellie, not for the horrid moment you just gave me when I saw your clothes on the ground."

It took him about five minutes to puzzle out a route up the tree. When he reached the branch Ellie was sitting on, he found her straddling the thick bough, looking both proud and mortified, a strange conflict of emotions that made her stare at him boldly while managing to blush at the same time.

"So, you climb trees too," Will said teasingly. "In naught but your shift and petticoat."

"Can't climb in heavy skirts," she replied saucily, flicking a twig at him.

He caught her hand. "Why, love?"

She leant back against the trunk and closed her eyes. "Don't you sometimes feel so trapped by everything? I couldn't breathe—I needed to get high."

"So you could see the wood for the trees?" He smiled, knowing that feeling all too well. "Did it work?"

"Not really. But you found me, so it has proved a happier adventure than I first thought."

He chuckled and swung up the branch a little above her to share her view. "My first impression of you was completely wrong, wasn't it?"

"Hmm?"

"I thought you a proper court lady, open to a little flirtation."

"Be very careful, my lord." Ellie frowned at him. "If you say something rude, I may just push you off your perch."

He laughed. "And you would too. You, Lady Eleanor, are a rebel. You made my mother sport in her gardens like a girl, charmed this year's most proper court lady and floored two of the country's finest men." She raised her eyebrow at that, making him laugh all the harder. "And now I find you scaling trees in my park like a monkey, practically naked."

She blushed. "I would ask you not to mention that."

"It's rather hard to ignore, sitting here with a view of your rather lovely figure."

She poked a twig in his side. "I think it's time we went down."

"After you, my lady." He made a decent bow despite the limitations of being twenty feet in the air.

Ellie decided, for modesty's sake, that going first was a splendid idea. She began a nimble descent, conquering the tree in five minutes, half the time it had taken her to get up. She brushed her hands nonchalantly together when she reached the ground, then looked about for her skirt. Will thumped to the ground beside her and grabbed her round the waist.

"Oh no, this is too good an opportunity to waste, my lady," he said, lifting her from her feet as he bent to kiss her.

"Will!" she protested, but not too hard. His arm was firm but not tight around her hips, holding her to him as if he would shelter her from all threats and difficulties.

"Don't be afraid, love. Just a kiss. You can't go running round my park like that without paying a penalty."

His kiss started light but soon turned serious as they clung together, their mutual passion flaring up. Feeling his hands sweeping down her spine, Ellie knew she was in serious trouble, close to forgetting all that stood between them.

"Will," she pleaded, turning her face so that her cheek lay on his chest, mouth out of his reach.

"Ellie, I . . . I want to make you mine." He ran his hands through her hair, which, thanks to his encouragement, had worked its way free of all pins and tumbled down to her hips.

"You can't."

He took a shuddering sigh. "No, I can't." With an effort, he pushed her away from his body and picked up her skirt, not looking at her as he held it out. "Put this on, please."

Quietly, she slipped back into her outer clothes, wondering at their behavior. If he hadn't cared enough about her to stop, she might well have succumbed, and then she would've added her own ruin to the rest of her problems. It was wrong to behave like that with any but a husband, but somehow her feelings for Will twisted all her normal beliefs and made wrong seem right.

"You're dangerous," he commented softly.

"So are you," she retorted.

"We've got ourselves into a fix, haven't we, love?"

She nodded.

"I can't have you. If it were just me, I'd say, let's run away together and forget the rest, but there's my family. . . ."

"I know."

"I have to think of them."

"I understand." She sighed. Long experience made it easy to accept that no one, not even the man who said he loved her, was ever going to put her first. "I apologize for my behavior."

A spark of his old mischief came back. "No apologies. I think I shall make today a holiday on the Lacey estate—a day when naked tree-climbing is obligatory for all tenants."

"I wasn't naked!"

"I'm sticking to my version of events. Besides, I have a very powerful imagination." He picked up her poor ruff. "Sadly, I think this has now expired."

In her haste, she'd ripped the light linen cloth nearly in two. She didn't have another and now could not go about properly dressed unless she begged one off Jane or the countess. That would make for an interesting conversation when it came to explaining how she had spoiled the old. She tweaked the ruff from his fingers and did her best to tuck it under her collar. He watched her in silence until she felt uncomfortable under his scrutiny.

"What?" she asked, rubbing her nose on the back of her hand in case she'd picked up a smudge.

"I'm going to marry Lady Jane, if she'll have me."

She'd known, of course, but to hear it stated felt like a knife in the gut. "I . . . I wish you both happiness."

"Happiness?" Will held out a hand to her, then dropped it. "Happiness, no. Contentment, perhaps?"

"I like Jane."

"Good. That helps. I don't know her yet, but if you like her, then there's something there."

"You should try to love her, Will, if you marry her. It's not fair otherwise." Ellie wished she didn't feel she owed it to them to be so understanding, so noble about this. Really she wanted to scream at him that he should choose her and hang the consequences.

Will stared at her like a starving man at a feast set out of reach. "I love you."

I love you too, she echoed silently. "That . . . that will fade once I'm gone."

His frown deepened. "No, it won't. You can't dismiss what I'm feeling so lightly. And you're not leaving."

"I have to." *Staying would kill me.*

He glared at her, all Earl of Dorset. "Where exactly do you think you are going?"

She gave a brittle laugh. "Oh, I don't know. That depends on Father: Oxford, another nobleman's house, a barn—you never can tell with him."

"A barn!"

"Will, what did you think happened when you turned us out four years ago?"

"You've been at Mountjoy's."

"For the last six months."

He shook his head, as if denying it would make it untrue. "No, not a barn."

"There are worse fates." *Like living in a house where the man you love is married to another.* She gestured across the park to the roofs visible above the trees. "This is as good as it will ever be for me—Lacey Hall, this village." And she knew it was true; even her optimism was unable to light the bleak future ahead. "I'm not saying this to make you feel sad for me; I've known all along our stay here is merely delaying my father's next spiral down. He's not quite well, you see. This alchemy—it's a kind of illness, resists all rational arguments."

"Ellie, I can't let you go knowing that."

"You already knew it, Will, when you told me to go before—twice now; you just had not thought what it would really mean for me."

He scrubbed his hand across his face. "I did, didn't I? I'm a blind fool, Ellie. Forgive me."

She shrugged, crossing her arms across her chest defensively. "Not your fault, Will. We'll manage—we always have."

"No." He spoke the word softly, then repeated it more firmly. "No, that's not good enough. No managing. No barns, ditches or God knows what." He seized her firmly by the shoulders. "By my faith, Ellie, I'm not letting that happen to you. You'll have to stay here. No engagement has been announced—I'll marry you instead."

Her heart performed a strange leap, then a swoop as her emotions shot from joy to despair. He was offering her her dream but with no way to realize it. And it was a proposal made only at the sword-point of necessity, pricking him to action. They both knew that a match between them was more than ineligible—it was laughable and would spell the end of his hopes of regaining the dignity of his house. A rash gesture, which, if she accepted, would lead them into misery. Her mind quickly conjured such a future—forget dreams of happiness despite darned clothes. Love was not always enough, as life with her father had taught her. She made herself wipe off the gilt of hope to see the solid, practical steel of the matter. Will's feelings would sour, turning to resentment as he saw in his wife's place the girl who had brought nothing to his family but her love. His family would come to hate her as she dragged their fortunes down. Her love was better than that. She had to make him see reason.

"And what of your family, your people?"

His face set in a grim expression. "They will have to tighten their belts."

"The dowries you promised your sisters? The funds to establish your brothers?"

"I'll manage."

She gave a wry smile at the echo of her words. "But I won't let your family be ruined again by a Hutton." She dipped a curtsy. "Thank you for your noble offer, my lord, but I fear I have to refuse."

"Ellie, I won't allow this!"

"You'll have to. All-powerful lord you might be, but last time I looked, they still required the bride to agree to the match."

"But I love you."

"And I you. That's why I can't marry you."

He pulled her in his arms and hugged her, running his chin over the top of her head. "Stubborn wench. You've not heard the last of this."

She squeezed him around the waist. "Obstinate lord. That's my final word on the subject."

From her window, Jane watched Will and Ellie walk back in from the garden. They'd dropped hands as they reached the path, not realizing they had been in sight of the house as they crossed the meadow, but still their bodies leant towards each other. There was a magic between them, the kind poets sang about, but Jane had not believed existed. She felt both jealous of their tenderness and sad for all of them that their paths were set away from love and bound for duty.

Nell appeared at her shoulder and gave a snort.

"My lord dallies with the alchemist's daughter, I see. You'll have to send her away when you marry, my lady."

"Did I ask your opinion, Nell?" Jane snapped. "And I would thank you not to slander my friend's reputation with your loose tongue."

Nell muttered something about loose tongues for loose women but didn't press the matter.

Jane turned back to her window. Now she saw James hurrying after his brother, waving a letter in his hand. He was dressed in a smart blue doublet and hose that made the most of his long, well-shaped legs. She smiled as he leapt a bench rather than take the more sedate detour. James was of an age with her—tall and with good-hearted manners. Attracted to him, Jane had found her thoughts turning to him rather more than they should. He made her laugh and bolstered her confidence with his outrageous flattery; even his matter-of-fact approach to life and love was a comfort. She knew she would have to confess her lapse with Raleigh to her husband before arriving at the marriage bed: if the groom were to have been James she imagined he would commiserate with her, then try to exceed Raleigh's performance; all she could picture of Will's reaction was coldly polite disappointment.

"Do you wish to wear the blue or the yellow gown today, mistress?" Nell asked, holding up the choices.

"The blue." Jane picked up her comb and began to dress for dinner. It was too bad they could not swap places: make James the eldest son, repair the family's fortunes with her dowry. Then Will, as the second son, could marry whom he wished. Life was never fair to the fools caught up in the messy business of surviving it.

A smash behind her caught her attention. She turned to find Nell staring weakly at a pitcher she had just dropped. Weakly? What was wrong with the girl? Normally she'd be putting the blame on the inadequate pottery as it hit the floor. Biting her tongue before she rapped out her usual reproof, Jane waited.

"I beg your pardon, my lady. I'm being clumsy today." Nell went on her knees to gather the pieces.

Jane's concern deepened. "Are you feeling unwell?"

"Nothing to speak of, just out of sorts."

She gave Nell an encouraging smile. She guessed that her maid was due a visit from her monthly curse, and she well knew how bad-tempered that could make a girl. "Don't worry—I'll tell them I broke it. It won't be taken out of your pay."

Nell gaped at her.

Had she really been so unkind to her maid that she did not expect even this small gesture from her?

"Thank you, my lady." Her poor maid looked completely at sea with this side of her mistress, so Jane decided to put her out of her misery.

She got to her feet, gesturing impatiently. "Then help me with my points or I'll be late for dinner."

Nell sprang back into her old manner at this command. Her face hardening, she dumped the shards into the washbasin and came to her mistress's side. "At once, my lady."

Standing at his study window, Will glared at the letter in his hand. The permission had come, the beautifully regal signature appended to the note, proper seal applied. Before Lady Jane had arrived, he had written to the Queen, as was his duty as one of her foremost peers, asking for her approval to court the Perceval daughter. Elizabeth had no objection. He had been hoping in one small corner of his heart that the Queen would throw an obstacle in his path, something to let him off this duty with no fault resting on him, though what good that would have been in the longer view, he did not know. If she had objected to Lady Jane, she would have laughed outright at the idea of marrying Ellie.

"All well, Will?" asked James astutely, watching his brother read the message.

"Never better," Will replied glumly, passing him the letter. "Cry 'Tally ho! Have at the rich bride!'" He collapsed in a chair. "God, I feel terrible."

"Not up to the hunt?"

"Hardly sport when she seems ready to walk into my trap."

James placed the letter carefully on the desk. "She's a good woman, Will. You're lucky."

"Yes, I know. She's a paragon. Beautiful, witty, wealthy—the noble trinity of virtues in the marriage market."

"But she's not the Lady Eleanor. How bad have you caught it, Will?"

Will met his brother's eyes. There was no mockery, only concern. "Bad, Jamie, really bad. She's everything I want: the key to my lock, the arrow to my bow—oh, and ten thousand other such pathetic poetic tropes, none of which comes close to describing what she means to me. When I'm with her, she opens up such wonderful hopes and feelings. I've never felt anything the least like this before. I know I shouldn't love her, but I do."

It was a sign of how seriously James was taking this that he did not scorn Will's lapse into the language of a lover. "And does she love you?"

Will picked up the tennis ball he kept on the desk and tossed it from hand to hand. "Yes."

"In truth, and not just because you're the earl?"

Will threw the ball at James for that insult, and with admirable reflexes, his brother caught it easily. "She loves me enough to turn down my rash offer of marriage this morning."

That surprised James. "Why did she do that?"

He gave a hollow laugh. "Because she knows it would ruin us. She was the one to talk of dowries and you and Tobias."

James tossed the ball back to Will. "I think I too love the lady for that."

"Don't!" growled Will.

"Don't what?"

"I can't . . . I can't take being teased about this. You are free to try for the lady when I'm not, but I have to warn you, I'd be insanely jealous if you did so."

James shook his head. "You have me all wrong, Will. I know her now and my feelings for the little Hutton are purely that of a brother. I wish her well." He cast a significant look at the Queen's letter. "I would that you could marry her."

"But I can't."

"No, you can't. Instead, you're getting a pearl of a lady—no bad bargain from where I stand."

Will stood up, hearing the bell ring in the hall, the signal that dinner was ready to be served. James didn't really understand. Not yet tortured over the fires of love, he could only imagine it as a weak glow, soon dismissed for another. There was little point trying to make him see.

"I want this business settled. I'll make a formal offer to Lady Jane today."

His brother couldn't resist the quip. "Two proposals in one day, Will? That's impressive, even for an earl."

"Oh, sneck up, Jamie! I'll laugh when your turn comes," Will replied, stalking from the room.

CHAPTER 19

NERVOUSLY FINGERING A BEAUTIFUL RUFF borrowed from Jane, Ellie found the atmosphere oppressive as they waited at the table for her father to appear. Will dispatched Turville to root him out of Walsingham's room, and till such time as he returned, the diners were left staring at the barren board. The countess made pleasant conversation with Henry and Jane, their discussion turning on current court gossip to which Ellie could not contribute, not being an intimate of the inner circle. James had given her a kind smile but was now trying not to look at Jane. Will was silent, his fist clenched around the handle of a tankard. He seemed furious, but with whom? Her father for being late? Her for refusing him?

"My apologies, my lords, ladies, gentlemen," her father said brightly, striding into the room with the energy of a much younger man.

"Now we may start," Will said gruffly. They all stood as he mumbled a hurried grace, then signaled to the servants.

"How is my patient?" the countess asked Sir Arthur as he took his seat in the middle of the table at Ellie's side.

"Well enough, my lady." He turned to Ellie, beaming at her. "I have good news, my love."

Ellie put down her spoon, bracing herself for the next disaster. "Good news, sir?"

"Walsingham is going to send me to the Tower."

Will spat out the mouthful of ale he had been drinking. "What!"

"The Tower?" Ellie said incredulously.

Her father nodded happily.

"As . . . as a prisoner?"

He laughed and patted her hand. "No, no, silly Ellie! As a guest of honor. We'll have lodgings in the White Tower."

It was worse than she could've dreamt. How could Walsingham have sold this incarceration to her father as an honor? "Why?"

"He wants me to experiment with my phoenix tears explosive. We need fire ships, apparently, as a way of defending our ports against a Spanish armada. Her Majesty is making preparations just in case, you know." Sir Arthur dug into the bowl of soup in front of him and took a satisfied slurp.

Ellie feared she was sounding like his echo, but every word he let fall shook her worse than his laboratory bombs. "An armada?"

"Flotilla of armed ships," her father explained breezily. "Of course, the Spanish will never succeed."

"They might," James said darkly, "if backed by enough ground forces to mount a proper invasion from the Low Countries." Cecil nodded in agreement, his expression pensive.

"Then fire ships it is," her father concluded, the light of enthusiasm burning bright in his eyes.

Ellie turned to Will, who was staring at her father with a

mixture of horror and amazement. He shook his head slightly and ripped off a piece of bread.

"What about your quest for gold, sir?" Ellie asked in a low voice, hoping she would not be overheard.

"Oh that." Sir Arthur waved a hand airily. "That can wait. Sir Francis explained how urgent this mission is—the service I will be doing my country by serving him. He's going to pay me!" He said the last comment with something like wonder in his voice.

"I don't know what to say." Ellie stared at her father, trying to track this strange behavior to its source. "You've never been diverted from your aim before. Not by me, not by anyone."

He smiled at her in that infuriatingly patronizing way of his. "Now, now, love, you are only a child. You cannot be expected to understand. I'll have a laboratory of my own, furnished with the best equipment. There are more secrets to unlock than that of gold. I'll be looking for the source of the very power that causes explosions—a matter little understood by scholars."

Dios, thought Ellie, he had another enthusiasm to follow. He'd not been cured of his gold fever, merely swapped it for one for which Walsingham had a use.

"When do we leave?" she asked quietly.

"As soon as may be," Sir Arthur replied. "How about tomorrow?"

"And what about Dame Holton?"

Her father frowned slightly, his eagerness having quite driven the drama of the last two nights from his mind. "Oh yes. You see, Ellie, it seems that we were quite wrong about her. She was playing host to a Catholic priest! Walsingham explained it all to me."

"And you are just going to abandon her?" Ellie tortured her

bread into tiny morsels, plucking at the pieces with her fingers as a way of stopping herself slapping her father in front of everyone.

"Well, no." Her father bent his head towards Will, whom Ellie suspected was listening in on their conversation. "The earl here seems a reasonable fellow. He'll do what's right."

Unbelievable! For a few minutes the night before last, Ellie had thought her father had risen above his own preoccupations to defend another, but the mood had not survived the heat of this new obsession. She raised her eyes in a wordless plea to Will.

"I have made arrangements, Lady Eleanor," Will said stiffly. "March is going to join his fellow priests in confinement at Banbury. Unless further proof against Dame Holton emerges, she'll be freed on a promise of keeping the peace."

"That . . . that sounds very wise," Ellie managed.

"Partly Cecil's idea," Will admitted with a wry smile. "Couldn't possibly think up something so enlightened myself, now, could I?"

"Oh, I don't know. You underestimate yourself, my lord."

"Do I, Lady Ellie?"

She nodded and smiled shyly at him.

"I won't forget you think so." His voice was almost a caress.

Ellie felt her cheeks redden. They'd let their tone become too intimate—and in the very public circumstances of the dinner table. Everyone had fallen silent; she guessed that they were straining to hear what passed at the head of the table. "What I mean, my lord, is that all who meet you think highly of your abilities."

"Do they, now?" broke in Sir Henry Perceval loudly. "And what abilities are they, sweeting? What *experience* have you of our host here? Anything you wish to share with the rest of us?" His innuendo was so broad you could have planked the Thames with it and walked across.

"I'm sure the lady refers to his nice judgment on the matter of our Catholic renegades," Cecil said quickly. "I saw him deal with March quite smartly this morning—good work, which I'll report to my father."

Ellie thanked her stars that Cecil was there to get her out of that hole, though she knew that Perceval had managed to tarnish her good name in front of his sister and Will's mother. She didn't have the courage to lift her eyes to look at them, so she picked up her spoon, her hand shaking, hoping no one else was going to comment on her behavior. The problem was that she didn't feel entirely innocent of the accusation. What decent girl would kiss the earl as she had done?

"Lady Jane, if I might beg a moment of your time after dinner?" Will asked, reducing the diners once more to silence.

Ellie put her spoon aside, her appetite quite fled.

"Of course, my lord. I am at your service," Jane replied coolly.

The earl led Jane into the glasshouse, a new feature for English gardens that had impressed her when she saw it the first time. It showed the earl kept abreast of progressive ideas and would spend money to benefit his estate. How fitting that he had brought his prospective bride here, she thought glumly, as with her money he could afford to build hundreds more.

Stopping in front of a display of tender spring blooms, he turned to face her.

"My lady, I have received permission from the Queen to

proceed with my suit. Will you do me the very great honor of being my wife?" He spoke rapidly, like a patient bolting a foul-tasting medicine.

Jane felt a sigh of disappointment inside. It was so . . . so passionless. If she were a better person she would refuse him for her friend's sake, but Jane was a realist; she knew she cared too much for her position and family expectations to make that gesture. Besides, who would really benefit? "Thank you, my lord, I accept."

"I will write to your father today telling him that we have come to an agreement. If you wish to enclose a note of your own, I would be happy to send it with the messenger."

Straight to practicalities.

"You are too kind, my lord."

The earl paused as if scenting the sarcasm she had not intended to let him hear.

"No, madam, it is you who are kind." He took her hand as an afterthought and placed a proper kiss on her fingers. Jane knew in her heart that he did not kiss Ellie like that, closedmouthed and dutiful. She slipped her hand free as soon as he released his grip.

"Pray excuse me, madam: with your permission, I would like to break the good news to my family immediately."

She nodded him away, then watched him walk swiftly back to the house. That must have taken all of five minutes from the moment they left the dining room together. Would he be as perfunctory about his marital duties? The thought made her shudder. She plucked the prize rose specimen from a pot on the bench and tore the petals off, rolling the seed head in her fingers until it was quite destroyed. Damn him.

Jane knew there would be one person more miserable than her

in Lacey Hall, but she took some finding. Finally, she tracked Ellie down to a nook off the library, hiding behind a heavy curtain.

"Room for two?" Jane asked softly.

Ellie tucked her feet up to make space. Without farthingale hoops she was able to sit with her knees up against her chest, a freedom that Jane quite envied her. She was forced to take a more ladylike seat with feet on the ground.

"I've news. I wanted you to hear it from me first," Jane began.

Ellie turned huge dark eyes to her, and Jane saw that she knew.

"I've agreed to marry Dorset." She was wedding the earl, but they both were aware that Ellie owned the man.

"Congratulations, my lady."

"Please, remember to call me Jane."

"I hope you will both be very happy together." Ellie managed the complete sentence before tears spilled from her eyes. Jane looked away, thinking it better to pretend not to notice.

"You promised to remain my friend." Jane knotted her fingers together in her lap.

"I . . . I will. Please give me a little time to . . . to get used to the idea."

"Will you write to me from London?"

Ellie cleared her throat, regaining control. "Of course. Where will you be?"

"Now this is settled, I'll return to court. My parents will join me there and we'll complete the arrangements."

"Arrangements?"

"The contract, the dowry—my wedding clothes."

"Ah yes."

"Ellie, I'm sorry."

Her friend turned her face to the window. "Don't be."

"No, I am, in more ways than I can count." She slipped a pearl brooch off her stomacher and pressed it into Ellie's cold hand. "For friendship."

Ellie closed her fingers around it. "For friendship."

Nell lay in wait for her prey that night in the back passage by the kitchen as the staff drank to the health of the new couple inside. The conditions were as near perfect as she could devise: Henry was hounding the alchemist's daughter, her mistress was playing the lute for the family and Turville was in his cups. But he was taking far too long about it. She wondered if she could lure him out of company with some excuse—a message, perhaps? Before she had to resort to such an obvious ploy, he got up from the kitchen table and reeled towards the outhouse. Nell wrinkled her nose: if it had to be a call to the privy that helped her, then she'd take what she could. Husbandless mothers couldn't be squeamish. Best to wait for the return journey, though.

He came back humming merrily as he negotiated the passageway with the elaborate care of the very drunk.

"One, two, three," Nell counted under her breath, before sallying out from her hiding place to collide with him. With a deliberate flourish of petticoats and ankles, she rebounded to the floor.

"Oh, Mistress Rivers, my apol—apples . . . apologies!" Turville steadied himself against the wall as he offered a hand to help her up. "Are you hurt?"

Nell feigned a groan. "My leg, sir."

Turville looked quite flustered, swaying like a tree in a gale. "I best get s-someone." He belched.

Fool!

"I think you should check I haven't broken anything," Nell prompted.

"Oh." The big man went down on his knees like a shire horse reclining in its stall. Tentatively, he ran a hand over her ankle. "Here?"

"Oh lud, sir! I fear the damage may be a little higher," she said breathily.

Turville crept closer and ran his hand up to her knee, stopping where her stocking met flesh. He ran his fingers around her garter. Nell could sense his embarrassed excitement at the liberty. "Here?"

"I don't think it's injured, but I do feel rather strange." Nell fluttered her eyelashes at him. "My heart is racing and I feel as though I have butterflies in my stomach."

"Really?" Turville had lost track of quite what he was supposed to be doing as his hand wandered somewhat higher. His breathing became heavy, wafting ale fumes over her. *Lovely.*

"Yes. I've never felt anything quite like this before." She rubbed at her chest, "accidentally" loosening her lacing. His eyes blearily followed her every move. Just a little more tickling and this trout would be hers. "Do . . . do you know what is wrong with me?"

"Oh yes, my dear," he panted.

"Is there a cure?" She leant back on her elbows so his face was now level with her breasts.

"I have . . . I have exactly what you need." He moved towards her, appearing intent on planting a kiss on her throat, but then at the last moment his arms gave out and he collapsed on top of her. She waited, gritting her teeth against the expected pawing. Next thing she heard were snores. Nell heaved, but to no avail: he was out cold. Wriggling, she managed to slide out sideways, leaving him facedown on the tiled floor. She straightened her clothing and looked down at the mountain of man that had crushed her.

"Fat-witted sot!" She delivered a sharp kick to the ribs, but he stirred not. Her plans ruined for the moment, she flounced away to see if Henry required her company.

The next morning Nell appeared in the kitchen to find most of the staff nursing hangovers from the previous night, heads in hands as they sat round the table eating a breakfast of bread and cold meat. No one looking, she gave them all a scornful glance. Her spirits had been restored after an interlude with Sir Henry, and she was feeling more positive about her plans for marriage but distinctly annoyed by the Dorset household. She still had a couple of months before she started to show. If not Turville, some other man would swim into her net.

Dorcas signed her to sit down and poured her a cup of small beer.

"You appear well, Nell—not like the rest of these poor sots."

Nell looked up at her through her lashes. "Well, mistress, I'm not used to strong drink. I feared to take too much." *Just listen to me,* she thought, amused by her playacting, *don't I sound the proper one!*

Dorcas patted the back of her hand. "Good girl."

Turville came in with none of his usual swagger. As soon as he caught sight of Nell, he blushed scarlet and cleared his throat awkwardly several times before taking a seat at the far end of the table. How much did he remember? Did he think they'd done it—there on the tiles? With a delirious feeling of relief, Nell realized that, if she played this right, she was safe already and without having had to suffer the man in her bed.

With a sideways glance at Dorcas, her unwitting ally in this affair, Nell buried her face in her apron and pretended to muffle a sob.

"Sweet chick, whatever is the matter?" Dorcas asked in consternation. The low conversation around the table faded, leaving Nell center stage.

"I . . . I can't," she whispered. "I cannot pretend to be happy any longer."

Dorcas placed her meaty arm around Nell's shoulders. "There now, it can't be that bad. Tell your Auntie Dorcas what's wrong."

"I cannot sit at the table with that m-man." She took a shuddering breath. "I feel . . . I feel so ashamed."

Dorcas glared at all the men around the table, searching for the culprit. From spitboy to footman, they looked puzzled, all except the steward, who was scrubbing his hand over his face as if trying to cudgel his brains into order.

"No, it can't be," Dorcas said in horror. "Not Master Turville!"

Nell let out a whimper of distress, rubbing at her empty ring finger. "Now I've done it, I can't hold my head up again in decent company."

Dorcas shot to her feet. "Master Turville, what have you to say for yourself?"

All eyes now turned to the steward.

"Mistress Dorcas?" He looked as happy as a man about to be taken out to be executed.

"You know what I'm talking about."

"I do?"

"You . . . you hypocrite, you! You, who sit in judgment over all of us, to go and ruin this poor maid—I would not believe it of you if the proof wasn't sitting beside me!"

The reaction from the other listeners ranged from scandalized sympathy from the women to amusement on the part of a number of the footmen who had suffered many a lecture on the subject of their wenching from the steward. Nell decided it was time for a noisy burst of weeping. She was immediately swept up in a huddle by the other girls and taken to the prize seat by the hearth.

"Oh, you poor darling!"

"Did he force you? Shall I get the master?"

"The wretch—I will tear his eyes out!"

Nell could tell they were all rather enjoying themselves; she wished she could join in.

"I cannot speak of it," she said breathily, thinking it best to keep the details of the encounter vague as she did plan to marry the man in the end and would have to live with him.

"Master Turville, what are you going to do about this?" demanded Dorcas, hands on her hips. The cook stood behind her with her ladle raised, the laundress unhooked her paddle from her girdle, the housemaid grabbed her broom.

"I can't remember what happened, mistress," Turville admitted humbly. Nell could tell he wished the whole pack of them to the ends of the earth. His authority had taken a fatal blow, and it had been so easy to do.

"That is no excuse!" screeched Dorcas.

"It makes it worse! He's a rogue—an out-and-out rogue!" capped the cook, a comely, stout woman. Word had been that she had set her sights on Turville before Nell had come along.

The women all muttered their agreement.

Turville got to his feet, trying to regain his dignity like a beggar pulling a ragged cloak around him to hide his nakedness. "Mistress Rivers, would you step aside with me?"

Nell was rather proud of her shiver—fear or revulsion: let them read it as they liked.

"You're not taking her anywhere on your own," Dorcas replied firmly. "Say what you have to say in front of witnesses."

Turville cast his eyes to the heavens then back to Nell. She thought she saw him grind his teeth before giving her the words she knew were her due.

"Dear lady, I know not what I can do to repair the damage I have done to your good name. I can plea excess of emotions as my only excuse."

"Excess ale if you ask me," muttered a footman in an undertone.

Turville ignored him. "Please forgive me."

Dorcas tutted. "Forgiveness? How like a man to think that's enough! She doesn't want to forgive you, Master Steward; she wants you to make a decent woman of her. You know what the vicar would say: if you want to taste the fruit, you should be prepared to buy the orchard."

The light of comprehension dawned in Turville's befuddled brain. He took another look at Nell sobbing in Dorcas's arms, the benefits of the arrangement making themselves all too plain as her breast heaved with emotion. "Mistress Rivers, dare I hope that after all that has passed between us, you would do me the honor of becoming my wife?"

Nell raised her eyes to him and gave him what she hoped appeared a tremulous smile. "Oh, sir, Master Turville . . . Affabel, I accept."

The listeners cheered. A reluctant grin broke out on Turville's face. He ran his hands through his thinning hair, smoothing it back. "I didn't wake expecting to be married by the end of the day, but I'd say I got myself a good bargain." He approached her and planted a kiss on her lips, pleased with his cleverness in netting a youthful, comely wife.

Nell quelled the impulse to wipe her mouth. He'd got a bargain all right—more than he'd anticipated. Two for the price of one.

Chapter 20

THREE WEEKS HAD PASSED since the Day of the Two Proposals, as Ellie had named it. She was now lodged in a small but finely furnished apartment in the White Tower, the high-walled square keep where royalty lodged when visiting the Tower of London. Her room had a view of the green and the grim walls behind, which lodged the less fortunate inmates of this place. There was little for her to do. Her father spent long hours in his laboratory and down at the wharf with his trial fire ships, rarely remembering to return even to eat. Ellie spent her days wandering the grounds, only venturing onto the riverbank when the guards were in sight, as it was not a safe part of London for a girl to walk alone. She didn't fit in any of the worlds that were contained within these battlements: neither prisoner nor soldier, she had no place. Perhaps when Walsingham paid her father, she could persuade him to rent lodgings within the city.

Perhaps. Perhaps not. He had a lover he did not wish to part from and her name was Science.

She wrote to Lady Jane as she had promised, finding her one consolation in the long letters she had plenty of time to pen. She received only short answers back, but they were full of news and sharp observations, enough to keep her going until the next installment. Jane complained of her new maid (the old one had surprised them all by wedding Will's steward)—piled invectives on her ambitious father, mocked her brother—so all was as usual. Only Will escaped her ire—in fact, he barely existed in the letters, walking across the stage like a minor player entitled Earl of Dorset, who had been given one line only by the playwright.

> *Dear Jane,*
>
> *Great excitement today: my father plans to launch his first fire ship on the Thames. Pray do not be alarmed: it is with the full permission of the warder and Sir Francis Walsingham and is only a small boat, so the shipping on our great river should not be unduly disturbed.*

Ellie raised her pen from the page. Her father was in his study, glimpsed through the door that stood open between them. He was striding to and fro, muttering to himself, as he ran through the final preparations.

> *He expects great things of this test and is already planning to give a lecture on the subject of explosive materials when we finally arrive at Oxford in triumph.*

She had begun to think they would never get to the university, not as long as Walsingham kept her father happy with his toys. That dream was disappearing, along with so many others Sir Arthur had clung to over the years.

> *I continue to stun the ravens with my erudition. They listen quite patiently as I declaim my favorite verses to them on my daily perambulation around my new home. Man with the white handkerchief waved to me again, so I spoke a little louder in order that he could hear. I hope I alleviated the boredom of his detention somewhat, but I am no closer to discovering his name—the guards are very close-lipped on the subject; they merely say he was once a military man in service to the Earl of Leicester.*
>
> *The Tower is a strange spot on God's busy earth. Just beyond our walls, the world is always rushing somewhere: beasts to market, people to work, ships to other countries. Within, we revolve around our same fixed mark, making no progress: all of us quite, quite lost.*

She was getting maudlin—she had to stop.

"Ellie, my love, have you seen my old notebook?" her father called.

Grateful for even this tedious errand, she leapt up. "I'll fetch it for you." She plucked it from the saddlebag where it had remained since they arrived. "Here it is."

"Thank you, my dear." He smiled faintly at her. "Do you wish to observe my experiment? It should be most interesting."

Better than staring at the walls all evening. "I would, sir. How are you going to launch the boat?"

"I'll row her out at high tide, light the fuse then cut her adrift. We've a ring of boats organized to keep others away from the site of the explosion."

These preparations alarmed her. It was not like her father to be so careful. "Will it be dangerous?"

"Think nothing of it, my dear." He tapped her nose. "Your old father knows what he's doing."

Why did that not comfort her?

Evening came, bringing the high tide. The river washed through Traitor's Gate, carrying the stench of the water right into the keep. Ellie walked two steps behind her father as he led Walsingham, the Tower warder, and other observers to the wharf. He was lapping up their obvious curiosity about the effectiveness of the explosive he had devised.

"The secret is in the proportion of gunpowder in my special preparation. A volatile mix, but with impressive results. I conducted a small trial in my laboratory and was very pleased with the damage it inflicted."

Yes, it had been spectacular: Ellie had spent the afternoon sweeping up the pieces.

A small vessel, guarded by two nervous soldiers, was moored at the steps. A larger rowing boat, powered by an experienced oarsman, waited to tow it out into the river channel. Sir Arthur lit a lantern to provide a flame for the fuse, then jumped aboard.

"Good fortune, sir!" called Walsingham.

So eager to prove himself, Sir Arthur only waved. He didn't even spare a glance for Ellie as he gave his final orders. "Take us out, Gridley," he told the boatman.

Ellie shivered despite the warm breeze. She moved apart from the watchers and began to pray for her father's safety. The lead boat became difficult to see, a dark shape low on the water, oars rising and falling like the flailing arms of a drowning man. The lanterns of the ring of boats keeping shipping clear of this stretch of river shone out like a fiery necklace. She wasn't sure exactly what was going to happen next.

Walsingham tapped his walking cane on the ground impatiently. His secretary made notes as his master muttered comments on the wind direction and the weather conditions.

Suddenly, a bright light flared in the darkness.

"That's it—that's the fuse lit!" announced Walsingham.

Night vision spoiled by the glare, Ellie could no longer see her father's boat or the fire ship, just the white snake burning rapidly away. Then—

Boom!

She turned her face as the fire ship exploded; blazing wooden splinters rained down on them even at their supposedly safe distance on the shore. She crouched, covering her head with her arms, waiting for the bombardment to stop. When she raised her eyes, she saw Walsingham getting to his feet.

"Oh, bravo!" he exclaimed, leading the other gentlemen in a round of applause.

Ellie's vision slowly recovered from the flash, but still she could see nothing on the water. The fire ship had been completely obliterated; the tow boat was nowhere in view.

"Sir Francis, where's my father?" Ellie asked in a panic, rushing to the water's edge.

"Patience, my lady. He'll be back in a moment to share his success with you," Walsingham said calmly.

"But I can't see him!"

"None of us can, my dear." The warder patted her arm. "Very impressive explosion, eh?"

"You don't understand—I can see the river, but I can't see the boat!" She turned to the water and cupped her hands around her mouth. "Father! Father!"

Catching her urgency, the warder gave Sir Francis an anxious look. "The girl's right, Walsingham. I can't see hide nor hair of it."

"Send word to the other boats," Walsingham ordered his secretary. "Tell them to look for survivors in the water."

Survivors!

Ellie let out a strangled sob. No, no. Her father had to be all right. He couldn't die in such a stupid way, so suddenly, without time to prepare.

The warder put an arm around her and drew her away from the water's edge. "Lady Eleanor, there's nothing for you to do here. Come back to my house and let my wife look after you until we've found your father."

She shook her head grimly. "I have to stay."

"It's high tide—he could be swept upstream a long way before someone pulls him out of the river," the warder said reasonably.

"I'll stay," she repeated.

The warder remained at her side as the search was made. Numb with shock, Ellie barely noticed when a guard draped a blanket over her shoulders. Walsingham had long since departed, murmuring something about word being sent to him at his town residence. And so she waited.

Gray dawn lit the eastern sky over the docks when the last boat returned with no survivors, just the body of the boatman. He had a deep gash across his forehead where debris had struck him, and burn marks on his arms and face. Ellie started to shake. The oarsman had been farther back in the boat than her father.

The warder placed a heavy hand on her shoulder. "Come, my dear, we have to assume Sir Arthur is lost but pray for a miracle."

"I'll stay." Ellie's voice was a thread fluttering in the wind, easily snapped.

"No, you won't," the warder said firmly. "You'll come with me now." He seized her by the elbow and towed her back into the Tower to his comfortable lodgings.

He passed her over to his wife and maid—a change of hands from cold masculine palms to soft female fingers. Her damp gown was removed and she was pressed down into a warm bed, quilts piled on top of her. She had the wild image that she was drowning and began to struggle.

"Hush now," crooned the lady. "Rest. I'll wake you if there is any news."

Ellie curled up into a ball, taking up as little space in the world as she could manage. She gazed at the white sheet covering her, counting the threads, staring at the tiny black dots between them until nothing remained but the weave.

When she woke, it took Ellie a few moments to remember, and for a few cruel seconds her father was still alive for her. Memory killed him again.

But it had not been certain. Perhaps there was word?

Jumping out of bed, she ran to the door, searching for someone to tell her the latest news. The hallway outside her room was empty. Frantic now, she hurried downstairs. There were voices in the warder's study. Not stopping to think about manners, she opened the door.

"Sir, has my father been found?"

The gentlemen gathered in the chamber turned to look at her in surprise at her interruption. Ellie's eyes were only for the warder until she saw Walsingham sitting opposite him.

"Child, you are not dressed," the warder said gently.

Ellie couldn't care less—a shift was sufficient covering for this news. What did it matter if she had bare feet and loose hair?

"Please, my father?"

The warder just shook his head.

Ellie refused to give up—refused to believe. "What is being done? Is the river being searched?"

Walsingham gestured to the warder. "Take her to your wife."

The warder approached Ellie and took her elbow. "Come, my dear. This is no place for you."

"But I must know what is being done to find him!" Panic swelled. He wasn't listening to her—what if her father was lying injured on some bank somewhere?

"Everything possible is being done, Lady Eleanor," Walsingham said stiffly. "We must know what went wrong."

"I don't care what went wrong! I just want my father." Her mouth was dry, her heart pounding. It could not be true. She wouldn't let it. "I must go and search myself if you won't."

The warder drew her away, taking her from the room like a naughty child. "My men have scoured the river and the banks, Lady Eleanor. The tide has turned twice since the accident. His body could be out to sea by now."

She shook her head, tears of fury glittering. "He's not dead, I tell you. He's not!"

The warder guided her into the kitchen, where his wife, a slight, elegant lady with a coil of dark hair beneath her neat cap, was standing with the cook discussing the week's meals. "Katherine, do something for her, will you?" He gently pushed Ellie towards the lady.

"Ah, love, come here." The warder's wife held out her arms, but Ellie stumbled away.

"I must get dressed—go and look."

The lady nodded. "Go and look if you must. I'll help you with your gown."

Offering a steadying arm, she led Ellie back to her bedroom. Ellie could see no sign of her clothes.

"You'll have to borrow something of mine," the warder's wife said. "Yours were singed in the explosion." She chose a black skirt and bodice from a clothes press and helped Ellie into them. They were far too fine for her, but Ellie didn't care about that. She shoved her feet into her shoes and turned to leave the room.

"Your hair?" the lady prompted gently, handing her a coif.

What did her appearance matter? Ellie tugged her hair into three parts and made a thick braid, then jammed the coif over the top. "I'm ready."

"Where do you want to start?" The warder's wife stood patiently at the door.

"What do you mean?"

"Upstream or downstream? In a boat or on the bank? All have been searched, you know. My husband saw to that, and he's very thorough."

Still desperate, Ellie felt some of the fight go out of her. It was hopeless—that was what the lady was saying. She swallowed.

"I'll start where I last saw him—on the wharf."

Nodding, the lady summoned two yeomen to accompany them out of the gates to the riverside. Ellie marched to the edge and stood on the brink of the Thames, staring across the brown expanse to the distant southern bank, warehouses partially obscured by the fleet of ships resting after long voyages. The river had an oily sheen and smelt foul, so different from the pure water upstream she had walked beside with her father as they left Windsor. What did she think she could achieve? It was useless.

"Shall I summon a boat?" the lady asked.

Ellie shook her head, tears spilling down her face.

"Do you want to go back inside?"

She nodded.

"Is there someone we can write to for you? A relative?"

It was only then that Ellie truly grasped that she was alone in the world—really alone. Her father, though a burden for much of her life, had at least given her a purpose, a family. Who was left?

"I . . . My father was not on good terms with his brother."

"Your mother's family?"

"She was from Spain, my lady. I know no one there."

"Ah, I see. Friends, then?"

Her best friends were about to marry each other; she could not spoil their chance for happiness by being a cuckoo in that nest. "No, my lady."

"Well, that can wait for now. Come inside. I'll have Cook make you something to eat."

Ellie let herself be led back towards the lodgings.

"Your father died a hero, Lady Eleanor," the warder's wife said, "giving his life in the service of his country."

A hero? *A hero?* Ellie began to laugh, a bitter outpouring that made her feel sick and desperate. He died as he lived—a fool for his craft. And this time he'd managed to kill someone else with him.

"Stop it! You'll make yourself ill!" The lady shook her by the shoulders.

But Ellie couldn't stop. Her stomach hurt so much she bent double, laughter turning to sobs. She knelt on the grass and gave in to her agony.

"Take her to her chamber," the lady ordered one of the yeoman. "She is overcome by grief."

The man picked her up like a bundle and hurried back inside. Ellie had quieted by the time she was placed on the bed. Sanity was creeping back. She could not turn away the only people who stood between her and the street by acting like this.

"I pray your pardon," she whispered, knowing the lady was hovering.

"No, my sweet, you need not ask for forgiveness. You rest. Mourn your father. We'll think about tomorrow when it comes."

She left the room, closing the door softly behind her.

Ellie stared at the ceiling, but that offered no answers to her predicament, so she sat up and looked about her. Her soul seemed to have fled, leaving behind but a husk of a body that was going through the motions of living. A writing desk stood under the window. She got to her feet and pulled out a piece of paper. Taking the quill in her fingers, she began her letter.

Chapter 21

Will was conscious that James waited for him outside the sovereign's presence chamber at Greenwich Palace, the Queen's favorite residence on the south bank of the Thames. Her private apartments were in a tower on the water's edge, and all during his audience he had been distracted by the reflections of the Thames rippling across the gilded ceiling. With fresh rushes rustling underfoot with every move, he had felt rather as if he was in the presence of a river goddess, not the Queen of England.

The court was about to go on summer progress. Only the monarch's essential ministers and servants were to accompany her, but that still meant an entourage of several hundred to travel about the country. Will was pleased not to be counted as indispensable, as it would be ruinously expensive to maintain appearances for so long a period. Besides, he had a wedding to prepare for—what joy.

In his audience with Elizabeth, the Queen was most understanding as to why he would want to be absent from her side for a few months. He escaped with nothing more onerous than having to kiss her pale hand.

"All well?" James asked when Will emerged.

"We can leave." Will set off at a quick march, eager to be gone before the Queen changed her mind.

"Home, then?"

"Yes, let's retreat."

"Did she say much to you?"

Will grimaced. "Congratulated me on winkling out March. Told me that she looked forward to hearing of further successes against Catholic conspirators."

James frowned, tugging at his newly clipped beard. "I trust you didn't mention that March escaped when he reached Banbury?"

"Er, no, I didn't. That wasn't my responsibility. The man kept to the letter of his promise to me, so I cannot fault him. I only hope he has the sense to head off for Rome and leave England in peace."

"And how likely is that, do you think?"

"About as likely as snow in July."

They took a turn around the courtyard, heading for the Percevals' set of rooms. Will was struck anew by the riverside palace's magnificent facade of mullioned bay windows and crenellated roof, which gave the appearance of a great glass castle afloat—a fit symbol of the dangerous voyage any took who ventured to court. As one of the favored mariners, the Percevals lodged in prime chambers, not far from those of the Queen.

Thinking of the state of his own heart, Will glanced at his brother, who had been unusually quiet the last few weeks. He'd been so wrapped up in his own depression on losing Ellie that he had not thought of how James was faring.

"So how is the widow in Cambridge, little brother?"

"What widow?" James kicked a stone from his path.

"Last I heard from Tobias you were enamoured of a lady there, or is that old news?"

"Ancient. It was but a dalliance. I didn't take up with her again after Windsor."

"Why not? Did she find someone of her own age to seduce?"

"Probably—but she was only a few years older than me, Will—not the decades I let Tobias believe."

Will chuckled. "So the affair ran its course."

"You could say I lost my taste for her charms."

"And they say women are fickle."

James gave a shrug, then turned the subject.

Will studied James as he talked animatedly about his hopes of soon joining Leicester's army, disappointed that he could get no rise out of his brother with his teasing; perhaps James's emotions had run deeper than he cared to admit?

"Jamie, you'd tell me if there was something the matter, would you not?" he asked, pausing at the door of the Percevals' chambers.

James's eyes shifted warily away from his face. "If I thought you could help."

"But . . ."

"Hadn't we better knock?" James took the decision out of his hands and rapped on the door. A manservant opened it and ushered them in.

"My lord!" Jane's father, Thaddeus Perceval, Earl of Wetherby, strode towards them. A head shorter than his son, he shared the same golden coloring of his children, though his beard was mostly silver. A formidable man, he reminded Will of a boulder bowling downhill with unstoppable momentum.

"We've come to bid you farewell, sir," Will explained. "The Queen has granted us leave from court, and I wish to return to my estates to prepare for the arrival of my wife."

"Grand. I've had my lawyer draw up deeds governing the betrothal and marriage, disposal of dowry and what's to be settled on my daughter if you die and so on. Would you care to sign it today or take it away to consult your own advisers?" He picked up a scroll of paper and waved it in the air.

"I think it best I study it at leisure, sir." Will plucked it from his fingers and handed it to James to look after. "I'll send it to you by messenger when I have completed the formalities."

Lord Wetherby clapped his hands, rubbing them enthusiastically. "Wedding in December, eh? I expect a grandson by harvest after next, then!" He laughed heartily. "Come along, come along, Jane'll be wondering what's keeping her lover."

He gestured them to proceed into the lady's apartment. Jane was waiting for them, looking breathtakingly beautiful in pale yellow as she stood against the heavy drape pulled back from the window. "My lord." She dipped a curtsy, then her smile brightened when she noticed he was not alone. "And Master Lacey."

Will kissed her hand. "Lady, we have come to say farewell. We're for Lacey Hall."

"Pray take my greetings to your mother and Lady Sarah—and that rogue Tobias, if he is at home."

Will returned her amused look. "Yes, he is. Running rings around my mother and teasing Sarah—it will not be a peaceful household, I fear. And where is your brother, my lady?"

Jane turned to her father. "Sir, is Henry here? I've not seen him this morning."

Her father grunted and walked to the window looking down on the river. "Nay, lass, he's off on some foolish errand to the Tower. Ran into Sir Francis Walsingham this morning—had news of an accident two nights since. One of Walsingham's men was killed in an explosion on the Thames—that alchemical fellow who was making a nuisance of himself at Windsor."

"What!" Will's world shook in a late shockwave from the blast.

"Sir Arthur Hutton?" Jane's face had gone very pale.

"Aye, that's the man. Blew himself to pieces, they say. No sign of him. Left Walsingham high and dry because he'd invented this grand formula for explosives, then died before he could record it. Very frustrating."

"And his daughter?"

Wetherby looked puzzled. "A daughter, is it? That explains why Henry hared off to the grieving family's side." He chuckled. "You mustn't worry about her: I expect someone will step in to see the lass is provided for."

Will was desperate to leave. He was standing here playing the dutiful suitor while across the river the wolves were circling Ellie. He had to find out for himself if she was safe. He turned to make his excuses to Jane only to find her already moving to the door.

"I must go to my friend, Father," she said brusquely.

Lord Wetherby stood in her path. "Nay, Jane, you stay here. Whatever this girl was in the past to you, she is quite out of your reach now. Your brother . . ." He changed his mind about what he would say, settling for something less direct. "You don't understand these things, but from now on it won't be decent for you to be seen with her. Your future husband, I'm sure, would not approve."

Will moved to Jane's side swiftly, tucking her hand in the crook of his elbow. "On the contrary, Lord Wetherby, Lady Eleanor is an entirely suitable companion for my wife. Henry won't find the welcome from her that you anticipate."

"Nonsense! From the hints he let drop the girl will have no choice but accept a protector—no money, no family."

"But she has friends. Come, lady, I'll escort you to the Tower and see what can be done." Will raised an imperious brow at Lord Wetherby. "If you have no objections, sir?"

"Humph! I suppose not. You're soon to have the responsibility for her, so I suppose you might as well start now. But if you're wrong about the Hutton girl, you will bring my Jane back immediately and cut all contact between them."

"I'm not wrong, sir."

"We'll see. You may know the lady, but you don't know my son. He can be very persuasive."

Ellie's last task for her father was to pack away his notebooks and writings in a large trunk for dispatch to Oxford. The apartment was no longer hers to stay in, so she had to clear their things. She could not keep much where she was going and he had spoken of acquaintances in New College so she was sending the papers there. That would please him, she thought: his work given respectful consideration by his fellow scholars.

Her hand hovered over the notebook he was using on the day of his death. Grief swamped her, and she lost track of what she was about.

He was dead. The worst of it was she kept forgetting, thinking him still just in the next room. People who had lost a limb said they could still feel it—that was what it was like, a phantom presence of completeness.

"Señor Jesucristo, sálvame," she whispered, stroking the calfskin binding on the notebook.

A tapping at the door disturbed her from her prayers. She looked up to see Sir Henry Perceval standing there, his face solemn but his eyes sharp, assessing her circumstances in one glance.

"My poor Lady Eleanor," he began, "I cannot tell you how sorrowful I was to hear of your loss."

Ellie struggled to her feet, clutching the notebook in front of her like a shield. He was the last person she wanted to see.

"Sir Henry."

"The warder told me you were to be found here. He said you were quite prostrate with grief."

Words felt like stones in her throat. "It is hard, sir."

"Yes, I know, sweeting, so hard, so unfair. Your father died in the service of our country, and yet you are to be put out of your lodgings here." He took a turn about the room, picking up books at random, muddling the piles she had spent the morning organizing so carefully.

"They are required for another, sir."

"And you? What is to become of you now?"

Ellie had plans, but Sir Henry was not to know them. "I'm going away, sir."

He stopped, put down the book he was holding and closed the distance between them. "Lady Ellie, you must know why I've come."

She took a step away, recalling her previous horrible encounters with him and determined not to get trapped again. "Sir, I do not want to hear this."

"But you must listen to me. I offer you so much—you can barely conceive of the comforts I can give you, the pleasure we can take together. Dorset can't do a fraction of what I can."

"Dorset?" squeaked Ellie in surprise.

Henry smiled sardonically. "I know you've been his lover, sweeting. I'd prefer it otherwise, but I am a man of the world and can overlook your lapse."

"He was not my lover!"

He cupped her cheek in his palm. "So sweet, you almost make me believe in your innocence."

"I'm untouched, sir!" she declared hotly, though why she was bothering to defend herself to him when she should be running, she could not fathom.

"We'll see, won't we?"

She batted his hand away with the notebook. "No, we will not. Go away, sir. I don't want or need your offers of protection."

"Oh, but you do."

He made a grab for her arm, but Ellie was too quick. She threw the book at his face then snatched up a glass alembic from the workbench and tossed it over her shoulder. It shattered on the wall behind him. "Just leave me alone!" Brass scales came next, then a pair of tongs. Henry ducked the bombardment and even had the nerve to laugh at her.

"Ellie! Ellie! You are magnificent!" he declared. "Such passion! Such fire!"

It was too much—on top of the loss of her father to have this . . . this vile beast stalk her.

"*Dios y sus ángeles!* I hate you!"

A pipette bounced off his forehead, spraying him with mercury.

"Come back, sweeting!"

A vial of some unidentified liquid exploded as she chucked it in his direction, spattering him with glass splinters. Taking advantage of the distraction, she reached the door, stumbled down the steps and fled. Her plans to leave had been brought abruptly forward. She was not going to stay in the same city as Henry a moment longer.

Will, James and Lady Jane arrived at the Tower to find Henry sitting among the ruins of what looked like numerous glass instruments and odd-shaped brass objects. He was thumbing through a book, dabbing at a cut on his cheek with a handkerchief.

"What happened here?" Jane asked.

Her brother looked up, showing no surprise to see them at the door. "Lady Eleanor has a temper."

Will barely restrained his urge to plant a fist in Henry's face. James put a hand on his arm.

"Let's find out where she is first," James said in a low voice.

"And where is she now?" Jane made the inquiry for him.

Henry shrugged. "Ran off after smashing her father's instruments. I'm waiting for her to come back." He flipped through the pages of the notebook. "You know, Sir Arthur really was quite mad—this is all nonsense. He repeats the same experiments several times and doesn't even notice."

"What did you say to her, Henry?" Jane asked coolly, picking her way through the glass shards.

"I offered her a shoulder to cry on."

"And?"

Henry glanced awkwardly at Will. "I say, Janie, I don't think I can talk about such things to you."

"I'm not stupid, Henry: you asked her to be your mistress and this was her answer." Jane ground a piece of glass under her toe.

Henry gave a self-mocking laugh. "You know something, Janie, I don't think she likes me very much."

"Only just realized, have you?"

"She likes someone else." Henry smirked at Will.

"Don't think in your anger with her you can make trouble between Dorset and me, Henry. I already know that Lady Eleanor and he hold each other in great affection."

With an evil glint in his eye, Henry beckoned her closer and bent his mouth to her ear. "And did you know that they were lovers?"

Jane reared back and slapped his face. "That is for my friend." She held up a palm to stop Will advancing on Henry. "He does this to torment you, my lord. Pray do not give him the satisfaction of provoking you."

Henry rubbed his cheek. "See what you're getting, my lord? She seems so meek and mild, doesn't she? But that's all show. She isn't what you think she is."

Impressed by her spirit, Will gave Jane his first genuine smile and kissed the reddened palm of her hand. "No, she isn't. I think she's quite splendid. Come, my lady, let's go seek our friend."

•❀•

The warder's wife greeted them in her parlour. Her kindly face was troubled, but she was obviously struggling to hide her upset.

"The Lady Eleanor? I'm afraid you're too late, my lord. She took a boat up the river but an hour since, leaving instructions for her father's things to be sent on to Oxford."

Will's alarm rocketed. To run off with the packing half done, Ellie must have been sincerely scared by Henry's actions. The man must not have told them the whole truth about what had happened. Will resolved to go back and teach him a lesson, then go fetch the silly girl and keep her safe as she should've been from the start!

Calmer than he was, Jane asked all the questions he should have thought to put to the lady. "Did she say where she was going, ma'am?" Jane asked.

"Yes, my lady. She said something about relatives in Gloucestershire. She'd intended to wait until she received an answer to her letter but then announced suddenly that she had to leave immediately." The warder's wife wrung her hands. "She wouldn't listen to reason; I fear her loss has overset her."

Jane glanced at Will, her look asking if he knew anything about these relatives, but he had no more knowledge than she did of Ellie's wider family.

"And do you know where they live?" Jane inquired.

The lady shook her head and Will's hopes plummeted. "But my husband will, for it was he who dispatched a messenger with the letter only yesterday. As I told Lady Eleanor, if she's not careful she'll overtake the man on the road and arrive before news of her father's death reaches his brother."

•❁•

Henry had not waited around for Will to exact punishment from his hide for scaring Ellie away.

"Can we leave the chamber like this?" Jane asked, gesturing to the mess in the tower room.

"I'll ask one of the yeomen to send someone to box up the last of the books and clear the glass," Will replied. "But it worries me that she didn't have a chance to finish it herself."

"Then we should put aside a few things that she might like later on."

They took a few sentimental mementos from the room that they thought Ellie would appreciate: her pearl brooch, a notebook belonging to her father that lay on the hearth, a book of verse, a sewing kit. The latter gave Will a bittersweet memory of her terrible embroidery skills. He took particular care of it, tucking it away in his doublet, and then escorted Jane to the boat waiting to return them to Greenwich.

"An uncle," mused Jane. "I thought Ellie was alone in the world."

"She mentioned that her father's obsession had driven a wedge between him and his family." Will drew his cloak around his shoulders, gazing back at the grim silhouette of the Tower against the cloudy sky. Rain spat angrily at the river, forming scattered rings on the surface.

James pulled a canvas sheet over Lady Jane's lap to give her more protection from the weather. "That's good news, isn't it? She's going to her uncle."

"But with no certainty that he'll take her in, sir," Jane said soberly.

Will clenched his fists in his lap. He had the unnerving sensation that of everyone only Jane understood him; his cold bride had become his ally. Despite this, the conviction had been growing that he couldn't go through with his plan to marry her. The prospect had been bearable when Ellie had been precariously safe with her father on their perch in the White Tower; now she'd been toppled from that nest there was no peace of mind until he knew she was happy. But to go after her to Gloucester would declare his unusual attachment to the lady, insulting Jane and ruining Ellie's reputation unless he married her.

Unless he married her. The very thought was both exhilarating and frightening, spitting in the face of all duties and responsibilities. But somehow he knew he'd already taken the decision; the hard part was telling everyone else.

Jane saw more than the earl realized as they took the chilly journey back to Greenwich. The man was torn between love and duty. Well, there was something she could do about that. The accident had changed everything: Ellie clearly needed Will far more than she did. He would carry on without the Perceval money, whereas it was by no means clear her friend would survive without him. As for herself, suitors were never difficult to find. How had she ever thought she could happily marry into a family where her friend loved her husband and she loved his brother?

She looked down with longing at James's hand resting on the bench next to hers. It sounded so ugly when put like that, but it was the unvarnished truth. Like some fiendishly complicated play, all the lovers were mixed up, and if she did not do something to untangle the knot, it was not going to end well.

But her father would not be pleased. She closed her eyes,

wincing at the remembered pain of beatings that he called discipline when she was a few years younger. He had always accused her of having an unfeminine spirit, too stubborn for her own good; too much like him, if the truth be told. She prayed her age would spare her now, for he was bound to think some wicked spirit had entered her when she point-blank refused to wed an earl.

I need to summon the bitter harridan who poured scorn on men, she thought ruefully, remembering her feelings when she arrived at court, before she met Ellie and James. *That Jane would get through this and snap her fingers at them all for their disapproval.*

The boat slipped into its moorings at the landing stage. James helped her ashore and the earl took her arm to escort her back to her rooms.

"My lord, might I have a word in private?" Jane asked haughtily. She couldn't do this in front of James—that was too much to demand of herself.

The earl looked taken aback by her tone but waved his brother to stand aloof. "Of course, my lady."

She waited until James was out of earshot. "It has come to my attention during our excursion that we will not suit." There, she had said it.

"What do you mean?" The earl drew back, letting her hand fall.

You are in love with my friend. No, she couldn't say that. "I wish to be released from this betrothal." No explanations—hard and unfeeling, that is what she had to be.

The earl ran his hand through his hair. "But the Queen—your father?"

"You do not want this match, sir, and neither do I."

He took a step towards her, dropping his voice. "Is this about what your brother said? Madam, I assure you that the lady and I have never been . . . were never . . ."

She held up a hand to stop him. "I have no wish to hear your excuses, sir. I wish to go my own way and leave you to yours."

She could see that he was drawing the conclusion that she thought ill of both him and Ellie when nothing could be further from the truth—she'd never liked either of them more than at that moment. That was why she had to let him think that.

"I have severe doubts about your moral character, sir. Your heart plays me false." That much was true.

The earl looked lost for words. He was in the position of trying to defend a match he did not want but thought he needed—hard to be sincere when everything was screaming for him to take the escape she offered.

"I bid you good day. I do not expect to see you again, my lord." *Take the hint, Dorset,* she silently urged him, holding herself rigid.

"You mean it?"

"I am immoveable, sir. Fortunately the betrothal papers have not yet been signed, so it is not too late to refuse your offer."

If her heart had not been so heavy with dread, she would have been tempted to laugh at the mixture of relief and chagrin on his face. He gave her a formal bow.

"I must admit to being confused at this sudden reversal, my lady, but I will take my dismissal if that is your wish."

"It is."

He backed away, nearly stumbling over the stone edging to the path. "Please forgive any distress I have caused you. I have always treated both you and the Lady Eleanor with the utmost respect and propriety."

And I am the fourth horseman of the Apocalypse, mused Jane, not believing for one moment that propriety had anything to do with his relationship with poor Ellie.

Giving her a final puzzled look, he turned and went in search of James.

Jane squeezed her hands together. She'd done the right thing, she was sure of that. Now all that remained was to convince her father.

Old Lord Fortescue ambled by on his equally ancient gelding, attended by a pair of smart grooms. In his seventies, a veteran of four marriages but with no surviving children, he was known to be on the prowl for a fifth wife. He touched his cap with his whip on seeing her standing there alone. She dipped a curtsy and forced a sweet smile. It appeared that her original plan was back on the table.

CHAPTER 22

THE JOURNEY TO SNOWSLIP, home of Ellie's uncle Paul in Gloucestershire, took a week and most of her remaining money as she had to spend it on hired horses and guides to take her through the unfamiliar countryside. The roads were worse than abysmal, passable only because it was summer and relatively dry; at other times of the year, the little village must be cut off from the world. Her journey had led her through Oxford, where she had not even stayed a night, as thoughts of her father were too painful, then out into the Vale of Evesham, a pretty spot of fruit trees and woodlands bordered by gentle hills. Now, arriving at the top of the valley in which Snowslip nestled, she was looking down on the roof of her uncle's manor house, a gentleman farmer's residence, tiled in local dark-gray slate and surrounded by working buildings, a dovecot, a barn and stables. Sheep grazed the tidy fields. In the corner of one pasture bordering a copse, two men were weaving hazel twigs to make a hurdle, their tunics hanging on a low branch of an elm tree as they worked in their shirtsleeves.

"This is the place?" she asked her guide, an old man she'd hired in Chipping Norton. Harding had been a good choice, friendly and reliable, but Ellie was well aware she should've at least taken a maid to accompany her. The truth was she had not been able to afford the luxury of respectability.

"Aye, lady, this is your uncle's farm. He'll be about the place—a hardworking man is Master Hutton, if a little narrow." The guide gave her a toothy grin, his white eyebrows twitching with a life of their own.

She smiled back. "Good. Then I'll call at the house and ask for him." By saying it out loud, Ellie prevented herself from making an ignoble flight. She had come this far; she couldn't turn back now.

"This way then, my lady. If you're sure."

Sure? Of course she wasn't sure! "Thank you, Harding."

Harding waited in the stable yard with the horses while Ellie went to the house to inquire if the family were at home. She wished she could stay with him, sitting in a patch of sunshine and chewing on a straw.

The old black oak door looked ancient, studded with nails that formed the letter "H" and a knocker in the shape of a fox. Taking a deep breath, she raised it and thumped twice. After only a moment's wait, a woman opened it to her—a maid, by the look of her sober gray garb and close-fitting coif. Ellie brushed her travel-stained gown nervously. Mud flecks showed up against the black cloth of the borrowed finery.

"Yes, mistress?" the woman asked quietly, showing neither suspicion nor recognition. Had her letter not arrived? Ellie wondered.

"I'm Eleanor Hutton," she blurted out.

The woman stood back. "Then you'd better come in."

"You were expecting me?" Ellie stepped into the cool passageway, the flagstones worn with age.

"We got your letter." She gestured to Ellie to proceed into the kitchen. This proved to be a tall, vaulted chamber, a remnant of the medieval great hall, the oldest part of the manor. A vast fireplace took up one wall, but only a small fire glowed at its center, enough to heat water but not the room. A bowl of summer salad sat on the scrubbed table, a batch of bread cooling under a cloth by the window. Everything was neat and plain.

"Are you thirsty?" the woman asked.

"Yes, yes, I am. Oh, and I left my guide in the stable yard."

"The boys will see to him." The woman poured Ellie a cup of water. "From our spring—it's quite fresh."

Ellie sipped and watched as the woman placed a plate of bread and salad before her.

"Eat."

"Thank you." Ellie picked up her spoon and knife. "Is my uncle or my aunt here?"

The woman turned from the fire, which she had been poking with a twig. "I'm your aunt, Eleanor. Aunt Hepzibah."

"Oh." Ellie got to her feet. "I apologize." She bobbed a curtsy, flustered at her mistake. "*Madre de Dios*. I didn't realize."

Aunt Hepzibah's eyes narrowed. "What did you say?"

Ellie swallowed. "I . . . I said that I ask your forgiveness for not recognizing you. I . . . I can't remember meeting you when I was little, and I thought . . . I don't know what I thought." She stared miserably down at her meal. The little flowers decorating the salad were the only cheerful things in the room.

"No, that foreign tongue you spoke—what did you say?"

Ellie ran through her words, only then remembering that she

had used one of her mother's favorite expressions, a habit when she was anxious.

"I said '*Madre de Dios.*'"

Aunt Hepzibah was ominously silent, obviously expecting more explanation.

"A Spanish phrase my mother taught me. It means 'mother of God.'"

Her aunt's eyebrows winged up to disappear under the low edge of her coif. "You take the Lord's name in vain?"

Had she? "I pray you forgive me. I had not considered it in that light."

"Be your word Yea, yea; Nay, nay. For whatsoever is more than that, cometh of evil!" thundered Aunt Hepzibah. She took the plate away from Ellie and switched the cup of water for one of brine out of the pickling barrel. "Wash your mouth out and pray to God to have mercy on your wicked tongue."

Ellie was astounded by the sudden change in this quiet woman, going from hospitable to hostile in a twinkling.

"I'm truly sorry for any offense I've given you."

"It's not a sin against me, girl, but against thy Maker!" She pushed the cup nearer. "Wash out your vile words."

A little afraid of the woman's temper, Ellie stood and went to the basin by the window. Hepzibah watched every move, as if expecting her to sprout horns and a tail at any moment. Realizing she would get no further in her introduction to the family unless she did this, Ellie took a cautious sip. It was beyond foul—the salt burning her tongue and throat. Quickly she spat it out.

"Again!"

Ellie wanted to ask why but instead did as she was bidden.

"I never want to hear such terrible words from you again, niece."

Ellie looked about her for the cup of water and took a step towards it.

"No!" Aunt Hepzibah blocked her path. "The lesson lasts as long as the taste, the better to remind you of your sinfulness."

Ellie sat back down. The woman was quite possibly mad—certainly strict beyond all reason. To punish a stranger within moments of meeting her for an unintentional misjudgment—it was too odd. Ellie could only hope her uncle was more reasonable.

Silence reigned in the kitchen as Hepzibah went about her tasks. Ellie wondered how long it would be until her uncle returned but dared not ask in case it sparked her aunt's temper again. The shadows were lengthening by the time she heard footsteps in the passageway—more than one person was approaching. Her aunt stood up straight, her hands folded demurely in front of her, waiting. The door opened and five people came into the room—an older man and four young ones aged somewhere between fifteen and twenty-five, all sharing the dark brown hair and stocky frame of their father. Ellie recognized two of them—tunics now replaced, they had been the laborers making the hurdles. She got to her feet, preparing herself for any manner of reception.

"This her?" the older man asked Aunt Hepzibah, nodding to Ellie.

"Aye, Husband." Hepzibah had reverted to her mouselike ways again.

"Niece, I dismissed your man. He's taken the horses back to Chipping Norton. You had paid for his services already." This was a statement, not a question.

"Yes, sir." Ellie wondered at the lack of greeting.

"Where is your maid?"

"I don't have one, sir." Was his rudeness intentional? He should at least introduce himself and his boys before beginning his interrogation.

"You traveled alone—from London?"

Ellie would be damned if she would justify herself to him. "As you see, sir."

The disapproval was almost tangible. She didn't need to look up to know that she was the focus of six pairs of scandalized eyes.

"Your father is dead?"

"Yes, sir." Ellie knotted her fingers together, praying that she would not weep in front of them.

"How?"

Ellie had explained the accident in her letter. Why was he asking her to rehearse it again if not to cause her pain?

"He died in an explosion while in the Queen's service."

"You've buried him already? He's only been dead these seven days."

Ellie looked out the window. A dove perched on the tiles of the gatehouse, cooing softly. "There was no body—it was lost in the Thames."

"So you came here—penniless and in disgrace."

She flicked her gaze back to him in shock. "Disgrace?"

"You—a young woman of what, eighteen?—have traveled alone for many days. You have not a shred of reputation left, girl."

"I'm sixteen."

"What?"

"I'm sixteen, sir."

"Old enough to know what you were doing was wrong. I can see you are as wrongheaded as my benighted brother."

Ellie had had enough. Whatever she had expected from her blood relations, it had not been this. She headed for the door.

"Where are you going, Eleanor?" barked her uncle. "I haven't finished talking to you."

She walked out into the yard, pushing blindly through the garden gate, and kept on going. She had no horse, no money, no plan—nothing but the desire to get away from these people.

Bees buzzed in the lavender spilling over the little path. She stepped over the border and continued on into the orchard. It provided some refuge, the tree canopy hiding the house and giving her somewhere to sit while she let her temper subside. That had been rash—to leave the room like that, no doubt inflaming her uncle's ire against her. She dropped her head on her knees, knowing that she would have to go back eventually and apologize. Next time she would be stronger; next time she would dig deeper and find that patience that had helped her survive all those years with her father.

Boots thumped on the grass beside her. Four pairs of feet ringed her.

"Cousin Eleanor?"

Reluctantly she looked up, shading her eyes against the slanting rays of the sun. One of the boys had spoken to her, the eldest, she guessed, as he stood in the middle, the natural leader of the quartet.

"Yes, Cousin?"

"We've been sent to fetch you."

"I see."

She took the offered hand and let him pull her to her feet.

"I'm Josiah, and this is Aaron, Titus and Zechariah."

She dipped a shallow curtsy. "Pleased to meet you."

Aaron, the thin-faced one with shrewd eyes, examined her impertinently. "Are you really a Catholic, Cousin?"

She guessed her aunt had been jumping to conclusions about her. "No, but my mother was."

"Are you a harlot?" asked Titus, seeming rather hopeful that she would answer in the affirmative. The question earned him a cuff from his oldest brother.

"No, I'm not," she replied stiffly.

"Father says you are."

"Then he'd be wrong."

"He's never wrong."

"Really? Then he must be perfect—and I thought only God was perfect."

That gave them something to think about.

"I don't think she is a Catholic or a harlot," said the last brother, Zechariah. He had the kindest face of them all, his eyes sparkled with humor lacking in the others. "I think she's just lost."

"Lost?" scoffed Josiah.

"Aye, a lost sheep." Zechariah held out his hand to her. "Come, Cousin, you've traveled far and must be tired."

"I am. Thank you."

"Say nothing around Father, be polite to Mother and you'll be all right, Cousin Eleanor."

"Ellie."

He shook his head. "Best not admit to that. Mother is already complaining that your name does not appear in the scriptures.

You would do better not to give her more ammunition to use against you."

"Is this a battle then?"

"Aye, a spiritual one that we fight each day. Any sign of weakness and the Devil will seize on it."

"And my name is a weakness?"

He paused at the threshold. "The lost sheep strayed through sin and willfulness, Eleanor. The family will expect true contrition if you are to remain with us."

So even Zechariah thought her a wretched creature, but was merely kinder than the rest.

"And what sins have I committed, Cousin?"

"You've been of the world and not held yourself apart as a true believer would, you cannot deny that."

"No, no, I don't, but neither have I heard of such a teaching before."

He smiled and patted her hand. "Then you have sinned in ignorance; there is hope for you. I'll tell Father."

Having mumbled an apology to her aunt and uncle for leaving so abruptly, Ellie was relieved that they did not press the matter. Hepzibah showed her to her room, saying that there would be no food for her that night so that she might fast and think on her sinfulness. Ellie closed the door to her chamber and put her small bag of necessaries on the narrow bed, grateful to be left alone. It was hard to know what was worst: her aunt's swings of temper, her uncle's blast of condemnation or Zechariah's mild-mannered conviction that she numbered among those who had strayed from righteousness.

•❁•

Ellie rose at dawn, hearing the family already about their business in the kitchen. A new day—perhaps she would be given a second chance? Brushing her hair and braiding it loosely, she went down the stairs to offer her help in preparing the morning meal. Her appearance in the kitchen was met with silence as the men looked up from their porridge. Her aunt took her arm and hurried her back to her room.

"You never," her aunt said tersely, "show your face in company with your hair about your ears. Only the wicked flaunt their charms. Do you not possess a coif like a decent woman?"

Ellie bit back a response that the Queen herself made much of her splendid red hair. "No, Aunt. Only a velvet hat."

"Then I will lend you one of mine."

With much tugging and muttering, Hepzibah hid every single strand of Ellie's hair under an ugly linen coif.

"Your dress is decent, but too fine for ordinary days. You may wear an old kirtle of mine."

Ellie feared she would say that. Her aunt was a head taller than her and twice her girth. The kirtle would swamp her. But if it bought her peace, the price of looking foolish was worth paying.

"Now you may go to the kitchen," her aunt said, nodding in approval at her transformed appearance.

After breakfast, the family met for prayers. Uncle Paul beseeched the Lord long and hard for the poor sinner who had been sent to them. Ellie pretended that it wasn't her he was referring to; the God she worshipped was very different from his—loving, merciful and understanding. Her Jesus suffered the children to come to him and made friends with Mary and Martha.

"Oh Lord, I wrestle with the Devil to win her soul for you." Uncle Paul held up his hands in mock battle with the air, face screwed up in concentration. "Help her to escape his wiles and return to the true path. May she renounce all female vanities, speak only of righteous things and bewail her manifold sins." Uncle Paul was sweating now, the droplets running down his cheeks into his beard. His words were met with "amens" and noises of agreement from the rest of the family. If she hadn't been so appalled, Ellie might have been impressed by their fervor. She closed her eyes, determined not to peek again, but suddenly, hands grasped her shoulders, making her squeak with alarm. Her uncle had grabbed her.

"Yea, Lord, the demons within her have her soul in their grasp. They cry out, turning from the true light. I cast them out in the name of Jesus Christ, our savior!" He rocked her violently to and fro before pushing her from her knees to the floor by the hearth. "See, she has been emptied of all corruption! She faints before the light of God! Hallelujah!"

"Hallelujah!" echoed his sons and wife.

Ellie got back to her knees, spitting out the mouthful of ash that she had picked up from the floor.

"Child, praise the Lord for your deliverance!" her uncle cried.

Ellie wanted only to be delivered from this madness. Doubtless they were sincere in their prayers, but they had left her far behind with their theatrics, spoiling any chance she might have had to say her own genuine words to God. But they were waiting for her to speak. She gathered herself and bowed her head.

"Padre, perdónanos nuestros pecados." Father, forgive us our trespasses.

"She's gibbering again!" Aunt Hepzibah exclaimed. "You must beat the Devil from her, Husband. She truly is possessed!"

Ellie raised weary eyes to her family. "No, mistress, it's not nonsense. I repeat the Lord's Prayer in Spanish as my mother taught me. I pray often in her tongue, as it was the first I learnt and comes most naturally to me."

"But Spanish is a Catholic language! Pray in good plain English like a decent Christian girl."

The objection was ridiculous—as if the Lord's Prayer could be sullied by being in another tongue!

"Very well." Ellie repeated the prayer in English, hoping this would satisfy them.

"I think you'd best beat her to be sure," said Josiah maliciously. "There is something very wrong about her."

"She's too bold—she tempts a man with her smiles and her hair," added Titus, pointing to the lock that had fallen from beneath her coif as a result of her being thrown to the floor by her uncle.

"You didn't spare the rod with us," Aaron argued. "And look how we turned out."

Uncle Paul rocked on the balls of his feet, eyeing the birch cane that hung by the back door. "I will think on't. My brother escaped chastisement, being the eldest and favorite of our parents, and so went on to steal from the family; mayhap his daughter is going the same way."

Ellie did not feel so much like a lost sheep now but a fox cub among a pack of hungry hounds. "My father did not steal."

"Are you accusing me of lying?" howled her uncle.

There was no safe answer to be given to that question.

"He mortgaged the land from under my nose—I'm still paying his debt. We lost our house in Gloucester thanks to him. He died without male heirs so it should have come to me and then Josiah; instead, some merchant bought it from him and has turned it into a shop!"

What could she say? She knew her father had been reckless, but it was not quite the same as stealing, surely?

"We offer you charity, opening our house to you, and you repay us by accusing us of falsehood and muttering Catholic curses under your breath!"

"They aren't curses."

"Go to your room. Read and ponder the scriptures for the morning, in particular the Gospel of Luke, chapter eleven, the six woes. If you pass my testing at noon, then you may escape the rod. Fail and you will be beaten to break your stubborn spirit." He handed her the family Bible. "Mark not a page; this book is worth more than your life. Many brave men died to bring you the scriptures in English for our instruction and salvation."

"I thought to help my aunt with the household tasks."

Her uncle stabbed his finger at the leather-bound book. "Your task is here. There is no work more important than that of a sinner's salvation."

On his return from Greenwich, Will couldn't bring himself to announce that the betrothal had been broken off. When his mother asked, he had merely muttered something about problems with the settlement. Will knew how much they all relied on him to save the family finances, so he was too embarrassed to admit he had lost the lady because she'd caught him hankering after another. What would his family say when he added to his failings by admitting he was contemplating marrying a girl without a penny to her name? James for one might never forgive him. Having received confirmation from the Tower Warder that Ellie had been taken in by her uncle, Will decided to give Ellie a chance to try a new life before going after her—it was only fair to both families. Then he would go and just check on her. If she seemed happy with her relatives, he would return home, announce that the alliance with Lady Jane was over and find a new rich bride to court, as his family would expect.

Waiting to see the harvest under way on his estate, it was late August by the time Will was free. He didn't tell anyone what he was about and took only Turville with him when he left for Gloucestershire. In his opinion, the less people knew about the mess he had made of his love life the better; he certainly didn't want the whole household speculating about it in his absence—there was enough talk already.

Will had not been alone with his old servant since the man's marriage to Nell Rivers. The long miles gave a natural opportunity for the subject to come up, but Turville spoke nothing of his new wife, seeming rather relieved to have the freedom to travel with his master.

"I trust you left your wife well?" asked Will.

"Well enough," Turville allowed, then gave him a flicker of a smile. "She's with child."

"So soon? Congratulations!"

"Aye, I'll be a father. The prospect fair terrifies me."

"You've been like a father to me and my brothers all these years, Turville—you have plenty of experience."

Turville was touched by Will's assertion. "Thank you, sir. You're fine boys, all of you, though I shouldn't call you boys now."

"And your wife likes it at Lacey Hall? I imagine it is quite a change for her, after serving the Lady Jane."

"She is . . . content," Turville managed, his cool tone betraying a deep chasm of doubt over which he tiptoed each day. "When you marry her old mistress and things look up for the estate, I think then she'll be truly happy."

"Ah." Will pondered taking Turville into his confidence. He'd find out sooner or later. "There's been a change in that particular plan. Lady Jane decided we wouldn't suit after all. The betrothal is not going ahead."

"What!" Turville looked quite dumbfounded. "But the dowry—the estate!" Will gave him a glance that effectively dried up his protests. There was only so much leeway he could allow even an old and trusted servant. "Of course, my lord. My Nell will be sorry to hear this, but we'll manage."

They rode into the village of Snowslip late on Saturday, finding poor accommodation in the local inn. The place seemed very quiet for a fine summer's evening—no one playing bowls on the green or sharing a patch of sunlight on the bench by the well. The men gathered in the taproom below spoke in sober tones, limiting themselves to only one tankard of indifferent ale. Will tucked in to his lamb pie, expecting any moment someone to call for news or ask their business, but to his surprise they kept themselves to themselves, showing no interest in the finely dressed gentleman and servant who had arrived at the hostelry.

"Very odd," he muttered to Turville.

"Aye, unnatural," agreed the steward.

"Landlord!" called Will, summoning their host. "Tell me, what's happening? The village is very quiet. Is there a fair nearby?"

The innkeeper, a small fellow with neat square hands and cropped silver hair, darted out from behind the bar. "No, sir, 'tis always thus. Can I get you anything else? We retire early before the Sabbath in these parts."

Will ignored the hint. "So where are the youngsters, the boys and girls?" He'd hoped for a glimpse of Ellie before he turned in for the night.

"At home, where they should be. We are a private people, sir, not given to drunkenness or debauchery as others are. Our choice, as the elect of God, is to live apart from the world, saving your presence, sir."

Will guessed he had just been consigned to the Devil. "Does everyone in Snowslip live in seclusion?"

The host's eyes flickered to the other men in the taproom. They had fallen silent and made no attempt to hide the fact that they were listening.

"We are peaceful and loyal men, sir," the host said warily. "We pay our taxes, attend church as we should."

Will frowned and pushed his chair back. "I never thought otherwise. I was merely wondering if all in your community followed your practices."

The innkeeper wrung out the cloth he was holding. "Aye, we're all part of the reformed church in this village, thanks be to God and Her Majesty."

"I seek a gentleman called Paul Hutton—is he one of you?"

Beside him, Turville took a sharp breath at the name.

The man's eyes widened in surprise. "Aye, that he is—an elder of our community. What have you to do with him?"

Will gave an easy smile. "That's between him and me, is it not? Thank you for your information. I wonder, would you have a boy available to take me to his house on the morrow?"

"No need of that. He'll be at matins." The host gestured to the stumpy-towered church on the far side of the green. "You can find him there yourself."

Turville waited until they reached their room on the first floor before letting out his barrage of questions.

"Hutton! What's he to us? The old fool died in the Thames, they said—why are you seeking others of that name?"

"Turville," Will said, his tone reproving.

"Sorry, my lord, but I can't believe . . . No, surely you have not . . ." Turville was putting the pieces together for himself. "Is this about the Spanish chit?"

"Lady Eleanor," corrected Will. "And yes, this is about her."

"We've traveled halfway across the country so you can dally with her?"

Will threw his boot at Turville. "I'm not here to dally—I'm here to find out if she's safe. If she's happy with her family, we'll leave."

"And if she's not?"

That was the question, wasn't it? Will chucked Turville the other boot for him to clean, then slid between the cold sheets, giving no reply.

CHAPTER 23

WILL POSITIONED HIMSELF AT THE BACK of the village church early so he could watch the parishioners file in. The vicar, a big man with a military bearing, greeted him briefly, but it was plain that he was not happy to find an outsider in his last pew. God's soldier in the fight against sin, he probably suspected the government had sent Will to check on the religious teaching in this community that held itself apart—on the hunt for signs of fanaticism. If Will had been there to spy, he would have reported that the minister's grip on the congregation was stern in its discipline. The interior of the church had been stripped of all but the effigies on the tombs, and even they had been defaced. The old paintwork had been covered with whitewash, the hangings long gone, only the hooks remaining, and the windows filled with plain glass. It left the worshipper awed but cold, pegged out before the judgment of God with nothing to hide behind.

As the hour for morning service approached, Will noted that the congregation assembled dressed in similar clothes of drab hues. The women wore coifs that clung close to their faces; the men carried felt hats. Their collars gave the merest nod to a frilled edging, a far cry from the elaborate ruffs in fashion at court. Sitting in his dark-green velvet doublet and cloak, Will felt increasingly conspicuous, a colorful drake among these humble ducks.

A minute to the hour, the last family arrived. At the head strode a capable looking man of medium height, heading for the front pew, the position of honor. He was followed by his gray-clad wife and four sons. Bringing up the rear was a small figure, struggling with a gown that was overlong and a coif that flopped in her eyes. A tendril of curly black hair had escaped to snake down her back. Ellie. Will almost laughed—she looked as out of place as he did among these serious citizens. Comforted by the sight of her after all these months, he sat back, prepared to pass the time during the sermon with pleasant thoughts anticipating her reaction when she saw him there.

But it was not to be. After an opening prayer making much of the purity of these people compared to the sinful inhabitants beyond the village boundary who approved of religious vestments and other works of the Evil One, the minister drew out a book. The congregation held itself in readiness.

"And now I will read out the penalties incurred during this week and the appropriate punishment given by the vestry court. Master Joseph Buntwell, for laughing at Widow Heron, six lashes and an hour at the village well drawing the water for the goodwives. Mistress Miriam Smith, for calling her neighbor a rude name, six lashes, to be administered by her husband."

A man towards the rear of the church raised his hand and was bidden to stand. "'Tis done already, Minister."

The vicar nodded and made a note in his book. "Eleanor Hutton . . . oh dear, oh dear." The congregation drew a collective breath. "I fear the list is very long this week, worse than last if that is possible. Singing on the Sabbath; falling asleep during prayers; walking alone without permission; rudeness to her guardians; unseemly dress; and something which most concerns me, speaking in strange tongues when she has been forbidden to use anything but English." The minister paused dramatically. "Rise, girl."

Ellie got to her feet, stumbling slightly as her shoe caught the hem of her skirt. Will stared at her in growing horror. Now he could see her in profile, he realized that she was painfully thin, her eyes ringed by dark circles, her hands cradled to her chest as if nursing them after blows.

"What have you to say for yourself, child? Your aunt and uncle have taken you in from the goodness of their hearts and you repay them with a stubborn spirit?"

She hung her head. Where was his Ellie with the pert replies and mischievous smile?

"We in the vestry ask ourselves if there is not something more at work in this girl." The minister turned to the congregation. "Her uncle claims she resisted when he tried to drive a demon from her. Have any of you more evidence that the girl is given over to the Evil One?"

A young man got to his feet. "I spoke to her last Wednesday at the stile near her uncle's manor. She attacked me—slapped my face and ran off." He pointed to a small cut under his eye. "I feared then that all was not well with her."

The minister frowned. "And why did you not report this to me?"

The man shuffled his feet, clearly hiding something. With a swell of outrage, Will suspected that his explanation was missing some pertinent details, such as what he meant by "speaking" to Ellie. Trying to kiss her, more like.

"I was not willing to bring the maid into more trouble," he offered.

"Kindness does her no favors, Master Miller." The minister waved to him to resume his seat. "Does anyone else wish to speak?"

Will wondered why Ellie was not saying something in her own defense. Her eyes were riveted to the floor, her manner distant as if she had put herself far away from this place, deep in her own mind where no one could reach her.

The minister addressed himself portentously to Ellie again. "You've been here two months, Eleanor Hutton, and we still look for signs of improvement in you. Instead all we get is continued proof of your rebellion. We have been pushed beyond all patience—our prayers have not been answered, which is proof if any needed it that sin has hardened your heart against the influence of goodness. Beatings and punishments have no influence on you."

Beatings! Will got to his feet.

"Yes, sir?" The minister glared at him for his interruption.

"You have beaten the Lady Eleanor?" Will demanded, his hand dropping to his riding crop.

Ellie's head jerked up. He saw her mouthing his name in disbelief.

"What is it to you, sir? And who are you to interfere with the proceedings of the vestry court?"

Enough was enough. He didn't need to talk to Ellie to know that she had to be miserable in this place, bullied for not fitting in with this gaggle of narrow-minded Puritans. They'd beaten her, for the love of God! Will pushed past the others in his row and strode down the aisle to stand next to Ellie's pew.

"Who am I? I am William Lacey, Earl of Dorset, Baron

Hancliffe, Sheriff of Berkshire—is that enough for you? And this lady is mine—you will not lay another finger on her." He held out his hand. "Come, love, let us leave these madmen to their twisted proceedings."

Looking frightened, Ellie took a hesitant step towards him, but then her uncle and his four sons rose to block her path.

"Eleanor, on peril of your immortal soul, you will not go with this man!" declared Uncle Paul. "Your ruin and eternal damnation will be complete if you move an inch."

Will gave the man a smile that was all teeth. "Come, come, sir, is marriage to me all that bad?" He heard Ellie gasp. He'd meant to propose in a more romantic setting, but his practical little Ellie would have to admit it was the expedient thing to do facing a hostile congregation.

"Marry my niece! I forbid it!" spluttered Uncle Paul.

That threat gave Will pause. Ellie was underage. It was quite possible that Hutton did have the official guardianship of her. But then he doubted that the farmer had thought to make a proper application to that end. How would a minor gentleman's objections stand against the wishes of an earl?

"The Queen herself will be the one to sanction this match, not you, sir," Will declared with more confidence than he felt. "Let the lady pass."

Ellie clenched her fingers together, ignoring the pain from the last chastisement. Would her uncle step back? Whatever the outcome—and she didn't really believe the offer of marriage would stand, not with Will already being betrothed—she couldn't stay here after this scene. She'd already plotted her departure, as every week her punishments were getting more and more severe. She had become the scapegoat for the community's sins: if a young man accosted her in a lane, thinking her by reputation a loose woman, she got the blame; when her cousin Josiah begged her to sing a hymn she was scolded, just as he had intended. To be called "love" by a nobleman in front of the entire village would probably result in her spending a week in the stocks.

But her uncle and cousins were not moving. Will shifted so he could meet her gaze around their backs; his eyes, the color of a May morning, dared her to defy them all.

"I fear your kinsfolk lack manners, my lady. Are you ready?"

Weeks of fear, months of humiliation, melted away in the warmth of his expression.

"A moment, sir." Bobbing a pert curtsy to her aunt, she picked up her skirts and hopped up on the pew. The congregation gaped at her in shock—never before had such antics been seen at the solemn Sabbath service. Undaunted, Ellie climbed onto the back of the seat and forced her way through the people behind, using their shoulders to steady herself. Stepping lightly from pew to pew, she made her way through the congregation before any gathered their wits to stop her. Will kept level with her progress down the main aisle, keeping her uncle and sons at bay with the threat of his riding crop. Reaching an empty bench at the rear, Ellie leapt down and ran to him.

"Ready now."

Grinning, he put his arm around her waist and spun her once. Waving his whip at the congregation he called: "Pray carry on with the service. We're done here."

The verger got quickly out of the way as Will pushed open the church door, towing Ellie out into the sunshine. She stumbled, feet catching on her hateful skirt that her aunt had not even allowed her to alter for her height, saying she didn't want her old kirtle ruined.

"'Swounds, Ellie, that's an ugly dress." Will picked her up, carrying her swiftly to the inn where his horse and Turville waited.

"I know. It's my aunt's." She grimaced.

"Say no more. Whatever were you doing with these people? They are all quite mad!"

Ellie laughed softly, drunk with happiness like a prisoner released early from jail. "I'm glad you think so. I was beginning to think that I must be the insane one, as they all agreed on how bad I am."

Will kissed her nose. "If you are bad, then the rest of us are doomed."

Turville narrowed his eyes when Will hurried into the stable yard carrying her. Ellie shrank against Will's chest, knowing that the steward hated her perhaps as much as her family.

"Saddle Barbary, Turville," ordered Will. "I predict we have about five minutes' worth of prayers and deliberation before they come after us."

"Aye, my lord."

"Do you have anything you would like to fetch from your uncle's?" Will asked her.

Ellie shook her head. "No, I cannot risk it. I came with very little."

"Excellent. Then let us shake the dust off our feet and leave this place as fast as possible." He plucked the horrible coif from her head and let it drop to the ground. "You'll ride with me?"

Ellie smiled, remembering their first ride on Barbary together. "Yes, my lord, gladly."

"Then let us go quickly before they gather their wits to wonder what an earl is doing with only one servant. I have no time to spare for the hours it would take to convince them of my claims."

Mounted on Barbary, her arms round Will's waist and her face buried in his back, Ellie felt a surge of pure happiness. She could not bring herself to care what the future held—the recent past had been so wretched. She no longer blamed her father for severing all ties with his family: they were a vile bunch, so holier-than-thou it had made her want to scream. She was immoral for having hair that refused to be tamed? Well, what about Titus groping her in the stable whenever he had a chance? Her prayers were unsuitable for God's ears because they were in Spanish? Then how could He bear to listen to Uncle Paul prosing on about the sinful merchants in Chipping Norton who had the temerity to bargain for a better price for his wool?

But Uncle Paul had achieved one thing she had not thought possible: he'd made her seriously miss her father's alchemy. His obsession for gold seemed not nearly as bad as his brother's fixation with godliness. Her father had never condemned the world for failing to live up to an unattainable level of perfection; he at least had died trying to serve his country, rather than consign it to the Devil.

"All right, my love?" Will asked, once they crested the hill and could look back down on the roof of the manor.

"Yes."

"No regrets?"

"Oh no."

"I'm afraid to say this, but your family is a disaster. You are the only decent one among them."

"Pray forgive me for my foolishness for having been born a Hutton," she said wryly.

He patted her hand, the only part of her he could reach, seated as they were. "I have a cure for that."

"Oh yes, my lord? Let me guess: you're going to turn back time and have me born elsewhere?"

"No, love, I'm going to change your name for you. As soon as I can persuade the Queen to grant me permission. Until then, I'm taking you home to my mother and will let her sort you out and teach you how to be a good Lacey wife."

She smiled. It was a lovely dream—and going to his family would be preferable to staying a moment longer with hers. But as for marriage—that was too much for her to expect.

"So, what do you think of my plan?"

"Splendid, my lord."

"Excellent. Carry on flattering me like that and I think you'll make the perfect wife, my lady."

Will was not expecting his homecoming to be pleasant. He had not said anything to Ellie—there was no point, as she could not change things—but when he rode up to the door with a waif-bride mounted pillion, he could tell that his family were somewhat perplexed. James was more than confused: he was furious. He stamped down the steps and stood by the mounting block, hands on hips, glaring up at his brother.

"Where did you find her?" he asked rudely. "I thought she'd gone to family."

Diego ran out of the stable to help Ellie descend. Her legs almost folded beneath her, as they had made long hours in the saddle with only one night's stop on the way. Will swung his leg over Barbary's flank and slid to the ground.

"She had. But that was not an acceptable arrangement."

"And what arrangement, pray, is this?" sneered James. "Do you think to insult your bride-to-be by bringing a paramour into the house? And what of our mother and sister? How are they to greet her?"

Will bit his cheek to prevent himself lashing out at his brother. James did not know the full story. Of course, this looked bad unless he had all the pieces of the picture.

"The Lady Eleanor is the only bride-to-be, Jamie. I ask you to treat her with courtesy."

"What about Jane?" James seized his brother by the shoulders, drawing him to his chest, hissing the words in his face. "Or have you forgotten her so easily because this girl bewitches you?"

Will squeezed his brother's wrists, putting pressure on so he had to let go.

"You forget yourself, James. I do not owe you an explanation, even though I had fully intended to give you one. My study in an hour." With that, he turned his back on his brother and offered his hand to a very quiet Ellie. "Come, love, you must be tired after our journey. I will ask my mother to attend you."

The countess did not question her son's actions before the servants watching the drama in the yard; she merely smiled at Ellie and led her towards her old room.

"Mother, if you would be so kind as to attend me in my study too," Will said with formal politeness. "I have something I wish to say to you."

The countess dipped her head, appearing the model of ladylike behavior. She waited until they were up the stairs and out of sight before peppering Ellie with questions. Where had Will found her? How was she after the loss of her father? Where was her baggage?

Why was she so thin? Ellie answered as best she could but all the while conscious of her fragile position in the household. She hated being the cause of a division between the brothers and feared the lady must resent her heartily.

"Lady Dorset, please believe me when I say that I do not mean to harm anyone in your family."

The countess shook her head and tutted as she helped her out of the horrid gray gown. "I know, my dear. Come, let me find you something to wear. This is fit only for the ragbag."

Ellie didn't think her aunt would like that, but then, her aunt had no more in common with the countess than a sheep with a thoroughbred palfrey.

"I will ask the servants to bring you something to eat in your chamber and water for a bath. If I know my son, he has barely stopped all day and you must be very tired."

Ellie thanked her, watching with something like wonder as the maids bustled around her, doing the tasks she was so used to performing herself. The hipbath was full and scented with oil, her meal served; all she had to do now was luxuriate in the hot water and count her blessings without worrying about tomorrow.

If only she could stop thinking about it.

Will paced the study, conscious of James's glare boring between his shoulder blades, but he refused to start his explanation until his mother arrived. She glided into the room and kissed his cheek.

"It is a joy to have you home, my dear," she said. "We were worried when we heard you had ridden off without a word to anyone."

He handed her to a chair. "Thank you, Mother. I couldn't speak before I left because I'd no idea what I would find at my destination."

"The Lady Eleanor?"

"Yes. I had to discover for myself what had happened to her."

James made a rude noise. "You've quite destroyed her, you know, Brother, bringing her back here. Everyone will draw the same conclusion as I as to what she means to you."

"Then everyone would be quite wrong, wouldn't they?" Will snapped back. "I intend to marry her."

The countess took a breath, marshaling her arguments. "You are promised to another, Will."

"No, I'm not. The Lady Jane saw fit to end our betrothal before it even began. She gave me my dismissal at Greenwich."

James jumped to his feet. "So long ago! And you didn't tell me?"

Will shrugged. "What's to tell? That she didn't think me good enough for the Percevals?"

"Is this true?"

"Why would I lie?"

James shook his head, reassessing his assumptions about his brother and the lady. "Why, the cold witch, to let it go so far!"

"James!" scolded his mother. "You cannot know what she was thinking."

"She was thinking that I was not moral enough for her, Mother." Will grimaced and poured three glasses of sherry.

"It's an insult to our family!" declared James. "I could wring her neck!"

Will had hoped his brother would swing to his defense once he knew that he had been jilted, but his vehemence surprised him. It was as if he took it far more personally than Will did.

"It is somewhat of an embarrassment, I suppose." Will sipped his sherry philosophically. "But I've begun to look on it as something of a blessed deliverance. And, besides, I wish to marry Ellie."

His mother turned the stem of her glass carefully in her fingers. "Will, she may have a Spanish title, but she has no dowry."

"I know."

"She's the alchemist's brat," slid in James, quoting Will's own words back at him.

"That's true."

"So why do you have to marry her?" asked his mother. "She's not . . . you know . . ."

Will smiled and shook his head. "No, Mother, you are not going to be a grandmother just yet."

"So why?"

"I love her."

His mother swallowed that unpalatable nugget of information. "I suppose I had guessed as much, but does she love you? How do you know you aren't just her port in the storm, a convenience now she's been left alone in the world?"

"Because she's refused me once, Mother, for my own good, no less. I let her go then, but I won't this time. I haven't called you here to discuss whether or not I'll marry her, just how we'll achieve this."

Will hated condemning his family to an uncertain future just so he could have his heart's choice, but he was not going to change his mind now. He would see them all right. It would take longer, be a struggle, but he would manage somehow. Cecil had mentioned the possibility of investing in a trading company; this year's harvest had been much better than the last; he just needed time and a lot of luck.

And with Ellie to help him, the prospect was not so terrible.

"Very well, my dear, let us think what must be done," his mother said bravely. "We'll need the Queen's permission; our position at court is such that we dare not go against her. And you're still a ward of Burghley; he must be consulted."

Will kissed her hand. "Thank you, Mother. James, are you with us?"

His brother threw back his head and gave a bitter laugh in surrender. "Why not? I wouldn't know what to do with a comfortable life, would I? Let's plan this madness. But I've one question."

"Yes?"

"Who's going to tell Tobias he won't be getting that horse after all?"

Will had not taken Ellie's agreement to his proposal for granted. He knew that once the euphoria of escaping her uncle's family faded, his lady would next think of saving him from himself. She had shown on more than one occasion that her instinct when facing trouble was to flee; this time he was determined she should stay the course and become his wife. Then they could work their way through the rest of the difficulties together.

The footman he had set to watch the corridor outside her room was in place when he finally came upstairs.

"Is the lady within?"

"Aye, my lord, she's not ventured out."

"Thank you. You're dismissed."

The footman bowed and headed for the servants' quarters. Will waited until he was sure the corridor was empty before tapping lightly on the door and slipping inside without waiting for an answer. As he had predicted, Ellie was not sleeping peacefully in her bed but sitting fully dressed in the window, her face resolute.

"Will!" She sprang to her feet. "What are you doing here at this hour?"

"Come to see you, of course." He waited by the door, knowing what was going to come next.

"Then maybe that's for the best. I wanted a private word." She toyed nervously with a pearl brooch on her stomacher.

"Oh yes?" Will plucked a flower from the vase on the bedside table and twirled it in his fingers.

"I . . . I've been thinking."

He smiled grimly. "I notice you do a lot of that."

"Well, yes, that's true. And I decided that this won't do. What about Jane?"

Will grimaced. "What about her? She ended the betrothal, not I."

"Oh, oh dear." Ellie frowned, assimilating that piece of information, putting it aside for later. "But still, I can't ruin your family." She let go of the brooch and brushed a finger over her father's notebook, which lay on the table beside her. "The Huttons have done that once already."

He would let her make all her arguments. "So what do you intend to do once you so nobly abandon me?"

"I . . . I thought that I could learn a trade. Dressmaking, perhaps." She gestured to the sewing kit that he had saved for her along with the other mementos of her old life.

He spluttered with laughter. "Ellie, you can't sew a straight stitch!"

She looked quite offended. "I'll have to learn. There's not much choice for a woman. Knowledge of Latin and Greek is not much in demand."

He moved in closer. "There is something you have that is most eagerly wanted."

She frowned at him, trying to keep her distance. If he put his arms around her, she would be lost. "What is that?"

"*My true love hath my heart, and I have his.* You have my heart, Ellie. You can't leave me to a loveless future—you aren't that cruel." He looped his arm round her waist and tucked the flower in her hair, petals pink against the dark locks.

"But, Will . . . !"

"No, it's no use. I've made up my mind, and my family has agreed. You promised to marry me in Snowslip, so there's no going back on your word. You're already the wife of my heart, so the ceremony is no more than a formality. As for dowry, there is more to life than money. I could be the richest earl in the kingdom and still be miserable."

Ellie wriggled in his embrace, trying to see his expression clearly. "So you want to be poor and miserable instead?"

He kissed her forehead lightly. "Not miserable."

"But when you tire of me and resent me for bringing nothing to this match—"

He placed a finger on her lips. "Hush, love. Have a little more faith in me. I am going into this with open eyes. It is not what I planned, but neither is it the end of the Dorsets' fortunes. We will work our way over the obstacles. My father was rich but lost it all. I'm poor now, but I'm convinced that with hard work and sound investments I can reverse our fate." He rubbed his nose against her cheek. "And I only have a chance of being wise if I have a practical-minded wife at my side."

"Oh, Will."

"Not 'Oh, Will.' I want to hear you say 'Yes, Will.'"

Ellie sighed, wondering why she was fighting this so hard when it was what they both wanted. It was time she made an investment of her own and trusted to love. "Then I suppose I must say it: yes, Will."

"Thank you, darling." Will ran his hands over her back, molding her to him. "I want to stay with you tonight. I fear if I leave you, you'll take it into your head to run off again."

"I won't," she promised, meaning it. Their fates were entangled now; there was no unlacing possible. "And you shouldn't stay."

"In my eyes, you are my wife. Take pity on your poor husband: I won't sleep unless I'm beside you. You're bound to get into more trouble if I leave you alone." He lifted her off her feet and carried her over to the bed.

"I think I'll be in more trouble if you stay."

"This isn't wrong. We are betrothed. There's no going back for us."

Ellie shivered in anticipation. "You mean it?"

He nibbled her fingertips. "Every word. Our future together starts here."

Chapter 24

The Queen was still holding court at Greenwich when the Dorset barge appeared at the river steps. First on shore was the earl, finely dressed in gold velvet, the same color as his hair and beard. His brother followed, his dark hair skimming the shoulders of his dark-blue doublet. Next came the younger children, a handsome pair in white (though the boy had a smudge on his knee from where he had fished over the side of the vessel). The Countess of Dorset descended arm in arm with a pretty dark-haired lady, both in severe black of mourning. If their clothes were old and only recently altered to fit the new styles, then no one was saying, because such a splendid family, one of the first in the realm, could be said to set the fashion, not slavishly follow it. Their retainers came next: an exotic blackamoor in green satin, a fierce red-haired man with a glower to sour milk, and six maids-in-waiting. There was much to entertain the onlookers as the baggage was unloaded, including the shrewish conversation between the red giant and the fairest of the maids, ending with him receiving a clip around the ear.

The family, however, was not there to see this altercation. They were met by Robert Cecil and conducted into the palace for an audience with the Queen. Waiting outside the royal apartments, Cecil drew Will aside.

"You are absolutely sure about this, my lord?" He glanced at Ellie, who was studying the pictures with great concentration, trying to pretend she didn't know they were discussing her.

"Yes, I am." Will laughed. "I'm a hopeless case, Cecil: there's no saving me from myself."

"She's a lovely girl, as I have always said, even when you held another opinion."

"Don't remind me," groaned Will.

"My father's agreed to the match—he won't stand in your way. Said you were entitled to choose the mother of your children even if you all had to live on turnips for the rest of your days."

Will sincerely hoped that wasn't to be his fate.

"He gave me some advice as to how this may be best presented to Her Majesty," Cecil continued. "So if you would trust me, I'll see what I can do."

Will held out his hand. "You have my thanks and my friendship, whatever the outcome, Cecil."

They shook hands with the sober expressions of men about to do battle.

Ellie was ready to flee, her usual response to tense situations where she had little hope of emerging the victor. The countess held on to her arm with grim determination.

"No, child, this cannot be avoided," she said in an undertone. "And don't look so terrified. Our Queen loves to hear a tale of true love as long as it doesn't affect her or her favorites. If Will were a

Raleigh, then we would have no hope. But a young earl in love with a scholar's daughter, who is secretly a Spanish countess—that sounds like a tale that might appeal to her humor."

Ellie had never considered her title a secret—rather a liability in a suspicious England. "Do you know the Queen well, my lady?"

"Not well. She's some years older than me, but I enjoyed my time at her court when my husband still mixed in those circles. She's a great dancer."

For Ellie, meeting the Queen was only a small step down from appearing before God himself. She felt completely inadequate and was sure the monarch would sense this immediately. But for Will and his family, who were risking their position at court for her, she would endure.

The door opened and they processed into the audience chamber. The Queen sat on her throne at the far end, her gown an amazing brocade of crimson and white, her ruff a pearl-white lace confection like nothing Ellie had ever seen before. She had a book in her hand and was studying two ornate globes on brass stands. Advisers clustered around her, a secretary working at a table piled with papers. Raleigh sat sprawl-legged in a chair at her side, looking distinctly bored, toying with a silver-gilt piece from a Wolf-and-Sheep game. A dwarf lady crouched at the Queen's feet playing with a tiny manlike creature—a monkey, Ellie guessed. From the expression in the Queen's dark eyes when she turned to the newcomers, she was intrigued to see what brought the Lacey family in force to court.

The Laceys and Ellie arrived at the foot of the throne and made their obeisance.

"My Lord Dorset," the Queen said, sounding amused by the

arrival of the entire family, "what brings you to court? I thought you were at home preparing for your nuptials." She spun one of the globes depicting the heavens, her long white fingers coming to rest on the constellation of Virgo.

Will touched his heart. "I fear that match did not prosper, Your Majesty."

Elizabeth dropped her hand, her full attention on the earl. "Indeed? But you do not look prostrate with grief."

"We parted on good terms, Your Majesty." Will thought it best not the mention the vitriolic letter he had received from Lord Wetherby, denouncing both him and the Lady Jane for wasting his time and tearing him away from his beloved hunting to attend court.

Raleigh yawned, though Ellie thought his air of smugness increased at news of the failed match with the Percevals.

The Queen examined Will's face for a moment, seeking clues to his state of mind. "I see. And why do you seek an audience today?"

Robert Cecil stepped forward. "Your Majesty, may we make known to you the Lady Eleanor Rodriguez, Countess of San Jaime, daughter of the late renowned scholar Sir Arthur Hutton?"

The Queen's gaze sharpened, her memory stirring. "The girl who translated Paracelsus?"

Ellie moved forward and swept her deepest curtsy. "Yes, Your Majesty."

"An impressive achievement for one so young. We were saddened to hear of your father's death in our service, child," Elizabeth said kindly. "We are glad to see that you are now an intimate of one of the finest families in our realm."

Cecil held himself in readiness, waiting for permission to speak.

"You have something further you wish to say, Master Cecil?"

"Yes, Your Majesty. My father believes it only appropriate that provision should be made for the lady since she lost her only relative in the explosion. Sir Arthur was a casualty of war, you might say."

Elizabeth frowned at the mention of provision. "One might," she said coolly.

"There was a debate whether a pension might be forthcoming from the Treasury, or, in view of the tender age of the lady, whether a marriage might be arranged on her behalf. That would save the government many long years of providing an annuity."

The Queen was no fool, but neither did she like spending money. "A match, you say. With one of Dorset's brothers perchance?" Her eyes swept the family, resting on the youngest, much to Tobias's alarm.

"With the earl himself, Your Majesty. Dorset and the lady conceived an affection for each other in their youth and have recently become reacquainted."

An affection? Ellie didn't think being run out of Will's house when she was twelve constituted a declaration of love, but held her tongue.

"I think this match would be acceptable to them both," Cecil concluded.

The Queen tapped her lips in thought. "You are prepared to marry the lady, Dorset?"

"I would be honored," Will replied swiftly.

"Your family agree?" The Queen studied the serene expression on the countess's face and the loyal stance of James at his brother's shoulder.

"They do."

Raleigh sat forward, his dislike for Will pricking him to speak. A lowly match would damage the Dorset influence at court permanently. "A romantic tale, Your Majesty. The poet in me wishes that such love not be thwarted."

The Queen smiled down on her favorite. "Then I grant my permission. The lady is your responsibility, Dorset."

Will refrained from hooting with delight. "You are most gracious, ma'am."

"I understand you will seek permission once more to return to prepare for your nuptials?"

"Indeed, Your Majesty."

"Then get thee gone. But make sure you return for the tilt at Michaelmas. I have a great desire to see if you can best my knights again."

Raleigh frowned, his fists curling on his knees.

Will knew when to take the bargain offered him. "I will be delighted to compete once more, ma'am. Master Raleigh, I look forward to measuring my lance against yours again."

"As do I," growled Raleigh.

The Lacey family retreated backwards from the audience chamber, then walked with all swiftness towards their private apartments. Only once they were out of public gaze did they allow themselves to give rein to their emotions. Will hugged Ellie, then his mother and Sarah. James pummeled Tobias, telling him he hadn't done too badly for a miniature barbarian brother. Cecil looked on, smiling at their antics.

"Robert, that was very well done of you," said the countess, kissing his cheek. "I predict a bright future for you if you can handle delicate matters so well."

"Thank you, my lady."

"You'll come for the wedding?" asked Will, clapping him on the shoulder.

"I'd not miss it for the world. I have great hopes that the lady will correct the vicar's Latin."

Ellie feigned a studious air. "Of course, if he needs it, sir."

Cecil took her hand. "Are you sure you want to marry this ignorant fellow even though he's an earl? Can't I lure you away from him?"

Ellie laughed and shook her head. "You know too much, sir; I look forward to the challenge of filling his empty head with my learning."

Will swooped on her from behind. "I vow we will have the most learned children in the land, wife."

"If not the richest," quipped James.

Epilogue

NELL THOUGHT THE WEDDING a most disappointing affair. The church had been packed with villagers, the atmosphere festive rather than refined, despite the presence of several noblemen. The earl and his bride had had to run the gauntlet under a harvest arch held by two giggling lines of girls, little Lady Sarah rubbing shoulders with the baker's wife and her sister—all very undignified. The bride had to make do with an altered gown belonging to her mother-in-law. A rich cloth-of-gold from Lady Dorset's trousseau, it reminded all that Ellie had brought nothing with her but a smile. Nell had no complaints against the lady herself—indeed, she anticipated that the young countess would be easy to handle and forgiving of faults—but she was enraged that she had ended up tied to a household with no money to spare. She had comforted herself on marrying her own dear spouse that she would soon be the housekeeper to an estate swelled with a decent dowry. Hard work would be a horrid memory. She could preside over an army of servants and never have to lift a finger. Now she was condemned to a future of early rising and back-breaking labor just so the neighboring gentry did not guess just how dire the state of the household budget was in truth.

She looked contemptuously at her husband, slouched over his ale at the kitchen table, drunk from having toasted the newly wedded couple since noon, a wreath of flowers dangling over one eye. He really was a sot. At least he would be too far in his cups to paw her tonight. She patted her rounded belly, feeling the child stir inside. The babe would soon give her an excuse to refuse Affabel completely; he always bowed to her wishes when she alluded to the mysteries of womanhood and childbearing. The only thing he had proved immovable on was his refusal to give up his wretched wolfhound. She could swear he loved that animal far more than he did her.

Feeling the need for some companionship, Nell caught the eye of the most handsome of the footmen. He at first looked startled at her sultry smile, then got the hint. She waited until he left the room, then followed, loosening her bodice as she went. There was no point in making him work for her; they would have to be quick before Turville noticed that they had both been absent.

Life was not how she thought it would be, but Lacey Hall did have its attractions.

Will and Ellie were not in their chamber as the guests at the wedding imagined. After being taken to the door and guided to the flower-strewn bed, the couple had slipped away, heading out to the deer park to enjoy the evening sunshine. Abandoning their wedding finery on the ground, they had climbed Ellie's favorite tree and were now sitting at its peak looking back on the house. In the meadow behind the stables, a black figure crouched low on the back of a white horse, streaking as one across the grass.

Ellie leant back against Will. "Did you know Diego rides your horse better than you do?"

"No, but I'm not surprised." Will ran his fingers around the neck of her shift.

"Will, we're up a tree!" Ellie reminded him.

"Hmm, I'm not sure it is possible," he mused. "Still, I'm ready to attempt it if you are?" He waggled his eyebrows at her suggestively.

"You, sir, are impossible. I am not going to tell my children I spent my wedding night on a branch!"

He nibbled her ear. "I very much hope you do not—I wouldn't want to shock them."

Ellie laughed and let him have his way with her earlobe.

Will began to think that tree-climbing had exhausted its attractions for him. "Ready to go down, love?"

"In a moment. We have all night."

He rubbed his palm in a circle on her stomach. "And all the next day. I'm not letting you out of our chamber once I get you inside."

"We'll starve." Ellie tickled the back of his hand with a leaf.

"No, we won't. I have left strict orders for trays of food to be left outside the door at regular intervals."

"My lord, I'm impressed: you think of everything."

"My lady, I only think of one thing—and that is you."

She snorted at his flowery compliment then settled back in his arms. "I truly regret, Will, that I did not bring my magic wand with me to make you rich like a hero from a folktale."

"Ah yes, but those kind of deals with the faerie folk always have a sting in the tail. I prefer you as you are."

"But your family . . ."

"We've been through this, love. We'll manage. Cecil and I have been talking about making an investment in a trading company together. There are great opportunities opening up with new shipping routes and settlements all over the globe."

"Where will you get the capital to invest?"

He kissed her chin lightly. "I can't believe, my practical madam, that we are spending our wedding night discussing finances. It is not very lover-like of you."

"Humph!"

He smiled at her disgruntled expression. "You know, I think your father really did make gold after all."

She wrinkled her nose in disgust. "Don't you start that, Will. He was chasing a rainbow."

"Yes, but he and your mother made you. And you are worth more to me than all the Spanish gold from the richest treasure ships." He waited for her to give her usual dismissal of his elegant phrases, but she was silent. "My love? Are you all right?"

"Oh, Will, that was so kind of you to say so." Ellie had tears in her eyes. "All through my life with him I just wanted him to look at me and see me clearly, but all he cared for were his experiments. I did not know what it was like to be valued until you."

Will was delighted he had slipped one of his compliments past her. He would have to try more in the future.

"And now it really is time for me to show you how much I appreciate you. I'll go first. Then I can catch you if you fall!"

Ellie was ahead of him. "No, you will not, my lord. You would just look up my petticoats."

"You, dear wife, forget you promised to obey me." Will swung down as quickly as he could, determined to reach the ground first.

"I will—as long as you promise to do everything I say," she called from her branch.

Will thumped to the ground and ran round to her side. She was sitting on the lowest limb waiting for him.

"And what is your command, my lady?" He held out his arms.

"Catch me!"

"Always." He caught her in his arms, letting her slide down his body. "On second thoughts, Wife, why waste a perfectly good bed of leaves?" He nuzzled her neck.

Ellie cupped the back of his head with her hands, stroking her fingers through his hair. "Why indeed?" She reached up on tiptoe to kiss him, putting everything she felt for him in the gesture.

He broke away to smile at her. "May I say, Countess, you are making an excellent start in your new position."

She laughed. "I would say the same about you—but only if you kiss me again."

"That will absolutely be my pleasure."

The QUEEN'S LADY

EVE EDWARDS

If you loved *The Other Countess*, you'll be eager to know what happens to Lady Jane Perceval. *The Queen's Lady* is her story.
COMING SPRING 2012!

Turn the page for a sneak preview.

Waiting in the cold passageway for her entrance, Jane shivered in her new dress. Despite the layers of chemise, kirtle, bodice, sleeves, stomacher and the rest, the February chill still managed to creep into her bones. Mary Radcliffe, another of the Queen's ladies, rubbed her arms.

"I swear I have goose pimples," she muttered, craning her neck to peek through the doorway. "When is it our turn?"

Jane listened for the musical cue. The courtier playing "Jupiter" was concluding his speech to the sovereign, and then it would be their chance to process across the stage, each wearing a mask and carrying a symbol of their divinity. Hers was a bow and arrow for the huntress; Mary Radcliffe bore a basket of apples, symbolizing love and temptation for Venus.

"If that windbag doesn't hurry up, I'm going to pelt him with my fruit," grumbled Mary.

"No need, I'll have shot him with my arrow before then," whispered Jane.

She felt a tingle of excitement: James Lacey had just entered with Raleigh and taken a seat near the Queen. James looked very serious in his black suit of doublet and long venetians, compared to the spangled finery of Raleigh in his gold-velvet jerkin worn over a white pinked doublet and puffy satin trunk hose.

The musicians struck up their tune. Jane took a breath to steady her nerves, then entered in her place in the procession of gods and goddesses. The sequined mask gave her the confidence to display herself before James after eighteen months apart. Would he recognize her? she wondered. She had never been entirely sure of his regard but thought he had liked her when she had been a guest at Lacey Hall. She had certainly felt a spark between them; had he?

The gods did a complete revolution of the room, bowing or curtsying on every count of twelve. Finally, they came together to hold a dramatic pose before the Queen, Jane in the front row holding aloft her bow and arrow as if to shoot the ceiling. She slid a look to the spectators and noticed with chagrin that James was studying his toe caps, seemingly indifferent to the masque.

The Queen led the applause. The actors in the masque dispersed to make way for the dancing to follow. Jane moved to one side, handing her bow and mask to a waiting page boy.

"La volta," demanded Elizabeth, signaling the musicians to play the strenuous dance that was one of her favorites. Though past fifty, she still reigned supreme as the foremost dancer at court. Raleigh immediately offered his services as her partner, lifting and turning Elizabeth as the steps demanded, her crimson skirts swishing as she leapt with the energy of a much younger woman. After they had completed a circuit of the floor, other couples joined the dance. Jane hovered at the edge, hoping James would look up and notice her, but he was still sunk in a brooding inspection of the floor.

"You wish to dance, Marchioness?" Jane's brother, Sir Henry

Perceval, appeared at her elbow. A large-built man with her fair coloring, he was never short of partners despite not being the heir to their father's earldom—that honor rested with their staid eldest brother, David, who rarely ventured from Yorkshire. Henry had served with Raleigh in Ireland and had been knighted for his military prowess.

Jane gave up on waiting for James. "How kind, brother, thank you."

Henry seized her by the waist and threw her into the first leap, her skirts belling as she landed. Too vigorous a dance, la volta did not allow for discussion between the participants, and Jane concentrated on keeping time while wondering at her brother's motives for asking her to partner him. His renewed interest in her presence at court was likely to herald an attempt by her family to use her once more. At the close of the music her suspicions were justified when Henry drew her aside.

"How are you faring as the Queen's lady, Janie?"

"Very well, thank you, Henry," she replied coolly, distrusting his use of his old nickname for her.

Henry signaled to a serving man to bring them wine. "I've been talking to your stepson." He said the word with a sneer.

"Oh? How is dear Richard?" Her tone was acidic, but a frisson of fear shivered down her spine—the Paton sons were in London. That was unlikely to mean good news for her.

"Spitting mad at you, sister. Something about a wedding ring and dower properties—I confess, I stopped listening after the first hour of his rant. Remarkable talent you have for making enemies."

"One we both inherited, I think."

Henry leaned back, considering her. "Father and I have been talking."

Here it came.

"We could help you against the Patons, gain your rights to your husband's estate."

"Could you now?" Jane sipped her wine, scanning the crowd for any sign of James. "And what would it cost me?"

"Nothing. We merely would like to explore with you the possibilities for another match. You surprised Father, landing a marquess; he has revised his opinion of your potential."

"How pleasing for him."

"He thinks if a marquess before, why not a duke next time?"

"Why not indeed? But for the fact that there are no dukes to be had in England at present."

"Who said anything about England?"

"Oh, I see. Father is thinking outside his usual patriotic prejudices. I suppose he has his eye on some trading advantage he thinks I can bring him."

Henry did not contradict her guess.

"You can tell him that this particular daughter is tired of being a pawn in his interminable game of chess. I do not want to be traded for a more valuable piece."

Henry laughed. "I knew you'd say that, which is why we had to look for an incentive that would make you cooperate."

Jane felt a pang of fear. "Incentive?"

"Ah, look, here's that Lacey fellow. James, isn't it?" Henry deliberately ignored her inquiry and tapped James on the shoulder as he made his way to the door. “Lacey, good to see you at court once more! You remember my sister, of course?”

Still on edge from Henry’s veiled threat, Jane felt her heart pounding in her chest. She could have done without her brother’s presence, but at least he had brought James to her side. She dipped a curtsy. “Sir.”

Disdainful brown eyes swept over her. “My lady, Sir Henry,” James said curtly, giving them both a shallow bow, evidently intent on escaping the chamber.

Henry refused to let him slip away so easily. “I don’t know if you’ve heard, my lord, but my sister is a widow now—a marchioness, no less.”

Henry had always been crass, but his bluntness made Jane cringe.

“My condolences, madam,” James murmured, his eyes skipping to the exit.

The musicians began another dance: a stately allemande.

“Happily, her mourning is past and she is quite able to participate in our revels,” Henry continued, enjoying his sister’s discomfort at the reluctance of the young lord to acknowledge her.

“Henry, please,” Jane murmured, finding his blatant begging a partner for her humiliating in the extreme.

“Come, come, sister.” Henry patted her wrist with maddening condescension. “You cannot spend the evening dancing only with your brother. Lent is upon us, and you won’t have another chance till April.”

Jane wished the floor would open and swallow her up. She had hoped for some sign that James had retained feelings for her, but he was as severe in manner as in dress. Her eyes now rested on his much-inspected toe caps.

"Good lord, you two are killjoys. I'll go find myself a merry partner and leave you to your gloomy corner." With a slight bow, Henry retreated, doubtless pleased with himself for dropping his sister in a socially impossible situation.

Jane took a step back. "I apologize, sir. I did not ask my brother to force you to dance, as you are obviously so unwilling to do so. I bid you good night."

The toe caps paused, then closed the distance she had opened up between them.

"No, he is right. It is our last chance. I would find the experience"—James paused, seeking the right word—*"enlightening."*

"How so?" Jane couldn't help a shiver of pleasure as he took her hand and led her onto the dance floor to join the procession. He was even more handsome than she remembered, his face firming into that of the man he was becoming, rather than remaining that of the youth she remembered. His hair curled at the temples and hung to his ruff, defying any attempt to order it.

"I'm intrigued to find out if you still think yourself so far above us poor Laceys, madam." The dance separated them before she could frame a reply. He returned to steer her through the next figure. "Ah, but of course you do: you are a marchioness now—a rung above my brother, the earl, and so far above me it hurts my neck just to catch a glimpse of your exaltedness. You must be very pleased with yourself."

It was worse than she had feared: "bitter" was too mild a word for what he felt towards her.

"I can explain, sir. I never considered myself superior to your family; far from it." Jane tried a conciliatory smile, but it slid right off his defenses.

"I'm delighted you see the truth, madam. You may have won the title, but you never had the nobility."

With that insult, the music changed to the faster, cheerful third section that concluded the allemande, giving Jane no opportunity to respond. She felt as if he had just slapped her. He'd unjustly lashed out at her, not giving her the chance to explain what had really happened between his brother and her all those months ago. A fury such as she had not felt in many years rose in her as he swung her cynically through the final measure, his eyes hard, his smile without mirth. The musicians struck the final chord and the dancers faced each other.

"It's been a pleasure, my lady," James drawled.

"You, sir," Jane said, quivering with anger, "are an arrogant swine!"

She did not even curtsy as she left, swishing her skirts as she passed as if to sweep him away like so much dirt. So much for her glorious reunion with the man of her dreams.

Published by Delacorte Press, an imprint of Random House Children's Books,
a division of Random House, Inc.